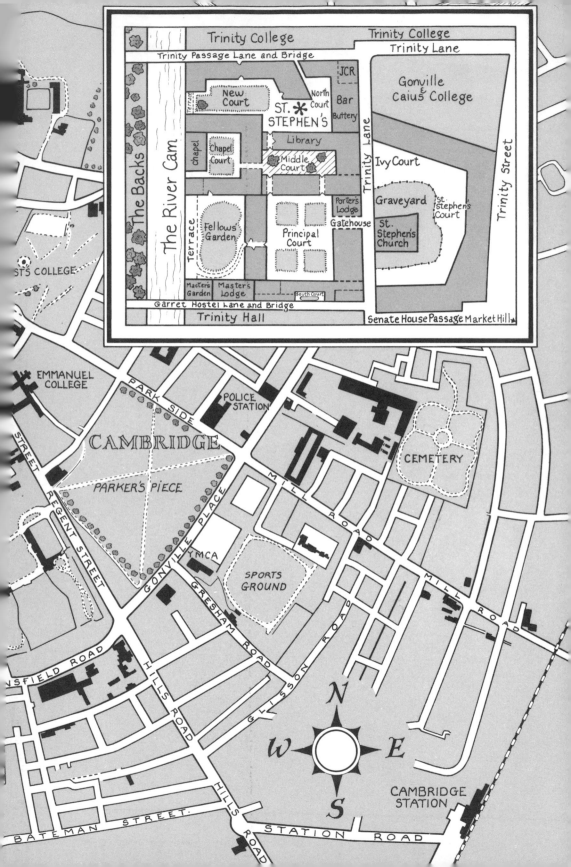

For the
SAKE OF ELENA

For the
SAKE OF ELENA

Elizabeth George

BANTAM BOOKS
NEW YORK · TORONTO · LONDON · SYDNEY · AUCKLAND

Grateful acknowledgment is made for permission to quote from "Epitaph for Fire and Flower"
by Sylvia Plath. From The Collected Poems of Sylvia Plath, *edited by Ted Hughes. Copyright*
© 1960 by the Estate of Sylvia Plath. Reprinted by permission of HarperCollins Publishers.

FOR THE SAKE OF ELENA
A Bantam Book / August 1992

Library of Congress Cataloging-in-Publication Data
George, Elizabeth.
    For the sake of Elena / Elizabeth George.
        p. cm.
    ISBN 0-553-08118-7
    I. Title.
PS3557.E478F6   1992
813'.54—dc20   91-34865
                                           CIP

Published simultaneously in the United States and Canada

PRINTED IN THE UNITED STATES OF AMERICA

BVG 0 9 8 7 6 5 4 3 2 1

For Mom and Dad,
who encouraged the passion
and tried to understand everything else

Dawn snuffs out star's spent wick,
Even as love's dear fools cry evergreen,
And a languor of wax congeals the vein
No matter how fiercely lit.

SYLVIA PLATH

Author's Note

Those familiar with the city of Cambridge and with Cambridge University will recognize that there is little enough space between Trinity College and Trinity Hall in the first place, let alone enough space to hold the seven courts and four hundred years of architecture which comprise my fictional St. Stephen's College.

I am indebted in any number of ways to a fine group of people who did their best to unlock for me the mysteries of Cambridge University from the standpoint of the senior fellows: Dr. Elena Shire of Robinson College, Professor Lionel Elvin of Trinity Hall, Dr. Mark Bailey of Gonville and Caius College, Mr. Graham Miles and Mr. Alan Banford of Homerton College.

I am additionally grateful to the undergraduates and postgraduates who did their best to school me in the finer points of life as a junior fellow: Sandy Shafernich and Nick Blain of Queens' College, Eleanor Peters of Homerton College, and David Derbyshire of Clare College. Most especially, I am deeply indebted to Ruth Schuster of Homerton College who orchestrated my visits to supervisions and lectures, who arranged for my attendance at formal dinner, who did additional photographic research for me, and who patiently and heroically answered countless questions about the city, the colleges, the faculties, and the University. Without Ruth I would have been a lost soul indeed.

I thank Inspector Pip Lane of Cambridge Constabulary for his assistance and suggestions in details of plot; Beryl Polley of Trinity Hall for introducing me to her boys on *L* staircase; and Mr. John East of C.E. Computing Services in London for all the information about the Ceephone.

And especially I thank Tony Mott for patiently listening to a brief and enthusiastic description of a murder site and recognizing it and giving it a name.

In the United States, I owe debts of gratitude to Blair Maffris, who always fields my questions on any aspect of art; to painter Carlos Ramos, who allowed me to spend a day with him in his studio in Pasadena; to Alan Hallback, who provided me with a beginner's course in understanding jazz; to my husband Ira Toibin, whose patience, support, and encouragement are the most important mainstays in my life; to Julie Mayer, who never gets tired of reading rough drafts; to Kate Miciak and Deborah Schneider—editor and literary agent—who continue to believe in the literary mystery.

If this book is at all accurate, it is owing to the good-natured involvement of this generous group. Any missteps and errors are mine alone.

For the

SAKE OF ELENA

1

Elena Weaver awakened when the second light went on in her bed-sitting room. The first light, twelve feet away on her desk, managed only to rouse her moderately. The second light, however, positioned to shine directly in her face from an angle-lamp on the bedside table, acted as efficiently as a blast of music or a jangling alarm. When it broke into her dream—an unwelcome interloper, considering the subject matter her subconscious had been pursuing—she bolted upright in bed.

She hadn't started out the previous night in this bed or even in this room, so for a moment she blinked, perplexed, wondering when the plain red curtains had been changed for that hideous print of yellow chrysanthemums and green leaves lounging on a field of what appeared to be bracken. They were drawn across a window which was itself in the wrong place. As was the desk. In fact, there shouldn't have been a desk in here at all. Nor should it have been strewn with papers, notebooks, several open volumes, and a large word processor.

This last item, as well as the telephone beside it, brought everything sharply into focus. She was in her own room, alone. She'd come in just before two, torn off her clothes, dropped exhausted into bed, and managed about four hours' sleep. Four hours . . . Elena groaned. No wonder she'd thought she was elsewhere.

Rolling out of bed, she thrust her feet into fuzzy slippers and quickly drew on the green woollen bathrobe that lay in a heap next to her jeans on the floor. The material was old, worn down to a feathery softness. Her father had presented her with a fine silk dressing gown upon her matriculation into Cambridge a year ago—indeed, he had presented her with an entire wardrobe which she had mostly discarded—but she had left it at his house on one of her frequent weekend visits, and while she wore it in his presence to appease the anxiety with which he seemed to watch her every move, she never wore it at any other time. Certainly not at home in London with her mother, and never here in college. The old green one was better. It felt like velvet against her bare skin.

She padded across the room to her desk and pulled open the curtains. It was still dark outside, and the fog which had lain upon the city like an oppressive miasma for the past five days seemed even thicker this morning, pressing against the casement windows and streaking them with a lacework of moisture. On the wide sill stood a cage with a small bottle of water hanging on its side, an exercise wheel in its centre, and an athletic-sock-turned-nest in its far right-hand corner. Curled into this was a dollop of fur the size of a tablespoon and the colour of sherry.

Elena tapped her fingers against the icy bars of the cage. She brought her face up to it, caught the mixed smells of shredded newspaper, cedar shavings, and pungent mouse droppings, and blew her breath softly in the direction of the nest.

"Muh-owz," she said. Again, she tapped against the bars of the cage. "Muh-owz."

Within the small mound of fur, a bright brown eye opened. The mouse lifted his head. His nose tested the air.

"Tibbit." Elena smiled in delight as his whiskers twitched. "Mornun, muh-owz."

The mouse scampered from his nest and came to inspect her fingers, clearly expecting a morning treat. Elena opened the cage door and picked him up, scarcely three inches of lively curiosity in the palm of her hand. She perched him on her shoulder, where he immediately began an investigation into the possibilities presented by her hair. This was quite long and quite straight, its colour identical to the mouse's fur. These facts seemed to offer the promise of camouflage, for he snuggled happily between the collar of Elena's robe and her neck, where he anchored himself onto the material and began to wash his face.

Elena did the same, opening the cupboard that housed the basin and switching on the light above it. She went on to brush her teeth, to bind her hair back with a bit of ribboned elastic, and to rustle through her clothes cupboard for her tracksuit and a jersey. She pulled on the trousers and went next door to the gyp room.

She flipped on the light and examined the shelf above the stainless steel sink. Coco Puffs, Wheetabix, Corn Flakes. The sight of all of them made her stomach roll uneasily, so she opened the refrigerator, pulled out a carton of orange juice, and drank directly from it. Her mouse put an end to his morning ablutions and scuttled back onto her shoulder in anticipation. As she continued to drink, Elena rubbed her index finger on the top of his head. His tiny teeth gnawed at the edge of her fingernail. Enough of affection. He was getting impatient.

"Awright," Elena said. She rooted through the refrigerator— grimacing at the rank smell of milk gone bad—and found the jar of peanut butter. A fingertip of this was the mouse's daily treat, and he set upon it happily when she presented it to him. He was still working the residue out of his fur when Elena returned to her room and placed him on her desk. She threw off her robe, pulled on a jersey, and began to stretch.

She knew the importance of warming up before her daily run. Her father had drummed it into her head with monotonous regularity ever since she had joined the University's Hare and Hounds Club in her first term. Still, she found it horrifically boring, and the only way she managed to complete the series of stretches was to combine them with something else, such as fantasizing, making toast, gazing out the window, or reading a bit of literature she'd been avoiding for ages. This morning she combined the exercising with toast and window gazing. While the bread was browning in the toaster on her bookshelf, she worked on loosening leg and thigh muscles, her eyes on the window. Outside, the fog was creating a billowing whirlpool round the lamppost in the centre of North Court, holding out the guarantee of an unpleasant run.

Out of the corner of her eye, Elena saw the mouse scooting back and forth across the top of her desk, pausing to raise himself on hind legs and sniff the air. He was nobody's fool. Several million years of olfactory evolution told him that more food was in the offing, and he wanted his share.

She glanced at the bookshelf to see the toast had popped up. She broke off a piece for the mouse and tossed it in his cage. He scrambled immediately in that direction, his tiny ears catching the light like diaphanous wax.

"Hey," she said, catching the little animal in his progress across two volumes of poetry and three Shakespearean criticisms. "Say g'bye, Tibbit." Fondly, she rubbed her cheek against his fur before replacing him in the cage. The piece of toast was nearly his size, but he managed to drag it industriously towards his nest. Elena smiled, tapped her fingers on the cage top, grabbed the rest of the toast, and left the room.

As the corridor's glass firedoor whooshed closed behind her, she put on the jacket of her tracksuit and pulled up its hood. She ran down the first flight of *L* staircase and swung round the landing by grasping the wrought iron banister and landing lightly in a crouch, taking the pressure of her weight in her legs and ankles, rather than in her knees. She took the second flight at a quicker pace, dashed across the entry, and flung open the door. The cold air hit her like water. Her muscles stiffened in reaction. She forced them to relax, running in place for a moment as she shook her arms. She breathed in deeply. The air—with the fog taking its origin in the river and the fens—tasted of humus and woodsmoke, and it covered her skin quickly with a watery down.

She jogged across the south end of New Court, sprinting through the two passageways to Principal Court. No one was about. No lights were on in rooms. It was wonderful, exhilarating. She felt inordinately free.

And she had less than fifteen minutes to live.

Five days of fog dripped off buildings and trees, made wet lattice on windows, created pools on the pavement. Outside St. Stephen's College, a lorry's hazard lights flashed in the mist, two small orange beacons like blinking cat's eyes. In Senate House Passage, Victorian lampposts reached long fingers of yellow light through the fog, and the Gothic spires of King's College first rose against then disappeared altogether into a backdrop of gloom the colour of grey doves. Beyond that, the sky still wore the guise of a mid-November night. Full dawn was yet an hour away.

Elena pounded from Senate House Passage into King's Parade. The pressure of her feet against the pavement sent an answering quiver up the muscles and bones of her legs and into her stomach. She pressed her palms against her hips, just where his had been last night. But unlike last night, her breathing was steady, not rapid and urgent and centred single-mindedly on that frantic rise to pleasure. Still, she could almost see his head thrown back. She could almost see him concentrating on the heat, the friction, and the slick profusion of her body's desire. She could almost see his mouth form the words *oh God oh God oh God oh God* as his hips thrust up and his hands pulled her down harder and harder against him. And then her name on his lips and the wild beating of his heart against his chest. And his breathing, like a runner.

She liked to think of it. She'd even been dreaming of it when the light went on in her room this morning.

She powered along King's Parade towards Trumpington, weaving in and out of the patchy light. Somewhere not far away, a breakfast was cooking, for the air held the faint scent of bacon and coffee. Her throat began to close uneasily in response, and she increased her speed to escape the odour, splashing through a puddle that sent icy water seeping through her left sock.

At Mill Lane, she made the turn towards the river. The blood was beginning to pound in her veins, and in spite of the cold, she had started to perspire. A line of sweat beneath her breasts was trickling towards her waist.

Perspiration's the sign that your body is working, her father would tell her. Perspiration, naturally. He would never say *sweat*.

The air seemed fresher as she approached the river, dodging two dust carts that were manned by the first living creature she had seen out on the streets this morning, a workman wearing a lime green anorak. He heaved a haversack onto the pushbar of one of the carts and lifted a thermos as if to toast her as she passed.

At the end of the lane, she darted onto the pedestrian bridge that spanned the River Cam. The bricks beneath her feet were slick. She ran in place for a moment, fumbling with the wrist of her track jacket to get a look at her watch. When she realised she'd left it back in her room, she cursed softly and jogged back across the bridge to have a quick look down Laundress Lane.

Damn, damn, double damn. Where is she? Elena squinted through the fog. She blew out a quick gust of breath in irritation. This wasn't the first time she'd had to wait, and if her father had his way, it wouldn't be the last.

"I won't have you running alone, Elena. Not at that hour of the morning. Not along the river. We won't have any discussion about this. If you'd care to choose another route . . ."

But she knew it wouldn't matter. Another route and he'd only come up with another objection. She should never have let him know that she was running in the first place. At the time, it had seemed an innocuous enough piece of information. *I've joined Hare and Hounds, Daddy.* But he managed to turn it into yet another display of his devotion to her. Just as he did when he got hold of her essays prior to supervisions. He'd read them, brow furrowed, his posture and expression both declaring: Look how concerned I am, see how much I love you, note how I treasure having you back in my life, I'll never leave you again, my darling. And then he'd critique them, guiding her through introductions and conclusions and points to be clarified, bringing her stepmother in for further assistance, sitting back in his leather chair with his eyes shining earnestly. *See what a happy family we are?* It made her skin crawl.

Her breath steamed the air. She'd waited more than a minute. Still no one emerged from the grey soup of Laundress Lane.

Stuff it, she thought, and ran back to the bridge. On the Mill Pool beyond her, swans and ducks etched out their shapes in the gauzy air while on the southwest bank of the pool itself a willow wept branches into the water. Elena gave one final glance over her shoulder, but no one was running to meet her, so she herself ran on.

Descending the slope of the weir, she misjudged the angle and felt the slight pull of a muscle in her leg. She winced, but kept going. Her time was shot to hell—not that she knew what her time was in the first place—but she might be able to make up a few seconds once she reached the causeway. She picked up her pace.

The pavement narrowed to a strip of tarmac with the river on its left and the wide, mist-shrouded expanse of Sheep's Green to its right. Here, the hulking silhouettes of trees rose out of the fog, and the handrails of footbridges made horizontal slashes of white where the occasional lights from across the river managed to cut through the gloom. As she ran, ducks plopped silently from the bank into the water, and Elena reached into her pocket for the last wedge of morning toast which she crumbled and tossed their way.

Her toes were driving steadily into the front of her running shoes. Her ears were starting to ache in the cold. She tightened the drawstring of her hood beneath her chin, and from her jacket pocket, she took a pair of mittens and pulled them on, blowing into her hands and pressing them against her chilled face.

Ahead, the river separated into two parts—main body and murky stream—as it flowed sluggishly round Robinson Crusoe's Island, a small mass of land thickly overgrown on its south end with trees and brush and its north end given to the repair of the colleges' sculls, canoes, rowboats, and punts. A bonfire had been lit in the area recently, for Elena could smell its remains in the air. Someone had probably camped illegally on the north section of the island during the night, leaving behind a residue of charred wood hastily extinguished by water. It smelled different from a fire that has died a natural death.

Curious, Elena looked through the trees as she dashed along the north end of the island. Canoes and punts piled one on top of another, their wood slick and glistening and dripping with the fog. But no one was there.

The path began the rise towards Fen Causeway, which marked the end of the first leg of her run. As always, she met the gradual acclivity with a fresh burst of energy, breathing steadily but feeling the building pressure in her chest. She was just beginning to adjust to the new speed when she saw them.

Two figures appeared ahead of her on the pavement, one crouched and the other stretched across the width of the path. They were shadowy and largely amorphous, and they seemed to tremble like uncertain holograms, backlit by the wavering, filtered light from the causeway about twenty yards away. Perhaps hearing Elena's approach, the crouched figure turned towards her, lifted a hand. The other didn't move.

Elena squinted through the fog. Her eyes went from one figure to the other. She saw the size. She saw the dimensions.

Townee, she thought, and rushed forward.

The crouched figure stood, backed off at Elena's approach, and seemed to disappear into the heavier mist near the footbridge that joined the path with the island. Elena stumbled to a stop and fell to her knees. She reached out, touched, and found herself frantically examining what amounted to nothing more than an old coat stuffed with rags.

In confusion, she turned, one hand on the ground, pushing herself to her feet. She drew in breath to speak.

As she did so, the heavy air splintered before her. A movement flashed on her left. The first blow fell.

It hit her squarely between the eyes. Lightning shot through her field of vision. Her body flew backwards.

The second blow crashed against her nose and cheek, cutting completely through the flesh and shattering the zygomatic bone like a piece of glass.

If there was a third blow, she did not feel it.

It was just after seven when Sarah Gordon pulled her Escort onto the wide section of pavement right next to the University Department of Engineering. In spite of the fog and the morning traffic, she'd made the drive from her home in less than five minutes, charging over Fen Causeway as if pursued by a legion of ghouls. She set the emergency brake, clambered out into the damp morning, and slammed the door.

She marched to the boot of the car where she began pulling out her equipment: a camp stool, a sketch pad, a wooden case, an easel, two canvases. When these objects lay on the ground at her feet, she stared into the boot, asking herself if she had forgotten anything. She concentrated on details—charcoal, temperas, and pencils in the case—and tried to ignore her increasing nausea and the fact that tremors weakened her legs.

She stood for a moment with her head resting against the grimy open lid of the boot and schooled herself to think only of the painting. It was something she'd contemplated, begun, developed, and completed times beyond counting ever since her childhood, so all the elements should have been old friends. The subject, the location, the light, the composition, the choice of media demanded her full concentration. She made an attempt to give it to them. The world of possibility was opening. This morning represented a sacred renaissance.

Seven weeks ago, she'd marked this day on her calendar, 13 November. She'd written *do it* across that small, white square of hope, and now she was here to put an end to eight months of paralysed inactivity, utilising the only means she knew to find her way back to the passion with which she'd once greeted her work. If only she could muster up the courage to overcome a minor setback.

She slammed home the boot lid and picked up her equipment. Each object found its natural position in her hands and under her arms. There wasn't even a panic-filled moment of wondering how she'd managed to carry everything in the past. And the very fact that some behaviours did seem to be automatic, like riding a bicycle, buoyed her for an instant. She walked back over Fen Causeway and descended the slope towards Robinson Crusoe's Island, telling herself that the past was dead, telling herself that she'd come here to bury it.

For too long she had stood numbly in front of an easel, incapable of thinking of the healing propensities inherent to the simple act of creating. All these months, she had created nothing except the means of her own destruction, collecting half a dozen prescriptions for pills, cleaning and oiling her old shotgun, preparing her gas oven, making a rope from her scarves and all the time believing that the artistic force within her had died. But all that was ended, as were the seven weeks of growing dread as 13 November approached.

She paused on the little bridge spanning the narrow stream that separated Robinson Crusoe's Island from the rest of Sheep's Green. Although it was daylight, the mist was heavy, and it lay against her field of vision like a bank of clouds. Through it, the rattling song of an adult male wren shot out from one of the trees above her, and the causeway traffic passed with the muted rise and fall of engines. A duck *wak-wacked* somewhere nearby on the river. A bicycle bell jingled from across the green.

To her left, the boat repair sheds were still closed and shuttered. Ahead of her, ten iron steps climbed up to Crusoe's Bridge and descended to Coe Fen on the east bank of the river. She saw that the bridge itself had been repainted, a fact she had not noticed before. Where once it had been green and orange and patchy with rust, now it was brown and cream, the cream a series of crisscrossing balusters that glistened luminescently through the mist. The bridge itself looked suspended over nothing. And everything round it was altered and hidden by the fog.

In spite of her determination, she sighed. It was impossible. No light, no hope, and no inspiration in this bleak, cold place. Be damned to Whistler's night studies of the Thames. To hell with what Turner could have made from this dawn. No one would ever believe she had come to paint this.

Still, this was the day she had chosen. Events had dictated that she come to this island to draw. Draw she would. She plunged across the rest of the footbridge and pushed open the creaking, wrought iron gate, determined to ignore the chill that seemed to be inching its way through every organ of her body.

Inside the gate, she felt the squish and ooze of mud sucking noisily against her plimsolls, and she shuddered. It was cold. But it was *only* the cold. And she picked her way into the copse created by alder, crack willow, and beech.

Condensation dripped from the trees. Drops splatted with a sound like slow-bubbling porridge onto the sorrel tarpaulin of autumn leaves. A thick, fallen branch undulated across the ground before her, and just beyond it, a small clearing beneath a poplar offered a view. Sarah made for this. She leaned her easel and canvases against the tree, snapped open her camp stool, and propped her wooden case next to it. The sketch pad she clutched to her chest.

Paint, draw, paint, sketch. She felt her heart thud. Her fingers seemed brittle. Her very nails ached. She despised her weakness.

She forced her body onto the camp stool to face the river, and she stared at the bridge. She made an assessment of every detail, trying to see each as a line or an angle, a simple problem in composition which needed to be solved. Like a reflex response, her mind began to evaluate what her eyes took in. With their late autumn leaves tipped by beads of moisture that managed to catch and reflect what little light there was, three alder branches acted as a frame for the bridge. They formed diagonal lines that first stretched above the structure then descended in a perfect parallel to the stairs which led down to Coe Fen where through a swirling mass of fog the distant lights from Peterhouse glimmered. A duck and two swans were misty forms on the river which was itself so grey—a duplication of the air above it—that the birds floated as if suspended in space.

Quick strokes, she thought, big bold impressions, use a smudge of charcoal to suggest greater depth. She made her first pass against the sketch pad, then a second, and a third before her fingers slipped, losing their grip on the charcoal which slid across the paper and into her lap.

She stared at the mess she had made of the drawing. She ripped it from the pad and began a second time.

As she drew, she felt her bowels begin to loosen, she felt nausea begin its process of gripping her throat. "Oh please," she whispered, and glanced about, knowing she had no time to get home, knowing also that she couldn't allow herself to be sick here and now. She looked down at her sketch, saw the inadequate, pedestrian lines, and crumpled it up.

She began a third drawing, forcing all her concentration on keeping her right hand steady. Seeking to hold her panic at bay, she tried to duplicate the angle of the alder branches. She tried to copy the crisscrossing of the bridge balusters. She tried to suggest the pattern of the foliage. The charcoal snapped in two.

She pushed herself to her feet. It wasn't supposed to be like this. The creative power was supposed to take over. Time and place were supposed to disappear. The desire itself was supposed to return. But it hadn't. It was gone.

You can, she thought fiercely, you can and you will. Nothing can stop you. No one stands in your way.

She thrust the sketch pad under her arm, grabbed her camp stool, and struck out southward on the island until she came to a small spit of land. It was overgrown with nettles, but it provided a different view of the bridge. This was the spot.

The ground was loamy, matted by leaves. Trees and bushes formed a web of vegetation behind which at a distance the stone bridge of Fen Causeway rose. Sarah snapped open the camp stool here. She dropped it to the ground. She took a step back and lost her footing on what seemed to be a branch that was hidden beneath a pile of leaves. Considering the location, she should have been more than prepared, but the sensation still unnerved her.

"Damn it," she said and kicked the object to one side. The leaves fell from it. Sarah felt her stomach heave. The object wasn't a branch, but a human arm.

2

Mercifully, the arm was attached to a body. In his twenty-nine years with the Cambridge Constabulary, Superintendent Daniel Sheehan had never had a dismemberment occur upon his patch, and he didn't want that dubious investigatory distinction now.

Upon receiving the telephone call from the station house at twenty past seven, he'd come barrelling down from Arbury with lights flashing and siren sounding, grateful for an excuse to leave the breakfast table where the tenth straight day of grapefruit wedges, one boiled egg, and one thin slice of unbuttered toast provoked him into snarling at his teenaged son and daughter about their clothing and their hair, as if they were not both wearing school uniforms, as if their heads were not well-groomed and tidy. Stephen glanced at his mother, Linda did the same. And the three of them tucked into their own breakfasts with the martyred air of a family too long exposed to the unexpected mood-swings of the chronic dieter.

Traffic had been locked at the Newnham Road roundabout, and only by driving half on the pavement was Sheehan able to reach the bridge of Fen Causeway at something other than the hedgehog speed at which the rest of the cars were moving. He could envision the clogged mess which every southern artery into the city had probably become by now, and when he braked his car behind the constabulary's scenes-of-crime van and heaved himself into the damp, cold air, he told the constable stationed on the bridge to radio the dispatcher for more men to help move traffic along.

He hated rubberneckers and thrill seekers equally. Accidents and murders brought out the worst in people.

Tucking his navy scarf more securely into his overcoat, Sheehan ducked under the yellow ribbon of the established police line. On the bridge, a half a dozen undergraduates leaned over the parapet, trying to get a look at the activity below. Sheehan growled and waved the constable over to deal with them. If the victim was a member of one of the colleges, he wasn't about to let the word out any sooner than he had to. An uneasy peace had reigned between the local constabulary and the University since a cocked-up investigation at Emmanuel last term. He didn't particularly want anything to disturb it.

He crossed the footbridge to the island, where a female constable was hovering over a woman whose face and lips were the colour of unbleached linen. She was sitting on one of the bottom iron steps of Crusoe's Bridge, one arm curved round her stomach and one fist bearing the weight of her head. She wore an old blue overcoat that looked as if it would dangle to her ankles, the front of it crusted with brown and yellow specks. Apparently, she'd been sick on herself.

"She found the body?" Sheehan asked the constable, who nodded in reply. "Who's made it so far?"

"Everyone but Pleasance. Drake kept him at the lab."

Sheehan snorted. Just another little tiff in forensic, no doubt. He raised his chin sharply at the woman in the overcoat. "Get her a blanket. Keep her here." He went back to the gate and entered the southern section of the island.

Depending upon how one looked at it, the place was either a dream-come-true or a crime-scene nightmare. Evidence abounded, everything from disintegrating newspapers to partially filled and discarded plastic sacks. The whole area looked like a common dumping ground with at least a dozen good—and obviously different—footprints pressed into the soggy earth.

"Hell," Sheehan muttered.

Wooden planks had been laid down by the scenes-of-crime team. They started at the gate and travelled south, disappearing into the fog. He picked his way along these, avoiding the regular splattering of water from the trees overhead. Fogdrops, his daughter Linda would have called them with that passion for linguistic accuracy which always surprised him into thinking that his real daughter had somehow been left behind at the hospital sixteen years ago and a pixy-faced poet left in her place.

He paused by a clearing where two canvases and an easel leaned against a poplar and a wooden case gaped open, collecting a skin of condensation on a neat row of pastels and eight hand-lettered tubes of paint. He frowned at this, looking from the river to the bridge to the great puffs of fog rising like a gas from the fen. As the subject for a painting, it reminded him of that French stuff he'd seen at the Courtauld Institute years ago, dots and swirls and dashes of colour that you could only figure out if you stood forty feet away and squinted like the devil and thought about how things might look if you needed specs.

Further along, the planks veered to the left, and he came upon his police photographer and the forensic biologist. They were bundled against the cold in overcoats and knitted caps, and they pranced about like two Russian dancers, hopping from foot to foot to keep the circulation going. The photographer looked as pale as he usually did prior to having to document a killing. The forensic biologist looked peeved. She hugged her arms to her chest, shifted from one foot to the other in a bobbling fashion, and glanced repeatedly and restlessly in the direction of the causeway as if in the belief that the killer lingered beyond them in the fog and only by plunging through it immediately could they hope to apprehend him.

As Sheehan reached them and began to ask his customary question—"What d'we have this time?"—he saw the reason for the forensic biologist's impatience. A tall figure was emerging from the mist beneath the crack willows, walking carefully with his eyes on the ground. In spite of the cold, his cashmere greatcoat was slung indifferently round his shoulders like a cape, and he wore no scarf to detract from the crisp, clean lines of his Italian suit. Drake, the head of Sheehan's forensic department, one-half of a bickering duo of scientists that had been aggravating him for the last five months. He was indulging in his flair for costume this morning, Sheehan noted.

"Anything?" he asked the scientist.

Drake paused to light a cigarette. He pinched the match with his gloved fingers, and deposited it in a small jar which he took from his pocket. Sheehan refrained from comment. The bloody man never went anywhere unprepared.

"We appear to be missing a weapon," he said. "I should think we're going to have to drag the river for a look."

Wonderful, Sheehan thought, and counted up the men and the hours it would take to complete the operation. He went to have a look at the body.

"Female," the biologist said. "Just a kid."

As Sheehan gazed down at the girl, he reflected upon the fact that there was none of the hush which one would expect to attend a death. Horns bellowed from the causeway; idling engines bawled; brakes squealed; voices called. Birds chirruped in the trees, and a dog yelped sharply in pain or play. Life was continuing, despite the proximity and the evidence of violence.

That the girl's death had been violent was unquestionable. Although much of her had been deliberately covered with fallen leaves, enough of her body was exposed to allow Sheehan to see the worst. Someone had beaten in her face. The tie of her track jacket's hood was wound round her neck. Whether she had died from head wounds or from strangulation would ultimately have to be determined by the pathologist, but one thing was clear: No one would be able to identify her from a simple glance at her face. It was battered.

Sheehan squatted for a careful, closer look. She lay on her right side, her face turned into the earth and her long hair falling forward and coiling on the ground. Her arms were in front of her, wrists together but unbound. Her knees were bent.

He gnawed thoughtfully at his lower lip, glanced at the river five feet away, looked back at the body. She was wearing a stained brown tracksuit and white athletic shoes with dirty laces. She looked trim. She looked fit. She looked like the political nightmare he had hoped she wouldn't be. He lifted her arm to see if there was any insignia on her jacket. His breath puffed out of him in a sigh of despair when he saw that a shield surmounted by the words *St. Stephen's College* had been sewn onto the material that covered her left breast.

"God damn," he muttered. He replaced her arm and nodded at the photographer. "Shoot her," he said and moved away.

He looked across Coe Fen. The fog seemed to be lifting, but it might have been the effect of growing daylight, a momentary illusion, or wishful thinking. Still, it didn't matter if the fog was there or not, for Sheehan was Cambridge born and bred, and he knew what lay beyond that opaque veil of shifting mist. Peterhouse. Across the street, Pembroke. To Pembroke's left, Corpus Christi. From there, to the north, the west, and the east sprang college after college. Surrounding them, servicing them, owing its very existence to the presence of the University was the city itself. And all of it—colleges, faculties, libraries, businesses, homes, and inhabitants—represented more than six hundred years of uneasy symbiosis.

A movement behind him and Sheehan turned to look into Drake's moody grey eyes. Obviously, the forensic scientist had known what to expect. He'd been long anticipating the opportunity to put the thumbscrews to his subordinate back in the lab.

"Unless she beat in her own face and made the weapon disappear, I doubt anyone will argue *this* a suicide," he said.

In his London office, New Scotland Yard's Superintendent Malcolm Webberly mashed out his third cigar in as many hours and surveyed his divisional DI's, wondering how merciful they would be about ignoring the egg which he was about to splatter upon his own face. Considering the length and volume of his diatribe only two weeks ago, he knew he could probably expect the worst. He certainly deserved it. He had expostulated with his team for at least thirty minutes about what he had caustically referred to as the Cross-Country Crusaders, and now he was about to ask one of his men to join them.

He evaluated the possibilities. They were sitting round the central table in his office. As usual, Hale was giving way to nervous energy, playing with a pile of paperclips which he appeared to be fashioning into a form of lightweight mail, perhaps with the anticipation of doing battle with someone armed with toothpicks. Stewart—the divisional compulsive—was using the pause in conversation to work on a report, a behaviour that was typical to him. Rumour had it that Stewart had somehow managed to perfect making love to his wife and filling out police reports simultaneously, and with just about the same degree of enthusiasm. Next to him, MacPherson was cleaning his fingernails with a broken-tipped pen knife, a this-too-shall-pass expression on his face, while on his left Lynley polished his reading spectacles with a snow-coloured handkerchief on which the heavily embroidered letter *A* adorned one corner.

Webberly had to smile at the irony of the situation. A fortnight ago, he had been expounding on the country's current penchant for peripatetic policing, using as fodder a piece in the *Times* which consisted of an expose on the amount of public funds being poured into the unnatural workings of the criminal justice system.

"Look at this," he had snarled, bunching the newspaper in his hand in such a way that made looking at it impossible. "We've got the Greater Manchester Force investigating Sheffield on suspicion of bribery because of that Hillsborough football cock-up. We've got Yorkshire in Manchester, looking at complaints against some senior officers. We've got West Yorkshire peeping at the serious crimes squad in Birmingham; Avon and Somerset dabbling round the Guilford Four in Surrey; and Cambridge-shire mucking out Northern Ireland, looking for dust under the beds of the RUC. No one's patrolling his own patch any longer and it's time that stopped!''

His men had nodded in thoughtful agreement, although Webberly wondered if any of them had really been listening. Their hours were long, their burdens tremendous. Thirty minutes given to their superintendent's political maundering were thirty minutes they could ill afford. That latter thought came to him later, however. At the moment, the craving for debate was upon him, his audience was captive, he was compelled to continue.

"This is miserable rubbish. What's happened to us? CC's are running like bashful milkmaids at the first sign of trouble from the press. They ask anyone and everyone to investigate their men rather than run their own force, conduct their own investigation, and tell the media to eat cow dung in the meantime. Who are these idiots that they don't have the gumption to wash their own dirty laundry?''

If anyone took umbrage with the superintendent's display of mixed metaphors, no one commented upon it. Instead, they bowed to the rhetorical nature of his question and waited patiently for him to answer it, which he did, in an oblique fashion.

"Just let them ask *me* to become part of this nonsense. I'll give them all a real piece of what-for.''

And now he had come to it, with a special request from two separate parties, direction from Webberly's own superior officer, and neither time nor opportunity to give anyone what-for.

Webberly pushed himself back from the table and lumbered to his desk where he pressed the intercom for his secretary. In response the slender box chattered with static and conversation. The former he was used to. The intercom had not worked properly since the hurricane of 1987. The latter, unfortunately, he was used to as well: Dorothea Harriman waxing warmly eloquent on the object of her not inconsiderable admiration.

"They're dyed, I tell you. Have been for years. That way there's no mascara to smudge up her eyes in pictures and such . . .'' An interruption of static. ''. . . can't tell *me* Fergie's anything . . . I don't care how many more babies she decides—''

"Harriman,'' Webberly interrupted.

"White tights would look the best . . . when she used to favour those god-awful *spots*. Thank God, she's given them a rest.''

"Harriman.''

"...darling hat she had on at Royal Ascot this summer, did you see?...*Laura Ashley?* No! I wouldn't be seen dead..."

Speaking of death, Webberly thought and resigned himself to a more primitive, stentorian, and decidedly effective manner of getting his secretary's attention. He strode to the door, yanked it open, and shouted her name.

Dorothea Harriman popped into the doorway as he returned to the table. She'd had her hair cut recently, quite short in the back and on the sides, a long glossy bit of blonde mane in the front that swept across her brow in a glitter of artificial gold highlighting. She wore a red wool dress, matching pumps, and white tights. Unfortunately, red favoured her as little as it did the Princess. But, like the Princess, she had remarkable ankles.

"Superintendent Webberly?" she asked, with a nod at the officers sitting round the table. It was a butter-wouldn't-melt look. All business, it declared. Every moment of *her* day was spent with her nose pressed directly upon the grindstone of her job.

"If you can tear yourself away from your current evaluation of the Princess..." Webberly said. His secretary's expression was a study in guilelessness. *Princess who?* was telegraphed across her innocent face. He knew better than to engage her in indirect combat. Six years of her adulation of the Princess of Wales had taught him he would lose in any attempt to shame her away from wallowing in it. He resigned himself to saying, "There's a FAX due from Cambridge. See about it. Now. If you get any calls from Kensington Palace, I'll keep them on hold."

Harriman pressed the very front of her lips together, but an imp's smile curled both corners of her mouth. "FAX," she said. "Cambridge. Right. In a tick, Superintendent." And she added as a parting shot, "Charles went there, you know."

John Stewart looked up, tapping the top of his pen reflectively against his teeth. "Charles?" he asked in some confusion, as if wondering whether the attention he had been giving to his report had somehow caused him to lose the drift of the conversation.

"Wales," Webberly said.

"Whales in Cambridge?" Stewart asked. "What sort of whales? Where? Have they opened an aquarium?"

"Wales as in princes of," Phillip Hale barked.

"The Prince of Wales is in Cambridge?" Stewart asked. "But that should be handled by Special Branch, not by us."

"Jesus." Webberly took Stewart's report from him and used it to gesture with as he spoke. Stewart winced when Webberly rolled it into a tube. "No Prince. No Wales. Just Cambridge. Got it?"

"Sir."

"Thank you." Webberly noted with gratitude that MacPherson had put away his pocket knife and that Lynley was regarding him evenly with those unreadable dark eyes that were so much at odds with his perfectly clipped blond hair.

"There's been a killing up in Cambridge that we've been asked to take on," Webberly said and brushed away both their objections and their comments with a quick, vertical chopping motion of his hand. "I know. Don't remind me. I'm eating my own words. I don't much like it."

"Hillier?" Hale asked astutely.

Sir David Hillier was Webberly's Chief Superintendent. If a request for the involvement of Webberly's men came from him, it was no request at all. It was law.

"Not altogether. Hillier approves. He knows about the case. But the request came directly to me."

Three of the DI's looked at each other curiously. The fourth, Lynley, kept his eyes on Webberly.

"I temporised," Webberly said. "I know your plates are full at the moment, so I can get one of the other divisions to take this. But I'd rather not do that." He returned Stewart his report, and watched as the DI assiduously smoothed the pages against the table top to remove the curled edges. He continued speaking. "A student's been murdered. A girl. She was an undergraduate at St. Stephen's College."

All four men reacted to that. A movement in the chair, a question cut off quickly, a sharp look in Webberly's direction to read his face for signs of worry. All of them knew that the superintendent's own daughter was a junior member of St. Stephen's College. Her photograph—giggling as she inexpertly punted both parents in an endless circle on the River Cam—stood on one of the filing cabinets in the room. Webberly saw the concern on their faces.

"It's nothing to do with Miranda," he reassured them. "But she knew the girl. That's part of the reason I got the call."

"But not the only reason," Stewart said.

"Right. The calls—there were two of them—didn't come from Cambridge CID. They came from the Master of St. Stephen's College and the University's Vice Chancellor. It's a tricky situation as far as the local police are concerned. The killing didn't occur in the college, so Cambridge

CID have the right to pursue it on their own. But since the victim's a college girl, they need the University's cooperation to investigate."

"Th' University won't gie it?" MacPherson sounded incredulous.

"They prefer an outside agency. From what I understand, they got their feathers ruffled over the way the local CID handled a suicide last Easter term. Gross insensitivity towards everyone concerned, the Vice Chancellor said, not to mention some sort of leaking of information to the press. And since this girl is apparently the daughter of one of the Cambridge professors, they want everything handled with delicacy and tact."

"Detective Inspector Empathy," Hale said with a curl of his lip. It was, they all knew, a poorly veiled attempt to imply antagonism and lack of objectivity. None of them were unaware of Hale's marital troubles. The last thing he wanted at the moment was to be sent out of the city on a lengthy case.

Webberly ignored him. "Cambridge CID aren't happy about the situation. It's their patch. They prefer to handle it. So whoever goes can't expect them to start killing the fatted calf. But I've spoken briefly to their superintendent—a bloke called Sheehan . . . he seems a decent sort—and they'll cooperate. He sees the University implying this is a town-and-gown situation and he's miffed about the idea that his team might be accused of prejudice against the students. But he knows that without the University's cooperation, any man he sends in will spend the next six months sifting through sawdust in order to find sand."

The sound of her light footsteps heralded Harriman. She presented Webberly with several sheets of paper on which the words *Cambridgeshire Constabulary* were printed along the top and in the right-hand corner a badge surmounted by a crown. She frowned at the collection of plastic coffee cups and foul-smelling ashtrays that sat on the table amid folders and documents. She clucked, tossed the cups into the waste bin by the door, and carried the ashtrays at arm's length from the room.

As Webberly read the report, he passed on the pertinent information to his men.

"Not much to work with so far," he said. "Twenty years old. Elena Weaver." He gave the girl's Christian name a Mediterranean pronunciation.

"A foreign student?" Stewart asked.

"Not from what I gathered from the Master of the College this morning. The mother lives in London and as I've said, the dad's a professor at the University, a bloke short-listed for something called the Penford Chair of History—whatever the hell that is. He's a senior fellow at St. Stephen's. A major reputation in his field, I was told."

"Thus the red carpet treatment," Hale interjected.

Webberly continued. "They've done no autopsy yet, but they're giving us an initial rough estimate of the time of death between midnight last night and seven this morning. Face beaten in with a heavy, blunt instrument—"

"Isn't it always?" Hale asked.

"—after which—according to the preliminaries—she was strangled."

"Rape?" Stewart asked.

"No indication of that yet."

"Midnight and seven?" Hale asked. "But you said she wasn't found in college?"

Webberly shook his head. "She was found by the river." He frowned as he read the rest of the information Cambridge Constabulary had sent. "She was wearing a tracksuit and athletic shoes, so they assume she was out running when somebody jumped her. The body was covered with leaves. Some sketch artist stumbled on her round a quarter past seven this morning. And, according to Sheehan, got sick on the spot."

"Nae on the body, I hope," MacPherson said.

"That certainly plays hell with trace evidence," Hale noted.

The others laughed quietly in response. Webberly didn't mind the levity. Years of exposure to murder hardened the softest of his men.

He said, "According to Sheehan they had enough evidence at the scene to keep two or three crime scene teams busy for weeks."

"How's that?" Stewart asked.

"She was found on an island, and it's used as a general trysting place, evidently. So they've at least half a dozen sacks of rubbish to analyse along with their tests on the body itself." He tossed the report onto the table. "That's the limit of what we know right now. No autopsy. No record of interviews. Whoever takes the case will be working from the bottom."

"It's a nice little mairder, nonetheless," MacPherson said.

Lynley stirred, reaching out for the report. He put on his spectacles, read it over, and having done so, he spoke for the first time.

"I'll take it," he said.

"I thought you were working on that rent boy case in Maida Vale," Webberly said.

"We tied it up last night. This morning, rather. Brought the killer in at half past two."

"Good God, laddie, take a breather sometime," MacPherson said.

Lynley smiled and rose. "Have any of you seen Havers?"

Detective Sergeant Barbara Havers sat at one of the green computers in the Information Room on the ground floor of New Scotland Yard. She stared at the screen. She was supposed to be scanning the PNC for information on missing persons—at least five years missing, if the forensic anthropologist was to be believed—in an attempt to narrow down the possibilities on a set of bones found beneath the basement foundation of a building being torn down on the Isle of Dogs. It was a favour for a mate at the Manchester Road police station, but her mind wasn't up to assimilating the facts on the screen, let alone comparing them to a list of dimensions of radius, ulna, femur, tibia, and fibula. Roughly, she rubbed her index finger and thumb through both eyebrows and glanced at the telephone on a nearby desk.

She ought to phone home. She needed to get her mother on the line or at least to speak with Mrs. Gustafson and see if everything was under control in Acton. But punching in those seven numbers and waiting with mounting anxiety for the phone to be answered and then facing the possible knowledge that things weren't working out any better than they had been for the last week . . . She couldn't do it.

Barbara told herself that there was no point to phoning Acton anyway. Mrs. Gustafson was nearly deaf. Her mother existed in her own cloudy world of long-term dementia. The chance of Mrs. Gustafson hearing the phone was as remote as her mother's ability to understand that the shrill double ringing coming from the kitchen meant that someone somewhere wanted to speak through that peculiar black instrument that hung from the wall. Hearing the noise, she was as likely to open the oven or go to the front door as she was to pick up the telephone receiver. And even if she managed that much, it was doubtful she'd recognise Barbara's voice or even remember who she was without endless, frustrating, hair-pulling prodding.

Her mother was sixty-three years old. Her health was excellent. It was only her mind that was dying.

Employing Mrs. Gustafson to stay with Mrs. Havers during the day was, Barbara knew, only at best a temporary and unsatisfactory measure. Seventy-two years old herself, Mrs. Gustafson had neither the energy nor the resources to care for a woman whose day had to be programmed and monitored as carefully as a toddler's. Three times already Barbara had come face-to-face with the impediments inherent to giving Mrs. Gustafson even limited guardianship over her mother. Twice she had arrived home later than usual to find Mrs. Gustafson sound asleep in the sitting room. While the television shrieked out a programme's laugh track, her mother floated in a mental fugue, once wandering at the bottom of the back garden, once swaying aimlessly outside on the front steps.

But the third incident, just two days ago, had rocked Barbara severely. An interview connected to the Maida Vale rent boy case had brought her close to her own neighbourhood, and she had gone home unexpectedly to see how things were going. The house was empty. At first she felt no panic, assuming Mrs. Gustafson had taken her mother for a walk and, in fact, feeling quite grateful that the older woman was even up to the challenge of controlling Mrs. Havers in the street.

Gratitude disintegrated with Mrs. Gustafson's appearance on the front steps less than five minutes later. She'd just popped home to feed her fish, she said, and added, "Mum's all right, i'nt she?"

For a moment, Barbara refused to believe what Mrs. Gustafson's question implied. "She isn't with you?" she asked.

Mrs. Gustafson raised one liver-spotted hand to her throat. A tremor shook the grey curls of her wig. "Just popped home to feed the fish," she said. "No more'n a minute or two, Barbie."

Barbara's eyes flew to the clock. She felt panic sweeping over her and with it came the wild scattering of a dozen different scenarios comprising her mother lying dead in the Uxbridge Road, her mother floundering through the crowds on the Tube, her mother trying to find her way to South Ealing Cemetery where both her son and her husband were buried, her mother thinking she were twenty years younger with an appointment at the beauty parlour to keep, her mother being assaulted, being robbed, being raped.

Barbara rushed from the house, leaving Mrs. Gustafson wringing her hands and wailing "It was just the fish" as if that could somehow excuse her negligence. She gunned her Mini and roared in the direction of the Uxbridge Road. She tore down streets and crisscrossed alleys. She stopped people. She ran into local stores. And she finally found her on the grounds of the local primary school where both Barbara and her long-dead younger brother had once been pupils.

The Headmaster had already phoned the police. Two uniformed constables—one male and one female—were talking with her mother when Barbara arrived. Against the windows of the school building itself, Barbara could see curious faces pressed. And why not, she thought. Her mother certainly presented a spectacle, wearing a thin summer house dress and slippers and nothing else at all save her spectacles, which were not on her nose but for some reason perched on the top of her head. Her hair was uncombed, her body smelled unwashed. She babbled, protested, and argued like a madwoman. When the female constable reached out for her, she dodged away adroitly and began running towards the school, calling for her children.

That had been just two days ago, yet another indication that Mrs. Gustafson was not the answer.

In the eight months since her father's death, Barbara had tried a variety of solutions to the problem of her mother. At first, she'd taken her to an adult day care centre, the very latest thing in dealing with the aged. But the centre couldn't keep their "clients" after seven at night, and the calls of policework made her hours irregular. Had he known of her need to fetch her mother by seven, Barbara's superior officer would have insisted that she take the time to do so. But that would have placed an unfair burden upon his shoulders, and Barbara valued her job and her partnership with Thomas Lynley too highly to jeopardise either by giving her personal problems priority.

She'd tried a variety of paid companions after that, four in succession who lasted a total of twelve weeks. She'd worked with a church group. She'd employed a series of visiting social workers. She'd contacted Social Services and arranged for home help. And at the last, she'd fallen back upon Mrs. Gustafson, their neighbour. Against the monitory recommendation of her own daughter, Mrs. Gustafson had stepped in as a temporary measure. But the fuse on Mrs. Gustafson's ability to deal with Mrs. Havers was a short one. And the fuse on Barbara's willingness to put up with Mrs. Gustafson's lapses was even shorter. It was only a matter of days before something blew.

Barbara knew the answer was an institution. But she couldn't live with the thought of placing her mother in a public hospital rife with inadequacies associated with the National Health. At the same time, she couldn't afford a private hospital, unless she won the football pools like a female Freddie Clegg.

She felt in her jacket pocket for the business card she'd placed there this morning. Hawthorn Lodge, it said. Uneeda Drive, Greenford. A single call to Florence Magentry and her problems would be solved.

"Mrs. Flo," Mrs. Magentry had said when she answered the door to Barbara's knock at half past nine that morning. "That's what my dears call me. Mrs. Flo."

She lived in a two-storey semi-detached piece of uninspired postwar housing which she optimistically called Hawthorn Lodge. Grey stucco relieved by a brick facade on the ground floor, the house featured woodwork the colour of oxblood and a five-paned bow window looking out on a front garden filled with trolls. The front door opened directly into a stairway. To the right of this a door revealed a sitting room into which Mrs. Flo led Barbara, chatting continually about the "amenables" which the house offered the dears who came to visit.

"I call it a visit," Mrs. Flo said, patting Barbara's arm with a hand that was soft and white and surprisingly warm. "Seems less permanent that way, doesn't it? Let me show you round."

Barbara knew she was looking for features that she could proclaim ideal. She ticked the items off in her mind. Comfortable furniture in the sitting room—worn but well-made—along with a television, a stereo, two shelves of books, and a collection of large and colourful magazines; fresh paint and wallpaper and gay prints on the walls; tidy kitchen and a dinette whose windows overlooked the back garden; four bedrooms upstairs, one for Mrs. Flo and the other three for the dears. Two loos, one up and one down, both glistening white with fixtures shining like silver. And Mrs. Flo herself, with her large-framed spectacles and her modern wedge-cut hair and her neat shirtwaister with a pansy brooch pinned at its throat. She looked like a smart matron, and she smelled of lemons.

"You've phoned up at just the right time," Mrs. Flo said. "We lost our dear Mrs. Tilbird last week. Ninety-three she was. Sharp as a pin. Went off in her sleep, bless her. Just as peaceful as ever you'd want someone's passing to be. She'd been with me a month short of ten years." Mrs. Flo's eyes became misty in her plump-cheeked face. "Well, no one lives forever, and that's a fact, isn't it? Would you like to meet the dears?"

The residents of Hawthorn Lodge were taking a bit of morning sun in the back garden. There were only two of them, one an eighty-four-year-old blind woman who smiled and nodded at Barbara's greeting after which she immediately fell asleep and the other a frightened-looking woman somewhere in her fifties, who clutched Mrs. Flo's hands and cowered back in her chair. Barbara recognised the symptoms.

"Can you cope with two?" she asked frankly.

Mrs. Flo smoothed down the hair of the hand clutcher. "They're no trouble to me, dear. God gives everyone a burden, doesn't He? But no one's burden is more than he can bear.''

Barbara thought of that now with her fingers still touching the card in her jacket pocket. Is that what she was trying to do, to slough off a burden that, from laziness or perverse selfishness, she didn't want to bear?

She avoided the question by evaluating everything that made the placement of her mother at Hawthorn Lodge right. She enumerated the positives: the proximity to Greenford Station and the fact that she would only have to change trains once—at Tottenham Court Road—if she placed her mother in this situation and herself took the small studio she'd managed to find in Chalk Farm; the greengrocer's stand right inside Greenford Station where she could buy her mother fresh fruit on the way to a visit; the common just a street away with its central walk lined with hawthorns which led to a play area of swings, see-saw, round-about, and benches where they could sit and watch the neighbourhood children romp; the string of businesses nearby—a chemist, a supermarket, a wine shop, a bakery, and even a Chinese take-away, her mother's favourite food.

Yet even as she listed every feature that encouraged her to phone Mrs. Flo while she still had a vacancy, Barbara knew she was deliberately avoiding a few of the qualities of Hawthorn Lodge which she hadn't been able to ignore. She told herself that nothing could be done about the unremitting noise from the A40, or about the fact that Greenford itself was a sandwich of a community squeezed between the railway and a motorway. Then there were the three broken trolls in the front garden. Why on earth should she even think of them, except that there was something so pathetic about the chipped nose on one, the broken hat on another, the armlessness of a third. And there was something chilling about the shiny patches on the sofa where oily, old heads had pressed against its back for too long. And the crumbs in the corner of the blind woman's mouth . . .

Minor things, she told herself, little hooks digging into the skin of her guilt. One couldn't expect perfection anywhere. Besides, all of these minor points of discomfiture were inconsequential when one compared them with the circumstances of their lives in Acton and the condition of the house in which they now lived.

The reality, however, was that this decision went far beyond Acton versus Greenford and far beyond keeping her mother at home or sending her away. The entire decision went right to the core of what Barbara herself wanted, which was simple enough: a life away from Acton, away from her mother, away from the burdens which, unlike Mrs. Flo, she did not believe she was equipped to bear.

Selling the house in Acton would give her the money to support her mother in Mrs. Flo's house. She would have the funds to set herself up in Chalk Farm as well. No matter that the Chalk Farm studio was little more than twenty-five feet long and twelve feet wide, little more than a converted potting shed with a terra cotta chimney and missing slates on the roof. It had possibilities. And that's all Barbara asked of life any longer, just the promise of possibility.

Behind her, the door opened as someone slipped an identification card through its locking device. She glanced over her shoulder as Lynley entered, looking quite rested despite their late night with the Maida Vale killer.

"Any luck?" he asked her.

"Next time I offer to do a bloke a favour, punch my lights, will you? This screen makes me blind."

"Nothing then, I take it?"

"Nothing. But I haven't exactly been giving it my all." She sighed, made a note of the last entry she'd read, and exited the programme. She rubbed her neck.

"How was Hawthorn Lodge?" Lynley asked her. He swung a chair over and joined her at the terminal.

She did her best to avoid his eyes. "Nice enough, I suppose. But Greenford's a bit out on the central line. I don't know how Mum would make the adjustment. She's used to Acton. The house. You know what I mean. She likes having her things about her."

She felt him watching her, but knew that he would not offer advice. Their positions in life were far too different for him to presume to make a suggestion. Still, Barbara knew he was only too aware of her mother's condition and the decisions she herself now faced because of it.

"I feel like a criminal," she said hollowly. "Why?"

"She gave you life."

"I didn't ask for it."

"No. But one always feels a responsibility to the giver. What's the best course to take? we ask. And is the best course the right one, or is it just a convenient escape?"

"God doesn't give burdens we cannot bear," Barbara heard herself mouth.

"That's a particularly ridiculous platitude, Havers. It's worse than saying things always work out for the best. What nonsense. Things work out for the worst more often than not, and God—if He exists—distributes unbearable burdens all the time. You of all people ought to know that."

"Why?"

"You're a cop." He pushed himself to his feet. "We've a job out of town. It'll be a few days. I'll go on ahead. You come when you can."

His offer irked her, filled as it was with the implicit understanding of her situation. She knew he wouldn't take another officer. He'd do his work and her own until she could join him. How utterly like him. She hated his easy generosity. It made her his debtor, and she did not possess—would never possess—the coin with which he might be repaid.

"No," she said. "I'll get things set up at home. I'll be ready in . . . How much time do I have? An hour? Two?"

"Havers . . ."

"I'll *go.*"

"Havers, it's Cambridge."

She jerked her head up, saw the undisguised satisfaction in his warm brown eyes. She shook her head darkly. "You're a real fool, Inspector."

He nodded, grinned. "But only for love."

3

Anthony Weaver pulled his Citroën to a halt on the wide gravel drive of his home in Adams Road. He stared through the windscreen at the winter jasmine that grew—neat and restrained—on the trellis to the left of the front door. For the last eight hours he'd been living in the region that lies just between a nightmare and hell, and now he was numb. It was shock, his intellect told him. Certainly, he'd begin feeling something again just as soon as this period of disbelief had passed.

He made no move to get out of the car. Instead, he waited for his former wife to speak. But stolidly sitting next to him in the passenger seat, Glyn Weaver maintained the silence with which she had greeted him at the Cambridge railway station.

She hadn't allowed him to drive to London to fetch her, to carry her suitcase, or to open a door. Nor had she allowed him to witness her grief. He understood. He'd already accepted the blame for their daughter's death. He'd taken on that responsibility the moment he'd identified Elena's body. Glyn had no need to hurl accusations at him. He would have agreed with every one.

He saw her eyes sweep over the front of the house, and he wondered if she would remark upon it. She hadn't been to Cambridge since helping Elena get settled into St. Stephen's in her first term, and even then she'd not set foot in Adams Road.

She would, he knew, see the house as indication of the combined elements of remarriage, inheritance, and professional egocentricity, a veritable showpiece of his success. Brick, three storeys, white woodwork, decorative tile cladding from second storey to roofline, a glass-enclosed morning room with a roof terrace atop it. This was a far cry from their claustrophobic newlywed digs, three rooms on Hope Street more than twenty years ago. This house was set alone at the end of a curved drive, not butted up to a neighbour's dwelling and squatting less than five feet from the street. This was the house of a tenured professor, a respected member of the history faculty. This was no ill-lit tenement of dying dreams.

To the right of the house, a copper beech hedge—brilliant with the sunset colours of autumn—walled off the back garden. Through an opening in the bushes, an Irish setter bounded joyfully towards the car. Seeing the animal, Glyn spoke for the first time, her voice low, without apparent emotion.

"This is her dog?"

"Yes."

"We couldn't keep one in London. The flat was too small. She always wanted a dog. She talked about a spaniel. She—"

Breaking off, Glyn got out of the car. The dog took two hesitant steps forward, tongue hanging out in a slap-dash canine grin. Glyn observed the animal but made no overt attempt to greet him. He took another two steps and snuffled round her feet. With a rapid blink, she looked back at the house.

She said, "Justine's made you a lovely place in the world, Anthony."

Between brick pilasters, the front door opened, its polished oak panels catching what little of the quickly fading afternoon light managed to seep through the fog. Anthony's wife, Justine, stood with one hand on the doorknob. She said, "Glyn. Come in. Please. I've made tea," after which she backed once again into the house, wisely offering no condolences where they would not be welcome.

Anthony followed Glyn into the house, carrying her suitcase up to the guestroom, and returning to find her and Justine standing in the sitting room, Glyn at the window overlooking the front lawn with its careful arrangement of white, wrought iron furniture glistening through the fog, and Justine by the sofa with the tips of her fingers pressed together in front of her.

His first and second wives could not have been more dissimilar. Glyn, at forty-six, was making no attempt to resist the encroachments of middle-age. Her face was worn, with crow's feet at her eyes, deep lines like trenches from nose to chin, tiny indentations shooting out from her lips, jawline losing definition from the pull of flesh beginning to sag. Grey streaked her hair, which she wore long, drawn back from her face in a severe chignon. Her body was thickening at the waist and hips, and she covered it with tweed and wool and flesh-coloured stockings and flat walking shoes.

In contrast, Justine, at thirty-five, still managed to suggest the fresh bloom of youth. Blessed with the sort of facial structure that would only enhance her looks as she grew older, she was attractive without being beautiful, with smooth skin, blue eyes, knife-edged cheekbones, a firm jaw. She was tall and lanky with a cascade of dusty blonde hair that hung, as it had from adolescence, loosely round her shoulders. Trim and fit, she wore the same clothes now in which she had gone off to work this morning, a tailored grey suit with a wide black belt, grey stockings, black pumps, a silver pin on her lapel. She was perfect, as always.

Anthony looked beyond her to the dining room where she had laid the table for afternoon tea. It served as demonstration of how Justine had spent the hours since he had telephoned her at the University Press to tell her of his daughter's death. While he had been to the morgue, to the police station, to the college, to his office, to the railway station, while he had identified the body and answered questions and accepted incredulous condolences and contacted his former wife, Justine had made her own preparations for the coming days of their mourning. The result of her efforts was spread across the burl-topped dining table.

On a linen cloth sat the entire tea service from their wedding china, a pattern of gilt-edged roses and curling leaves. Among the plates and cups and silver and crisp white napkins and vases of flowers lay a poppy seed cake, a platter of delicate afternoon sandwiches, another of thinly sliced bread and butter, fresh scones, strawberry jam, and clotted cream.

Anthony looked at his wife. Justine smiled fleetingly, saying again with an airy motion at the table, "I've made tea."

"Thank you, darling," he said. The words felt unnatural, badly rehearsed.

"Glyn." Justine waited for the other woman to turn. "May I offer you something?"

Glyn's eyes slid to the table, from there to Anthony. "Thank you. No. I couldn't possibly eat."

Justine turned to her husband. "Anthony?"

He saw the trap. For a moment, he felt suspended in the air, like the rope in an endless tug-of-war. Then he went to the table. He chose a sandwich, a scone, a slice of cake. The food tasted like sand.

Justine came to his side and poured the tea. Its steam rose in the air with the fruity scent of the modern, herbal blend she preferred. The two of them stood there with the food spread out before them, the silver gleaming, and the flowers fresh. Glyn remained by the window in the other room. No one moved towards a chair.

"What did the police tell you?" Glyn asked. "They never phoned me."

"I told them not to."

"Why?"

"I thought I should be the one to—"

"You?"

Anthony saw Justine set down her teacup. He saw that her eyes remained on its rim.

"What happened to her, Anthony?"

"Glyn, sit down. Please."

"I want to know what happened."

Anthony set his plate down next to the cup of tea which he had not tasted. He returned to the sitting room. Justine followed. He sat on the sofa, motioned his wife down next to him, and waited to see if Glyn would move from the window. She did not do so. Next to him, Justine began twisting her wedding band.

Anthony recited the facts for Glyn. Elena was out running, someone killed her. She was beaten and strangled.

"I want to see the body."

"No. Glyn. You don't."

Glyn's voice wavered for the first time. "She was my daughter. I want to see the body."

"Not as she is now. Later. When the morticians—"

"I'll see her, Anthony."

He could hear the tight elevation in her voice and knew from experience where it would lead. He headed her off with, "One side of her face is bashed in. The bones are showing. She doesn't have a nose. Is that what you want to see?"

Glyn fumbled in her handbag and brought out a tissue. "Damn you," she whispered. Then, "How did it happen? You told me—you promised me—she wouldn't run alone."

"She phoned Justine last night. She said she wasn't going to run this morning."

"She phoned . . ." Glyn's glance moved from Anthony to his wife. "You ran with Elena?"

Justine stopped twisting her wedding band, but she kept her fingers on it, as if it were a talisman. "Anthony asked me to. He didn't like her running along the river when it was dark, so I ran as well. Last night she phoned and said she wouldn't be running, but evidently, for some reason she changed her mind."

"How long has this been going on?" Glyn asked, her attention going back to her former husband. "You said Elena wouldn't be running alone, but you never said that Justine—" She abruptly shifted gears. "How could you do that, Anthony? How could you entrust your daughter's well-being to—"

"Glyn," Anthony interposed.

"She wouldn't be concerned. She wouldn't watch over her. She wouldn't take care to see that she was safe."

"Glyn, for God's sake."

"It's true. She's never had a child, so how could she know what it's like to watch and wait and worry and wonder. To have dreams. A thousand and one dreams that won't come to anything because *she* didn't run with Elena this morning."

Justine hadn't moved on the sofa. Her expression was fixed, a glazed mask of good breeding. "Let me take you to your room," she said and got to her feet. "You must be exhausted. We've put you in the yellow room at the back of the house. It's quiet there. You'll be able to rest."

"I want Elena's room."

"Well, yes. Of course. That's no trouble at all. I'll just see to the sheets . . ." Her voice drifting off, Justine left the room.

Glyn said at once, "Why did you give her Elena?"

"What are you saying? Justine is my wife."

"That's the real point, isn't it? How much do you care that Elena's dead? You've got someone right here to cook up another."

Anthony got to his feet. Against her words, he summoned up the image of Elena as he last had seen her from the window of the morning room, offering him a grin and a final wave from her bicycle as she pedalled off to a supervision after their lunch together. It had been just the two of them, eating their sandwiches, chatting about the dog, sharing an hour of love.

He felt anguish swell. Re-create Elena? Fashion another? There was only one. He himself had died with her.

Blindly, he pushed past his ex-wife. He could still hear her low, harsh words continue as he left the house even though he couldn't distinguish one from another. He stumbled to his car, fumbled the keys into the ignition. He was reversing down the driveway when Justine ran outside.

She called his name. He saw her caught for a moment in the headlamps before he plunged his foot onto the accelerator and, with a sputter of gravel, clattered into Adams Road.

He felt his chest heaving, his throat aching as he drove. He began to weep—dry, hot, tearless sobs for his daughter and his wives and the mess he'd made of every part of his life.

He was on Grange Road and then on Barton Road and then, blessedly, out of Cambridge itself. It had grown quite dark and the fog was thick, especially in this area of fallow, open fields and winter-dying hedges. But he drove without caution, and when the countryside gave way to a village, he parked and threw himself out of the car only to find that the temperature had fallen further, encouraged by the bitter East Anglian wind. He'd left his overcoat at home. All he wore was a suit jacket. But that was of no account. He turned up its collar and began to walk, past a kissing gate, past half a dozen thatched cottages, stopping only when he came to her house. He crossed the street then to get some distance from the building. But even through the fog, he could see in the window.

She was there, moving across the sitting room with a mug in her hand. She was small, so slender. If he held her, she would be practically nothing in his arms, just a fragile heartbeat and a glowing life that consumed him, fired him, and had once made him whole.

He wanted to go to her. He needed to talk to her. He wanted to be held.

He stepped off the kerb. As he did so, a car skidded by, horn honking in warning, a stifled shout from inside. It brought him back to his senses.

He watched her go to the fireplace where she fed wood into the flames as he once had done, turning from the fire to find her eyes on him, her smile a benediction, her hand held out.

"Tonio," she'd murmur, his name underscored with love.

And he'd answer her even as he did this moment. *"Tigresse."* Just a whisper. *"Tigresse. La Tigresse."*

Lynley arrived in Cambridge at half past five and drove directly to Bulstrode Gardens where he parked the Bentley in front of a house that reminded him of Jane Austen's home in Chawton. Here was the same symmetry of design—two casement windows and a white front door below, three evenly spaced windows in the same positions above. Possessing a pantiled roof and several plain chimneys, the house was a rectangular, solid, uninteresting piece of architecture. Lynley didn't, however, feel the same disappointment upon seeing it that he had felt in Chawton. One expected Jane Austen to have lived in a snug, whimsically atmospheric thatched cottage surrounded by a garden filled with flowerbeds and trees. One didn't expect a struggling lecturer from the divinity faculty to maintain a wife and three children in that kind of wattle-and-daub heaven.

He got out of the car and shrugged into his overcoat. The fog, he noted, managed to obscure and romanticise features of the house that spoke of a growing indifference and neglect. In lieu of a garden, a semi-circular driveway of leaf-strewn pebbles curved round the front door, and the inner part of the semi-circle comprised an overgrown flowerbed which was separated from the street by a low, brick wall. Here, nothing had been done to prepare the ground for autumn or winter, so the remains of summer plants were lying blackened and dying against a solid sheet of unturned soil. A large hibiscus was fast overpowering the garden wall, trailing among the yellowed leaves of narcissi which should long ago have been cleared away. To the left of the front door an actinidia had worked its way up to the roof and was sending out tendrils to cover one of the lower windows, while to the right of the door, the same species of plant was creating an inert mound of disease-spotted leaves. As a result, the front of the house bore a lopsided appearance at odds with the symmetry of its design.

Lynley passed beneath a birch at the edge of the drive. From a neighbouring house, he could hear faint music, and somewhere in the fog a door slammed like the crack of a pistol shot. Sidestepping an overturned large-wheeled tricycle, he mounted the single step to the porch and rang the bell.

Its noise was answered by the shouting of two children who raced to the front door with the accompanying clatter of some sort of popping toy. Hands which could not yet successfully manage the doorknob pounded frantically instead on the wood.

"Auntie Leen!" Either the boy or the girl was doing the shouting. It was difficult to tell.

A light went on in the room to the right of the front door, sending an insubstantial oblong of illumination onto the driveway through the mist. A baby began crying. A woman's voice called out, "Just a moment."

"Auntie Leen! Door!"

"I know, Christian."

Above his head, the porchlight went on, and Lynley heard the sound of the deadbolt turning. "Step back, darling," the woman said as she opened the door.

The four of them were framed by the architrave, and held in a sideways diffusion of gold light from the sitting room that would have done credit to Rembrandt. Indeed, just for a moment, they looked very much like a painting, the woman in a rose cowl-necked sweater against which she held an infant wrapped in a cranberry shawl while two toddlers clutched the legs of her black wool trousers, a boy with a misshapen bruise beneath his eye and a girl with the handle of some sort of wheeled toy in her hand. This, apparently, was the source of the popping sound Lynley had heard, for the toy was domed in transparent plastic and when the child pushed it along the floor, coloured balls flew up and hit the dome like noisy bubbles.

"Tommy!" Lady Helen Clyde said. She took a step back from the door and urged the two children to do the same. They moved like a unit. "You're in Cambridge."

"Yes."

She looked over his shoulder as if in the expectation of seeing someone with him. "You're alone?"

"Alone."

"What a surprise. Come in."

The house smelled strongly of wet wool, sour milk, talcum powder, and nappies, the odours of children. It was filled with the detritus of children as well, in the form of toys strewn across the sitting room floor, storybooks with torn pages gaping open on the sofa and chairs, discarded jumpers and playsuits heaped on the hearth. A stained blue blanket was bunched onto the seat of a miniature rocking chair, and as Lynley followed Lady Helen through the sitting room into the kitchen at the rear of the house, the little boy ran to this, grabbed it, and clutched it. He peered at Lynley with defiant curiosity.

"Who's he, Auntie Leen?" he demanded. His sister remained at Lady Helen's side, her left hand fixed like an extra appendage to her aunt's trousers while her right hand made the climb to her face and her thumb found its way into her mouth. "Stop that, Perdita," the boy said. "Mummy says not to suck. You baby."

"Christian," Lady Helen said in gentle admonition. She guided Perdita to a child-sized table beneath a window where the little girl began to rock in the tiny ladder-back chair, her thumb in her mouth, her large dark eyes fixed with what looked like desperation on her aunt.

"They're not dealing with a new baby sister very well," Lady Helen said quietly to Lynley, shifting the crying infant to her other shoulder. "I was just taking her up to be fed."

"How's Pen doing?"

Lady Helen glanced at the children. The simple look said it all. No better.

She said, "Let me take the baby up. I'll be back in a moment." She smiled. "Can you manage?"

"Does he bite?"

"Only girls."

"That's a comforting thought."

She laughed and went back through the sitting room. He heard her footsteps on the stairs and the sound of her voice as she murmured to the baby, gentling its cries.

He turned back to the children. They were twins, he knew, just over four years old, Christian and Perdita. The girl was older by fifteen minutes, but the boy was larger, more aggressive, and, from what Lynley could see, unlikely to respond to friendly overtures from strangers. That was just as well, considering the times in which they lived. Nonetheless, it didn't make for a comfortable situation. He had never been at his best with toddlers.

"Mummy's sick." Christian accompanied this announcement by bashing his foot into the door of a kitchen cupboard. One, two, three savage little kicks, whereupon he discarded his blanket on the floor, opened the cupboard, and began pulling out a set of copper-bottomed pots. "The baby made her sick."

"That happens sometimes," Lynley said. "She'll get better soon."

"*I* don't care." Christian pounded a pan against the floor. "Perdita cries. She wet the bed last night."

Lynley glanced at the little girl. Curly hair tumbling into her eyes, she rocked without speaking. Her cheeks worked in and out round her thumb. "She didn't mean to, I imagine."

"Daddy won't come home." Christian selected a second pan which he banged unmercifully into the first. The noise was teeth-jarring, but it didn't seem to bother either one of the children. "Daddy doesn't like the baby. He's cross with Mummy."

"What makes you think that?"

"I like Auntie Leen. She smells good."

Here, at least, was a subject about which they could converse. "She does indeed."

"You like Auntie Leen?"

"I like her very much."

Christian seemed to feel this planted the seeds of friendship between them. He scrambled to his feet and shoved a pot and its cover into Lynley's thigh.

"Here," he said. "You do this way," and he demonstrated his skill at noise-making by slamming another cover onto a pot of his own.

"Really, Tommy! Are you encouraging him?" Lady Helen closed the kitchen door behind her and went to rescue her sister's pots and pans. "Sit with Perdita, Christian. Let me get your tea."

"No! I play!"

"Not at the moment, you don't." Lady Helen detached his fingers from the handle of a pot, lifted him up, and carried him to the table. He kicked and squalled. His sister watched him, round-eyed and rocking. "I've got to get their tea," Lady Helen said to Lynley over Christian's wailing. "He won't settle till he's eaten."

"I've come at a bad time."

She sighed. "You have."

He felt his spirits sink. She knelt and began gathering the pots from the floor. He joined her. In the unforgiving kitchen light, he could see how pale she was. The natural blush of colour was faded from her skin, and there were faint smudges like newly bruised flesh beneath her eyes. He said, "How much longer will you be here?"

"Five days. Daphne comes on Saturday for her two weeks. Then Mother for two. Then Pen's on her own." She brushed a lock of chestnut hair off her cheek. "I can't think how she's going to cope alone, Tommy. This is the worst she's ever been."

"Christian said his father's not here much."

Lady Helen pressed her lips together. "Quite. Well. That's putting it mildly."

He touched her shoulder. "What's happened to them, Helen?"

"I don't know. Some sort of blood score. Neither one of them will talk about it." She smiled without humour. "The sweet bliss of a marriage made in heaven."

Unaccountably stung, he removed his hand.

"I'm sorry," she said.

His mouth quirked in a smile. He shrugged and put the last pot in its place.

"Tommy." He looked her way. "It isn't any good. You know that, don't you? You shouldn't have come."

She got to her feet and began removing food from the refrigerator, carrying four eggs, butter, a wedge of cheese, and two tomatoes to the cooker. She rummaged in a drawer and dragged out a loaf of bread. Then quickly, without speaking, she made the children's tea while Christian occupied himself by scribbling on the table top with a stubby pencil he'd removed from between the pages of a telephone directory on a jumble-covered work top nearby. Perdita rocked and sucked blissfully with her eyes at half-mast.

Lynley stood by the kitchen sink, watching Lady Helen. He hadn't removed his overcoat yet. She hadn't offered to take it from him.

What, he wondered, had he hoped to accomplish by coming to her at her sister's house when she was plagued by worry and worn by the effort of caring for two children and an infant who were not even hers? What had he hoped? That she would fall gratefully into his arms? That she would see him as her blessed salvation? That her face would light with joy and desire? That her defences would crumble and her spirit surrender—finally, irrefutably, once and for all? Havers was right. He was such a fool.

"I'll be off, then," he said.

She turned from the stove where she was scooping scrambled eggs onto two Beatrix Potter plates. "Back to London?" she asked.

"No. I'm here on a case." He told her what little he knew about it, concluding with, "They've given me digs at St. Stephen's."

"So you can relive your own undergraduate days?"

"Bedders and gyp rooms and night keys from the porter."

She took the plates to the table along with the toast, grilled tomatoes, and milk. Christian fell to like a victim of famine. Perdita rocked. Lady Helen placed a fork in her hand, touched her dark head, and rubbed her fingers gently against the child's downy cheek.

"Helen." He found some comfort in saying her name. She looked up. "I'll be off now."

"Let me see you out."

She followed him back through the sitting room to the front door. It was colder in this part of the house. He looked at the stairway.

"Shall I say hello to Pen?"

"I don't think so, Tommy." He cleared his throat, nodded. As if she read his expression, she touched his arm lightly. "Please understand."

He knew instinctively that she wasn't talking about her sister. "I suppose you can't get away for dinner."

"I can't leave her alone with them. God only knows when Harry's coming home. He's staying for formal dinner at Emmanuel tonight. He may sleep there as well. He's done that already four nights this past week.''

"Will you phone me at the college if he comes home?''

"He won't—''

"Will you phone?''

"Oh, Tommy.''

He felt a sudden, overpowering surge of hopelessness which prompted him to say, "I volunteered for this case, Helen. When I knew it was Cambridge.''

As soon as the words were out, he despised himself. He was resorting to the worst form of emotional blackmail. It was manipulative, dishonest, and unworthy of them both. She didn't respond. In the shadows of the hallway, she was darkness and light. The glossy unbroken curve of hair to her shoulders, the cream of her skin. He reached out, caressed the line of her jaw. She came into the shelter of his overcoat. He felt her arms slip warmly round him. He rested his cheek on the top of her head.

"Christian said he likes you because you smell good,'' he whispered.

Against his chest, he could feel her smile. "Did he?''

"Yes.'' He let himself hold her for a moment longer before he pressed his lips to the top of her head. "Christian was right,'' he said and released her. He opened the front door.

"Tommy.'' She crossed her arms in front of her. He said nothing, waiting, willing her to take some sort of first step.

"I'll phone,'' she said. "If Harry turns up.''

"I love you, Helen.'' He walked to his car.

Lady Helen returned to the kitchen. For the first time in the nine days that she had been in Cambridge, she looked at the room dispassionately, seeing it as an outside observer would see it. *Dissolution,* it declared.

Despite the fact that she had scrubbed it herself only three days ago, the yellow linoleum floor was once again grimy, patched with spilled food and drink from the children's meals. The walls looked greasy, with grey handprints smeared like directional indicators against the paint. Work tops acted as storage space for anything that couldn't be fitted anywhere else. A stack of unopened mail, a wooden bowl of apples and browning bananas, half a dozen newspapers, a plastic jar of kitchen utensils and brushes, and a children's colouring book and crayons shared the area with a wine rack, an electric mixer, a toaster, and a shelf of dusty books. Beneath the burners on the cooker, the remains of boil-overs lay like sour slop, and cobwebs collected on three empty wicker baskets atop the refrigerator.

Lady Helen wondered what Lynley must have thought, seeing all this. It was quite a change from the only other time he had been in Bulstrode Gardens for a quiet summer dinner in the back garden, preceded by drinks on a lovely terrace that had since been turned into a sandbox and play area now choked with toys. Her sister and Harry Rodger had been live-in lovers then, consumed with each other and fueled by the delights of early love. They were virtually oblivious of everything else. They exchanged meaningful glances and knowing smiles; they touched each other fondly at the slightest excuse; they fed each other small morsels of food and shared a drink. They had their own lives by day—Harry lecturing at the University and Pen working for the Fitzwilliam Museum—but by night they were one.

Their devotion to each other had seemed excessive and embarrassing to Lady Helen at the time, too cloying to be in particularly good taste. But now she questioned the nature of her own reaction to such an overt display of love. And she admitted the fact that she would rather see her sister and Harry Rodger clinging and cooing than witness what they had come to over the birth of their third child.

Christian was still noisily addressing himself to his tea. His toast fingers had become dive bombers, and with accompanying sound effects which he supplied at maximum volume, he was flying them gustily into his plate. Eggs, tomatoes, and cheese dripped down the front of his playsuit. His sister had only picked at her own meal. At the moment, she was sitting motionless in her chair with a Cabbage Patch doll laid across her lap. She was studying it pensively, but she did not touch it.

Lady Helen knelt by Perdita's chair as Christian shouted, "Ka-boom! Ka-plowy!" Eggs splashed across the table. Perdita blinked as a bit of tomato hit her on the cheek.

"Enough, Christian," Lady Helen said, taking his plate from him. He was her nephew. She was supposed to love him and under most circumstances she could say that she did. But after nine days, her patience was at its lowest ebb, and if she'd ever had compassion for the unspoken fears that underlay his behaviour, she found that she couldn't summon it at the moment. He opened his mouth for a howl of protest. She reached across the table and covered it with her hand. "Enough. You're being a wicked little boy. Stop this right now."

That beloved Auntie Leen would speak to him in such a manner seemed to surprise Christian momentarily into cooperation. But only for a moment. He said, "Mummy!" and his eyes filled with tears.

Without the slightest qualm, Lady Helen seized the advantage. "Yes. Mummy. She's trying to rest, but you're not making it very easy for her, are you?" He fell silent and she turned to his sister. "Won't you eat something, Perdita?"

The little girl kept her eyes on her doll which lay inertly across her lap, with cheeks shaped like marbles and a placid smile on her lips. The appropriate picture of infancy and childhood, Lady Helen thought. She said to Christian, "I'm going up to check on Mummy and the baby. Will you keep Perdita company for me?"

Christian eyed his sister's plate. "She din't eat," he said.

"Perhaps you can persuade her to have a bit."

She left them together and went to her sister. In the upper corridor, the house was quiet, and at the top of the stairs she took a moment to lean her forehead against the cold pane of a window. She thought of Lynley and his unexpected appearance in Cambridge. She had a fairly good idea of what his presence presaged.

It had been nearly ten months since he had made the wild drive to Skye in order to find her, nearly ten months since the icy day in January when he had asked her to marry him, nearly ten months since she had refused. He had not asked her again, and in the intervening time they had somehow reached an unspoken agreement to try to retreat to the easy companionship which they once had shared. It was a retreat that brought little satisfaction to either of them, however, for in asking her to marry him, Lynley had crossed an undefined boundary, altering their relationship in ways neither of them could have possibly foreseen. Now they found themselves in an uncertain limbo in which they had to face the fact that while they could call themselves friends for the rest of their lives if they chose to do so, the reality was that friendship had ended between them the moment Lynley took the alchemical risk of changing it into love.

Their every meeting since January—no matter how innocent or superfluous or casual—had been subtly coloured by the fact that he had asked her to marry him. And because they had not spoken of it again, the subject seemed to lie like quicksand between them. One wrong step and she knew she'd go under, caught in the suffocating mire of attempting to explain to him that which would hurt him more than she could bear.

Lady Helen sighed and pulled back her shoulders. Her neck felt sore. The cold window had made her forehead feel damp. She was tired to the bone.

At the end of the corridor, her sister's bedroom door was closed, and she tapped on it quietly before letting herself in. She didn't bother to wait for Penelope to answer her knocking. Nine days with her sister had taught her that she would not do so.

The windows were closed against the nighttime fog and cold air, and an electric fire in addition to the radiator made the room claustrophobic. Between the closed windows sat her sister's king-size bed, and, looking ashen-faced even in the soft light of the bedside table, Penelope lay holding the infant to her swollen breast. Even when Lady Helen said her name, she kept her head tilted back against the headboard, her eyes squeezed shut, her lips pressed into a scar line of pain. Her face was sheened with sweat which was forming rivulets that ran from her temples to her jaws, then dripped and formed new rivulets on her bare chest. As Lady Helen watched, a single inordinately heavy tear trickled down her sister's cheek. She didn't wipe it away. Nor did she open her eyes.

Not for the first time, Lady Helen felt the frustration of her own uselessness. She had seen the condition of her sister's breasts, with their cracked and bleeding nipples; she had heard her sister cry out as she expressed the milk. Yet she knew Penelope well enough to know that nothing she might say could make a difference to her once she was bent upon a course of action. She *would* breast-feed this baby until its sixth month, no matter the pain or the cost. Motherhood had become a fine point of honour, a position from which she would never retreat.

Lady Helen approached the bed and looked at the baby, noticing for the first time that Pen wasn't holding her. Rather, she had placed the infant on a pillow and it was this which she held, pressing the baby's face to her breast. The baby sucked. Soundlessly, Pen continued to weep.

She hadn't been out of the room all day. Yesterday, she had managed ten listless minutes in the sitting room with the twins squabbling at her feet while Lady Helen changed the sheets on her bed. But today she had remained behind the closed door, stirring herself only when Lady Helen brought the baby to be fed. Sometimes she read. Sometimes she sat in a chair by the window. Most of the time she wept.

Although the baby was now a month old, neither Pen nor her husband had yet named the child, referring to it as *the baby, she,* or *her.* It was as if not naming the baby made her presence in their lives a less permanent feature. If she didn't have a name, she didn't really exist. If she didn't exist, they hadn't created her. If they hadn't created her, they didn't have to examine the fact that whatever love, lust, or devotion moved her making seemed to have disappeared between them.

Fist curled, the infant gave over sucking. Her chin was wet with a thin greenish film of mother's milk. Releasing a fractured breath, Pen pushed the pillow away from her breast, and Lady Helen raised the baby to her own shoulder.

"I heard the door." Pen's voice was weary and strained. She did not open her eyes. Her hair—dark like her children's—lay in a limp mass pressed to her skull. "Harry?"

"No. It was Tommy. He's here on a case."

Her sister's eyes opened. "Tommy Lynley? What did he want here?"

Lady Helen patted the baby's warm back. "To say hello, I suppose." She walked to the window. Pen shifted in bed. Lady Helen knew she was watching her.

"How did he know where to find you?"

"I told him, of course."

"Why? No, don't answer. You wanted him to come, didn't you?" The question had the ring of an accusation. Lady Helen turned from the window where the fog was pressing like a monstrous, wet cobweb against the glass. Before she could answer, her sister continued. "I don't blame you, Helen. You want to get out of here. You want to get back to London. Who wouldn't?"

"That's not true."

"Your flat and your life and the silence. God oh God, I miss the silence most of all. And being alone. And having time to myself. And privacy." Pen began to weep. She fumbled among creams and unguents on the bedside table for a box of tissues. "I'm sorry. I'm a mess. I'm no good for anyone."

"Don't say that. Please. You know it isn't true."

"Look at me. Just please *look* at me, Helen. I'm good for nothing. I'm just a baby machine. I can't even be a proper mother to my children. I'm a ruin. I'm a slug."

"It's depression, Pen. You do see that, don't you? You went through this when the twins were born, and if you remember—"

"I didn't! I was fine. Perfectly. Completely."

"You've forgotten how it was. You've put it behind you. As you'll do with this."

Pen turned her head away. Her body heaved with a sob. "Harry's staying at Emmanuel again, isn't he?" She flashed a wet face in her sister's direction. "Never mind. Don't answer. I know he is."

It was the closest thing to an opening Pen had given her in nine days.

Lady Helen took it at once, sitting down on the edge of the bed. "What's happening here, Pen?"

"He's got what he wants. Why hang about to examine the damage?"

"Got . . . ? I don't understand. Is there another woman?"

Pen laughed bitterly, choked back a sob, and then deftly changed the subject. "You know why he's come up from London, Helen. Don't pretend you're naive. You know what he wants, and he intends to get it. That's the real Lynley spirit. Charge right towards the goal."

Lady Helen didn't reply. She laid Pen's daughter on her back on the bed, feeling warmed by the baby's fist-waving, leg-kicking grin. She wrapped the tiny fingers round one of her own and bent to kiss them. What a miracle she was. Ten fingers, ten toes, sweet miniature nails.

"He's here for more reasons than to solve some little murder and you ought to be ready to head him off."

"That's all in the past."

"Don't be such a fool." Her sister leaned forward, grabbed onto her wrist. "Listen to me, Helen. You've got it all right now. Don't throw it away because of a man. Get him out of your life. He wants you. He means to have you. He'll never give it up unless you spell it out for him. So do it."

Lady Helen smiled in what she hoped was a loving fashion. She covered her sister's hand with her own. "Pen. Darling. We aren't play-acting at *Tess of the D'Urbervilles*. Tommy isn't in hot pursuit of my virtue. And even if he were, I'm afraid he's about—" She laughed lightly. "Let me try to remember . . . Yes, he's just about fifteen years too late. Fifteen years exactly on Christmas Eve. Shall I tell you about it?"

Her sister pulled away. "This isn't a joke!"

Lady Helen watched, feeling surprised and helpless, as Pen's eyes filled again. "Pen—"

"No! You're living in a dream world. Roses and champagne and cool satin sheets. Sweet little babies delivered by the stork. Adoring children sitting on mama's knee. Nothing smelly or unpleasant or painful or disgusting. Well, take a good look round here if you mean to get married."

"Tommy hasn't come to Cambridge to ask me to marry him."

"Take a good long look. Because life's rotten, Helen. It's filthy and lousy. It's just a way to die. But you don't think of that. You don't think of anything."

"You're not being fair."

"Oh, I dare say you think about screwing him, though. That's what you hoped for when you saw him tonight. I don't blame you. How could I? He's supposed to be quite the performer in bed. I know at least a dozen women in London who'll be only too happy to attest to that. So do what you want. Screw him. Marry him. I only hope you're not so stupid as to think he'd be faithful to you. Or your marriage. Or to anything, in fact."

"We're only friends, Pen. That's the beginning and end of it."

"Maybe you just want the houses and cars and servants and money. And the title, of course. We mustn't forget that. Countess of Asherton. What a brilliant match. At least one of us will end up making Daddy proud." She turned on her side and switched out the light on the bedside table. "I'm going to sleep now. Put the baby to bed."

"Pen."

"No. I'm going to sleep."

4

"It was always clear that Elena Weaver had the potential for a first," Terence Cuff said to Lynley. "But I suppose we say that about most undergraduates, don't we? What would they be doing here if they didn't have the potential to take firsts in their subjects?"

"What was hers?"

"English."

Cuff poured two sherries and handed one to Lynley. He nodded towards three over-stuffed chairs that were grouped round a gateleg table to the right of the library's fireplace, a two-tiered demonstration of one of the more flamboyant aspects of late Elizabethan architecture, decorated with marble caryatids, Corinthian columns, and the coat of arms of Vincent Amberlane, Lord Brasdown, the college founder.

Before coming to the lodge, Lynley had taken a solitary evening stroll through the seven courts that comprised the western two-thirds of St. Stephen's College, pausing in the fellows' garden where a terrace overlooked the River Cam. He was a lover of architecture. He took pleasure in the evidence of each period's individual caprice. And while he had always found Cambridge itself to be a rich source of architectural whimsies—from Trinity Great Court's fountain to Queens' Mathematical Bridge—St. Stephen's College, he discovered, merited special attention. It spanned five hundred years of design, from the sixteenth-century Principal Court, with its buildings of red brick and freestone quoins, to the twentieth-century, triangular North Court, where the junior combination room, the bar, a lecture hall, and the buttery were contained in a series of sliding glass panels framed by Brazilian mahogany. St. Stephen's was one of the largest colleges in the University, "bound by the Trinities" as University brochures described it, with Trinity College to its north, Trinity Hall to its south, and Trinity Lane bisecting its west and east sections. Only the river running along its western boundary kept the college from being entirely hemmed in.

The Master's Lodge sat at the southwest end of the college grounds, abutting Garret Hostel Lane and facing the River Cam. Its construction dated from the 1600's, and like its predecessors in Principal Court, it had escaped the ashlar refacing that had been so popular in Cambridge in the eighteenth century. Thus, it maintained its original brick exterior and contrasting stone quoins. And like much of the architecture of the period, it was a happy combination of classical and Gothic details. Its perfect balance spoke of the influence of classical design. Two bay windows jutted out on either side of the front door, while a row of dormer windows topped by semi-circular pediments rose from a pitched slate roof. A lingering love of the Gothic showed itself in that roof's crenellation, in the pointed arch that comprised the building's entry, and in the fan vaulting of that entry's ceiling. It was here that Lynley came to keep his appointment with Terence Cuff, Master of St. Stephen's and a graduate of Exeter College, Oxford, where Lynley himself had been a student.

Lynley watched Cuff settle his lanky frame into one of the overstuffed chairs in the panelled library. He couldn't remember having heard about Cuff during his own time at Oxford, but as the man was some twenty years Lynley's senior, this fact could hardly constitute an indication of Cuff's failure to distinguish himself as an undergraduate.

He seemed to wear confidence with the same ease with which he wore his fawn trousers and navy jacket. It was clear that while he was deeply—perhaps even personally—concerned about the murder of one of the junior members of the college, he did not look upon Elena Weaver's death as a statement about his competence as college head.

"I'm relieved that the Vice Chancellor agreed to Scotland Yard's coordinating the investigation," Cuff said, setting his sherry on the gateleg table. "Having Miranda Webberly at St. Stephen's helped. It was easy enough to give the Vice Chancellor her father's name."

"According to Webberly, there was some concern about the way a case was handled by the local CID last Easter term."

Cuff rested his head against his index and forefinger. He wore no rings. His hair was thick and ash grey. "It was a clear-cut suicide. But someone from the police station leaked to the local press that it looked to him like a hushed-up murder. You know the sort of thing, an allegation that the University's protecting one of its own. It developed into a small but nasty situation fanned by the local press. I'd like to avoid that happening again. The Vice Chancellor agrees."

"But I understand the girl wasn't killed on University property, so it stands to reason that someone from the city may have committed the crime. If that's the case, you're heading into a nasty situation of another sort no matter what anyone wants from New Scotland Yard."

"Yes. Believe me, I know."

"So the Yard's involvement—"

Cuff stopped Lynley with the abrupt words: "Elena was killed on Robinson Crusoe's Island. Are you familiar with it? A short distance from Mill Lane and the University Centre. It's long been a gathering place for young people, somewhere they go to drink and smoke."

"Members of the colleges? That seems a bit odd."

"Quite. No. Members of college don't need the island. They can drink and smoke in their common rooms. The graduates can go to the University Centre. Anyone who wants to get up to anything else can do as much in his own bed-sit. We've a certain number of rules, naturally, but I can't say they're enforced with any regularity. And the days of the proctors patrolling are gone."

"Then I gather the island's mostly used by the city."

"The south end, yes. The north end's used to repair rivercraft in the winter."

"College boats?"

"Some."

"So students and locals might have occasion to bump into one another there."

Cuff didn't disagree. "An unpleasant run-in between a member of a college and someone from the city? A few choice epithets, the word *townee* hurled like an execration, and a killing as revenge?"

"Was Elena Weaver likely to have had that sort of run-in?"

"You're thinking of an altercation that led up to a lying-in-wait."

"It's a possibility, I should think."

Cuff looked over the top of his glass to an antique globe standing in one of the library's bay windows. The light from the room created the globe's duplicate—slightly contorted—on the imperfect pane. "To be frank, that doesn't sound at all like Elena. And even if that weren't the case, if we're talking about a killer who knew her and waited for her, I doubt it was someone from the city. As far as I know, she had no city relationship close enough to lead to murder.''

"An arbitrary killing then?''

"The night porter indicates she left the college grounds round a quarter past six. She was by herself. It would certainly be convenient to reach the conclusion that a young girl out running was victimised by a killer she didn't know. Unfortunately, I tend to think that's not the case.''

"Then you believe it was someone who knew her? A member of one of the colleges?''

Cuff offered Lynley a cigarette from a rosewood case on the table. When Lynley demurred, he lit one himself, looked away for a moment and said, "That seems more likely.''

"Have you any ideas?''

Cuff blinked. "None at all.''

Lynley noted the determined tone behind the words and led Cuff back to their original topic. "You mentioned that Elena had potential.''

"A telling statement, isn't it?''

"It does tend to suggest failure rather than success. What can you tell me about her?''

"She was in Part IB of the English tripos. I believe her coursework concentrated on the history of literature this year, but the senior tutor would be able to tell you exactly, if you need to know. He's been involved with Elena's adjustment here in Cambridge from her first term last year.''

Lynley raised an eyebrow. He knew the purpose of the senior tutor. It was far more personal than academic. So the fact that he had been involved with Elena Weaver suggested adjustment problems that went beyond a confused undergraduate's learning to cope with the mysteries of the University's system of education.

"There were troubles?''

Cuff took a moment to tap the ash from his cigarette into a porcelain ashtray before saying, "More so than most. She was an intelligent girl and a highly skilled writer, but quite soon into Michaelmas term last year she began missing supervisions, which sent the first red flag up.''

"And the other red flags?''

"She stopped attending lectures. She went to at least three supervisions drunk. She was out all night—the senior tutor could tell you how many times, if you feel it's important—without signing out with the porter.''

"I take it that you wouldn't have considered sending her down because of her father. Is he the reason why she was admitted to St. Stephen's in the first place?''

"Only partially. He's a distinguished academic, and we'd naturally give his daughter serious consideration. But beyond that, as I said she was a clever girl. Her A-levels were good. Her entrance papers were solid. Her interview was—all things considered—more than adequate. And she certainly had good reason to find the life at Cambridge overwhelming at first.''

"So when the flags came up . . . ?''

"The senior tutor, her supervisors, and I met to develop a plan of action. It was simple enough. Other than attending to her studies, putting in appearances at lectures, and turning in signed chits that indicated she'd been to her supervisions, we insisted she have more contact with her father so that he could monitor her progress as well. She began spending her weekends with him.'' He looked faintly embarrassed as he continued. "Her father suggested that it might be additionally helpful if we allowed her to keep a pet in her room, a mouse actually, in the hope it would develop her sense of responsibility and no doubt get her back to the college at night. Apparently she had quite a fondness for animals. And we brought in a young man from Queens'—a chap called Gareth Randolph—to act as an undergraduate guardian and, more importantly, to get Elena involved in an appropriate society. Her father didn't approve of that last item, I'm afraid. He'd been dead set against it from the very first.''

"Because of the boy?''

"Because of the society itself. DeaStu. Gareth Randolph's its president. And he's one of the more high-profile handicapped students in the University.''

Lynley frowned. "It sounds as if Anthony Weaver was concerned that his daughter might become romantically linked with a handicapped boy.'' Here was potential for trouble indeed.

"I've no doubt of that,'' Cuff said. "But as far as I was concerned, becoming involved with Gareth Randolph would have been the best thing for her.''

"Why?''

"For the obvious reason. Elena was handicapped as well.'' When Lynley said nothing, Cuff looked perplexed. "Surely you know. You would have been told.''

"Told? No.''

Terence Cuff leaned forward. "I'm terribly sorry. I thought you'd been given the information. Elena Weaver was deaf.''

•   •   •

DeaStu, Terence Cuff explained, was the informal name given to the Cambridge University Deaf Students Union, a group that met weekly in a small, vacant conference room in the basement of Peterhouse Library at the bottom of Little St. Mary's Lane. On the surface, they were a support group for the not insignificant number of deaf students who attended the University. Beyond that, they were committed to the idea of deafness being a culture in itself, rather than a handicap.

"They're a group with a great deal of pride," Cuff explained. "They've been instrumental in promoting tremendous self-esteem among the deaf students. No shame in signing rather than speaking. No dishonour in being unable to read lips."

"Yet you say that Anthony Weaver wanted his daughter to stay away from them. If she herself was deaf, that hardly makes sense."

Cuff got up from his chair and went to the fireplace, where he lit the coals that formed a small mound in a metal basket. The room was growing cold, and while the action was reasonable, it also bore the appearance of temporising. Once the fire was lit, Cuff remained standing near it. He sank his hands into his trouser pockets and studied the tops of his shoes.

"Elena read lips," Cuff explained. "She spoke fairly well. Her parents—her mother especially—had devoted themselves to enabling her to function as a normal woman in a normal world. They wanted her to appear for all intents and purposes as a woman who could hear. To them, DeaStu represented a step backwards."

"But Elena signed, didn't she?"

"Yes. But she'd only begun that as a teenager when her secondary school called in Social Services after failing to convince her mother of the need to enroll Elena in a special programme to learn the language. Even then, she wasn't allowed to sign at home. And as far as I know, neither of her parents ever signed with her."

"Byzantine," Lynley mused.

"To our way of thinking. But they wanted the girl to have a good chance to make her way in the hearing world. We might disagree with the way they went about it, but the final result was that she ended up with lip-reading, speech, and ultimately signing. In effect, she had it all."

"Those are the things she could do," Lynley agreed. "But I wonder where she felt she belonged."

The mound of coals shifted slightly as the fire took them. Cuff rearranged them deftly with a poker. "No doubt you can see why we were willing to make allowances for Elena. She was caught between two worlds. And as you yourself have pointed out, she wasn't brought up to fit completely into either.''

"It's such an odd decision for an educated person to make. What's Weaver like?''

"A brilliant historian. A fine mind. A man of deep, committed professional integrity.''

Lynley didn't miss the oblique nature of the answer. "I understand he's in line for some sort of advancement as well.''

"The Penford Chair? Yes. He's been short-listed for it.''

"What is it, exactly?''

"The University's main chair in the area of history.''

"An offer of prestige?''

"More. An offer to do exactly what he wants for the rest of his career. Lecture when and if he wants, write when and if he wants, take on graduate students when and if he wants. Complete academic freedom along with national recognition, the highest possible honours, and the esteem of his fellows. If he's selected, it shall be the finest moment of his career.''

"And would his daughter's spotty record here at the University have impeded his chances of being selected?''

Cuff shrugged off both question and implication, saying, "I haven't been a member of the search committee, Inspector. They've been reviewing potential candidates since last December. I can't tell you exactly what they're looking into.''

"But might Weaver have thought the committee would judge him in an ill light because of her problems?''

Cuff replaced the poker and ran his thumb over its dull, brass head. "I've always felt it's wise to stay clear of the interior lives and beliefs of the senior fellows,'' he replied. "I'm afraid I can't be of any help to you in this direction of enquiry.''

Only after he finished speaking did Cuff look up from the handle of the poker. And once again in their interview, Lynley clearly read the other man's reluctance to part with information.

"You'll be wanting to see where we've put you, no doubt,'' Cuff said politely. "Let me ring the porter.''

It was shortly after seven when Lynley rang the bell at Anthony Weaver's home off Adams Road. With an expensive-looking metallic blue

Citroën parked in its drive, the house was not a great distance from St. Stephen's College, so he had walked, crossing the river on the modern concrete and iron crescent of Garret Hostel Bridge and passing beneath the horse chestnut trees that littered Burrell's Walk with enormous yellow leaves sodden with the fog. The occasional bicycle rider passed him, muffled against the cold in knit hat, scarf, and gloves, but otherwise the path that connected Queen's Road with Grange Road was largely deserted. Lampposts provided sporadic illumination. Holly, fir, and box hedgerows—broken up by intermittent fencing that ran the gamut from wood to brick to iron—served as boundaries for the walk. Beyond them stood the russet mass of the University Library, into which shadowy figures scurried for last minutes of work prior to its closing.

The houses in Adams Road were all set behind hedges. Trees surrounded them, leafless silver birches that stood like pencil sketches against the fog, poplars whose bark displayed every variation of the colour grey, alders not yet offering their leaves to the coming winter. It was quiet here. Only the gurgle of water pouring into an outdoor drain broke into the stillness. The night air was tinged with the friendly fragrance of woodsmoke, but at the Weaver house the only scent outdoors came from the dampening wool of Lynley's own overcoat.

It was largely no different inside.

The door was opened by a tall, blonde woman with a face of chiselled, refined composure. She looked far too young to be Elena's mother, and she didn't appear particularly struck by grief. Lynley thought, as he looked at her, that he'd never seen anyone with such perfect posture. Every limb, bone, and muscle seemed locked into position, as if an unseen hand had arranged her stance at the door just moments before he knocked upon it.

"Yes." She said it as a statement, not a question. No part of her face moved other than her lips.

He produced his warrant card, introduced himself, and asked to see the dead girl's parents.

At this the woman stepped back from the door. She said only, "I'll fetch Anthony," and left him standing on the bronze and peach Oriental carpet of a parquet-floored entrance hall. To his left a door opened into a sitting room. To his right a glass-enclosed morning room held a wicker table that was set with linen and china for breakfast.

Lynley took off his overcoat, laid it over the polished handrail of the stairway, and went into the sitting room. He paused, feeling unaccountably put off by what he saw. Like the hall, the sitting room was floored in parquet, and like the hall the parquet was covered with an Oriental carpet.

On it sat grey leather furniture—a sofa, two chairs, and a chaise longue—and tables with pedestals of peach-veined marble and tops of glass. The watercolours on the walls had obviously been chosen, mounted, and framed to match the room's colour scheme, and they hung precisely centred over the sofa: the first, a bowl of apricots on a windowsill behind which shone a sky of robin's egg blue and the second, a slim grey vase of salmon-coloured oriental poppies with three blooms fallen to the ivory surface upon which the vase stood. Both of them were signed with the single word *Weaver*. Either husband, wife, or daughter had an interest in art. A slender glass tea table against one wall held an arrangement of silk tulips. Next to this was a single copy of *Elle* and a photograph in a silver frame. Other than these last two objects and the watercolours, there was nothing in the room to indicate that anyone actually lived in it. Lynley wondered what the rest of the house was like, and walked to the tea table to look at the photograph. It was a wedding portrait, perhaps ten years old, judging from the length of Weaver's hair. And the bride—looking solemn and celestial and surprisingly young—was the woman who had just answered the door.

"Inspector?" Lynley turned from his perusal of the picture as the dead girl's father came into the room. He walked quite slowly. "Elena's mother is asleep upstairs. Shall I wake her for you?"

"She's taken a pill, darling." Weaver's wife had come to the doorway where she hesitated, one hand touching the silver lily pinned to the lapel of her jacket.

"I've no need to see her at the moment if she's asleep," Lynley said.

"The shock," Weaver said and added unnecessarily, "She's just come up from London this afternoon."

"Shall I make coffee?" Weaver's wife asked. She'd ventured no further into the room.

"Nothing for me," Lynley said.

"Nor for me. Thank you, Justine. Darling." Weaver smiled at her briefly—the effort it cost him rode directly on the surface of the behaviour itself—and he held out a hand to indicate that she was to join them. She entered the sitting room. Weaver went to the fireplace where he lit a gas fire beneath an artful arrangement of artificial coals. "Please sit down, Inspector."

As Weaver himself chose one of the two leather chairs and his wife took the other, Lynley observed the man who had lost his daughter that day and saw in him the subtleties that illustrate the manner in which men are permitted to face before strangers the worst of their grief. Behind his thick wire-rimmed spectacles, his brown eyes were blood-shot, with crescents of red lining their lower lids. His hands—rather small for a man of his height—trembled when he gestured, and his lips, which were partially obscured by a dark, clipped moustache, quivered as he waited for Lynley to speak.

He was, Lynley thought, so different from his wife. Dark, his body thickening at the waist with advancing middle age, his hair beginning to show strands of scattered grey, his skin creasing on the forehead and webbing beneath the eyes. He wore a three-piece suit and a pair of gold cufflinks, but despite his rather formal attire, he managed to seem completely out of place in the cool, crafted elegance that surrounded him.

"What can we tell you, Inspector?" Weaver's voice was as unsteady as his hands. "Tell me what we can do to help. I need to know that. I need to find this monster. He strangled her. He beat her. Have they told you that? Her face was . . . She was wearing her gold chain with the little unicorn I'd given her last Christmas, so I knew it was Elena the moment I saw her. And even if she hadn't been wearing the unicorn, her mouth was partly open and I saw her front tooth. I saw that much. I saw that tooth. The little chip in it. That tooth."

Justine Weaver lowered her eyes and clasped her hands in her lap.

Weaver pulled his spectacles from his face. "God help me. I can't believe that she's dead."

Despite his presence in their home as a professional come to deal with the crime, Lynley was not untouched by the other man's anguish. How many times had he witnessed this very scene played out in the last thirteen years? And still he felt no more able to assuage grief than he had as a detective constable, facing his first interview with the hysterical adult daughter of a woman who'd been bludgeoned to death by her own, drunk husband. In every case, he'd allowed grief free rein, hoping by this means to offer victims the meagre solace of knowing that someone shared their need to see justice done.

Weaver continued to speak. As he did so, his eyes filled with tears. "She was tender. Fragile."

"Because she was deaf?"

"No. Because of me." When Weaver's voice cracked, his wife looked his way, pressed her lips together, and once more lowered her eyes. "I left her mother when Elena was five, Inspector. You're going to learn that eventually, so you may as well know it right now. She was in bed, asleep. I packed my bags and I left and I never went back. And

I had no way to explain to a five-year-old child—who couldn't even *hear* me—that I wasn't leaving her, that it wasn't her fault, that the marriage itself was so filled with unhappiness that I couldn't bear to live in it any longer. And Glyn and I were at fault for that. Not Elena, never once Elena. But I was her father. I left her, betrayed her. And she struggled with that—and with the idea that somehow *she* was at fault—for the next fifteen years. Anger, confusion, lack of confidence, fear. Those were her demons.''

Lynley didn't even need to formulate a question to guide Weaver's discourse. It was as if the man had only been waiting for an appropriate opportunity for self-flagellation.

"She could have chosen Oxford—Glyn was determined she'd go to Oxford, she didn't want her here with me—but Elena chose Cambridge instead. Can you know what that meant to me? All those years she'd been in London with her mother. I'd tried to be there for her as best I could, but she held me at a distance. She'd only let me be a father in the most superficial ways. Here was my chance to be a real father to her again, to mend our relationship, to bring to some sort of''—he searched for a word—''some sort of fulfillment the love I felt for her. And my greatest happiness was feeling the bond begin to grow between us over this last year and sitting here and watching while Justine helped Elena with her essays. When these two women . . . '' He faltered. ''These two women in my life . . . these two women together, Justine and Elena, my wife and my daughter . . . '' And finally he allowed himself to weep. It was a man's horrible, humiliated sobbing, one hand covering his eyes, the other clutching his spectacles.

Justine Weaver didn't stir in her chair. She looked incapable of movement, carved out of stone. Then a single breath eased from her and she raised her eyes and fastened them on the bright, artificial fire.

"I understand Elena had difficulties in the University at first,'' Lynley said as much to Justine as to her husband.

"Yes,'' Justine said. ''The adjustment for her . . . from her mother and London . . . to here . . . '' She glanced uneasily at her husband. ''It took a bit of time for her to—''

"How could she have made the change easily?'' Weaver demanded. ''She was struggling with her life. She was doing her best. She was trying to be whole.'' He wiped his face with a crumpled handkerchief which afterwards he continued to grasp—crushed—in his hand. He placed his spectacles back on his nose. ''But that didn't matter. Not a bit of it to me. Because she was a joy. An innocent. A gift.''

"Her troubles didn't cause you embarrassment, then? Professional embarrassment?"

Weaver stared at him. His expression altered in a single instant from ravaged sorrow to disbelief. Lynley found the sudden change disquieting, and despite the occasion for both grief and outrage, he found himself wondering if he was being entertained by a performance of some sort.

"My God," Weaver said. "What are you suggesting?"

"I understand you've been short-listed for a rather prestigious position here at the University," Lynley said.

"And what does that have to do with—"

Lynley leaned forward to interrupt. "My job is to obtain and evaluate information, Dr. Weaver. In order to do that, I have to ask questions you might otherwise prefer not to hear."

Weaver worked this over, his fingers digging into the handkerchief balled into his fist. "Nothing about my daughter was an embarrassment, Inspector. Nothing. Not a single part of her. And nothing she did."

Lynley tallied the denials. He reflected upon the rigid muscles in Weaver's face. He said, "Had she enemies?"

"No. And no one who knew her could have hurt Elena."

"Anthony," Justine murmured hesitantly, "you don't think she and Gareth . . . Might they have had a falling out?"

"Gareth Randolph?" Lynley said. "The president of DeaStu?" When Justine nodded, he went on with, "Dr. Cuff told me he'd been asked to act as a guardian to Elena last year. What can you tell me about him?"

"If he was the one, I'll kill him," Weaver said.

Justine took up the question. "He's an engineering student, a member of Queens' College."

Weaver said, more to himself than to Lynley, "And the engineering lab is next to Fen Causeway. He has his practicals there. His supervisions as well. What is it, a two-minute walk from Crusoe's Island? Across Coe Fen, a one-minute run?"

"Was he fond of Elena?"

"They saw a great deal of each other," Justine said. "But that was one of the stipulations set up by Dr. Cuff and her supervisors last year: attendance at DeaStu. Gareth saw to it that she went to the meetings. He took her to a number of their social functions as well." She shot her husband a wary look before she finished carefully with, "Elena liked Gareth well enough, I dare say. But not, I imagine, the way he liked her. And he's a lovely boy, really. I can't think that he—"

"He's in the boxing society," Weaver continued. "He's got a blue in boxing. Elena told me that."

"Could he have known that she would be running this morning?"

"That's just it," Weaver said. "She wasn't supposed to run." He turned to his wife. "You told me she wasn't going to run. You said that she'd phoned you."

His words had the ring of an accusation. Justine's body retreated fractionally, a reaction that was almost imperceptible considering her upright posture in the chair. "Anthony." She said his name like a discreet entreaty.

"She phoned you?" Lynley repeated, perplexed. "How?"

"On a Ceephone," Justine said.

"Some sort of visual phone?"

Anthony Weaver stirred, moved his eyes off his wife, and pushed himself out of his chair. "I've one in the study. I'll show you."

He led the way through the dining room, through a spotless kitchen fitted with an array of gleaming appliances, and down a short corridor that led to the rear of the house. His study was a small room that faced the back garden, and when he switched on the light, a dog began to whine beneath the window outside.

"Have you fed him?" Weaver asked.

"He wants to be let in."

"I can't face it. No. Don't do that, Justine."

"He's just a dog. He doesn't understand. He's never had to—"

"Don't do it."

Justine fell silent. As before, she remained by the door while Lynley and her husband went into the room.

The study was quite different from the rest of the house. A worn floral carpet covered the floor. Books crowded onto sagging shelves of cheap pine. A collection of photographs leaned against a filing cabinet, and a set of framed sketches hung on the wall. Beneath the room's single window stood Weaver's desk, large, grey metal, and utterly hideous. Aside from a pile of correspondence and a set of reference books, on it rested a computer, its monitor, a telephone, and a modem. This, then, constituted the Ceephone.

"How does it work?" Lynley asked.

Weaver blew his nose and shoved his handkerchief into his jacket pocket. He said, "I'll phone my rooms in the college," and walked to the desk, where he switched on the monitor, punched several numbers on the telephone, and pressed a data key on the modem.

After a few moments, the monitor screen divided into two sections, split horizontally by a thin, solid band. On the bottom half appeared the words: *Jenn here.*

"A colleague?" Lynley asked.

"Adam Jenn, my graduate student." Weaver typed quickly. As he did so, his message to the student was printed on the top half of the screen. *Dr. Weaver phoning, Adam. I'm demonstrating the Ceephone for the police. Elena used it last night.*

Right appeared on the bottom half of the screen. *Shall I stand by then? Do they want to see something special?*

Weaver cast Lynley a querying look. "No, that's fine," Lynley said. "It's clear how it works."

Not necessary, Weaver typed.

OK, the response. And then after a moment, *I'll be here the rest of the evening, Dr. Weaver. Tomorrow as well. And as long as you need me. Please don't worry about anything.*

Weaver swallowed. "Nice lad," he whispered. He switched off the monitor. All of them watched as the messages on the screen slowly faded away.

"What sort of message did Elena send you last night?" Lynley asked Justine.

She was still at the door, one shoulder against the jamb. She looked at the monitor as if to remember. "She said only that she wasn't going to run this morning. She sometimes had trouble with one of her knees. I assumed she wanted to give it a rest for a day or two."

"What time did she phone?"

Justine frowned pensively. "It must have been a bit after eight because she asked after her father and he wasn't yet home from the college. I told her he'd gone back to work for a while and she said she'd phone him there."

"Did she?"

Weaver shook his head. His lower lip quivered, and he pressed his left index finger to it as if by that action he could control further displays of emotion.

"You were alone when she phoned?"

Justine nodded.

"And you're certain it was Elena?"

Justine's fine skin seemed to tauten across her cheeks. "Of course. Who else—?"

"Who knew the two of you ran in the morning?"

Her eyes went to her husband, then back to Lynley. "Anthony knew. I suppose I must have told one or two of my colleagues."

"At?"

"The University Press."

"Others?"

Again, she looked at her husband. "Anthony? Do you know of anyone?"

Weaver was still staring at the monitor of the Ceephone, as if in the hope that a call would come through. "Adam Jenn, probably. I'm sure I told him. Her friends, I should think. People on her staircase."

"With access to her room, to her phone?"

"Gareth," Justine said. "Of course she would have told Gareth."

"And he has a Ceephone as well." Weaver looked sharply at Lynley. "Elena didn't make that call, did she? Someone else did."

Lynley could feel the other man's growing need for action. Whether it was spurious or genuine he could not tell. "It's a possibility," he agreed. "But it's also a possibility that Elena simply preferred to create an excuse to run alone this morning. Would that have been out of character?"

"She ran with her stepmother. Always."

Justine said nothing. Lynley looked her way. She averted her eyes. It was admission enough.

Weaver said to his wife, "You didn't see her at all when you were out this morning. Why, Justine? Weren't you looking? Weren't you watching?"

"I had the call from her, darling," Justine said patiently. "I wasn't expecting to see her. And even if I had been, I didn't go along the river."

"You ran this morning as well?" Lynley asked. "What time was this?"

"Our usual time. A quarter past six. But I took a different route."

"You weren't near Fen Causeway."

A moment's hesitation. "I was, yes. But at the end of the run, instead of the beginning. I'd made a circuit of the city and came across the causeway from east to west. Towards Newnham Road." With a glance at her husband, she made a slight change of position as if she were girding herself with strength. "Frankly, I hate running along the river, Inspector. I always have. So when I had the opportunity to take another route, I did just that."

It was, Lynley thought, the nearest thing to a revelation that Justine Weaver was likely to make in front of her husband about the nature of her relationship with his daughter Elena.

•   •   •

Justine let the dog into the house directly after the Inspector left. Anthony had gone upstairs. He wouldn't know what she was doing. Since he wouldn't come back down for the rest of the night, what could it hurt, Justine wondered, to let the dog sleep in his own wicker basket? She would get up early in the morning to let the animal out before Anthony even saw him.

It was disloyal to go against her husband this way. Justine knew her mother would never have done such a thing once her father had made his wishes known. But there was the dog to consider, a confused, lonely creature whose instincts told him something was wrong but who couldn't know what or understand why.

When Justine opened the back door, the setter came at once, not bounding across the lawn as was usual, but hesitantly, as if he knew that his welcome was at risk. At the door with his auburn head lowered, the dog raised hopeful eyes to Justine. His tail wagged twice. His ears perked up, then drooped.

"It's all right," Justine whispered. "Come in."

There was something comforting about the *snick-snicking* of the dog's nails on the floor as he pursued the smells on the kitchen tiles. There was something comforting about all his sounds: the yelp and the growl when he played, the *snarf* when he dug and got soil in his nose, the long sigh when he settled into his bed at night, the low hum when he most wanted someone's attention. He was in so many ways just like a person, a fact that Justine had found most surprising.

"I think a dog would be good for Elena," Anthony had said prior to her arrival in Cambridge last year. "Victor Troughton's bitch had a litter not long ago. I'll take Elena by and let her have her pick of the lot."

Justine hadn't protested. Part of her had wanted to. Indeed, the protest was practically automatic since the dog—a potential source of mess and trouble—would be living in Adams Road, not in St. Stephen's College with Elena. But another part of her had sparked alive to the idea. Other than a blue parakeet who had been mindlessly devoted to Justine's mother, and a won-at-a-fête goldfish that on its first night in her possession had suicidally flung itself out of its overfilled bowl to become stuck on a wallpaper daffodil behind the sideboard when she was eight years old, Justine had never owned what she thought of as a real pet—a dog to tag

along scruffily at her heels or a cat to curl at the foot of her bed or a horse
to ride in the back lanes of Cambridgeshire. These weren't deemed healthy
by either of her parents. Animals carried germs. Germs were not appropriate. And propriety was everything once they'd come into her great-
uncle's fortune.

Anthony Weaver had been her break with all that, her permanent
declaration of impropriety and adulthood. She could still see her mother's
mouth trembling round the words: "But what on earth can you possibly
be thinking, Justine? He's . . . well, he's Jewish." She could still manage
to feel that searing, quite physical stab of satisfaction right between her
breasts at the pale-cheeked consternation with which her mother greeted
the news of her impending marriage. Her father's reaction had been less
of a pleasure.

"He's changed his surname. He's a Cambridge don. He's got a solid
future. That he's been married before is a bit of a problem, and I'd be
happier if he weren't so much older than you. But, all things considered,
he's not a bad catch." He crossed his legs at the ankles and reached for
his pipe and the copy of *Punch* which he'd long ago decided was appropriate gentleman's Sunday afternoon reading. "I'm damned glad about
that surname, however."

Anthony hadn't been the one to change it. His grandfather had done
so, altering just two letters. The original *i-n* became *a-v,* and there he
was, born anew, not a Weiner from Germany, but a Weaver, an English-
man. Weaver, of course, was not exactly an upper-class name, but Anthony's grandfather couldn't have known or understood that at the time,
any more than he could have understood the delicate sensibilities of the
class to which he aspired, sensibilities that would prevent him from ever
breaking through the barrier constructed by his accent and his choice of
profession. The upper crust, after all, did not generally rub social elbows
with their tailors, no matter the proximity of their tailors' shops to Savile
Row.

Anthony had told her all this, not long after they'd met at the University Press where as an assistant editor newly graduated from Durham
University, she'd been assigned the task of shepherding a book on the
reign of Edward III through the final stages of the publication process.
Anthony Weaver had been the editorial force behind the volume, a collection of essays written by lofty medievalists from round the country. In
the final two months of the project, they had worked closely together—
sometimes in her small office at the Press, more often in his rooms in St.

Stephen's College. And when they weren't working, Anthony had talked, his conversation drifting round his background, his daughter, his former marriage, his work, and his life.

She'd never known a man so capable of sharing himself in words. From a world in which communication constituted a single lift of the eyebrows or a twitch of the lips, she'd fallen in love with his willingness to speak, with his quick warm smile, with the way he engaged her directly with his eyes. She wanted nothing more than to listen to Anthony, and for the last nine years, she'd managed just that, until the circumscribed world of Cambridge University had no longer been enough for him.

Justine watched as the Irish setter rooted in his toy box and brought out a worn black sock for a game of tug-of-war on the kitchen tiles. "Not tonight," she murmured. "In your basket. Stay here." She patted the dog's head, felt the soft caress of a warm, loving tongue on her fingers, and left the kitchen. She paused in the dining room to remove a loose thread that dangled from the tablecloth, and once again in the sitting room to turn off the gas fire and watch the flames' quick, sucking disappearance between the coals. Then, nothing more to keep her from doing so, she went upstairs.

In the half-darkened bedroom, Anthony was lying on the bed. He'd removed his shoes and his jacket, and Justine went automatically to place the former in their rack, the latter on its hanger. That done, she turned to face her husband. The light from the corridor glittered on the snail-track of tears that forked across his temple and disappeared into his hair. His eyes were closed.

She wanted to feel pity or sorrow or compassion. She wanted to feel anything save a recurrence of the anxiety that had first gripped her when he'd driven away from the house that afternoon, abandoning her to deal with Glyn.

She walked to the bed. Gleaming Danish teak, it was a modern platform with side tables attached. On each of these, mushroom-shaped brass lamps squatted, and Justine switched on the one by her husband's head. He brought his right arm up to cover his eyes. His left hand reached out, seeking hers.

"I need you," he whispered. "Be with me. Stay here."

She didn't feel her heart open as it would have a year ago. Nor did she feel her body stir and awaken to the implicit promise behind his words. She wished she could have used the moment as other women in her position would have done, by opening the little drawer in his side table, taking up the box of condoms, and saying, "Throw these away, if you need me so much." But she didn't do that. Whatever self-assurance powered that kind of behaviour, she'd used up her stock of it long ago. What she had left was what remained once all the positives were gone. For an age, it seemed, she had been filled with outrage, distrust, and a need for vengeance that nothing had yet been able to satiate.

Anthony turned on his side. He pulled her down to sit on the bed and laid his head in her lap, his arms round her waist. In a rote reaction, she stroked his hair.

"It's a dream," he said. "She'll be here this weekend and the three of us will be together again. We'll take a drive to Blakeney. Or practise shooting for the pheasant hunt. Or just sit and talk. But we'll be a family. Together." Justine watched the tears slide across his cheek and drop onto the fine grey wool of her skirt. "I want her back," he whispered. "Elena. *Elena.*"

She said the only thing which she knew to be the single, absolute truth at this point. "I'm sorry."

"Hold me. Please." His hands slid beneath her jacket and tightened against her back. After a moment, she heard him breathe her name. He held her closer and eased her blouse from the waistband of her skirt. His hands were warm on her back. They smoothed the way to unfasten her bra. "Hold me," he said again. He pushed the jacket from her shoulders and lifted his mouth to nuzzle her breasts. Through the thin silk of her blouse, she felt first his breath, then his tongue, then his teeth on her nipple. She felt her nipple harden. "Just hold me," he whispered. "Just hold me. Please."

She knew that making love was one of the most normal, life-affirming reactions to a grievous loss. The only thing she couldn't keep herself from wondering was whether her husband had already engaged in a life-affirming reaction to his grievous loss today.

As if he sensed her resistance, he backed away from her. His spectacles were on the bedside table, and he put them on. "I'm sorry," he said. "I don't even know what I'm doing any longer."

She stood. "Where did you go?"

"You didn't seem to want—"

"I'm not talking about right now. I'm talking about this afternoon. Where did you go?"

"For a drive."

"Where?"

"Nowhere."

"I don't believe you."

He looked away from her, to the teak chest of drawers with its sleek, cool lines.

"It's starting again. You went to see her. You went to make love. Or did you just communicate—how was it between you?—soul to soul?"

He returned his gaze to her. His head shook slowly. "You choose your moments, don't you?"

"That's avoidance, Anthony. That's a play for guilt. But it's not going to work, not even tonight. Where were you?"

"What do I have to do to convince you it's over? You wanted it that way. You named your terms. You got them. All of them. It's over."

"Is it?" She played her trump card smoothly. "Then where were you last night? I phoned your rooms in the college, right after I spoke to Elena. Where were you, Anthony? You lied to the Inspector, but surely you can tell your wife the truth."

"Lower your voice. I don't want you to wake Glyn."

"I don't care if I wake the dead."

She recoiled from her words as immediately as he did. They served to throw water onto the fire of her anger, as did her husband's broken response.

"If only you could, Justine."

5

In the London suburb of Greenford, Detective Sergeant Barbara Havers slowly drove her rusting Mini down Oldfield Lane. In the passenger's seat, her mother huddled like an unstrung marionette within the many folds of a dusty black coat. Round her neck Barbara had tied a jaunty red and blue scarf before they'd left Acton. But sometime during the drive, Mrs. Havers had worked the big square knot loose, and now she was using the scarf as a muff, twirling it tighter and tighter round her hands. Even in the lights from the dashboard, Barbara could see that behind her spectacles her mother's eyes were large and frightened. She hadn't been this far from her home in years.

"There's the Chinese take-away," Barbara pointed out. "And see, Mum, there's the hairdresser's and the chemist's. I wish it was daylight so we could go to the common and have a sit on one of the benches there. But we'll do it soon enough. Next weekend, I should guess."

In response, her mother hummed. Half-shrunk into the door, she made an unconsciously inspired choice of music. Barbara couldn't have named the origin of the song, but she could put the first seven words to the tune. *Think of me, think of me fondly* . . . Something she'd heard on the radio enough times over the past few years, something which her mother had doubtless heard as well and had called upon in this moment of uncertainty to give definition to what she was feeling behind the muddled facade of her dementia.

I am *thinking of you,* Barbara wanted to say. *This is for the best. It's the only option left.*

Instead, she said with a desperately forced heartiness, "Just look how wide the pavement is here, Mum. You don't see that sort of pavement in Acton, do you?"

She didn't expect an answer and didn't get one. She turned the car onto Uneeda Drive.

"See the trees along the street, Mum? They're bare now, but in the summer think how pretty they'll be." They wouldn't, of course, create that sort of leafy tunnel one often saw along the streets of the finer neighbourhoods in London. They were planted too far apart for that. But they managed to break the bleak monotony created by the line of stucco-and-brick, semi-detached houses, and for this reason alone Barbara noted them with gratitude. As she did the front gardens, pointing them out to her mother as they slowly cruised by, pretending to see details that the darkness obscured. She chatted amiably about a family of trolls, some plaster ducks, a birdbath, and a flowerbed of winter pansies and phlox. It didn't matter that she hadn't seen any of this. Her mother wouldn't recall that in the morning. She wouldn't even recall it in a quarter of an hour.

Indeed, Barbara knew that her mother didn't remember the conversation they'd had about Hawthorn Lodge soon after her arrival home this afternoon. She had telephoned Mrs. Flo, had made the arrangements for her mother to become one of the lodge "visitors," and had gone home to pack her mother's belongings.

"Now Mummy won't need everything with her at first," Mrs. Flo had said kindly. "Just bring a suitcase with a bit of this and that, and we'll move her in gradual. Call it a little visit, if you think she'll take to that."

After years of listening to her mother plan holidays which they would never take, Barbara wasn't oblivious of the irony of packing the suitcase and talking about a visit to Greenford. It was a far cry from the exotic destinations that had occupied her mother's disjointed thinking for so long. But the very fact that she had given herself so much to the idea of taking a holiday had made the sight of the suitcase less frightening than it otherwise might have been.

Her mother had noticed, however, that Barbara wasn't packing any of her own things into the large vinyl case. She'd even gone to Barbara's room and rustled through her clothes, bringing back an armload of trousers and pullovers that comprised the staple of Barbara's wardrobe.

"You'll be wanting these, lovey," she'd said. "Especially if it's

Switzerland. *Is* it Switzerland? I've wanted to go there for such a long time. Fresh air. Barbie, think of the air.''

She'd explained to her mother that it wasn't to be Switzerland, adding the fact that she herself could not go. She'd ended with the lie: ''But it's only a visit. Only for a few days. I'll be with you at the weekend,'' and with the hope that somehow her mother would hold on to those thoughts long enough to get her installed in Hawthorn Lodge without trouble.

But now Barbara saw that confusion had vanquished the moment of rare lucidity during which she'd listed the advantages of a stay with Mrs. Flo and the disadvantages of any further reliance upon Mrs. Gustafson. Her mother was chewing at her upper lip as her bewilderment increased. As if from the primary chink in a sheet of glass from which a starburst of breakage grows, dozens of tiny lines radiated from her mouth and formed a fretwork up her cheeks to her eyes. Her hands twisted in the muff of the scarf. The tempo of her humming accelerated. *Think of me, think of me fondly* . . .

''Mum,'' Barbara said as she pulled to the kerb at the nearest spot she could find to Hawthorn Lodge. There was no response other than the humming. Barbara felt her spirits plummet. For a time this afternoon, she had thought this transition was going to be easy. Her mother had even seemed to greet the idea with anticipation and excitement, as long as it was labelled a holiday. Now Barbara saw that it promised to be as wrenching an experience as she had previously expected.

She thought about praying for the strength to carry her plans through to their completion. But she didn't particularly believe in God, and the thought of calling upon Him at convenient moments to suit her own needs seemed as useless as it was hypocritical. So she garnered what little resolution she had, pushed open her door, and walked round to help her mother from the car.

''Here we go, Mum,'' she said with a cheerful bravado that she summoned from a repertoire of inadequate coping skills. ''Let's meet Mrs. Flo, shall we?''

In one hand she grasped her mother's suitcase. In the other, she held her mother's arm. She eased her down the pavement towards the grey stucco promise of permanent salvation.

''Listen, Mum,'' she said as she rang the front bell. From inside the house, Deborah Kerr was singing ''Getting to Know You,'' perhaps in preparation for the new visitor. ''They've got music on. Hear it?''

''Smells of cabbage,'' her mother said. ''Barbie, I don't think a cabbage-house is suitable for a holiday. Cabbage is common. This won't do at all.''

"It's coming from next door, Mum.''

"I can smell cabbage, Barbie. I wouldn't book us a room in a cabbage-hotel.''

Barbara heard the growing, querulous anxiety in her mother's voice. She prayed for Mrs. Flo to come to the door and rang the bell again.

"We don't serve cabbage in our home, Barbie. Never to guests.''

"It's all right, Mummy.''

"Barbie, I don't think—''

Mercifully, the porchlight snapped on. Mrs. Havers blinked in surprise and shrank back against Barbara.

Mrs. Flo still wore her neat shirtwaister with the pansy pin at her throat. She looked as fresh as she had that morning. "You've arrived. Splendid.'' She stepped out into the night and took Mrs. Havers' arm. "Come and meet the dears, love. We've been talking about you and we're dressed and ready and excited to meet you.''

"Barbie . . .'' Her mother's voice was a plea.

"It's all right, Mum. I'm right behind you.''

The dears were in the sitting room, where a videotape of *The King and I* was playing. Deborah Kerr sang melodiously to a group of precious-looking Oriental children. The dears—on the couch—swayed in time to the music.

"Here we are, my dears,'' Mrs. Flo announced, her arm going round Mrs. Havers' shoulders. "Here's our new visitor. And we're all ready to get to know her, aren't we? Oh I wish Mrs. Tilbird were here to share the pleasure, don't you?''

Introductions were made to Mrs. Salkild and Mrs. Pendlebury, who remained, shoulder to shoulder, on the couch. Mrs. Havers hung back, casting a panicked glance in Barbara's direction. Barbara smiled at her reassuringly. The suitcase she carried seemed to pull upon her arm.

"Shall we take off your nice coat and scarf, dear?'' Mrs. Flo reached for the top button of the coat.

"Barbie!'' Mrs. Havers shrilled.

"Now it's all right, isn't it?'' Mrs. Flo said. "There's not a thing to worry about. We're all so anxious to have you join us for a bit.''

"I smell cabbage!''

Barbara placed the suitcase on the floor and came to Mrs. Flo's rescue. Her mother was clutching onto the top button of her coat as if it were the Hope diamond. Spittle gathered at the corners of her mouth.

"Mum, it's the holiday you've wanted," Barbara said. "Let's go upstairs so you can see your room." She took her mother's arm.

"It's usually a bit difficult for them at first," Mrs. Flo said, perhaps noting Barbara's own incipient panic. "They get riled a bit at the change. It's perfectly normal. You're not to worry about it."

Together they guided her mother from the room as all the Oriental children chimed "day . . . by . . . day" in unison. The stairway was too narrow to allow them to climb it three abreast, so Mrs. Flo led the way, continuing to chat in a light-hearted manner. Underneath her words, Barbara heard the calm determination in her voice, and she marvelled at the woman's patient willingness to spend her life caring for the elderly and infirm. She herself only wanted to get out of the house as quickly as possible, and she despised that feeling of emotional claustrophobia.

Guiding her mother up the stairway did nothing to ameliorate Barbara's need for escape. Mrs. Havers' body had gone rigid. Each step was a project. And although Barbara murmured, encouraged, and kept a supportive hand fixed round her mother's arm, it was like leading an innocent animal to its death in a slaughterhouse in those last horrible moments when it first catches on the air the unmistakable scent of blood.

"The cabbage," Mrs. Havers whimpered.

Barbara tried to steel herself against the words. She knew there was no smell of cabbage in the house. She understood that her mother's mind was clinging to the last rational thought it had produced. But when her mother's head lolled back against Barbara's shoulder and she saw the milky pattern tears made through the face powder which she had donned impulsively in girlish preparation for her long-coveted holiday, Barbara felt the crushing grip of guilt.

She doesn't understand, Barbara thought. She'll never understand.

She said, "Mrs. Flo, I don't think—"

At the top of the stairs, Mrs. Flo turned and held up a hand, palm out, to stop her words. "Give it a moment, dear. This isn't easy for anyone, is it?"

She crossed the landing and opened one of the doors at the rear of the house where a light was already burning to welcome the new dear. The room had been furnished with a hospital bed. Otherwise it was as normal-looking as any other bedroom Barbara had ever seen and, admittedly, far more cheerful than her mother's room in Acton.

"Look at the lovely wallpaper, Mummy," she said. "All those daisies. You like daisies, don't you? And the rug. Look. There're daisies on the rug as well. And you've got your own basin. And a rocker by the window. Did I tell you that you can see the common from this window, Mum? You'll be able to watch the children playing ball.'' Please, she thought, please. Just give me a sign.

Clinging to her arm, Mrs. Havers mewled.

"Give me her case, dear," Mrs. Flo said. "If we pop things away quickly, she'll settle all the sooner. The less disruption, the better for Mum. You've brought photos and little mementoes for her, haven't you?''

"Yes. They're on the top.''

"Let's have them out first, shall we? Just the photos for now, I think. A quick bit of home.''

There were only two photos, together in a hinged frame, one of Barbara's brother and the other of her father. As Mrs. Flo flipped open the suitcase, took the frame out, and opened it upon the chest of drawers, Barbara realised suddenly that she'd been in such a hurry to clear her mother out of her life that she hadn't thought to include a picture of herself. She grew hot with the shame of it.

"Now, doesn't that look nice?'' Mrs. Flo said, stepping back from the chest of drawers and cocking her head to one side to admire the photographs. "What a sweet little boy. Is he—''

"My brother. He's dead.''

Mrs. Flo clucked sympathetically. "Shall we have her coat off now?''

He was ten, Barbara thought. There was no member of the family at his bedside, not even a nurse to hold his hand and make his passing gentle. He died alone.

Mrs. Flo said, "Let's just slip this off, dearie.''

Next to her, Barbara felt her mother cringe.

"Barbie . . . '' A note of unquestionable defeat sounded in the two syllables of her name.

Barbara had often wondered what it had been like for her brother, whether he'd slipped away easily without rising from his final coma, whether he'd opened his eyes at the last to find himself abandoned by everyone and everything save the machines and tubes and bottles and gadgets that had been industriously prolonging his life.

"Yes. That's a good girl. A button. Now another. We'll get you settled and have a nice cup of tea. I expect you'd like that. A slice of cake as well?''

"Cabbage.'' Mrs. Havers drew the word out. It was nearly indistinguishable, like a faint cry, distorted, from a great distance.

Barbara made the decision. "Her albums," she said. "Mrs. Flo, I've forgotten my mother's albums."

Mrs. Flo looked up from the scarf which she'd managed to untangle from Mrs. Havers' hands. "You can bring them later, dear. She won't want everything all at once."

"No. These are important. She's got to have her albums. She's collected . . ." Barbara stopped for a moment, knowing in her mind that what she was doing was foolish, feeling in her heart that there was no other answer. "She's planned holidays. She's got them done up in albums. She works on them every day. She'll be lost and—"

Mrs. Flo touched her arm. "My dear, do listen. What you're feeling is natural. But this is for the best. You must see that."

"No. It's bad enough, isn't it, that I forgot a picture of myself. I can't leave her here without those albums. I'm sorry. I've taken up your time. I've made a mess of everything. I've just . . ." She wouldn't cry, she thought, not with her mother needing her and Mrs. Gustafson to be spoken to and arrangements to be made.

She went to the chest of drawers, snapped closed the framed photographs, and returned them to the suitcase which she swung off the bed. She took a tissue from her pocket, using it to wipe her mother's cheeks and her nose.

"Okay, Mum," she said. "Let's go home."

The choir was singing the *Kyrie* as Lynley crossed Chapel Court and approached the chapel itself which, fronted by an arcade, comprised most of the court's west range. Although it clearly had been built to be admired from Middle Court, which stood to its east, eighteenth-century calls for college expansion had enclosed the seventeenth-century chapel into a quadrangle of buildings of which it was the focal point. Even through the mist and the darkness, it could hardly have been otherwise.

Ground lights glowed against the Weldon stone ashlar exterior of the building, which—if it hadn't been designed by Wren—was surely a monument to his love of classical ornamentation. The facade of the chapel rose from the middle of the arcade, defined by four Corinthian pilasters which supported a pediment both broken and penetrated by a clock and a lantern cupola. Decorative swags looped from the pilasters. An *oeil-de-boeuf* glittered on each side of the clock. At the centre of the building hung an oval entablature. And all of it represented the concrete reality of

Wren's classical ideal, balance. Where, at its north and south ends, the chapel did not fill in the entirety of the west range of the court, the arcade framed the river and the backs beyond it. The effect was lovely at night with the river mist rising to swirl round the low wall and lap at the columns. In sunlight, it would have been magnificent.

Like a coincidental accent to this thought, a trumpet fanfare played. The notes were pure and sweet on the cold night air. As Lynley pulled open the chapel door at the southeast corner of the building—unsurprised to find that the middle entry was merely an architectural device unintended for use—the choir answered the fanfare with another *Kyrie*. He entered the chapel as a second fanfare began.

To the height of the arched windows which rose to a plaster dog-tooth cornice, the walls were panelled in golden oak beneath which matching pews faced the solitary central aisle. Lined up in these were the members of the college choir, their attention fixed on a solitary trumpeter who stood at the foot of the altar, completing the fanfare. She was quite dwarfed by the gilded baroque reredos, framing a painting of Jesus calling Lazarus from the dead. She lowered her instrument, saw Lynley, and grinned at him as the choir burst into the final *Kyrie*. A few crashing bars from the organ followed. The choir master jotted notes in his music.

"Altos, rubbish," he said. "Sopranos, screech-owls. Tenors, howling dogs. The rest of you, a pass. The same time tomorrow evening, please."

General moaning greeted his evaluation of their work. The choir master ignored this, shoved his pencil into his thatch of black hair, and said, "The trumpet was excellent, however. Thank you, Miranda. That will be all, ladies and gentlemen."

As the group disbanded, Lynley walked down the aisle to join Miranda Webberly, who was cleaning her trumpet and repacking it into its case. "You've gone off jazz, Randie," he said.

Her head popped up. Her top knot of curly ginger hair bounced and bobbled. "I never!" she answered.

She was dressed in her usual style, Lynley noted, a baggy sweat suit which she hoped would both elongate and camouflage her short, plump body at the same time as its colour—a deep heliotrope blue—would darken the shade of her own pale eyes.

"Still in the jazz society then?"

"Absolutely. We have a gig on Wednesday night at Trinity Hall. Will you come?"

"Wouldn't miss it."

She grinned. "Good." She snapped the trumpet case closed and set it on the edge of a pew. "Dad phoned. He said I ought to expect one of his men to come crawling round this evening. Why're you alone?"

"Sergeant Havers is handling some personal business. She'll be along later. Tomorrow morning, I should guess."

"Hmmm. Well. D'you want a coffee or something? I expect you want to talk. The buttery's still open. Or we could go to my room." Despite the casual sound of the latter invitation, Miranda's cheeks coloured. "I mean if you want to talk privately. You know."

Lynley smiled. "Your room."

She struggled into a huge pea jacket—tossing a "Ta, Inspector" over her shoulder when he helped her get it on—wrapped a scarf round her neck, and picked up her trumpet case. She said, "Right. Come on, then. I'm over in New Court," and headed down the aisle.

Instead of crossing Chapel Court and using the formal passageway between the east and south buildings—"These're called the Randolph digs," Miranda informed him. "After the architect. Ugly, aren't they?"— she led him along the arcade and into a doorway at its north end. They went up a short flight of stairs, down a corridor, through a fire door, down another corridor, through another fire door, down another flight of stairs. All the time Miranda talked.

"I don't know yet how I feel about what's happened to Elena," she said. It sounded like a discourse she'd been having with herself most of the day. "I keep thinking I should feel outrage or anger or grief, but so far I've not felt anything at all. Except guilty for not feeling what I ought to feel and sort of disgustingly self-important now that Daddy's involved— through you, of course—and that puts me 'in the know.' How despicable really. I'm a Christian, aren't I? Shouldn't I mourn her?" She didn't wait for Lynley to reply. "You see, the essential problem is that I can't quite grasp that Elena's dead. I didn't see her last night. I didn't hear her leave this morning. That's a fair description of how we lived on a regular basis anyway, so everything seems perfectly normal to me. Perhaps if I had been the one to find her, or if she'd been killed in her room and our bedder had found her and come screaming in to get me—kind of like a film, you know?—I would have seen and known and been moved somehow. It's the absence of feeling that's worrying me. Am I turning to stone? Don't I even care?"

"Were you particularly close to her?"

"That's just it. I should have been closer than I was. I should have made a bigger effort. I've known her since last year."

"But she wasn't a friend?"

Miranda paused at the doorway that led out of the north Randolph building and into New Court. She wrinkled her nose. "I wasn't a runner," she said obscurely, and shoved open the door.

A terrace overlooked the river to their left. A cobbled path to their right ran between the Randolph building and a lawn. An enormous sweet chestnut tree stood in the lawn's centre, beyond which loomed the horseshoe-shaped building that comprised New Court, three storeys of blazing Gothic revival decorated with two-centred cusp windows, arched doorways whose doors wore heavy iron studs, battlements on the roofline, and a steepled tower. Although it was constructed from the same ashlar stone as the Randolph building which it faced, it could not have been stylistically more dissimilar.

"It's this way," Miranda said, and led him along the path to the southeast corner of the building. There, winter jasmine was growing enthusiastically up the walls. Lynley caught its sweet fragrance the instant before Miranda opened a door next to which the discreet letter *L* was carved into a small block of stone.

They went up two flights of stairs at Miranda's quick pace. Her room was one of two bed-sitting rooms that faced each other on a short corridor, sharing a gyp room, a shower, and a toilet.

Miranda paused in the gyp room to fill a kettle and put it on to boil. "It'll have to be instant," she said with a little grimace. "But I've a bit of whisky and we can tart it up with that if you like. As long as you don't tell Mummy."

"That you've taken to drink?"

She rolled her eyes. "That I've taken to anything. Unless it's a man. You can tell her what you'd like about that. Make up something good. Put me in a black lace negligee. It'll give her hope." She laughed and went to the door of her room. She'd wisely locked it, he noted with approval. She wasn't the only daughter of a superintendent of police for nothing.

"I see you've managed to snare yourself deluxe accommodations," he said as they entered, and indeed by Cambridge standards she had. For the bed-sit comprised two rooms, not one: a small inner chamber where she slept; a larger outer chamber for sitting. This latter was capacious enough to accommodate two undersized sofas and a small walnut dining table that acted as substitute for a desk. There was a bricked-in fireplace in one corner of the room and an oak window seat overlooking Trinity Passage Lane. On the seat itself a wire cage stood. Lynley went to inspect the tiny prisoner who was engaged in running furiously on a squeaking exercise wheel.

Miranda set her trumpet case next to the armchair and dumped her coat nearby. She said, "That's Titbit," and went to the fireplace to fiddle with an electric fire.

Lynley looked up from removing his own coat. "Elena's mouse?"

"When I heard what happened, I fetched him from her room. It seemed the right thing to do."

"When?"

"This afternoon. Perhaps . . . a bit after two."

"Her room wasn't locked?"

"No. Not yet at least. Elena never locked up." On a set of shelves in an alcove were several bottles of spirits, five glasses, three cups and saucers. Miranda fetched two of the cups and one of the bottles and took them to the table. "That could be important, couldn't it?" she said. "That she didn't lock her room."

The little mouse left off running and scampered from the wheel to the side of the cage. His whiskers twitched, his nose quivered. His paws grasping the slender metal bars, he raised himself up and sniffed eagerly at Lynley's fingers.

"It could be," he said. "Did you hear anyone in her room this morning? Later on, I imagine, perhaps at seven or half past."

Miranda shook her head. She looked regretful. "Earplugs," she said.

"You wear earplugs to bed?"

"Have done since . . . " She hesitated, appearing embarrassed for a moment before she sloughed the feeling off and continued with, "It's the only way I can sleep, Inspector. Got used to them, I suppose. Unappealing as the devil, but there it is."

Lynley filled in the blanks of Miranda's awkward justification, admiring her for the plucky effort at bravado. The struggle that was the Webberly marriage was no particular secret to anyone who knew the superintendent well. His daughter would have begun wearing earplugs at home, wanting to block out the worst of her parents' nighttime quarrels.

"What time did you get up this morning, Randie?"

"Eight," she said. "Give or take ten minutes." She smiled wryly. "Give ten minutes, then. I had a lecture at nine."

"And when you got up, what did you do? Shower? Bathe?"

"Hmm. Yes. Had a cup of tea. Ate some cereal. Made some toast."

"Her door was shut?"

"Yes."

"Everything seemed normal? No sign that anyone had been in?"

"No sign. Except . . . " The kettle began to whistle in the gyp room. She hooked the two cups and a small jug over her fingers and went to the door, where she paused. "I don't know that I would have noticed. I mean, she had more visitors than I did, you see."

"She was popular?"

Miranda picked at a chip in one of the cups. The pitch of the kettle's whistle seemed to intensify a degree. She looked uncomfortable.

"With men?" Lynley asked.

"Let me get the coffee," she said.

She ducked out of the room, leaving the door open. Lynley could hear her movements in the gyp room. He could see the closed door across the hall. From the porter, he'd obtained the key to that now-locked door, but he felt no inclination to use it. He considered this sensation, so at odds with how he believed he ought to feel.

He was going at the case backwards. The rational dictates of his job told him that, despite the hour of his arrival, he should have spoken to the Cambridge police first, to the parents next, to the finder of the body third. That accomplished, he should have sifted through the victim's belongings for a possible clue to her killer's identity. All textbook stuff, labelled *proper procedure,* as Sergeant Havers would have undoubtedly pointed out. He couldn't have listed reasons why he wasn't adhering to it. He merely felt that the nature of the crime itself suggested a personal involvement, perhaps, more than that, a settling of scores. And only an understanding of the central figures involved could reveal exactly what those personal involvements and those settled scores were.

Miranda returned, cups and jug on a pink tin tray. "Milk's gone off," she announced, putting the cups into their saucers. "Sorry. We'll have to make do with the whisky. But I've a bit of sugar. Would you like some?"

He demurred. "Elena's visitors?" he asked. "I assume they must have been men."

She looked as if she'd been hoping he'd forgotten the question while she was making the coffee. He joined her at the table. She sloshed some whisky into both of their cups, stirred them with the same spoon, which she licked and then continued to hold, slapping it into her palm as she spoke.

"Not all," she said. "She was best mates with the girls in Hare and Hounds. They came by now and then. Or she'd go off with them to a party somewhere. She was a great one for parties, Elena was. She liked to dance. She said she could feel the vibrations from the music if it was loud enough.''

"And the men?" Lynley asked.

The spoon slapped noisily against her palm. She screwed up her face. "Mummy would be happy if I had only a tenth of whatever Elena had. Men liked her, Inspector.''

"Something which you find difficult to understand?"

"No. I could see why they did. She was lively and funny and she liked to talk and to listen, which is awfully odd when you think she couldn't really *do* either, could she? But somehow she always gave the impression that when she was with you, she was only and completely interested in you. So I could see how a man . . . You know.'' She flipped the spoon back and forth to complete her sentence.

"Creatures of ego that we are?"

"Men like to believe they're the centre of things, don't they? Elena was good at letting them think they are."

"Particular men?"

"Gareth Randolph for one," Miranda said. "He was here to see her lots. Two or three times every week. I could always tell when Gareth came to call because the air got heavy, he's so intense. Elena said she could feel his aura the moment he opened the door to our staircase. Here comes trouble, she'd say if we were in the gyp room. And thirty seconds later, there he would be. She said she was psychic when it came to Gareth." Miranda laughed. "Frankly, I think she could smell his cologne.''

"Were they a couple?"

"They went about together. People paired their names.''

"Did Elena like that?"

"She said he was just a friend.''

"Was there someone else special?"

She took a drink of her coffee and added more whisky to it, shoving the bottle across to him when she was through. "I don't know if he was special, but she saw Adam Jenn. Her father's graduate student. She saw a good bit of him. And her dad stopped by lots, but I suppose he doesn't count, does he, because he was only here to keep tabs on her. She hadn't done well last year—have they told you that?—and he wanted to make sure there was no repeat performance. That's how Elena put it, at least. Here comes my keeper, she'd say when she saw him from the window.

Once or twice she hid in my bed-sit just to tease him and came out laughing when he started to react because she wasn't in her room when she'd said she'd be there to meet him.''

"I take it she didn't like the plan they'd come up with to keep her at the University.''

"She said the best part about it was the mouse. Tibbit, she called him, companion of my cell. She was like that, Inspector. She could make a joke out of anything.''

Miranda seemed to have completed her recital of information, for she sat back in her chair Indian style with her legs tucked under her on the seat, and she drank more coffee. But her look at him was a chary one which indicated that something was being withheld.

"Was there someone else, Randie?''

Miranda squirmed. She examined a small basket of apples and oranges on the table, and after that the posters on the wall above it. Dizzy Gillespie, Louis Armstrong, Wynton Marsalis in concert, Dave Brubeck at the piano, Ella Fitzgerald at the mike. She hadn't abandoned her love of jazz. She glanced at him again, poking the handle of the teaspoon into her mop of hair.

"Someone else?'' Lynley repeated. "Randie, if you know something more—''

"I *don't* know anything else absolutely for sure, Inspector. And I can't tell you every little thing, can I, because something I tell you— some little detail—might not even mean anything. But if you took it to heart, people might get hurt, mightn't they? Dad says that's the biggest danger in policework.''

Lynley made a mental note to discourage Webberly from waxing philosophical with his daughter in the future. "That's always possible,'' he agreed. "But I'm not about to arrest someone just because you mention his name.'' When she said nothing, he leaned across the table and tapped his finger against her coffee cup. "Word of honour, Randie. All right? Do you know something else?''

"What I know about Gareth and Adam and her father came from Elena,'' she said. "That's why I told you. Anything else in my head is nothing but gossip. Or something I maybe saw and didn't understand. And that can't be helpful. That could make things go wrong.''

"We're not gossiping, Randie. We're trying to get at the truth behind her death. The facts, not conjectures.''

She didn't immediately respond. She stared at the bottle of whisky on the table. Its label bore a greasy fingerprint stain. She said, "Facts aren't conclusions. Dad always says that."

"Absolutely. Agreed."

She hesitated, even looked over her shoulder as if to make sure they were still alone. "This is about seeing, nothing more," she said.

"Understood."

"All right." She straightened her shoulders as if in preparation, but she still didn't look as if she wanted to part with the information. "I think she had a row with Gareth on Sunday evening. Only," she added in a rush, "I can't know for sure because I didn't *hear* them, they talked with their hands. I just caught a glimpse of them in Elena's room before she shut the door and when Gareth left he was in quite a temper. He banged his way out. Only it could mean nothing because he's so intense anyway that he'd be acting like that even if they'd been discussing the poll tax."

"Yes. I see. And after their argument?"

"Elena left as well."

"What time was this?"

"Round twenty to eight. I never heard her come back." Miranda seemed to read heightened interest in his face, for she went on hastily. "I don't think Gareth had anything to do with what's happened, Inspector. He has a temper, true, and he's on a tight string, but he wasn't the only one . . . " She gnawed at her lip.

"Someone else was here?"

"Noooo   not exactly."

"Randie—"

Her body slumped. "Mr. Thorsson then."

"He was here?" She nodded. "Who is he?"

"One of Elena's supervisors. He lectures in English."

"When was this?"

"I saw him here twice, actually. But not on Sunday."

"Day or night?"

"Night. Once probably round the third week of the term. Then again last Thursday."

"Could he have been here more often?"

She looked reluctant to answer, but she said, "I suppose, yes. But I just saw him twice. Twice is all, Inspector." *Twice is the fact,* her voice implied.

"Did she tell you why he came to see her?"

Miranda shook her head slowly. "I think she didn't much like him because she called him Lenny the Lech. Lennart. He's Swedish, see. And that's all I know. Truly. Really.''

"That's the fact, you mean.'' Even as he said it, Lynley felt sure that Miranda Webberly—daughter of her father—could have produced half a dozen conjectures to go with it.

Lynley went through the gatehouse, stopping briefly in the porter's lodge before stepping out into Trinity Lane. Terence Cuff had wisely seen to it that the rooms set aside for visitors to the college were in St. Stephen's Court, which along with Ivy Court was across the narrow lane from the rest of the college. And unlike the rest of the college, it had neither porter nor gatehouse, so it wasn't locked at night, thereby giving visitors more freedom of movement than the junior members of the college had.

A plain wrought-iron fence separated this part of the college from the street. It ran north to south, forming a line of demarcation that was interrupted by the west wall of St. Stephen's Church. This random rubble building was one of the original parish churches in Cambridge, and its stone quoins, buttresses, and Norman tower seemed strangely at odds with the neat Edwardian brick building that partially encircled it.

Lynley pushed open the iron gate. A second fence inside marked the boundary of the churchyard. There, graves lay dimly illuminated by the same ground lights that shone cones of yellow against the walls of the church where moths fluttered weakly with sodden wings in the glow. The fog had grown even heavier during the time he had spent with Miranda, and it transformed sarcophagi, gravestones, tombs, bushes, and trees into colourless silhouettes laid against a slowly shifting background of mist. Along the wrought iron fence that separated St. Stephen's Court from the churchyard, perhaps a hundred or more bicycles stood, their handlebars gleaming, slick with the damp.

Passing these, Lynley made his way to Ivy Court, where the porter had earlier shown him to his room at the top of *O* staircase. It was quiet inside the building itself. These rooms, the porter had told him, were used only by the senior members of the college. They comprised studies and conference rooms where supervisions took place, gyp rooms and smaller rooms with beds for kipping. Since most of the senior fellows lived away from the college, the building was largely unpopulated at night.

Lynley's room encompassed one of the building's Dutch gables, and it looked out into Ivy Court and St. Stephen's graveyard. With brown carpet squares on the floor, stained yellow walls, and faded floral curtains at the window, it wasn't a particularly uplifting environment. Clearly, St. Stephen's did not expect visitors to embark upon an extended stay.

Left alone there earlier by the porter, he'd found himself slowly examining its contents, touching a musty-smelling armchair, opening a drawer, running his fingers along the empty, adjustable bookshelves that lined one wall. He ran water in the basin. He tested the strength of the single steel rod in a cupboard for holding clothes. He thought about Oxford.

The room had been different but the feeling was the same, that sensation of having the entire world opening up before him, revealing its mysteries even as it held out the promise of satisfactions to come. The blessing of relative anonymity had filled him with the sense of having been newly born. Empty shelves, blank walls, drawers that held nothing. Here, he had thought, he would make his mark. No one need know of his title and background, no one need know of his risible angst. The secret lives of one's parents had no place in Oxford. Here, he had thought, he would be safe from the past.

He chuckled now to think of how tenaciously he had held on to that final, adolescent belief. He had actually seen himself moving into a golden future in which he had to do absolutely nothing to deal with what had led up to it. How we flee our personal realities, he thought.

His suitcase was still on the desk in the recess made by the gable. It took him less than five minutes to unpack, after which he sat, feeling the room's chill and his own restless need to be elsewhere. He sought distraction by writing out his first day's report, a job that would usually be completed by Sergeant Havers but one that he set upon automatically now, grateful for a diversion that would keep thoughts of Helen at bay, if only for an hour or so.

"One call. Yes, sir," the porter had said as he passed through the lodge.

She's phoned, Lynley thought. Harry's come home. And his mood began to lift accordingly, only to plummet to earth when the porter handed him the message. Superintendent Daniel Sheehan of the Cambridge Constabulary would meet with him at half past eight in the morning.

There was nothing from Helen.

He wrote steadily, filling in page after page with the details of his meeting with Terence Cuff, with the impressions he'd formed after his conversation with Anthony and Justine Weaver, with a description of the Ceephone and the possibilities it presented, with the facts he'd managed to glean from Miranda Webberly. He wrote far more than he needed to write, forcing himself to address the murder in a stream-of-consciousness fashion which Havers would rightfully scorn but which also served to focus his mind on the killing and kept it from wandering to areas that would only intensify his nerve-aching frustration. At the end, however, the effort was a failure. For after an hour of writing, he set down his pen, removed his spectacles, rubbed his eyes, and thought immediately of Helen.

He could sense that he was fast approaching the limit of his capacity for friendship with her. She'd wanted time. He'd given it, month after month, believing that any false move on his part would cause him to lose her forever. As much as possible, he'd tried to refashion himself into the man who had once been her comrade in laughter, a casual companion willing to engage in whatever madcap adventure she'd cared to propose, from hot-air ballooning in the Loire to spelunking in the Burren. It didn't particularly matter, as long as she was there. But he was finding that the pretence of fraternal affection was growing daily more difficult to maintain, and the words *I love you* were no longer a means of defining the nature of the close friendship between them. Instead, they were fast becoming a gauntlet which he repeatedly threw down before her, demanding a satisfaction that she did not appear willing to give.

She continued to see other men. She never told him this directly, but he knew it intuitively. He read it in her eyes when she spoke of a play she had seen, a drinks party she'd attended, a gallery she'd visited. And while he sought out other women in what amounted to a momentarily successful effort to drive the thought of Helen from his mind, he could not drive her spirit from his heart any more than he could obliterate the connection that tied her to his soul. He had closed his eyes upon more than one lover, imagining the body beneath his to be Helen's, hearing Helen's cries, feeling Helen's arms, tasting the miracle of Helen's mouth. And more than once, he had cried out with the pleasure of his body's fleeting moment of release, only to be filled with desolation in the very next instant. It was no longer enough to take and give pleasure. He wanted to make love. He wanted to own love. But not without Helen.

His nerves felt strung. His arms and legs ached. He pushed away from the desk and went to the basin where he splashed water on his face and examined himself dispassionately in the mirror.

Cambridge would be their battleground, he decided. Whatever was to be won or lost, it would happen here.

Back at the desk, he flipped through the pages he had written, reading his words but assimilating nothing. He closed the notebook with a snap and slapped it down.

The air in the room seemed suddenly close, too much hung with the opposing odours of fresh disinfectant and old tobacco smoke. It felt oppressive. He leaned over the desk top, shoved the window up all the way, and let the damp night air wash over his cheeks. Below him the graveyard—half-hidden by the fog—cast up a faint, fresh scent of pine from its trees. The ground there would spring with fallen needles, and as he breathed in their fragrance, he could almost imagine the spongy feel of them beneath his feet.

A movement at the fence caught his attention. At first he thought the wind was rising to shift the fog away from bushes and trees. But as he watched, a figure melted out of the shadow of one of the spruces, and he saw that the movement had not come from within the graveyard at all, but from its perimeter where someone was easing stealthily between the bicycles, away from him, head lifted to examine the windows of the court's east range. Woman or man, Lynley couldn't tell, and when he switched off his desk lamp to have a better look, the figure froze as if preternaturally aware of being watched even at a distance of some twenty yards. Then Lynley heard the sound of a car's engine idling in Trinity Lane. Voices called out a laughing good night. A horn tooted happily in response. With a grinding of gears, the car roared off. The voices faded as their owners walked away, and the shadow below became both substance and movement again.

Whoever it was, stealing one of the bicycles didn't appear to be its objective. It headed for a doorway on the east range of the court. A lantern-shaped lamp, overhung with the ivy for which the court was named, provided scant illumination there, and Lynley waited for the figure to enter the milky penumbra directly in front of the door, hoping that whoever it was might toss a quick look over a shoulder and give him a glimpse of face. It didn't happen. Instead, the figure hurried soundlessly to the doorway, shot out a pale hand to grasp the knob, and disappeared into the building. But just for a moment as the shadowy form passed beneath the light, Lynley saw hair, rich, dark, and plentiful.

A woman suggested an assignation, with someone no doubt anxiously waiting behind one of those sightless, darkened windows. He waited for one of them to brighten with light. It did not happen. Instead, less than two minutes after she had disappeared into the building, the door opened again and the woman re-emerged. This time she paused for an instant beneath the light in order to pull the door shut behind her. The faint glow outlined the curve of a cheek, the shape of a nose and chin. But only for a moment. Then she was gone, moving across the court, fading back into the darkness by the graveyard. She was as silent as the mist.

6

Cambridge police headquarters faced Parker's Piece, a vast green crisscrossed by intersecting paths. Joggers ran here, their breaths gusting out in fibrous clouds, while on the grass two dalmatians—tongues flapping happily—chased after an orange Frisbee thrown by a whip-thin bearded man whose bald head shone in the morning sun. All of them seemed to be rejoicing in the disappearance of the fog. Even pedestrians rushing by on the pavement held up their faces to let the sunlight strike them for the first time in days. Although the temperature was no higher than it had been on the previous morning, and a brisk wind made the chill cut close, the fact that the sky was blue and the day was bright served to make the cold stimulating instead of insufferable.

Lynley paused outside the dun brick-and-concrete structure that housed the main offices of the local police. A glass-enclosed notice board stood in front of the doors, on which were fastened posters about child safety in cars, drinking and driving, and an organisation called Crimestoppers. Over this last had been taped a hand-out giving the superficial details of Elena Weaver's death and asking for information from anyone who might have seen her yesterday morning or Sunday night. It was a hastily composed document with a grainy, photocopied picture of the dead girl upon it. And it had not been generated by the police. *DeaStu* and a telephone number were printed prominently at the bottom of the page. Lynley sighed when he saw this. The deaf students were launching their own investigation. That wouldn't make his job any less complicated.

A blast of warm air hit him when he opened the doors and entered the lobby where a young man garbed in black leather was arguing with a uniformed receptionist about a traffic ticket. On one of the chairs, his companion waited, a girl in moccasins and what appeared to be an Indian bedspread. She kept murmuring, "Come on, Ron. Cripes. Come *on*," with her feet drumming impatiently on the black tile floor.

The constable working reception cast a thankful look in Lynley's direction, perhaps appreciative of the diversion. He broke into the young man's "You listen here, mate. I bloody don't intend to—" with "Sit down, lad. You're getting in a twist over nothing," after which he nodded to Lynley, saying, "CID? Scotland Yard?"

"It's that obvious, then?"

"Colour of the skin. Police pallor, we call it. But I'll have a glance at your ID all the same."

Lynley produced his warrant card. The constable examined it before pressing the release on the locked door which separated the lobby from the station proper. A buzzer sounded, he nodded Lynley inside. "First floor," he said. "Just follow the signs." He resumed his argument with the boy in leather.

The superintendent's office was at the front of the building, over-looking Parker's Piece. As Lynley approached it, the door opened and an angular woman with a geometric haircut took up a position within its frame. Arms akimbo, elbows pointed like spikes, she scrutinised him from head to foot. Obviously, reception had phoned ahead.

"Inspector Lynley." She spoke with the same sort of inflection one uses when naming a social disease. "The superintendent's scheduled for a meeting with Chief Constable in Huntingdon at half past ten. I shall ask you to keep that in mind when you—"

"That'll do, Edwina," a voice called from the inner office.

Her lips minced their way round a glacial smile. She stepped to one side and allowed Lynley to pass her. "Of course," she said. "Coffee, Mr. Sheehan?"

"Yes." As he spoke, Superintendent Daniel Sheehan came across the room to meet Lynley at the door. He offered a large beefy hand, a companion in bulk to the rest of him. His grip was firm, and in spite of the fact that Lynley represented a Scotland Yard invasion into his patch, his smile offered fellowship. "Coffee for you, Inspector?"

"Thank you. Black."

Edwina nodded curtly and disappeared. Her high heels cracked sharp reports in the hall. Sheehan snorted a chuckle. "Come in. Before the lions have at you. Or at least the lioness. Not all of my troops are taking your visit well.''

''That's a reasonable reaction.''

Sheehan motioned him not to one of the two plastic chairs which faced his desk but to a blue vinyl-covered sofa which along with a pressed wood coffee table apparently constituted the conference area of his office. A map of the city centre hung on the wall there. Each of the colleges was outlined in red.

While Lynley took off his overcoat, Sheehan went to his desk where, in apparent defiance of gravity, a stack of folders leaned precariously towards the rubbish container on the floor. As the superintendent gathered up a loose collection of papers and fastened them together with a paperclip, Lynley regarded him, caught between curiosity and admiration at finding Sheehan so calm in the face of what could easily be interpreted as a declaration of his CID's incompetence.

Sheehan certainly didn't appear unflappable on the surface. His ruddy complexion suggested a quick temper. His thick fingers promised notable fists. His barrel chest and massive thighs seemed suitable to a brawler. And yet his easy manner contradicted his physique. As did his words, which were perfectly dispassionate. His choice of topic suggested that he and Lynley had spoken to each other before, establishing some sort of camaraderie. It was an oddly non-political approach to what could have been an uneasy situation. Lynley liked him for choosing it. It revealed him to be direct and confident of who and what he was.

''I can't say we didn't bring this on ourselves,'' Sheehan said. ''It's a problem in forensic that should have been resolved two years back. But my CC doesn't like to get involved in departmental squabblings, and as a result the chickens, if you'll pardon the cliché and don't mind wearing feathers, have come home to roost.''

He snagged one of the plastic chairs, returned to the sofa, and dropped his collection of papers onto the table where a manila folder labeled *Weaver* already lay. He sat. The chair creaked under his weight.

''I'm not happy as a sod myself about having you here,'' he admitted. ''But I wasn't surprised when the Vice Chancellor rang me and said the University wanted the Yard. Forensic made a real balls-up of an under-graduate suicide last May. The University doesn't want a re-play. I can't say I blame them. What I don't much like is the implication of bias, though. They seem to think that if a student pops off, the local CID are as likely to say good riddance to another gown as they are to investigate.''

"I was told you had a leak in the department that caused the University bad press last term."

Sheehan gave a grunt of confirmation. "A leak from forensic. We've got two prima donnas out there. And when one disagrees with the other's conclusions, they fight it out in the press instead of the lab. Drake—the senior man—called the death a suicide. Pleasance—the junior—called it murder, based on the propensity for a suicide to stand before a mirror to cut his throat. This suicide did it while lying on his bed, and Pleasance wouldn't buy it. The trouble started from there." Sheehan lifted a thigh with another grunt and drove his hand into his trouser pocket. He brought out a packet of chewing gum and balanced it on his palm. "I've been after my CC to separate those two—or fire Pleasance—for exactly twenty-one months now. If the Yard's involvement in this case can manage to bring that about, I'll be a happy man." He offered the gum. "Sugarless," he said, and when Lynley shook his head, "Don't blame you a bit. Stuff tastes like rubber." He popped a folded piece into his mouth. "But it manages to give the illusion of food. If only I could convince my stomach."

"Dieting?"

Sheehan smacked his palm against his bulging waistline where his stomach overhung the belt on his trousers. "It's got to go. I'd a heart attack last year. Ah. Here's the coffee."

Edwina marched into the room with a cracked wooden tray held in front of her on which plumes of steam rose from two brown mugs. She set the coffee on the table, looked at her watch, and said with a brief, meaningful glance in Lynley's direction, "Shall I buzz you in time to leave for Huntingdon, Mr. Sheehan?"

"I'll manage, Edwina."

"Chief Constable expects you—"

"—at half past ten. Yes." Sheehan reached for his coffee and raised it to his secretary in a salute. He offered a smile of both thanks and dismissal. Edwina looked as if she wished to say more, but she left the room instead. The door, Lynley saw, did not quite catch behind her.

"We don't have much more than the preliminaries for you," Sheehan said with a lift of his coffee mug towards the papers and the folder on the table. "We can't get her into autopsy until late this morning."

Lynley put on his spectacles, saying, "What do you know?"

"Not much so far. Two blows to the face causing a sphenoidal fracture. That was the initial damage. Then she was strangled with the tie cord of her tracksuit's hood."

"All this occurred on an island, as I understand it."

"Only the killing itself. We've got a good-sized blood splatter on the footpath that runs along the riverbank. She would have been attacked there first, then dragged across the footbridge onto the island. When you go out there, you'll see that it'd be no problem. The island's only separated from the west bank of the river by a bit of a ditch. Dragging her off the footpath would have been a matter of fifteen seconds or less, once she was unconscious."

"Did she put up a fight?"

Sheehan blew across the top of his coffee mug and took a gusty slurp. He shook his head. "She was wearing mittens, but we've got no hairs or skin caught in the material. It looks to us like someone caught her by surprise. But forensic are taping her tracksuit to see what's what."

"Other evidence?"

"A plethora of crap that we're sorting through. Disintegrating newspapers, half a dozen empty cigarette packs, a wine bottle. You name it, it's there. The island's a local hang-out, has been for years. We've probably got two generations of rubbish to sift through."

Lynley opened the folder. "You've narrowed time of death between half past five and seven," he noted and looked up. "According to the college, the porter saw her leaving the grounds at a quarter past six."

"And the body was found not long after seven. So you've actually less than an hour to play with. Nice and narrow," Sheehan said.

Lynley flipped through to the crime scene photographs. "Who found her?"

"Young woman called Sarah Gordon. She'd gone there to sketch."

Lynley raised his head sharply. "In the fog?"

"My thought as well. You couldn't see ten yards. I don't know what she was thinking. But she had a whole kit of stuff with her—couple of easels, a case of paints and pastels—so she was obviously setting up for a good long stay. Which was cut a bit short when she found the body instead of inspiration."

Lynley looked through the pictures. The girl lay mostly covered by a mound of sodden leaves. She was on her right side, her arms in front of her, her knees bent, and her legs slightly drawn up. She might have been sleeping save for the fact that her face was turned towards the earth, her hair falling forward to leave her neck bare. Round this, the ligature cut into her skin, so deeply in places that it seemed to disappear, so deeply in places that it suggested a rare, brutal, and triumphant sort of strength, a surging of adrenaline through a killer's muscles. Lynley studied the

pictures. There was something vaguely familiar about them, and he wondered if the crime were a copy of another.

"She certainly doesn't look like an arbitrary body dump," he said.

Sheehan leaned forward to get a look at the picture. "She wouldn't
be, would she? Not at the hour in the morning. This wasn't any arbitrary
killing. This was a lying-in-wait."

"Quite. There's some evidence of that." He told the superintendent
about Elena's alleged call to her father's house the night before she
died.

"So you're looking for someone who knew her movements, what
her schedule would be that morning, and the fact that her stepmother
wouldn't go running along the river at a quarter past six if she had the
chance not to. Someone close to the girl, I should guess." Sheehan picked
up a picture and then another, looking at them with an expression of
marked regret on his face. "I always hate to see a young girl like this
die. But especially this way." He tossed the pictures back. "We'll do
what we can at our end to help you—matters being what they are in
forensic. But if the body's any indication, Inspector, aside from someone
who knew the girl well, I should say you're looking for a killer who's
craw-filled with hate."

Sergeant Havers emerged from the buttery and descended the stairs
from the terrace only moments after Lynley emerged from the library
passage which connected Middle Court to North Court. She flipped her
cigarette into a bed of asters and sank both hands into the pockets of her
coat. Pea-soup green, it hung open to reveal navy trousers going baggy
at the knees, a purple pullover, and two scarves—one brown and one
pink.

"You're a vision, Havers," Lynley said when she joined him. "Is
this the rainbow effect? You know the sort of thing. Rather like the
greenhouse effect but more immediately apparent?"

She rummaged in her bag for a packet of Players. She shook one
out, lit it, and reflectively blew smoke in his face. He did his best not to
lap up the aroma. Ten months without smoking and he still felt the urge
to rip the cigarette from his sergeant's hand and smoke it to the nub.

"I thought I ought to blend in with the environment," Havers said.
"You don't like it? Why? Don't I look academic?"

"You do. Certainly. By someone's definition."

"What could I hope to expect from a bloke who spent his formative years at Eton?" Havers asked the sky. "If I'd shown up in a top hat, striped trousers, and cutaway, would I have passed muster with you?"

"Only if you had Ginger Rogers on your arm."

Havers laughed. "Sod you."

"Sentiments returned." He watched her flick a bit of ash to the ground. "Did you get your mother settled at Hawthorn Lodge?"

Two girls passed them, holding a muted conversation, their heads together over a piece of paper. Lynley saw that it was the same hand-out which had been posted in front of the police station. His eyes went back to Havers, who kept her own on the two girls until they disappeared round the herbaceous border that marked the entrance to New Court.

"Havers?"

She waved him off, puffing on her cigarette. "I changed my mind. It didn't work out."

"What have you done about her?"

"Carrying on with Mrs. Gustafson for a bit. I'll see how it goes." She brushed her hand aimlessly over the top of her head, ruffling her short hair. The cold air made it crackle. "So. What d'we have here?"

For the moment, he submitted himself to her desire for privacy and gave her what facts he had gleaned from Sheehan. When he was finished telling her what he knew so far, she said:

"Weapons?"

"For beating her, they don't know yet. Nothing was left at the scene, and they're still working on possible trace evidence on the body."

"So we've got the ubiquitous unidentified blunt object," Havers said. "And the strangulation?"

"The tie from the hood of her jacket."

"The killer knew what she would wear?"

"Possibly."

"Photos?"

He handed her the folder. She put her cigarette between her lips, opened the folder, and squinted through the smoke at the pictures that lay on top of the report. "Have you ever been to Brompton Oratory, Havers?"

She looked up. The cigarette bobbed as she spoke. "No. Why? Are you getting some of that old-time religion?"

"There's a sculpture there. The martyred St. Cecilia. I couldn't quite put my finger on what it was about this body when I first saw the pictures, but on the way back here it came to me. It's the sculpture of St. Cecilia."

Over her shoulder, he fingered through the pictures to find the one he wanted. "It's the way her hair sweeps forward, the position of her arms, even the ligature round her neck."

"St. Cecilia was strangled?" Havers asked. "I thought martyrdom was more your basic lion-attack in front of a crowd of cheering, down-thumbing Romans."

"In this case—if I recall it correctly—her head was half-severed and she waited two days to die. But the sculpture only shows the cut itself, which looks like a ligature."

"Jesus. No wonder she got into heaven." Havers dropped her cigarette to the ground and crushed it out. "So what's your point, Inspector? Do we have a killer hot after duplicating all the sculptures in Brompton Oratory? If that's what's going on, when he gets to the crucifixion, I hope I'm off the case. *Is* there a crucifixion sculpture in the Oratory, by the way?"

"I can't remember. But all the Apostles are there."

"Eleven of them martyrs," she said reflectively. "We've got big trouble. Unless the killer's only looking for females."

"It doesn't matter. I doubt anyone would buy the Oratory theory," he said and guided her in the direction of New Court. As they walked, he listed the points of information he had gathered from Terence Cuff, the Weavers, and Miranda Webberly.

"The Penford Chair, blighted love, a good dose of jealousy, and an evil stepmother," Havers commented when he was done. She looked at her watch. "All that in only sixteen hours by yourself on the case. Are you sure you need me, Inspector?"

"No doubt of that. You pass for an undergraduate better than I. I think it's the clothes." He opened the door to *L* staircase for her. "Two flights up," he said and took the key from his pocket.

From the first floor, they could hear music playing. It grew louder as they climbed. The low moan of a saxophone, the answering call of a clarinet. Miranda Webberly's jazz. In the second-floor corridor, they could hear a few tentative notes blown from a trumpet as Miranda played along with the greats.

"It's here," Lynley said and unlocked the door.

Unlike Miranda's, Elena Weaver's was a single room, and it overlooked the buff brick terrace of North Court. Also unlike Miranda's, it was largely a mess. Cupboards and drawers gaped open; two lights burned; books lay strewn across the desk, their pages fluttering in the sudden breeze from the door. A green robe formed a heap on the floor along with a pair of blue jeans, a black camisole, and a balled-up bit of nylon that seemed to be dirty underwear.

The air felt close and overheated, fusty with the odour of clothes needing to be washed. Lynley walked to the desk and cracked open a window as Havers took off her coat and scarves, dumping them on the bed. She went to the walled-in fireplace in the corner of the room where a row of porcelain unicorns lined the mantel. Fanning out above them, posters hung, again depicting unicorns, the occasional maiden, and an excessive amount of phantasmagorical mist.

Across the room, Lynley glanced into the clothes cupboard which was largely a jumble of neon-coloured, elasticised garments. The odd exception of a pair of neat tweed trousers and a floral dress with a delicate lace collar hung away from the rest.

Havers came to his side. Wordlessly, she examined the clothing. "Better bag all this to make a match of any fibres they pull off her tracksuit," Havers said. "She would have kept it in here." She began removing the clothing from its hangers. "Odd, though, isn't it?"

"What?"

She flicked a thumb towards the dress and the trousers at the end of the rod. "Which part of her was playing dress-up, Inspector? The vamp in neon or the angel in lace?"

"Perhaps both." At the desk, he saw that a large calendar served as a blotter, and he moved the texts and the notebooks to one side to have a look at it. "A stroke of possible good fortune here, Havers."

She was stuffing garments into a plastic sack which she'd removed from her shoulder bag. "What sort?"

"A calendar. She hasn't removed the old months. She's merely folded them back."

"Score a point for our side."

"Quite." He reached for his spectacles in the breast pocket of his jacket.

The first six months of the calendar represented the latter two-thirds of Elena's first year at the University, Lent and Easter terms. Most of her notations were clear. Lectures were listed by subject: from *Chaucer— 10:00* on every Wednesday to *Spenser—11:00* the following day. Supervisions seemed to bear the name of the senior fellow with whom she would be meeting, a conclusion Lynley reached when he saw the name *Thorsson* blocking out the same period of time every week in Easter term. Other notations patched in more details of the dead girl's life. *DeaStu* appeared with increasing regularity from January through May, indicating Elena's adherence to at least one of the guidelines set down by the senior tutor, her supervisors, and Terence Cuff for her social rehabilitation. Attended by specific times, the titles *Hare and Hounds* and *Search and Pellet* suggested her membership in two of the University's other societies. And *Dad's*, sprinkled liberally throughout every month, gave evidence of the amount of time Elena spent with her father and his wife. There was no indication that she saw her mother in London at any time other than on holidays.

"Well?" Havers asked as Lynley searched through the months. She popped the last piece of clothing from the floor into the sack, twisted it closed, and wrote a few words on a label.

"It looks fairly straightforward," he said. "Except . . . Havers, tell me what you make of this." When she joined him at the desk, he pointed out a symbol that Elena used repeatedly throughout the calendar, a simple pencil-sketch of a fish. It first appeared on the eighteenth of January and continued with regularity three or four times each week, generally on a weekday, only sporadically on a Saturday, rarely on a Sunday.

Havers bent over it. She dropped the sack of clothes to the floor. "Looks like the Christianity symbol," she said at last. "Perhaps she'd decided to be born again."

"That would have been a quick recovery from reprobation," Lynley replied. "The University wanted her in DeaStu, but no one's mentioned a word about religion."

"Perhaps she didn't want anyone to know."

"That's clear enough. She didn't want someone to know something. I'm just not sure it had anything to do with discovering the Lord."

Havers seemed willing to pursue another tack. "She was a runner, wasn't she? Maybe it's a diet. These are the days she had to eat fish. Good for the blood pressure, good for the cholesterol, good for the . . . what? Muscle tone or something? But she was thin anyway—you can tell that much from the size of her clothes—so she wouldn't have wanted anyone to know."

"Heading towards anorexia?"

"Sounds good to me. Body weight. Something a girl like her—with everyone's fingers in her personal pie—could control."

"But she would have had to cook it herself in the gyp room," Lynley said. "Surely Randie Webberly would have noticed that and mentioned it to me. And anyway, don't anorexics simply stop eating?"

"Okay. It's the symbol of some society then. A secret group that's up to no good. Drugs, alcohol, stealing government data. This *is* Cambridge after all, alma mater of the UK's most prestigious group of traitors. She may have been hoping to follow in their footsteps. Fish could have been an acronym for their group.''

"Foolish Intellectuals Squashing Hedonism?''

Havers grinned. "You're a finer detective than ever I thought.''

They continued flipping through the calendar. The notations were unchanging from month to month, tapering off in the summer when only the fish appeared—and that a mere three times. Its final appearance was the day before her murder, and the only other marking of any note was a single address written on the Wednesday before she died: *31 Seymour Street* and the time *2:00*.

"Here's something," Lynley said, and Havers jotted it down in her notebook along with *Hare and Hounds, Search and Pellet,* and a rough copy of the fish. "I'll handle it," she said, and began to go through the drawers of the desk as he turned to the cupboard that housed the washbasin. This contained a cornucopia of possessions and illustrated the manner in which one usually stores belongings when space is at a minimum. There was everything from laundry detergent to a popcorn popper. But nothing revealed very much about Elena.

"Look at this," Havers said as he was closing the cupboard and moving on to one of the drawers built into the wardrobe next to it. He looked up to see that she was holding out a slim, white case decorated with blue flowers. A prescription label was affixed to its centre. "Birth control pills," she said, sliding out the thin sheet still encased in its plastic cover.

"Hardly something surprising to find in the room of a twenty-year-old college girl," Lynley said.

"But they're dated last February, Inspector. And not one of them taken. Looks like there was no man in her life at the present. Do we eliminate a jealous lover as the killer?''

This was, Lynley thought, certainly support for what both Justine Weaver and Miranda Webberly had said last night about Gareth Randolph: Elena hadn't been involved with him. The pills, however, also suggested a consistent refusal to get involved with anyone, something which might have set the wheels of a killer's rage in motion. But surely she would have talked about that with someone, looking to someone for support or advice if she had been having trouble with a man.

Across the hall, the music ended. A few last wavering, live notes sounded on the trumpet before, after a moment of muffled activity, the squeak of a door replaced the other sounds.

"Randie," Lynley called.

Elena's door swung inward. Miranda stood there, bundled up for the outdoors in her heavy pea jacket and navy sweat suit with a lime-green beret perched rakishly on her head. She was wearing high-topped black athletic shoes. Socks decorated to look like slices of watermelon peeked out from the top of them.

Glancing at her attire, Havers said meaningfully, "I rest my case, Inspector," and then to the girl, "Good to see you, Randie."

Miranda smiled. "You got here early."

"Necessity. I couldn't let his lordship muddle through on his own. Besides"—this with a sardonic look in Lynley's direction—"he hasn't quite got the flavour of modern university life."

"Thank you, Sergeant," Lynley said. "I'd be lost without you." He indicated the calendar. "Will you look at this fish, Randie? Does it mean anything to you?"

Miranda joined him at the desk and inspected the sketches on the calendar. She shook her head.

"She hadn't been doing any cooking in the gyp room?" Havers asked, obviously testing out her diet theory.

Miranda looked incredulous. "Cooking. Fish, you mean? Elena cooking *fish*?"

"You would have known it, right?"

"I would have got sick. I hate the smell of fish."

"Then some society that she belonged to?" Havers was going for theory number two.

"Sorry. I know she was in DeaStu and Hare and Hounds and probably one or two other societies as well. But I'm not sure which." Randie looked through the calendar as they themselves had done, chewing absently on the edge of her thumb. "It's too often," she said when she'd gone back to January. "No society has this many meetings."

"A person, then?"

Lynley saw her cheeks flush. "I wouldn't know. Really. She never said that there was anyone *that* special. I mean special enough for three or four nights a week. She never said."

"You can't know for certain, you mean," Lynley said. "You don't know for a fact. But you lived with her, Randie. You knew her far better than you think. Tell me the sorts of things Elena did. Those are merely facts, nothing more. I'll build upon them."

Miranda hesitated a long moment before saying, "She went out a lot at night by herself."

"For entire nights?"

"No. She couldn't do that because after last December they made her check in and out with the porter. But she got back to her room late whenever she went out . . . I mean when it was one of those secret going-outs. She was never here when I went to bed on those nights."

"Secret going-outs?"

Miranda's ginger hair bobbed as she nodded. "She went by herself. She always wore perfume. She didn't take books. I thought there must have been someone she was seeing."

"But she never told you who it was?"

"No. And I didn't like to pry. I don't think she wanted anyone to know."

"That doesn't suggest a fellow undergraduate, does it?"

"I suppose not."

"What about Thorsson?" Her eyes dropped to the calendar. She touched the edge of it reflectively. "What do you know about his relationship with Elena? There's something to it, Randie. I can see that on your face. And he was here Thursday night."

"I only know . . . " Randie hesitated, sighed. "This is what she said. It's only what she *said*, Inspector."

"All right. That's understood." Lynley saw Havers flip over a page of her notebook.

Miranda watched the sergeant write. "She said he was trying to make it with her, Inspector. He'd been after her last term, she said. He was after her again. She hated him for it. She called him smarmy. She said she was going to turn him over to Dr. Cuff for sexual harassment."

"And did she do so?"

"I don't know." Miranda twisted the button on her jacket. It was like a little talisman, infusing her with strength. "I don't know that she ever got the chance, you see."

Lennart Thorsson was in the process of completing a lecture in the English Faculty on Sidgwick Avenue when Lynley and Havers finally caught him up. The popularity of both his material and his manner of presenting it was attested by the size of the hall in which he spoke. It held at least one hundred chairs. All of them were filled, mostly by women. Ninety percent of them appeared to be hanging upon Thorsson's every word.

There was much to hang on, all of it delivered in perfect, virtually unaccented English.

The Swede paced as he talked. He didn't use notes. He seemed to take inspiration from intermittently running his right hand through the thick, strawberry-blond hair which tumbled onto his forehead and round his shoulders in an appealing mess, a complement to the drooping moustache that curved round his mouth in a style that befitted the early 1970's.

"So in the royalty plays, we examine the issues that Shakespeare himself was intent upon examining," Thorsson was saying. "Monarchy. Power. Hierarchy. Authority. Dominion. And in our examination of these issues we cannot avoid a scrutiny of that which comprised the question of status quo. How far is Shakespeare writing from a perspective to conserve the status quo? How does he do it *if* he does it? And if he's cleverly spinning an illusion in which he merely wears the guise of adherence to these social constrictions of his day—while all the time espousing an insidious subversion of the social order—how is he doing *that*?"

Thorsson paused to let the furious note-takers catch up with the flow of his thoughts. He turned on his heel briskly and paced again. "And then we go further to begin our examination of the obverse position. We ask to what extent is Shakespeare openly contesting the existing social hierarchies? From what standpoint is he contesting them? Is he implying an alternative set of values—a subversive set of values—and if he is, what are they? Or"—Thorsson pointed a meaningful finger at his audience and leaned towards them, his voice more intense—"is Shakespeare doing something even more complex? Is he questioning and challenging the foundation of this country—his country—itself—authority, power, and hierarchy—in order to imply a refutation of the premise on which his entire society was founded? Is he projecting different ways of living, arguing that if possibility is circumscribed only by existing conditions, then man makes no progress and effects no change? Because is not Shakespeare's real premise—present in *every* play—that all men share equality? And does not every king in every play reach that point at which his interests are in alignment with humanity at large and no longer with kingship? 'I think the King is but a man, as I am.' As . . . I . . . am. This, then, is the point we examine. Equality. The king and I are equals. We are but men. There is no defensible social hierarchy, here or anywhere. So we agree that it was possible for Shakespeare, as an imaginative artist, to store and dwell upon ideas which would not be talked about for centuries, projecting himself into a future he did not know, allowing us to see at last that the reason his works are valid today is simply because we have not yet even begun to catch up to his thinking.''

Thorsson strode to the podium and picked up a notebook which he closed decisively. ''Next week then. *Henry V.* Good morning.''

For a moment, no one stirred. Paper crackled. A pencil dropped. Then, with what appeared to be reluctance, the audience roused itself with a collective sigh. Conversation rose as people headed for the exits while Thorsson stuffed his notebook and two texts into a haversack. As he removed his black academic gown and balled it up to join the textbooks, he spoke to a tousle-haired young woman still sitting in the front row. Then, after taking a moment to tap one finger against her cheek and laugh at something she'd said, he came up the aisle towards the door.

''Ah,'' Havers said, *sotto voce.* ''Your basic Prince of Darkness.''

It was a particularly apt sobriquet. Thorsson didn't favour black, he wallowed in it, as if in the attempt to generate a deliberate contrast to his fair skin and hair. Pullover, trousers, herringbone jacket, overcoat, and scarf. Even his boots were black, with pointed toes and high heels. If he was intent upon playing the role of youthful, indifferent rebellion, he couldn't have chosen a more successful costume. However, when he reached Lynley and Havers and began, with a sharp nod, to move past them, Lynley saw that while Thorsson might well have been a rebel, he wasn't a youth. Crow's feet shot out from the corners of his eyes, and a few grey strands wove through his abundant hair. Middle thirties, Lynley decided. He and the Swede were of an age.

''Mr. Thorsson?'' He offered his warrant card. ''Scotland Yard CID. Do you have a few minutes?''

Thorsson looked from Lynley to Havers and back to Lynley, who made the introductions. He said, ''Elena Weaver, I take it?''

''Yes.''

He slung his haversack over one shoulder and, with a sigh, roughly drove a hand through his hair. ''We can't talk here. Have you got a car with you?'' He waited for Lynley's nod. ''Let's go to the college.'' He turned abruptly and walked out the door, flinging his scarf back over his shoulder.

''Nice exit, that,'' Havers said.

''Why do I imagine he excels at them?''

They followed Thorsson down the hall, down the stairs, and into the open cloister which had been created by a well-intentioned modern architect who had designed the three-sided faculties building to stand upon columns of reinforced concrete round a rectangle of lawn. The resulting structure hovered above the ground, suggesting impermanence and offering no protection from the wind which at this moment was gusting through the columns.

"I've a supervision next hour," Thorsson informed them.

Lynley smiled pleasantly. "I certainly hope we're done by then." He motioned Thorsson in the general direction of his car which he'd parked illegally at the northeast entrance to Selwyn College. They walked to it three abreast on the pavement, with Thorsson merely nodding indifferently to students who called out to him from passing bicycles.

It wasn't until they reached the Bentley that the Shakespearean lecturer addressed them again. And then it was only to say, "This is what the British police are driving? *Fy fan!* No wonder the country's going to hell."

"Ah, but my motor makes up for it," Havers replied. "Average a ten-year-old Mini with a four-year-old Bentley and you come up with seven years of equality, don't you?"

Lynley smiled inwardly. Havers had taken Thorsson's lecture directly into her caustic little heart. "You know what I mean," she continued. "A car by any other name rolls down the street."

Thorsson didn't look amused.

They got into the car. Lynley headed up Grange Road to make the circuit that would take them back into the centre of the city. At the end of the street, as they waited to make the right turn onto the Madingley Road, a lone bicyclist rolled past them, heading out of town. It took more than a moment for Lynley to recognise the rider, Helen's brother-in-law, the absent Harry Rodger. He was pedalling towards his home, his coat flapping like great woollen wings round his legs. Lynley watched him, wondering if he'd spent the entire night at Emmanuel. Rodger's face seemed pasty, save for his nose which was red and matched the colour of his ears. He looked perfectly miserable. Seeing him, Lynley felt a quick surge of concern only indirectly related to Harry Rodger. It centred itself on Helen and a need to get her away from her sister's home and back to London. He shoved the thought aside and made himself concentrate on the conversation between Havers and Lennart Thorsson.

"His writing illustrates the artist's struggle to work out a utopian vision, Sergeant. A vision that goes beyond a feudal society and deals with all mankind, not just a select group of individuals who happen to be born with a silver spoon on which to suck. As such, the body of his work is prodigiously—no, miraculously—subversive. But most critical analysts don't wish to see it that way. It scares them witless to think that a sixteenth-century writer might have had more social vision than they . . . who of course have no social vision at all.''

"Shakespeare was a closet Marxist then?''

Thorsson made a snort of derision. "Simplistic snobbery,'' he responded. "And hardly what I'd expect from—''

Havers turned in her seat. "Yes?''

Thorsson didn't finish his thought. There was no need. *Someone of your class* hung among them like an echo, four words that robbed his liberal literary criticism of virtually all of its meaning.

They rode the rest of the distance without conversation, threading through the lorries and taxis on St. John's Street to make their way down the narrow gorge of Trinity Lane. Lynley parked near the end of Trinity Passage, just outside the north entrance to St. Stephen's College. Unlocked and pushed open during the day, it offered immediate access to New Court.

"My rooms are this way,'' Thorsson said, striding towards the west range of the court which was built on the river. He slid back a slat of wood to uncover his name, painted in white on a black sign by the door, and he entered to the left of the crenellated tower where woodbine grew thickly on the smooth stone walls. Lynley and Havers followed, Lynley having acknowledged Havers' knowing look at *L* staircase directly across the lawn on the east range of the court.

Ahead of them, Thorsson pounded up the stairs, his boots barking in staccato against the bare wood. When they caught him up, he was unlocking a door upon a room whose windows overlooked the river, the blazing autumn of the Backs, and Trinity Passage Bridge where at this moment a group of tourists were taking pictures. Thorsson crossed to the windows and dropped his haversack onto a table beneath them. Two ladder-back chairs faced each other there, and he draped his overcoat across the back of one of them and went to a large recess in one corner of the room where a single bed stood.

"I'm done for,'' he said, and lay down on his back across the plaid counterpane. He winced as if the position were uncomfortable for him. "Sit if you want.'' He gestured to an easy chair and a matching sofa at the foot of the bed, both of them covered with material the colour of wet mud. His intention was clear. The interview that he wished to be conducted on his turf would also be conducted precisely on his terms.

After nearly thirteen years on the force, Lynley was used to encountering displays of bravado, specious or otherwise. He ignored the invitation to sit and took a moment to inspect the collection of volumes in a break-front bookcase at one side of the room. Poetry, classic fiction, literary criticism printed in English, French, and Swedish, and several volumes of erotica, one of which lay open to a chapter entitled "Her Orgasm." Lynley smiled wryly. He liked the subtle touch.

At the table, Sergeant Havers was opening her notebook. She produced a pencil from her shoulder bag, and looked at Lynley expectantly. On the bed, Thorsson yawned.

Lynley turned from the bookcase. "Elena Weaver saw a lot of you," he said.

Thorsson blinked. "Hardly a cause for suspicion, Inspector. I was one of her supervisors."

"But you saw her outside of her supervisions."

"Did I?"

"You'd been to her room. More than once, I understand." Speculatively and as obviously as possible, Lynley ran his eyes the length of the bed. "Did she have her supervisions in here, Mr. Thorsson?"

"Yes. But at the table. I find that young ladies do far better thinking on their bums than on their backs." Thorsson chuckled. "I can see where you're heading, Inspector. Let me put your mind at rest. I don't seduce school girls, even when they invite seduction."

"Is that what Elena did?"

"They come in here and sit with their pretty legs spread and I get the message. It happens all the time. But I don't take them up on it." He yawned again. "I admit I've had three or four of them once they've graduated, but they're adults by then and they know the score proper. A bit of dirty hard cock for the weekend, that's all. Then off they go, warm and tingly, with no questions asked and no commitments made. We have a good time—they probably have a far better time than I, to be frank—and that's the end of it."

Lynley wasn't blind to the fact that Thorsson hadn't answered his question. The other man was continuing.

"Cambridge senior fellows who have affairs with school girls fit a profile, Inspector, and it never varies. If you're looking for someone likely to stuff Elena, look for middle-aged, look for married, look for unattractive. Look for generally miserable and outstandingly stupid."

"Someone completely unlike you," Havers said from the table.

Thorsson ignored her. "I'm not a madman. I'm not interested in being ruined. And that's what's in store for any *djavlar typ* who makes a mess of himself with an undergraduate—male or female. The scandal's enough to make him miserable for years."

"Why do I have the impression that scandal wouldn't bother you in the least, Mr. Thorsson?" Lynley asked.

Havers added, "Did you actually harass her for sex, Mr. Thorsson?"

Thorsson turned onto his side. He put his eyes on Havers and kept them there. Contempt drew down the corners of his mouth.

"You went to see her Thursday night," Havers said. "Why? To keep her from doing what she threatened she'd do? I don't imagine you much wanted her to give your name over to the Master of the College. So what did she tell you? Had she already filed a formal complaint for harassment? Or were you hoping to stop her from doing that?"

"You're a fucking stupid cow," Thorsson replied.

Lynley felt quick anger shoot blood to his muscles. But Sergeant Havers, he saw, was not reacting. Instead, she twirled an ashtray slowly beneath her fingers, studying its contents. Her expression was bland.

"Where do you live, Mr. Thorsson?" Lynley asked.

"Off the Fulbourn Road."

"Are you married?"

"Thank God, no. English women don't exactly heat my blood."

"Are you living with someone?"

"No."

"Did anyone spend the night with you Sunday? Was anyone with you Monday morning?"

Thorsson's eyes danced away for a fractional instant. "No," he said. But like most people he did not lie well.

"Elena Weaver was on the cross country team," Lynley went on. "Did you know that?"

"I might have known. I don't recall."

"She ran in the morning. Did you know that?"

"No."

"She called you 'Lenny the Lech.' Did you know that?"

"No."

"Why did you go to see her Thursday night?"

"I thought we could sort things out if we talked like two adults. I discovered I was wrong."

"So you knew she was intending to turn you in for harassing her. Is that what she told you Thursday night?"

Thorsson hooted a laugh. He dropped his legs over the side of the bed. "I see the game now. You're too late, Inspector, if you're here to sniff up a motive for her murder. That one won't do. The bitch had already turned me in."

•   •   •

"He's got motive," Havers said. "What happens to one of these University blokes if he gets caught with his hands in some pretty thing's knickers?"

"Thorsson was fairly clear on that. At the least, I imagine he finds himself ostracised. At the most, dismissed. No matter its politics, ethically the University's a conservative environment. Academics won't tolerate one of their fellows becoming entangled with a junior member of his college. Especially a student he's seeing for supervisions."

"But why would Thorsson even care what they thought? When d'you think he'd ever find the need to go rubbing elbows with his fellow scholars?"

"He may not need to rub social elbows with them, Havers. He may not even want to. But he's got to rub academic elbows all the time, and if his colleagues cut him off, he's ruined his chances for advancement here. That would be the case for all the senior fellows, but I imagine Thorsson has a finer line to walk to move along in his career."

"Why?"

"A Shakespearean scholar who's not even English? Here? At Cambridge? I dare say he's fought hard to get where he is."

"And might fight even harder to keep himself there."

"True enough. No matter Thorsson's superficial disdain for Cambridge, I can't think he'd want to endanger himself. He's young enough to have his eye on an eventual professorship, probably a chair. But that's lost to him if he's involved with a student."

Havers dumped some sugar into her coffee. She munched thoughtfully on a toasted teacake. At three other steel-legged tables in the airy buttery, seven junior members of the college huddled over their own mid-morning snacks with sunlight from the wall of windows streaking down their backs. The presence of Lynley and Havers did not appear to interest them.

"He had opportunity as well," Havers pointed out.

"If we discount his claim that he didn't know Elena ran in the morning."

"I think we can, Inspector. Look how many times her calendar indicates she met with Thorsson. Are we supposed to believe that she never once mentioned the cross country team to him? That she never talked about her running? What utter rot."

Lynley grimaced at the bitterness of his own coffee. It tasted cooked—like a soup. He added sugar and borrowed his sergeant's spoon.

"If an investigation was pending, he'd want to put an end to it, wouldn't he?" Havers was continuing. "Because once Elena Weaver came forward to put the thumbscrews to him, what was to stop a dozen other sweet young things from doing the same?"

"If a dozen other sweet young things even exist. If, in fact, he's guilty at all. Elena may have charged him with harassing her, Sergeant, but let's not forget that it remained to be proved."

"And it can't be proved now, can it?" Havers pointed a knowing finger at him. Her upper lip curled. "Are you actually taking the male position in this? Poor Lenny Thorsson's been falsely accused of dandling some girl because he rejected her when she tried to get him to take off his trousers? Or at least unzip them?"

"I'm not taking any position at all, Havers. I'm merely gathering facts. And the most cogent one is that Elena Weaver had already turned him in, and as a result an investigation was pending. Look at it rationally. He's got *motive* spelled out in neon lights above his head. He may talk like an idiot, but he doesn't strike me as a fool. He would have known he'd be placed at the top of the list of suspects as soon as we learned about him. So if he did kill her, I imagine he'd have set himself up with an iron-clad alibi, don't you?"

"No, I don't." She waved her teacake at him. One of its raisins dropped with a plop into her coffee. She ignored it and continued. "I think he's clever enough to know we'd be having a conversation just like this. He knew we'd be saying he's a Cambridge don, he's a far sight off dim, he'd never kill Elena Weaver and hand himself over to the rozzers on a platter now, would he? And look at us, will you. Playing right into his hands." She bit into her teacake. Her jaws worked it furiously.

Lynley had to admit that there was a certain skewed logic to what Havers was suggesting. Still, he didn't like the fire with which she suggested it. That hot edge of feeling nearly always implied a loss of objectivity, the bane of effective policework. He had encountered it too often in himself to let it go ignored in his partner.

He knew the source of her anger. But to address it directly would be to give a distinction to Thorsson's words that was undeserved. He sought another tack.

"He would know about the Ceephone in her room. There's that. And according to Miranda, Elena left the room prior to the time Justine received the call. If he'd been in her room before—and he admits that he had—then he probably knew how to use the phone as well. So he could have made the call to the Weavers.''

"Now you're onto something," Havers said.

"But unless Sheehan's forensic team give us trace evidence that we can connect to Thorsson, unless we can pin down the weapon used to beat the girl before she was strangled, and unless we can connect that weapon to Thorsson, we've got nothing much more than our natural dislike of him.''

"And we've plenty of that.''

"In spades.'' He shoved his coffee cup to one side. "What we need is a witness, Havers.''

"To the killing?''

"To something. To anything.'' He stood. "Let's look up this woman who found the body. If nothing else, at least we'll find out what she was planning to paint in the fog.''

Havers drained her coffee cup and wiped the greasy crumbs from her hands onto a paper napkin. She headed for the door, shrugging into her coat, with her two scarves dragging along the floor behind her. He said nothing else until they were outside on the terrace above North Court. And even then he chose his words carefully.

"Havers, as to what Thorsson said to you.''

She looked at him blankly. "What he said, sir?''

Lynley felt an odd strip of sweat on the back of his neck. Most of the time he didn't give a thought to the fact that his partner was a woman. At the moment, however, that fact couldn't be avoided. "In his room, Havers. The . . . '' He sought a euphemism. "The bovine reference?''

"Bo . . . '' Under her thick fringe of hair, her brow creased in perplexity. "Oh, *bovine*. You mean when he called me a cow?''

"Ah . . . yes.'' Even as he said it, Lynley wondered what on earth he could possibly come up with to soothe her feelings. He needn't have worried.

She chuckled quietly. "Don't give it a thought, Inspector. When an ass calls me a cow, I always consider the source.''

7

"And what's this one, Christian?" Lady Helen asked. She held up a piece of the large wooden puzzle that lay on the floor between them. Carved from mahogany, oak, fir, and birch, it was a softly hued map of the United States, a gift to the twins on their fourth birthday sent from America by their aunt Iris, Lady Helen's oldest sister. The puzzle reflected Lady Iris' taste more than it said anything about her devotion to her niece and nephew. "Quality and durability, Helen. That's what one looks for," she would say stolidly, as if in the expectation that Christian and Perdita would be playing with toys right into their dotage.

Bright colours would have attracted the children more strongly. They certainly would have gone further to hold their attention. But after a few false starts, Lady Helen had managed to turn putting the puzzle together into a game which Christian was playing like a zealot as his sister watched. Perdita sat snugly against Lady Helen's side, her thin legs splayed out in front of her, her scuffed shoes pointed northeast and northwest.

"Cafilornia!" Christian announced triumphantly, after spending a moment studying the shape his aunt held for him. He beat his feet on the floor and crowed. He was always successful with the oddly shaped states. Oklahoma, Texas, Florida, Utah. No problem there. But Wyoming, Colorado, and North Dakota were blatant invitations to a fit of temper.

"Wonderful. And its capital is . . . ?"

"New York!"

Lady Helen laughed. "Sacramento, silly face."

"Sackermenno!"

"Quite. Now put it in. Do you know where it goes?"

After a futile attempt to pound it into the spot left for Florida, Christian slid it across the board to the opposite coast. " 'Nother, Auntie Leen," he said. "I can do more."

She selected the smallest piece and held it up. Wisely, Christian squinted down at the map. He plunged his finger into the empty spot to the east of Connecticut.

"Here," hc announced.

"Yes. But can you name it?"

"Here! Here!"

"Are you stalling, darling?"

"Auntie Leen! Here!"

Next to Lady Helen, Perdita stirred. "Rose-ila," she whispered.

"Roads Island!" Christian shrieked. With a whoop of triumph, he lunged for the state which his aunt still held.

"And the capital?" Lady Helen kept the puzzle piece away from him. "Come along. You knew it yesterday."

"Lantic Ocean!" he bellowed.

Lady Helen smiled. "Close enough, I suppose."

Christian tugged the piece from her fingers and smashed it into the puzzle face downward. When it didn't fit, he tried it upside down. He pushed his sister away when she leaned forward to help him, saying, "I c'n do it, Perdy," and managing to get it right on a third clumsy, sticky-handed try.

" 'Nother," he demanded.

Before Lady Helen could accommodate him, the front door opened and Harry Rodger entered the house. He glanced into the sitting room, his eyes lingering on the baby who kicked and burbled on a heavy quilt next to Perdita on the floor.

"Hullo, everyone," he said as he took off his overcoat. "Got a kiss for Dad?"

Squealing, Christian barrelled across the room. He flung himself against his father's legs. Perdita didn't move.

Rodger swung his son up, kissed him noisily on the cheek, and set him back on the floor. He pretended to paddle him, demanding, "Have you been bad, Chris? Have you been a bad boy?" Christian shrieked with glee. Lady Helen felt Perdita shrink closer beside her and glanced down to see that she was sucking her thumb, eyes fixed on her sister, fingers kneading her palm.

"We're doing a puzzle," Christian told his father. "Auntie Leen 'n me."

"And what about Perdita? Is she helping you?"

"No. Perdita won't play. But Auntie Leen and I play. Come see." Christian dragged on his father's hand, urging him into the sitting room.

Lady Helen tried to feel neither anger nor aversion as her brother-in-law joined them. He hadn't come home last night. He hadn't bothered to phone. And those two facts eradicated whatever sympathy she might have felt upon looking at him and seeing that, whether the illness was of the body or the spirit, he was obviously unwell. His eyes looked yellow. His face was unshaven. His lips were chapped. If he wasn't sleeping at home, he certainly didn't look as if he were sleeping anywhere else.

"Cafilornia." Christian poked at the puzzle. "See, Daddy? Nevada. Puta."

"Utah," Harry Rodger said automatically, and to Lady Helen, "How's everything here, then?"

Lady Helen was acutely aware of the presence of the children, especially of Perdita quivering against her. She was also aware of her own need to rail at her brother-in-law. But she said merely, "Fine, Harry. How lovely to see you."

He responded with a vague smile. "Right. I'll leave you to it, then." Patting Christian on the head, he left the room, escaping in the direction of the kitchen.

Christian began to wail immediately. Lady Helen felt herself growing hot. She said, "It's all right, Christian. Let me see about your lunch. Will you stay here with Perdita and little sister for a moment? Show Perdita how to put the puzzle together."

"I want Daddy!" he screamed.

Lady Helen sighed. How well she had come to understand that fact. She turned the puzzle over and dumped it onto the floor, saying, "Look, Chris," but he began flinging pieces into the fireplace. They splattered into the ashes under the grate and spewed clouds of debris out onto the carpet. His screams grew louder.

Rodger stuck his head back into the room. "For God's sake, Helen. Can't you shut him up?"

Lady Helen snapped. She sprang to her feet, stalked across the room, and shoved her brother-in-law back into the kitchen. She closed the door upon Christian's wailing.

If Rodger was surprised by her sudden vehemence, he did not react to it. He merely went back to the work top where he had been in the process of going through the collection of two days' post. He held a letter up to the light, squinted at it, discarded it, picked up another.

"What's going on, Harry?" she demanded.

He looked her way briefly before returning to the post. "What on earth are you talking about?"

"I'm talking about you. I'm talking about my sister. She's upstairs, by the way. You might want to look in on her before you trot back to the college. I take it that you *are* trotting back, aren't you? Somehow this visit doesn't quite have the aura of permanence round it."

"I've a lecture at two."

"And after that?"

"I'm attending formal dinner tonight. And really, Helen, you are beginning to sound rather drearily like Pen."

Lady Helen marched to him, ripped the stack of letters from his hand, and threw them on the work top. "How dare you," she said. "You egocentric little worm. Do you think we're all of us here for your convenience?"

"How astute you are, Helen." Penelope spoke from the doorway. "I wouldn't have thought it." She halted her way into the room, one hand against the wall and the other folded into the throat of her dressing gown. Two streaks of damp from her swollen breasts discoloured the pink material, turning it fuchsia. Harry's eyes fell on these before shifting away. "Don't like the sight?" Penelope asked him. "Too real for you, Harry? Not quite what you wanted?"

Rodger went back to his letters. "Don't start, Pen."

She gave a wavering laugh. "I didn't start this. Correct me if I'm wrong, but you were the one. Wasn't that you? All those days. All those nights. Talking and urging. They're like a gift, Pen, our gift to the world. But if one of them should die . . . That was you, wasn't it?"

"And you won't let me forget it, will you? For the last six months you've been taking your revenge. Well, fine then. Do it. I can't stop you. But I *can* decide not to stay for the abuse."

Penelope laughed again, more weakly this time. She leaned for support against the refrigerator door. One hand climbed to her hair which lay, limp and oily, against her neck. "Harry, how amusing. If you want some abuse, climb into this body. Oh, but you did that, didn't you? Any number of times."

"We're *not* going to—"

"Talk about it? Why? Because my sister's here and you don't want her to know? Because the children are playing in the other room? Because the neighbours might notice if I scream loud enough?''

Harry slapped down his letters. Envelopes slithered across the work top. "Don't put this on me. You made up your mind."

"Because you gave me no peace. I didn't even feel like a woman any longer. You wouldn't even touch me if I didn't agree to—"

"No!" Harry shouted. "God damn it, Pen. You could have said no."

"I was just a sow, wasn't I? Fodder for the rut."

"That's not quite accurate. Sows wallow in the mud, not in self-pity."

"Stop it!" Lady Helen said.

In the sitting room, Christian shrieked. The thin wail of the baby joined in his cries. Something hit the wall with a tremendous clatter, suggesting the body of the puzzle being hurled in a rage.

"Just look at what you're doing to them," Harry Rodger said. "Take a good long look." He headed for the door.

"And what are you doing?" Penelope shrilled. "Model father, model husband, model lecturer, model saint. Running away as usual? Working up your revenge? She hasn't let me have it for the last six months so I'll make her pay now when she's weak and ill and I can get her a good one? Just the moment when I can best let her know what a nothing she is?"

He whirled to face her. "I've had it with you. It's time you decided what you want instead of constantly digging into me for what you have." Before she could answer, he was gone. A moment later, the front door slammed. Christian howled. The baby cried. In response, fresh growing wet spots seeped through Penelope's dressing gown. She began to weep.

"I don't want this life!"

Lady Helen felt an answering rush of pity. Tears stung her eyes. Never had she felt so at a loss for something to say that might comfort.

For the first time she understood her sister's long silences, her vigils at the window, and her wordless weeping. But what she could not understand was the initial act that had brought Penelope to this point. It constituted a kind of surrender so foreign to her that she found herself recoiling from its significance.

She went to her sister, took her into her arms.

Penelope stiffened. "No! Don't touch me. I'm leaking all over. It's the baby . . . ''

Lady Helen continued to hold her. She tried to frame a question and wondered where to start and what she could ask that would not betray her growing anger. The fact that her rage was multi-directional served to make the act of concealing it only that much more difficult.

She felt it first for Harry and for the needs of ego that would prompt a man to urge for the breeding of another child, as if what was being created were a demonstration of the father's virility, and not an individual with decided needs of its own. She felt it also for her sister and for the fact that she had given in to that sense of duty inbred in women from the beginning of time, a duty which told them that the possession of a functioning womb necessarily served as a definition of self.

The initial decision to have children—one which no doubt had been made with joy and commitment by both Penelope and her husband—had proved her sister's undoing. For in leaving behind her career to care for the twins, she had, over time, allowed herself to become a dependent, a woman who believed she had to hold onto her man. So when he had made the request for another child, she had acquiesced. She had done her duty. After all, what better way to keep him than to give him what he wanted?

That none of this had been necessary, that all of it rose from her sister's inability or unwillingness to challenge the constrictive definition of womanhood to which she had decided to adhere, served to make her current situation even more untenable. For Penelope was wise enough at the heart of the matter to know that she was assenting to living a life in which she did not believe, and that was, undoubtedly, a large part of the wretchedness she was now experiencing. Her husband's parting words had instructed her to make a decision. But until she learned to redefine herself, circumstances and not Penelope would do the deciding.

Her sister sobbed against her shoulder. Lady Helen held her and tried to murmur comfort.

"I can't stand it," Penelope wept. "I'm suffocating. I'm nothing. I don't have an identity. I'm just a machine."

You're a mother, Lady Helen thought, while in the next room, Christian continued to scream.

It was noon when Lynley and Havers pulled to a stop on the twisting high street of the village of Grantchester, a collection of houses, pubs, a church, and a vicarage separated from Cambridge by the University's rugby fields and a long stretch of farmland lying fallow for the winter behind a hawthorn hedgerow that was beginning to brown. The address on the police report had looked decidedly vague: *Sarah Gordon, The*

School, Grantchester. But once they reached the village, Lynley realised that no further information was going to be necessary. For between a row of thatched cottages and the Red Lion Pub stood a hazel-coloured brick building with bright red woodwork and numerous skylights set into a pitched tile roof. From one of the pillars that stood on either side of the driveway hung a bronze-lettered sign that said merely *The School.*

"Not bad digs," Havers commented, shouldering open her door. "Your basic loving renovation of an historical property. I've always hated people with the patience for preservation. Who is she, anyway?"

"An artist of some sort. We'll find out the rest."

The space for the original front door now accommodated four panels of glass through which they could see lofty white walls, part of a sofa, and the blue glass shade of an arching brass floorlamp. When they slammed the car doors and started to walk up the drive, a dog came to these windows and began to yap wildly.

The new front door was set towards the rear of the building, recessed into part of a low, covered passage which connected the house to the garage. As they approached, it was opened by a slender woman wearing faded jeans, a man-sized work shirt of ivory wool, and a rose-coloured towel like a turban on her head. One hand held this in place as with the other she restrained her dog, a scruffy mongrel with lopsided ears—one at attention and the other at ease—and a thatch of khaki hair flopping into its eyes.

"Don't be afraid. He never bites," she said as the dog tried to lunge away from the hold she had on his collar. "He just likes visitors." And to the dog, "Flame, sit," a mild command which he blithely ignored His tail wagged frantically.

Lynley produced his warrant card, introducing himself and Havers. He said, "You're Sarah Gordon? We'd like to talk to you about yesterday morning."

At the request, her dark eyes seemed to grow even darker for an instant, although it may have been the result of her movement into a shadow cast by the overhanging roof. "I don't know what more I can add, Inspector. I told the police as much as I could."

"Yes, I know. I've read the report. But I find it sometimes helps to hear everything firsthand. If you don't mind."

"Of course. Please. Come in." She stepped back from the door. Flame made a leap of happy greeting in Lynley's direction, planting mitt-sized paws against his thighs. Sarah Gordon said, "No! Flame, stop it at once!" and pulled the dog back. She picked him up—he was a frantic, squirming, tail-wagging armful—and carried him into the room they had seen from the street, where she put him into a basket to one side of the fireplace, saying, "Stay," and patting him on the head. His eager glance darted from Lynley to Havers to his mistress. When he saw that everyone intended to remain in the room with him, he gave one more delighted bark and settled his chin on his paws.

Sarah went to the fireplace where a haphazard stack of wood was burning. It crackled and popped as the flames hit pockets of resin and sap. She threw on another piece before turning to face them.

"Was this actually a school?" Lynley asked her.

She looked surprised. Obviously, she had expected him to plunge directly into her discovery of Elena Weaver's corpse on the previous morning. Nonetheless, she smiled, glanced around, and answered. "The village school, yes. It was quite a mess when I bought it."

"Did you remodel it yourself?"

"A room here and there, when I could afford it and when I had the time. It's largely finished now except for the back garden. This"—she extended her hand to indicate the room in which they stood—"was the last. A bit different from what one would expect to see inside a building of this age, I suppose. But that's why I like it."

As Havers began unwrapping the first of her scarves from her throat, Lynley glanced around. The room was indeed an unexpected pleasure, with its extensive display of lithographs and oils. Their subjects were people: children, adolescents, old men playing cards, an elderly woman looking out a window. Their compositions were figurative and metaphorical at once; their colours were pure and bright and true.

In combination with a bleached oak floor and an oatmeal sofa, the overall effect of a room filled with this much art should have been much like a museum and just about as friendly. But as if with the intention of easing the unwelcoming nature of her environment, Sarah Gordon had draped a red mohair blanket across the back of the sofa and covered the floor with a motley braided rug. If this were not enough to declare the room lived in, a copy of *The Guardian* was spread out in front of the fireplace, a sketch box and easel lay near the door, and the air—most unmuseumlike of all—bore the unmistakable, rich odour of chocolate. This seemed to be emanating from a thick green jug on the bar at one end of the room. It sat next to a mug. A trail of steam rose from both.

Seeing the direction of his gaze, Sarah Gordon said, "It's cocoa. An anti-depressant, I find. I've needed rather a lot of it since yesterday. May I offer you some?"

He shook his head. "Sergeant?"

Havers demurred and went to sit on the sofa, where she dropped her scarves, shed her coat, and wrestled her notebook from her shoulder bag. A large orange cat, materialising from behind the open front curtains, leaped agilely to join her and settled, paws working, directly on her lap.

Sarah fetched her cup of cocoa and hurried to Havers' rescue. "Sorry," she said, scooping the cat under one arm. She herself took a place at the other end of the sofa, putting her back to the light. She buried her free hand in the cat's thick fur. The other—raising the cocoa to her lips—trembled noticeably. She spoke as if with the need to excuse this.

"I've never seen a dead body before. No, that's not absolutely true. I've seen people in coffins but that's after they've been scoured, washed, and painted by an undertaker. I suppose that's the only way we can bear death, isn't it, if it looks like a modestly altered state of life. But this other . . . I'd like to forget that I saw her, but she seems to be branded right into my brain." She touched the towel wrapped round her head. "I've taken five showers since yesterday morning. I've washed my hair three times. Why am I doing that?"

Lynley sat in an armchair opposite the sofa. He didn't bother to try to frame an answer to the question. Everyone's reaction to an exposure to violent death was peculiar to his individual personality. He'd known young detectives who wouldn't bathe until a case was solved, others who wouldn't eat, still others who wouldn't sleep. And while the vast majority of them became immune to death over time, seeing a murder investigation merely as a job to be done, the layman never saw it that way. The layman took it personally, like a deliberate insult. No one wanted a sudden reminder of life's grim and remarkable transiency.

He said, "Tell me about yesterday morning."

Sarah placed the mug on a side table and buried her other hand in the cat's fur. It didn't seem so much a gesture of affection as a means of holding onto something for solace or support. With typical feline sensitivity, the cat apparently knew this, for his ears flattened and he gave a throaty growl which Sarah ignored. She began to pet him. He attempted to launch himself in the direction of the floor. She said, "Silk, be good," and tried to hold onto him, but he yowled once, spit, and jumped off her lap. Sarah looked stricken. She watched the cat stroll over to the fire where, completely indifferent to his act of desertion, he settled himself on the newspaper and began to wash his face.

"Cats," Havers said in eloquent explanation. "Aren't they just exactly like men."

Sarah appeared to evaluate the comment gravely for its merit. She sat as if she held the cat in her lap, slightly bent forward, her hands on her thighs. It was a particularly self-protective position. "Yesterday morning," she said.

"If you will," Lynley said.

She went through the facts quickly, adding very little to what Lynley had read in the police report. Unable to sleep, she had risen at a quarter past five. She had dressed, eaten a bowl of cereal. She had read most of the previous day's paper. She had sorted through and gathered up her equipment. She had arrived at Fen Causeway shortly before seven. She had gone onto the island to do some sketches of Crusoe's Bridge. She had found the body.

"I stepped on her," she said. "I . . . It's awful to think about. I realise now that I should have wanted to help her. I should have tried to see if she was still alive. But I didn't."

"Where was she exactly?"

"At the side of a small clearing, towards the south end of the island."

"You didn't notice her at once?"

She reached for her cocoa and cradled the mug between her hands. "No. I'd gone there to do some sketching, and I was intent upon getting something done. I'd not worked—no, let me be truthful for once, I'd not produced anything of possible *merit*—in a number of months. I felt inadequate and paralysed, and I'd been harbouring a tremendous fear that I'd lost it altogether."

"It?"

"Talent, Inspector. Creativity. Passion. Inspiration. What you will. Over time, I'd grown to believe it was gone. So I decided a number of weeks ago to stop procrastinating. I was determined to put an end to busying myself with projects round the house—being afraid of failure, really—and to start working again. I chose yesterday as the day." She appeared to anticipate Lynley's next question, for she went on with, "It was just an arbitrary choice of days, actually. I felt if I marked the calendar, I'd be making a commitment. I thought if I chose the date in advance, I could begin again without any further false starts. It was important to me."

Lynley looked round the room again, more carefully this time, studying the collection of lithographs and oils. He couldn't help comparing them to the watercolours he had seen in Anthony Weaver's house. Those had been clever, nicely executed, safe. These were a challenge, both in colour and design.

"This is all your work," he said, a statement, not a question, for it was obvious that everything had been created by the same gifted hand.

She used her cocoa mug to point towards one of the walls. "This is all my work, yes. None of it recent. But all of it mine."

Lynley allowed himself to revel in an instant's gratification which rose from the knowledge that he couldn't have been handed a better potential witness. Artists were trained observers. They couldn't create without observation. If there had been something to see on the island, an object out of kilter, a shadow worth noticing, Sarah Gordon would have seen it. Leaning forward, he said:

"Tell me what you recall about the island itself."

Sarah looked into her cocoa as if replaying the scene there. "Well. It was foggy, very wet. Tree leaves were actually dripping. The boat repair sheds were closed. The bridge had been repainted. I remember noticing that because of the way it caught the light. And there was . . . " She hesitated, her expression thoughtful. "Near the gate, it was quite muddy, and the mud was . . . churned up. I'd call it furrowed, actually."

"As if a body had been dragged through it? Heels to the ground?"

"I suppose. And there was rubbish on the ground by a fallen branch. And . . . " She looked up. "I think I saw the remains of a fire as well."

"There by the branch?"

"In front of it, yes."

"And on the ground, what sort of rubbish?"

"Cigarette packs, mostly. A few newspapers. A large wine bottle. A sack? Yes, there was an orange sack from Peter Dominic. I remember that. Could someone have spent some time waiting for the girl?"

He ignored the question, saying, "Anything else?"

"The lights from the Peterhouse lantern cupola. I could see them from the island."

"Anything that you heard?"

"Nothing out of the ordinary. Birds. A dog, I think, somewhere in the fen. It all seemed perfectly normal to me. Except that the fog was heavy, but you'll have been told that."

"You heard no sound from the river?"

"Like a boat? Someone rowing away? No. I'm sorry." Her shoulders sagged a bit. "I wish I could give you something more. I feel monumentally egocentric. When I was on the island, I was thinking only of my drawing. I'm still thinking mostly of my drawing, in fact. What an ugly little item in my personal make-up.''

"Unusual to go sketching in the fog," Havers noted. She had been writing rapidly, but now she looked up, addressing their prime interest in coming to speak to the woman: What sort of artist goes sketching in the fog?

Sarah didn't disagree. "It was more than unusual. It was a little bit mad. And anything I might have managed to create wouldn't exactly be like the rest of my work, would it?''

There was truth in this. In addition to the use of bright, crisp, sun-inspired colours, Sarah Gordon's images all were clearly defined, from a group of Pakistani children sitting on the worn front steps of a paint-peeling tenement to a nude woman reclining beneath a yellow umbrella. Not one of them featured the gauzy absence of definition or the lack of hue that drawing in the morning fog suggested. Not one of them, additionally, depicted a landscape.

"Were you attempting a change in style?" Lynley asked.

"From *The Potato Eaters* to *Sunflowers*?" Sarah got to her feet and went to the bar where she poured herself more cocoa. Flame and Silk looked up from their respective positions, alert to the possibility of a treat. She went to the dog, squatted next to him, ran her fingers across his head. His tail thumped appreciatively, and he settled his chin back onto his paws. She sat on the floor next to his basket, cross-legged, facing Lynley and Havers.

She said, "I was willing to try just about anything. I don't know if you can understand what it feels like to believe you may have lost the ability and the will to create. Yes''—as if she expected disagreement—"the will, because it *is* an act of will. It's more than being called upon by some convenient artistic muse. It's making a decision to offer up a bit of one's essence to the judgement of others. As an artist, I'd told myself that I didn't care how my work was evaluated. I'd told myself that the creative act—and not how it was received or what anyone did with the finished product—was absolutely paramount. But somewhere along the line, I stopped believing in that. And when one stops believing that the act itself is superior to anyone's analysis of it, then one becomes immobilised. That's what happened to me.''

"Shades of Ruskin and Whistler, as I recall their story," Lynley said.

For some reason, she flinched at the allusion. "Ah, yes. The critic and his victim. But at least Whistler had his day in court, didn't he. He did have that much." Her eyes went from one piece of art to another, slowly, as if with the need to convince herself that she indeed had been their creator. "I'd lost it: the passion. And without that, what you have is only mass, the objects themselves. Paint, canvas, clay, wax, stone. Only passion gives them life. Otherwise, they're inert. Oh, you may draw or paint or sculpt something, anyway. People do it all the time. But what you draw or paint or sculpt without passion is an exercise in competence and nothing more. It's not an expression of self. And that's what I wanted back—the willingness to be vulnerable, the power to feel, the ability to risk. If it meant a change in technique, an alteration in style, a shift in media, I was more than willing to try it. I was willing to try anything."

"Did it work?"

She bent over the dog and rubbed her cheek against the top of his head. Somewhere in the house, the telephone began to ring. An answering machine switched on. A moment later the low tones of a man's voice floated to them, leaving a message that was indistinguishable from where they sat. Sarah seemed indifferent both to the identity of her caller and to the fact of the call itself. She said, "I hadn't the chance to find out. I made several preliminary sketches in one location on the island. When they didn't work out—they were dreadful, to be honest—I went to another spot and stumbled on the body."

"What do you remember of that?"

"Just that I stepped backwards onto something. I thought it was a branch. I kicked it aside and saw it was an arm."

"You hadn't noticed the body?" Havers clarified.

"She was covered by leaves. My attention was on the bridge. I can't say I even watched where I was walking."

"In what direction did you kick her arm?" Lynley asked. "Towards her? Away from her?"

"Towards her."

"You didn't touch her other than that?"

"God, no. But I should have done, shouldn't I? She may have been alive. I should have touched her. I should have checked. But I didn't. Instead, I was sick. And then I ran."

"In what direction? Back the way you came?"

"No. Across Coe Fen."

"In the fog?" Lynley asked. "Not back the way you'd come?"

At the opening of her shirt, Sarah's chest and neck began to redden. "I'd just stumbled upon a girl's body, Inspector. I can't say I was feeling very logical at the time. I ran across the bridge and through Coe Fen. There's a path that comes out next to the Department of Engineering. That's where I'd left my car.''

"You drove from there to the police station?"

"I just kept running. Down Lensfield Road. Across Parker's Piece. It isn't very far.''

"But you could have driven.''

"I could have done. Yes.'' She offered no defence. She looked at her painting of the Pakistani children. Flame stirred beneath her hand and gave a gusty sigh. Roused, she said, "I wasn't thinking clearly. I'd been in a welter of nerves already because I'd gone to the island in order to draw. To *draw*, you see. To do something I'd been unable to do for months. That was everything to me. So when I found the body, I simply didn't think. I should have seen if the girl was still alive. I should have tried to help her. I should have kept to the paved path. I should have driven my car to the police station. I know all that. I'm filled with *should*'s. I have no excuse for behaving as I did. Except that I panicked. And believe me, I feel wretched enough about that.''

"At the Department of Engineering, were there lights on?''

She looked back at him although her eyes didn't focus. She seemed to be trying to conjure up a picture of the events in her mind. "Lights. I think so. But I can't be certain.''

"Did you see anyone?''

"On the island, no. And not on the Fen, there was too much fog. I passed some bicyclists when I got to Lensfield Road, and there was traffic, of course. But that's all I remember.''

"How did you come to choose the island? Why didn't you do your sketching here in Grantchester? Especially once you saw the fog in the morning.''

The red flush on her skin deepened in hue. As if aware of this, she raised her hand to the neck of her shirt and played with the material in her fingers until she had buttoned it. "I don't know how to explain it to you except to say that I'd chosen the day, I'd planned in advance on the island, and to do anything less than what I planned seemed like admitting defeat and running away. I didn't want to do that. I just couldn't face it. It sounds pathetic. Rigid and obsessive. But that's the way it was.'' She got to her feet. "Come with me,'' she said. "There's really only one way that you might understand completely.''

Leaving her cocoa and her animals behind, she led them to the rear of the house where she pushed open a door that was only partially closed and admitted them into her studio. It was a large, bright room whose ceiling comprised four rectangular skylights. Lynley paused before entering, letting his eyes wander over everything, seeing how the room acted as mute corroboration to all that Sarah Gordon had told them.

The walls were hung with enormous charcoal sketches—a human torso, a disembodied arm, two interlocking nudes, a man's face in three-quarter profile—all the sort of preliminary studies an artist does before setting out upon a new work. But instead of acting as rough ideas for a finished product that was also on display, beneath them leaned a score of incomplete canvases, project after project begun and discarded. A large worktable held a mass of artistic paraphernalia: coffee tins filled with clean, dry brushes like camel-hair flowers; bottles of turps, linseed oil, and Damar varnish; a box of unused dry pastels; more than a dozen hand-labelled tubes of paint. It should have been a chaotic mess, with daubs of paint on the table and smudgy fingerprints on the bottles and tins, and squeeze-points on the tubes. Instead, everything was arranged as neatly and precisely as if it were on display in a Castle Museum exhibit devoted to a fanciful day-in-the-life-of presentation.

The air held no odour of paint or turpentine. No sketches piled here and there on the floor to make the suggestion of rapid artistic inspiration and equally rapid artistic rejection. No finished paintings stood waiting for the varnish that would complete them. It was apparent that someone cleaned the room regularly, for the bleached oak floor shone as if it were under glass and nowhere was there the slightest sign of dust or dirt. Just signs of disuse, and they were everywhere. Only a single easel holding a canvas stood covered with a paint-splodged cloth beneath one of the skylights, and even it looked as if it hadn't been touched in ages.

"This was once the centre of my world," Sarah Gordon said with simple resignation. "Can you understand, Inspector? I wanted it to be the centre again."

Sergeant Havers, Lynley saw, had wandered to one side of the room where above a work top had been built a series of storage shelves. These held cartons of carousels for photographic slides, dog-eared sketch pads, fresh containers of pastels, a large roll of canvas, and a variety of tools—from a set of palette knives to a pair of stretching pliers. The work top itself was covered by a large sheet of plate glass with a roughened surface to which Sergeant Havers touched her fingertips tentatively, a question on her face.

"Grinding colours," Sarah Gordon told her. "That's what it's for. I used to grind my own colours."

"You're a purist then," Lynley said.

She smiled with much the same resignation as he had heard in her voice. "When I first began to paint—this was years ago—I wanted to own each part of the finished piece. I wanted to *be* each painting. I even milled the wood to make the stretcher bars for my canvases. That's how pure I was going to be."

"You lost that purity?"

"Success taints everything. In the long run."

"And you had success." Lynley went to the wall where her large charcoal sketches were hanging, one on top of the other. He began to browse through them. An arm, a hand, the line of jaw, a face. He was reminded of the Queen's collection of Da Vinci's studies. She was very talented.

"After a fashion. Yes. I had success. But that meant less to me than peace of mind. And ultimately peace of mind was what I was seeking yesterday morning."

"Finding Elena Weaver put an end to that," Sergeant Havers remarked.

As Lynley was looking through her sketches, Sarah had gone to stand near the covered easel. She had raised a hand to adjust its linen shroud—perhaps with the hope of keeping them from seeing how far the quality of her work had disintegrated—but she stopped and said without looking in their direction: "Elena Weaver?" Her voice sounded oddly uncertain.

"The dead girl," Lynley said. "Elena Weaver. Did you know her?"

She turned to them. Her lips worked without making any sound. After a moment, she whispered, "Oh no."

"Miss Gordon?"

"Her father. Anthony Weaver. I know her father." She felt for the tall stool at one side of the easel and sat upon it. She said, "Oh my God. My poor Tony." And as if answering a question which no one had spoken, she gestured round the room. "He was one of my students. Until early last spring when he began all the politicking for the Penford Chair, he was one of my students."

"Students?"

"I offered classes locally for a number of years. I don't any longer, but Tony . . . Dr. Weaver took most of them. He was a private student of mine as well. So I knew him. For a time we were close." Her eyes filled. She blinked the tears away quickly.

"And did you know his daughter?"

"After a fashion. I met her several times—early last Michaelmas term—when he brought her with him to act as a model for a life-drawing class.''

"But you didn't recognise her yesterday?''

"How could I? I didn't even see her face.'' She lowered her head, raised a hand quickly, and brushed it over her eyes. "This is going to destroy him. She was everything to him. Have you talked to him yet? Is he . . . ? But of course you've talked to him. What am I asking?'' She raised her head. "Is Tony all right?''

"No one takes well the death of a child.''

"But Elena was more than a child to him. He used to say that she was his hope of redemption.'' She looked round the room, her expression filling with self-contempt. "And here I've been—poor little Sarah—wondering if I can begin to draw again, wondering if I'll ever create another piece of art, wondering . . . while all the while Tony . . . How could I possibly be any more selfish?''

"You're not to blame for trying to get your career back on track.''

It was, he thought, the most rational of desires. He reflected on the work he had seen hanging in her sitting room. It was crisp and clean. One somehow expected that of a lithograph, but to achieve such purity of line and detail in oil seemed remarkable. Each image—a child playing with a dog, a weary chestnut seller warming himself over his metal-drum brazier, a bicyclist pumping along in the rain—spoke of assurance in every stroke of the brush. What would it be like, Lynley wondered, to believe one had lost the ability to produce work so palpably excellent? And how could a desire to recapture that ability ever be construed as an act of selfishness?

It seemed odd to him that she would even consider it so, and as she led them back to the front of the house, Lynley became aware of a vague disquiet in his evaluation of her, the same sort of disquiet he had felt when confronted with Anthony Weaver's reaction to his daughter's death. There was something about her, something in her manner and her words, that gave him pause. He couldn't put his finger on what it was about her that nagged at his subconscious, yet he knew intuitively that something was there, like a reaction that was too much planned in advance. A moment later, she gave him the answer.

As Sarah Gordon opened the front door for them, Flame leaped out of his basket, began to bark, and came tearing along the passage, intent upon a gambol in the outdoors. Sarah leaned forward, grabbed onto his collar. As she did so, the towel fell from her head, and damp curling hair the rich colour of coffee streamed round her shoulders.

Lynley stared at the image of her, caught in the doorway. It was the hair and the profile, but mostly the hair. She was the woman he had seen last night in Ivy Court.

Sarah headed for the lavatory the moment after she closed and locked the front door. With a gasp of urgency, she hurried through the sitting room, through the kitchen beyond it, and barely made it to the toilet. She vomited. Her stomach seemed to twist as previously sweet cocoa, hot and sour now, burned in her throat. It shot up towards her nose when she attempted to breathe. She coughed, gagged, and continued to vomit. Cold sweat broke out on her forehead. The floor seemed to dip, the walls to sway. She squeezed her eyes shut.

Behind her, she heard a soft whimper of sympathy. A nudge on her leg followed it. Then a head rested on one of her extended arms, and warm breath wafted against her cheek.

"It's all right, Flame," she said. "I'm all right. Don't worry. Have you brought Silk with you?"

Sarah chuckled weakly at the thought of the cat's developing a sudden change in personality. Cats were so like people. Compassion and empathy were not exactly in their line. But dogs were different.

Blindly, she reached for the mongrel and turned her face towards him. She heard his tail thump against the wall. He licked her nose. She was struck by the thought that it didn't matter to Flame who she was, what she'd done, what she'd managed to create, or whether she made a single lasting contribution to life at all. It didn't matter to Flame if she never put brush to canvas again. And there was comfort in that. She wanted to feel it. She tried to believe that there was nothing more in her life which she had to do.

The last spasm passed. Her stomach settled uneasily. She got to her feet and went to the basin where she rinsed her mouth, raised her head, and caught sight of her reflection in the mirror.

She raised a hand to her face, traced the lines on her forehead, the incipient creases from her nose to her mouth, the matrix of small, scarlike wrinkles just above her lower jaw. Only thirty-nine. She looked at least fifty. Worse, she felt sixty. She turned from the sight.

In the kitchen, she ran the water against her wrists until it felt cold. Then she drank from the tap, splashed her face again, and dried it on a yellow tea towel. She thought about brushing her teeth or trying to get some sleep, but it seemed like too much trouble to climb the stairs to her room and far too much trouble to smear toothpaste onto a brush and run it energetically round her mouth. Instead, she went back to the sitting room where the fire still burned and Silk still basked in uninterested contentment before it. Flame followed, returning to his basket from which he watched her throw more wood on the fire. Through his bushy fur, she could see that he'd scrunched up his face in what she always thought of as his worried expression, turning his eyes into shapes like roughly modified diamonds.

"I'm all right," she told him. "Really. It's true."

He didn't look convinced—after all, he knew the truth since he'd witnessed most of it and she'd told him the rest—but he made four revolutions in his basket, dug around in his blanket, and sank into its folds. His eyelids began to droop at once.

"Good," she said. "Have a bit of a kip." She was grateful that at least one of them could.

To distract herself from the idea of sleep and from everything that conspired to keep her from sleeping, she went to the window. It seemed that with every foot away from the fire, the temperature in the room dropped another ten degrees. And while she knew that this couldn't possibly be the case, her arms went round herself anyway. She looked outside.

The car was still there. Sleek, silver, it winked in the sun. For the second time, she wondered if they had really been the police. When she'd first opened the front door to them, she'd thought they'd come with a request to see her work. That hadn't happened in ages and never without an appointment, but it seemed the only reasonable explanation for the appearance of two strangers who'd arrived in a Bentley. They'd been mismatched as a couple: the man tall, handsome in a refined sort of way, astonishingly well-dressed, and possessing an unmistakably public school voice; the woman short, quite plain, looking more thrown together than Sarah herself was, with an accent that bore the distinct inflections of the working class. Still, even for a few minutes after they had identified themselves, Sarah continued to think of them as man and wife. It was easier to talk to them that way.

But no matter her story, they hadn't believed her. She could see it in their faces. And who could blame them? Why would anyone run across Coe Fen in the fog instead of dashing back the way she'd come? Why would someone who had just found a body tear by her own car and sprint to the police station instead of simply driving there? It didn't make sense. She knew that very well. And so did they.

Which went far to explain why the Bentley was still parked in front of her house. The police officers themselves were not in sight. They'd be questioning her neighbours, verifying her story.

Don't think of it, Sarah.

She forced herself away from the window and went back to the studio. On a table near the door, her answering machine stood, blinking to announce a message on the tape. She stared at it for a moment before she remembered having heard the phone ringing while she was talking to the police. She pressed the button to play.

"Sarah. Darling. I've got to see you. I know I have no right to ask. You've not forgiven me. I don't deserve forgiveness. I'll never deserve it. But I need to see you. I need to talk to you. You're the only one who knows me completely, who understands, who has the compassion and tenderness and . . . " He began to weep. "I was parked in front of your house most of Sunday evening. I could see you through the window. And I . . . Monday I came by but I didn't have the courage to come to the door. And now . . . Sarah. Please. Elena's been murdered. Please see me. Please. Phone me at the college. Leave a message. I'll do anything. Please see me. I beg you. I need you, Sarah."

Numbly, she listened as the unit switched itself off. Feel something, she told herself. But nothing stirred in her heart. She pressed the back of her hand to her mouth and bit on it, hard. And then a second time and a third and a fourth until she tasted the vague salinity of her blood rather than the chalk and lotion of her skin. She forced a memory forward. Something, anything. It didn't matter what. It merely had to suffice as a smokescreen to keep her mind occupied with thoughts she could bear to face.

Douglas Hampson, her foster brother, seventeen years old. Wanting him to notice her. Wanting him to talk to her. Wanting him. That musty shed at the bottom of his parents' garden in King's Lynn where even the smell from the sea couldn't supplant the odours of compost, mulch, and manure. But they hadn't cared, had they? She, desperate for an indication of someone's approval and affection. He, eager to do it because he was seventeen and randy and if he returned from one more school holiday without having had a good roger to talk about with his mates he'd never live it down.

They'd chosen a day when the sun beat down on the streets and the pavements and most especially on the old tin roof of that garden shed. He'd kissed her with his tongue and as she wondered if this was what people called making love—because she was only twelve and although she should have known at least something about what men and women actually did with those parts of their bodies that were so different from each other's, she didn't at all—he grappled first with her shorts, then with her knickers and all the time he breathed like a dog who's had a good run.

It was over quickly. He was hard and hot and she wasn't ready, so there was nothing in it for her but blood, suffocation, and searing pain. And Douglas stifling a groan when he came.

He stood up immediately afterwards, cleaning himself on her shorts and tossing them back to her. He zipped his jeans and said, "This place smells like a toilet. I've got to get out of here." And out he went.

He didn't answer her letters. He responded with silence when she phoned the school and wept out a tedious declaration of her love. Of course, she hadn't loved him at all. But she had to believe that she did. For nothing else excused that mindless invasion of her body which she had allowed without protest on that summer afternoon.

In her studio, Sarah moved away from the answering machine. For a smokescreen memory, she couldn't have chosen better than to conjure Douglas Hampson up out of the pit. He wanted her now. Forty-four years old, twenty years married, an insurance adjuster well on his way into mid-life crisis, he wanted her now.

Come on, Sarah, he would say when they met for lunch as they often did. I can't just sit here and look at you and pretend I don't want you. Come on. Let's do it.

We're friends, she'd respond. You're my brother, Doug.

Bugger the brother business. You didn't think about that once.

And she would smile at him fondly—because she was fond of him now—and not try to explain what that *once* had cost her.

It was not enough—the memory of Douglas. In spite of herself, she moved across the studio to the covered easel and gazed at the portrait she'd begun all those months ago to act as companion piece to the other. She'd intended it as a Christmas present for him. She hadn't yet known there would be no Christmas.

He was leaning forward as she so often had seen him, one elbow on his knee, his spectacles dangling from his fingers. His face was lit with the zeal which always came upon him when he talked about art. His head cocked to one side, himself caught in the act of arguing a fine point of composition, he looked boyish and happy, a man living fully for the first time in his life.

He wore no three-piece suit but a paint-splattered work shirt with half the collar turned up and a rip in the cuff. And as often as not when she stood close in front of him to study the way the light hit his hair, he'd reach out and pull her to him and laugh at her protest which wasn't much of a protest and hold her in his arms. His mouth on her neck and his hands on her breasts and the painting forgotten in the shedding of clothes. And the way he looked at her, beautifying her body, every moment of the act his eyes upon hers. And his voice that whisper *oh my god my dear love . . .*

Sarah steeled herself against the force of the memory and made herself evaluate the painting as a simple piece of art. She thought about finishing it, dwelling on the idea of a possible exhibition and of finding a way to put paint to canvas and making it mean something beyond a neophyte's obedient exercise in technique. She could do it, after all. She *was* a painter.

She reached towards the easel. Her hands were shaking. She drew them back, fists clenched into balls.

Even if she filled her mind with a dozen other thoughts, her body still betrayed her. At the end of everything, it would neither avoid nor deny.

She looked back at the answering machine, heard his voice and his plea.

But her hands still trembled. Her legs felt hollow.

And her mind had to accept what her body was telling her. There are things far worse than finding a dead body.

8

Lynley was just tucking into his shepherd's pie when Sergeant Havers came into the pub. The temperature had begun to fall outside and the wind to rise, and Havers had reacted to the weather accordingly, wrapping one of her scarves three times round her head and pulling up the other to cover her mouth and nose. She looked like a bandit from Iceland.

She paused in the doorway, eyes sweeping over the considerable—and boisterous—lunchtime crowd seated beneath the collection of antique scythes, hoes, and pitchforks which decorated the pub walls. She nodded in Lynley's direction when she saw him and went to the bar, where she divested herself of her outer garments, ordered her meal, and lit a cigarette. Tonic water in one hand and a bag of vinegar crisps in the other, she wove her way through the tables and joined him in the corner. Her cigarette dangled between her lips, growing ash.

She dumped her coat and scarves next to his on the bench and slumped into a chair facing him. She shot a look of irritation at the stereo speaker directly above them which was currently offering "Killing Me Softly" by Roberta Flack at a disturbing volume. Havers was no lover of musical trips down memory lane.

Over the din created by music, conversation, and clattering crockery, Lynley said, "It's better than Guns and Roses."

"Only just," Havers replied. Using her teeth for a start, she tore open her crisps and spent the next few moments munching, while her cigarette's smoke wafted into Lynley's face.

He looked at it meaningfully. "Sergeant . . ."

She scowled. "I wish you'd take it up again. We'd get on better if you did."

"And I thought we were marching blissfully arm-in-arm towards retirement."

"Marching, yes. I don't know about bliss." She moved the ashtray to one side. It began offering its smoke to a blue-haired woman with six noticeable hairs growing out of her chin. From the table she was sharing with a three-legged wheezing Corgi and a gentleman in only marginally better condition, she scathed Havers with a glare over the top of her gin and bitters. Havers muttered in defeat, took a final hit of the cigarette, and crushed it out.

"So?" Lynley said.

She picked a piece of tobacco off her tongue. "She checks out completely with two of her neighbours. The woman next door"—she grabbed her notebook from her shoulder bag and flipped it open—"'a Mrs. Stamford . . . Mrs. *Hugo* Stamford, she insisted, and spelled it out just in case I'd fluffed my O-levels. She saw her loading up the boot of her car sometime round seven yesterday morning. In a real hurry, Mrs. Stamford said. Preoccupied as well because when she went out for the morning milk, she called a hello but Sarah didn't hear her. Then"—she turned the notebook to read it sideways—"'a bloke called Norman Davies who lives across the road. He saw her fly by in her car round seven as well. He remembers because he was walking his collie and the dog was doing its business on the pavement instead of in the street. Our Norman was all in a flutter about that. He didn't want Sarah to think he'd just blithely allow Mr. Jeffries—that's the dog—to foul the footpath. He nattered on for a bit about her being in the car in the first place. Not good for her, he wanted me to know. She needs to get back to walking. She was always a walker. What's happened to the g'el? What's she doing in the car? He didn't much like your motor, by the way. Gave it a bit of a sneer and said whoever drove it is sending the country straight to Arab-dominated oil hell, never mind the North Sea. Quite a talker. I'm lucky I got away before teatime."

Lynley nodded but didn't reply. "What's up?" she asked him.

"Havers, I'm not sure."

He said nothing more as a teenaged girl dressed like one of Richard Crick's milkmaids delivered the sergeant's meal to the table. It was cod, peas, and chips which Havers doused thoroughly with vinegar while she eyed the waitress and said, "Shouldn't you be in school?"

"I'm old for my looks," the girl replied. She wore a large garnet stud through her right nostril.

Havers snorted. "Right." She dug into her fish. The girl disappeared with a flounce of her petticoats. Havers said in reference to his last comment, "I don't like the sound of that, Inspector. I've got the feeling you're keyed in to Sarah Gordon." She looked up from her food as if in the expectation of reply. When he said nothing, she went on with, "I expect it's because of that St. Cecilia business. Once you found out she's an artist, you decided that she arranged the body unconsciously."

"No. It's not that."

"Then what?"

"I'm sure I saw her last night at St. Stephen's College. And I can't account for it."

Havers lowered her fork. She sipped some tonic water and scraped a paper napkin across her mouth. "Now that's an interesting bit. Where was she?"

Lynley told her about the woman who had emerged from the shadows of the graveyard while he watched from his window. "I couldn't get a clear look at her," he admitted. "But the hair's the same. So's the profile. I'd swear to it."

"What would she have been doing there? You're nowhere near Elena Weaver's room, are you?"

"No. Ivy Court's used by the senior fellows. It's mostly studies where professors do their work and hold supervisions."

"So what would she—"

"My guess is that Anthony Weaver's rooms are there, Havers."

"And?"

"If that's the case—and I'll check it out after lunch I should imagine that she went to see him."

Havers forked up a generous portion of chips and peas, chewed on them thoughtfully before replying. "Are we doing some serious quantum leaping here, Inspector? Going from A to Z with twenty-four letters unaccounted for?"

"Who else would she have gone to see?"

"How about practically anyone in the college? Better yet, how about the possibility that it wasn't Sarah Gordon? Just someone with dark hair. It could have been Lennart Thorsson if he didn't get in the light. The colour's not right but he's got hair enough for two women."

"But this was clearly someone who didn't want to be seen. Even if it was Thorsson, why would he have been hiding?"

"Why would she, for that matter?" Havers returned to her fish. She took a bite, chewed, and pointed her fork in his direction. "Okay, I'm easy. Let's play it your way. Let's say Anthony Weaver's study is there. Let's say Sarah Gordon went to see him. She said he'd been her student, so we know she knew him. She was calling him Tony, so let's say she knew him well. She admitted as much. What have we got, then? Sarah Gordon going to offer her former student—a friend—some words of comfort upon the death of his daughter." She lowered her fork, rested it on the edge of her plate, and offered the counterpoint to her own argument. "Except that she didn't know his daughter was dead. She didn't know the body she'd found was Elena Weaver's until we told her this morning."

"And even if she did know who it was and lied to us about it for some reason, if she wanted to offer Weaver condolences, why didn't she go to his house?"

Havers speared up a soaking chip. "All right. Let's change the story. Perhaps Sarah Gordon and Anthony—*Tony*—Weaver have been boffing each other on an on-going basis. You know the sort of thing. Mutual passion for art leading to mutual passion for each other. Monday night was one of their previously arranged assignations. There's your reason for her stealth. She didn't know it was Elena Weaver she'd found, and she was showing up for a bit of the regular go. All things considered, Weaver wouldn't have had the presence of mind to phone her up and cancel their session, so she got to his rooms—if they *are* his rooms— only to find he wasn't there."

"If they had an assignation, wouldn't she have waited for at least a few minutes? More importantly, wouldn't she have a key to his rooms to let herself in?"

"How do you know she doesn't have a key?"

"Because she was in and out in less than five minutes, Sergeant. I'd say two minutes at the very most. Does that suggest unlocking a door and having a bit of a wait for your lover? And why on earth would they meet in his rooms in the first place? On his own admission, he has a graduate student working there. Beyond that, he's been short-listed for a prestigious chair in history which I don't imagine he'd care to jeopardise by having at a woman who's not his wife right there in the college. Selection committees tend to be peculiar about that sort of thing. If a love affair's at the heart of this, why wouldn't Weaver just go to see her in Grantchester?"

"What are we saying here, Inspector?"

Lynley pushed his plate to one side. "How often does it happen that the finder of the body turns out to be the killer just trying to cover his tracks?''

"About as often as the killer turns out to be a member of the immediate family." Havers forked up more fish, piled two chips on top of it. She regarded him shrewdly. "Perhaps you might tell me exactly where you're heading. Because her neighbours have just got through clearing her no matter what you say, and I'm getting that Westerbrae feeling of discomfort with where you're leading us. If you know what I mean."

He did. Havers had ample reason to question his ability to remain objective. He sought to justify his leery feelings about the artist. "Sarah Gordon finds the body. She appears at Weaver's rooms that night. I don't like the coincidence."

"What coincidence? Why does it even have to be coincidence? She didn't recognise the body. She went to see Weaver for other reasons. Maybe she wanted to woo him back to art. That's a big deal to her. Maybe she wanted it to be a big deal to him."

"But she was trying not to be seen."

"According to your appraisal, Inspector. On a foggy night when she might only have been trying to stay warm." Havers crumpled up her crisp bag and rolled it in her palm. She looked concerned and, at the same time, intent upon not showing the extent of that concern. "I think you've made a hasty decision here," she said carefully. "I'm wondering why. You know, I had a fair good look at Sarah Gordon myself today. She's dark, she's thin, she's attractive. She reminded me of someone. I wonder if she reminded you of someone as well."

"Havers—"

"Inspector, listen to me. Look at the facts. We know Elena started running at a quarter past six. Her stepmother told you that. The porter confirmed it. From her own report—now verified by her neighbours— Sarah left her own house just round seven. And the police report has her popping into the station to report finding the body at twenty past. So please take a look at what you're suggesting, all right? First, that for some reason, although she left St. Stephen's at a quarter past six, it took Elena Weaver forty-five minutes to run from her college to Fen Causeway—what is it, less than a mile? Second, that when she got there, for reasons unknown, Sarah Gordon beat her in the face with something which she managed to get rid of, then strangled her, then covered her body with leaves, then got sick, and then dashed to the police station to divert suspicion. All in just over fifteen minutes. And we haven't even addressed the question of *why*. Why would she kill her? What on earth was her motive? You're always lecturing me on motive, means, and opportunity, Inspector. So tell me how Sarah Gordon fits in.''

Lynley couldn't do so. Nor could he argue that any part of what they knew had occurred was a wildly improbable coincidence illustrating undeniable culpability. For everything Sarah Gordon told them about her reasons for going to the island in the first place had the ring of veracity. And that she was committed to her art seemed easily understandable when one considered the quality of her work. This being the case, he forced himself to evaluate Sergeant Havers' pointed questions.

He wanted to argue that Sarah Gordon's resemblance to Helen Clyde was purely superficial, a combination of dark hair, dark eyes, fair skin, a slender frame. But he couldn't lie about the fact that he was drawn to her because of other similarities—a straightforward manner of speaking, a willingness to examine the self, a commitment to personal growth, the ability to be alone. And yet beneath it all, something frightened and vulnerable. He didn't want to believe that his difficulties with Helen would once again result in a form of professional myopia in which he forged obdurately ahead, not to pin guilt upon a man with whom Helen was sleeping this time, but to concentrate on a suspect to whom he was drawn for reasons having nothing to do with the case, all the time ignoring signposts leading him elsewhere. Yet he had to admit that Sergeant Havers' points about the time frame in which the crime was carried out obviated Sarah Gordon's guilt immediately.

He sighed, rubbing his eyes. He wondered if he had actually seen her at all the previous night. He had been thinking of Helen only moments before he walked to the window. Why not transport her through the means of imagination from Bulstrode Gardens to Ivy Court?

Havers rustled through her shoulder bag to bring out a packet of Players which she flipped onto the table between them. Instead of lighting up, however, she looked at him.

''Thorsson's the stronger candidate,'' she said. And when he started to speak, she cut him off with, ''Hear me out, sir. You're saying his motive's too obvious. Fine. So apply a variation of that objection to Sarah Gordon. Her admitted presence at the crime scene is too obvious. But if we're going to go with one of them—if only for the moment—my money's on the man. He wanted her, she refused him, she turned him in. So why's your money on the woman?''

"It isn't. Not entirely. It's just her coincidental connection to Weaver that makes me uneasy."

"Fine. Be uneasy. Meanwhile, I vote we pursue Thorsson until we've a reason not to. I say we check out *his* neighbours to see if anyone saw him skipping out in the morning. Or returning for that matter. We see if the autopsy gives us anything else. We see what that address on Seymour Street is all about."

It was solid policework, Havers' expertise. He said, "Agreed."

"That easily? Why?"

"You handle that half of it."

"And you?"

"I'll see if the rooms at St. Stephen's are Weaver's."

"Inspector—"

He took a cigarette from the pack, handed it to her, and struck a match. "It's called compromise, Sergeant. Have a smoke," he said.

When Lynley pushed open the wrought iron gate at the south entrance to Ivy Court, he saw that a wedding party was posing for photographs in the old graveyard of St. Stephen's Church. It was a curious group, with the bride done up in whiteface and wearing what appeared to be part of a privet hedge on her head, her chief attendant swathed in a blood-red burnoose, and the best man looking like a chimney sweep. Only the groom wore conventional morning dress. But he was alleviating any concern this might have caused by drinking champagne from a riding boot which he'd apparently removed from the foot of one of the guests. The wind whipped everyone's clothing about, but the play of colours— white, red, black, and grey—against the slick lichenous green of the old slate gravestones had its own distinct charm.

This the photographer himself seemed to see, for he kept calling out, "Hold it, Nick. Hold it, Flora. Right. Yes. Perfect," as he snapped away with his camera.

Flora, Lynley thought with a smile. No wonder she was wearing a bush on her head.

He dodged past a heap of fallen bicycles and walked across the court to the doorway through which he had seen the woman disappear on the previous night. Nearly hidden by a tangle of goldheart ivy, a sign, still fresh with having been recently hand-lettered, hung on the wall beneath an overhead light. It contained three names. Lynley felt that quick, brief rush of triumph which comes with having one's intuition affirmed by fact. Anthony Weaver's was the first name listed.

Only one of the other two he recognised. *A. Jenn* would be Weaver's graduate student.

It was Adam Jenn, in fact, whom Lynley found in Weaver's study when he climbed the stairs to the first floor. The door stood ajar, revealing an unlit triangular entry off of which opened a narrow gyp room, a larger bedroom, and the study itself. Lynley heard voices coming from within the study—low questions from a man, soft responses from a woman—so he took the opportunity to have a quick look at the two other rooms.

To his immediate right, the gyp room was well-equipped with a stove, a refrigerator, and a wall of glass-fronted cupboards in which sat enough cooking utensils and crockery to set up housekeeping. Aside from the refrigerator and the stove, everything in the room appeared to be new, from the gleaming microwave to the cups, saucers, and plates. The walls were recently painted, and the air smelled fresh, like baby powder, a scent which he tracked to its source: a solid rectangle of room deodoriser hanging on a hook behind the door.

He was intrigued by the perfection of the gyp, so at odds with what he envisaged Anthony Weaver's professional environment would be, considering the state of his study at home. Curious to see if some stamp of the man's individuality evidenced itself elsewhere, he flipped on the light-switch of the bedroom across the entry and stood in the doorway surveying it.

Above wainscoting painted the colour of forest mushrooms rose walls which were papered in cream with thin brown stripes. Framed pencil sketches hung from these—a pheasant shoot, a fox hunt, a deer chased by hounds, all signed with the single name *Weaver*—while from the white ceiling a pentagonal brass fixture shed light on a single bed next to which stood a tripod table holding a brass reading lamp and a matching diptych frame. Lynley crossed the room and picked this up. Elena Weaver smiled from one side, Justine from the other, the first a candid snapshot of the daughter joyfully romping with an Irish setter puppy, the second an earnest studio portrait of the wife, her long hair carefully curled back from her face and her smile close-lipped as if she wished to hide her teeth. Lynley replaced it and looked around reflectively. The hand that had outfitted the kitchen with its chromium appliances and ivory china had apparently seen to the decoration of the bedroom as well. On impulse, he pulled back part of the brown and green counterpane on the bed to find only a bare mattress and unslipped pillow beneath it. The revelation was not the least surprising. He left the room.

As he did so, the study door swung open and he found himself face-to-face with the two young people whose murmured conversation he had heard a few moments earlier. The young man, his broad shoulders emphasised by an academic gown, reached out for the girl when he caught sight of Lynley, and he pulled her back against him protectively.

"Help you with something?" His words were polite enough but the frigid tone conveyed an entirely different message, as did the young man's features which quickly altered from the relaxed repose that accompanies friendly conversation to the sharpness that signals suspicion.

Lynley glanced at the girl who was clutching a notebook to her chest. She wore a knitted cap from which bright blonde hair spilled. It was drawn low on her forehead, hiding her eyebrows but heightening the colour of her eyes which were violet and, at the moment, very frightened.

Their responses were normal, admirable in the circumstances. An undergraduate in the college had been brutally murdered. Strangers would be neither welcomed nor tolerated. He produced his warrant card and introduced himself.

"Adam Jenn?" he said.

The young man nodded. He said to the girl, "I'll see you next week, Joyce. But you've got to get on with the reading before you do the next essay. You've got the list. You've got a brain. Don't be so lazy, okay?" He smiled as if to mitigate the negativity of the final comment, but the smile seemed rote, merely a quick curving of the lips that did nothing to alter the wariness in his hazel eyes.

Joyce said, "Thank you, Adam," in that breathy sort of voice which always manages to sound as if it's extending an illicit invitation. She smiled her goodbye and a moment later they heard her clattering noisily down the wooden stairs. It wasn't until the ground-floor staircase door opened and shut upon her departure that Adam Jenn invited Lynley into Weaver's study.

"Dr. Weaver's not here," he said. "If you're wanting him, that is."

Lynley didn't respond at once. Rather, he strolled to one of the windows which, like the sole window in his own room in the building, was set into one of the ornate Dutch gables overlooking Ivy Court. Unlike his room, however, no desk stood in the recess. Instead, two comfortably battered armchairs faced each other at an angle there, separated by a chipped piecrust table on which lay a copy of a book entitled *Edward III: The Cult of Chivalry*. Anthony Weaver was its author.

"He's brilliant." Adam Jenn's assertion had the distinct ring of defence. "No one in the country comes close to touching him in medieval history."

Lynley put on his spectacles, opened the volume, and leafed through a few of the densely worded pages. Arbitrarily, his eyes fell on the words *but it was in the abysmal treatment of women as chattels subjugated to the political whims of their fathers and brothers that the age developed its reputation for a diplomatic manoeuvring far superseding any transitory—or spurious—demotic concerns it may have actively promulgated.* Having not read university writing in years, Lynley smiled in amusement. He'd forgotten that tendency of the academician to voice his pronouncements with such egregious pomposity.

He read the book's dedication, *For my darling Elena,* and tapped the cover closed. He removed his spectacles.

"You're Dr. Weaver's graduate student," he said.

"Yes." Adam Jenn shifted his weight from one foot to the other. Beneath his black academic gown, he wore a white shirt and freshly laundered jeans that had been carefully pressed with creases down the front. He drove his fists into the rear pockets of these and waited without speaking, standing next to an oval table across which were spread three open texts and half a dozen handwritten essays.

"How do you come to be studying under Dr. Weaver?" Lynley removed his overcoat and placed it over the back of one of the old armchairs.

"Decent luck for once in my life," Adam said.

It was a curious non-answer. Lynley raised an eyebrow. Adam read this as Lynley intended and continued.

"I'd read two of his books as an undergraduate. I'd heard him lecture. When he was short-listed for the Penford Chair at the beginning of Easter term last year, I came to ask him if he'd direct my research. To have the Penford Chair as advisor . . ." He gazed round the room as if its jumble of contents would provide him with an adequate explanation of the importance of Weaver's place in his life. He settled with, "You can't go higher."

"Then this is all a bit of a risk on your end, isn't it, hooking yourself up with Dr. Weaver so soon? What if he doesn't get the appointment?"

"It's worth the risk as far as I'm concerned. Once he gets the Chair, he'll be flooded with requests to direct graduates' studies. So I got to him first."

"You seem relatively sure of your man. I'd always gathered these appointments are largely political. A change in the academic climate and a candidate's finished.''

"That's true enough. Candidates walk a tightrope. Alienate the search committee, offend some muckety-muck, and they're done for. But committee'd be fools not to award it to him. As I said, he's the best medievalist in the country and they're not going to find anyone to argue with that.''

"I take it he's unlikely to alienate or offend?''

Adam Jenn laughed boyishly. *"Dr. Weaver?"* was his reply.

"I see. When should the announcement take place?''

"That's the odd thing.'' Adam shook a heavy lock of sandy hair off his forehead. "It should have been announced last July, but the committee went on and on about extending the deadline, and they started checking everyone out like they were looking for red skeletons in somebody's closet. Stupid, they are.''

"Perhaps merely cautious. I've been given to understand that the Chair's a fairly coveted advancement.''

"It *represents* historical research at Cambridge. It's the place they put the best.'' Two thin lines of crimson ran along Adam's cheekbone. No doubt he pictured himself in the Chair in the distant future when Weaver retired.

Lynley moved to the table, glancing down at the essays that were spread across it. "You share these rooms with Dr. Weaver, I've been told.''

"I put in a few hours most days, yes. I run my supervisions here as well.''

"And that's been going on for how long?''

"Since the beginning of term.''

Lynley nodded. "It's an attractive environment, far nicer than what I remember from my days at university.''

Adam looked round the study at the general mess of essays, books, furniture, and equipment. Obviously, *attractive* wouldn't have been the first word to spring to his lips had he been asked to evaluate the room. Then he seemed to combine Lynley's comment with his initial sight of him a few moments earlier. His head turned towards the door. "Oh, you mean the gyp and the bedroom. Dr. Weaver's wife fixed them up for him last spring.''

"In anticipation of the Chair? An elevated professor needs a proper set of rooms?''

Adam grinned ruefully. "That sort of thing. But she didn't manage to get her way in here. Dr. Weaver wouldn't let her.'' He added this last as if to explain the difference between the study and its companion rooms and concluded with a mildly sardonic, "You know how it is," in a brotherhood-of-men fashion in which the connotation was clear: Women need to have their fancies tolerated, men are the ones with the sainted toleration.

That Justine Weaver's hand had not seen to the study was apparent to Lynley. And while it did not actually resemble the disordered sanctum at the rear of Weaver's house, the similarities to it could not be ignored. Here was the same mild chaos, the same profusion of books, the same air of habitation which the Adams Road room possessed.

One form of academic work or another seemed to be in progress everywhere. A large pine desk served as the heart for labour, holding everything from a word processor to a stack of black binders. The oval table in the room's centre had the function of conference area, and the gable recess acted as a retreat for reading and study, for in addition to the table which displayed Weaver's own book, a small case beneath the window, within an arm's length of both the chairs, held additional volumes. Even the fireplace with its cinnamon tiles served a purpose beyond providing heat from an electric fire, for its mantel functioned as a clearing house for the post, and more than a dozen envelopes lined up across it, all bearing Anthony Weaver's name. A solitary greeting card stood like a bookend at the far side of the serried collection of letters, and Lynley picked it up, a humorous birthday card with the word *Daddy* written above the greeting and the round-lettered signature *Elena* beneath it.

Lynley replaced it among the envelopes and turned to Adam Jenn, who still stood by the table, one hand in his pocket and the other curved round the shoulder rail of one of the chairs. "Did you know her?"

Adam pulled out the chair. Lynley joined him at the table, moving aside two essays and a cup of cold tea in which a thin, unappetising film was floating.

Adam's face was grave. "I knew her."

"Were you here in the study when she phoned her father Sunday night?"

His eyes went to the Ceephone which sat on a small oak desk next to the fireplace. "She didn't phone here. Or if she did, it was after I left."

"What time was this?"

"Round half past seven?" He looked at his watch as if for verification. "I had to meet three blokes at the University Centre at eight, and I stopped by my digs first."

"Your digs?"

"Near Little St. Mary's. So it must have been somewhere round half past seven. It might have been a bit later. Perhaps a quarter to eight."

"Was Dr. Weaver still here when you left?"

"Dr. Weaver? He wasn't here at all Sunday evening. He'd been in for a while in the early afternoon, but then he went home for dinner and didn't come back."

"I see."

Lynley reflected on this piece of information, wondering why Weaver had lied about his whereabouts on the night before his daughter's death. Adam appeared to realise that for some reason this detail was important in the investigation, for he went on earnestly.

"He could have come in later, though. It's out of line for me to claim that he didn't come back in the evening. Actually, I might have missed him. He's been working on a paper for about two months now— the role of monasteries in medieval economics—and he might have wanted to go over a bit of the research again. Most of the documents are in Latin. They're hard to read. It takes forever to sort everything out. I imagine that's what he was doing here Sunday evening. He does that all the time. He's always concerned about getting the details right. He'd want to have them perfect. So if something was on his mind, he probably came back on the spur of the moment. I wouldn't have known and he wouldn't have told me."

Outside of Shakespeare, Lynley couldn't recall having heard anyone protest quite so much. "Then he usually didn't tell you if he'd be coming back?"

"Well, now let me think." The young man drew his eyebrows together, but Lynley saw the answer in the manner in which he pressed his hands nervously against his thighs.

He said, "You think a great deal of Dr. Weaver, don't you?" *Enough to protect him blindly* remained unspoken, but there was no doubt that Adam Jenn recognised the implied accusation behind Lynley's question.

"He's a great man. He's honest. He has more natural integrity than any half a dozen other senior fellows at St. Stephen's College or anywhere else." Adam pointed at the envelopes lining the mantelpiece. "All of those have come in since yesterday afternoon when the word went out about what happened to . . . what happened. People love him. People care. You can't be a bastard and have people care about you so much."

"Did Elena care for her father?"

Adam's gaze flicked to the birthday card. "She did. Everyone does. He involves himself with people. He's always here when someone has a problem. People can talk to Dr. Weaver. He's straight with them. Sincere."

"And Elena?"

"He worried about her. He took time with her. He encouraged her. He went over her essays and helped her with her studies and talked to her about what she was going to do with her life."

"It was important to him that she be a success."

"I can see what you're thinking," Adam said. "A successful daughter implies a successful father. But he's not like that. He didn't just take time with *her*. He took time with everyone. He helped me get my housing. He lined up my undergraduate supervisions. I've applied for a research fellowship and he's helping me with that. And when I've a question with my work, he's always here, ready. I've never got the feeling that I'm taking up his time. D'you know how valuable a quality that is in a person? The streets round here aren't exactly paved with it."

It wasn't the panegyric to Weaver which Lynley found interesting. That Adam Jenn should so admire the man who was directing his graduate studies was reasonable. But what underlay Adam Jenn's avowals was something far more telling: He'd managed to deflect every question about Elena. He'd even managed to avoid using her name.

Outside, faint laughter from the wedding party floated up from the graveyard. Someone shouted, "Give us a kiss!" and someone else, "Don't you wish!" and the splintering sound of breaking glass suggested a champagne bottle's abrupt demise.

Lynley said, "Obviously, you're quite close to Dr. Weaver."

"I am."

"Like a son."

Adam's face took on more colour. But he looked pleased.

"Like a brother to Elena."

Adam ran his thumb rapidly back and forth along the edge of the table. He reached up and rubbed his fingers along his jaw.

Lynley said, "Or perhaps not really like a brother. She was an attractive girl, after all. You would have seen a great deal of each other. Here in the study. At the Weavers' house as well. And no doubt in the combination room from time to time. Or at formal dinner. And in her own room."

Adam said, "I never went inside. Just to get her. That's all."

"I understand you took her out."

"To foreign films at the Arts. We went to dinner occasionally. We spent a day in the country."

"I see."

"It's not what you're thinking. I didn't do it because I wanted . . . I mean I couldn't have . . . Oh *hell*."

"Did Dr. Weaver ask you to take Elena out?"

"If you have to know. Yes. He thought we were suited."

"And were you?"

"No!" The vehemence driving the word seemed to cause it to reverberate in the room for an instant. As if with the need to disguise the strength of his reply in some way, Adam said, "Look, I was like a hired escort to her. There was nothing more to it than that."

"Did Elena want a hired escort?"

Adam gathered up the essays that lay on the table. "I've too much work here. The supervisions, my own studies. I've no time in my life for women at the moment. They add complications when one least expects it, and I can't afford the distraction. I've hours of research every day. I've essays to read. I've meetings to attend."

"All of which must have been difficult to explain to Dr. Weaver."

Adam sighed. He crossed his ankle on his knee and picked at the lace of his gym shoe. "He invited me to his house the second weekend of term. He wanted me to meet her. What could I say? He'd taken me on as a graduate. He'd been so willing to help me. How could I not give him help in return?"

"In what way were you helping him?"

"There was this bloke he preferred she didn't see. I was supposed to run interference between them. A bloke from Queens'."

"Gareth Randolph."

"That's him. She'd met him through the deaf students' union last year. Dr. Weaver wasn't comfortable with them going about together. I imagine he hoped she might . . . you know."

"Learn to prefer you?"

He dropped his leg to the floor. "She didn't really fancy this bloke Gareth anyway. She told me as much. I mean, they were mates and she liked him, but it was no big deal. All the same, she knew what her father was worrying about."

"What was that?"

"That she'd end up with . . . I mean marry . . ."

"Someone deaf," Lynley finished. "Which, after all, wouldn't be that unusual a circumstance since she was deaf herself."

Adam pushed himself off his chair. He walked to the window and stared into the courtyard. "It's complicated," he said quietly to the glass.

"I don't know how to explain him to you. And even if I could, it wouldn't make any difference. Whatever I'd say would just make him look bad. And it wouldn't have anything to do with what happened to her."

"Even if it did, Dr. Weaver can't afford to look bad, can he? Not with the Penford Chair hanging in the balance."

"That's not it!"

"Then it really can't hurt anyone if you talk to me."

Adam gave a rough laugh. "That's easy to say. You just want to find a killer and get back to London. It doesn't make any difference to you whose lives get destroyed in the process."

The police as Eumenides. It was an accusation he'd heard before. And while he acknowledged its partial accuracy—for there had to be a disinterested hand of justice or society crumbled—the convenience of the allegation afforded him a moment's sour amusement. Pushed right to the edge of truth's abyss, people always clung tenaciously to the same form of denial: I'm protecting someone else by withholding the truth, protecting someone from harm, from pain, from reality, from suspicion. It was all a variation of an identical theme in which denial wore the guise of self-righteous nobility.

He said, "This isn't a singular death taking place in a void, Adam. It touches everyone she knew. No one stays protected. Lives have already been destroyed. That's what murder does. And if you don't know that, it's time you learned."

The young man swallowed. Even across the room, Lynley could hear him do so.

"She took it all as a joke," he said finally. "She took everything as a joke."

"In this case, what?"

"That her father was worried she'd marry Gareth Randolph. That he didn't want her to hang round the other deaf students so much. But most of all, that he . . . I think it was that he loved her so much and that he wanted her to love him as much in return. She took it as a joke. That's the way she was."

"What was their relationship like?" Lynley asked, even though he knew how unlikely it was that Adam Jenn would say anything to betray his mentor.

Adam looked down at his fingernails and began to worry the cuticles by pushing his thumb against them. "He couldn't do enough for her. He wanted to be involved in her life. But it always seemed—" He shoved his hands back into his pockets. "I don't know how to explain."

Lynley recalled Weaver's description of his daughter. He recalled Justine Weaver's reaction to the description. "Not genuine?"

"It was like he felt he had to keep pouring on the love and devotion. Like he had to keep showing her how much she meant to him so that maybe she'd come to believe it someday."

"He would have wanted to take special pains with her because she couldn't hear, I should think. She was in a new environment. He'd have wanted her to succeed. For herself. For him."

"I know what you're getting at. You're heading back towards the Chair. But it's more than that. It went beyond her studies. It went beyond her being deaf. I think he believed he had to prove himself to her for some reason. But he was so intent on doing that that he never even saw her. Not really. Not entirely."

The description moulded perfectly to Weaver's agonising on the previous night. It was so often the circumstance that grew from divorce. A parent partnered in an unremittingly bleak marriage feels caught between the needs of a child and the needs of self. If he stays in the marriage solely to meet the needs of the child, he reaps the benefits of society's approval, but his self erodes. Yet if he leaves the marriage solely to meet the needs of self, the child is damaged. What is required is a masterful balancing act between these disparate needs, a balancing act in which a marriage can end, former partners can establish more productive lives, and the children can escape without irreparable harm in the process.

It was, Lynley thought, the Utopian ideal, utterly improbable because feelings were involved whenever a marriage came to an end. Even when people were acting in the only manner possible to preserve their peace of mind, it was in the very *need* for peace of mind that guilt lay its most virulent seeds. Most people—and he admitted he was one of them—invariably gave power to social condemnation, allowing their behaviour to be guided by guilt, living their lives dominated by a Judaeo-Christian tradition which taught them that they had no right to happiness or to anything else save a life in which considerations of self were secondary to complete devotion to others. The fact that men and women did indeed lead lives of quiet desperation as a result generally went ignored. For as long as they led their lives for others, they achieved the approval of everyone else who—in equally quiet desperation—was engaged in doing the very same thing.

The situation was worse for Anthony Weaver. To achieve peace of mind—which society told him was not his due in the first place—he had ended a marriage only to find that the guilt attendant to divorce was exacerbated by the fact that, in escaping unhappiness, he had not merely left behind a small child who loved and depended upon him. He had left behind a handicapped child as well. And what kind of society would ever forgive him that? He stood to lose no matter what he'd done. Had he stayed in his marriage and devoted his life to his daughter, he could have felt self-righteous and nobly miserable. In opting at a try for peace of mind, he had reaped the harvest of guilt whose seeds were planted within what he—and society—considered a base and selfish need.

Upon close examination, guilt was the prime mover behind so many kinds of devotion. Lynley wondered if it underlay Weaver's devotion to his daughter. In his own mind, Weaver had sinned. Against his wife, Elena, and society itself. Fifteen years of guilt had grown out of his sin. Proving himself to Elena, smoothing the way for her, capturing her love, had apparently been the only expiation he saw for himself. Lynley felt a profound pity at the thought of the other man's struggle to gain acceptance as what he already was: his daughter's father. He wondered if Weaver had ever garnered the courage and taken the time to ask Elena if such extremes of behaviour and such torment of spirit were actually necessary to obtain her forgiveness.

"I don't think he ever really knew her," Adam said.

Lynley wondered if Weaver really knew himself. He got to his feet. "What time did you leave here last night after Dr. Weaver phoned you?"

"A bit after nine."

"You locked the door?"

"Of course."

"The same on Sunday night? Do you always lock it?"

"Yes." Adam nodded his head towards the pine desk and its collection of equipment—word processor, two printers, floppy disks, and files. "That lot's worth a fortune. The study door's double bolted."

"And the other doors?"

"The gyp and bedroom don't have locks, but the main entry door does."

"Did you ever use the Ceephone in here to contact Elena in her room? Or at Dr. Weaver's home?"

"Occasionally, yes."

"Did you know Elena ran in the morning?"

"With Mrs. Weaver." Adam pulled a face. "Dr. Weaver wouldn't let her run alone. She didn't care for having Mrs. Weaver tag along, but the dog went as well, so it made the situation bearable. She loved the dog. And she loved to run."

"Yes," Lynley said thoughtfully. "Most people do."

He nodded his goodbye and left the room. Two girls were sitting on the staircase outside the door, their knees drawn up, their heads together over an open textbook. They didn't look up as he passed them, but their conversation ceased abruptly, only to resume once he reached the lower landing. He heard Adam Jenn's voice call, "Katherine, Keelie, I'm ready for you now," and went out into the chill autumn afternoon.

He looked across Ivy Court at the graveyard, thinking about his meeting with Adam Jenn, wondering what it must have been like to be caught between the father and the daughter, wondering most of all what that violent *No!* had meant when he asked the young man if he and Elena had been suited to each other. And still he knew nothing more about Sarah Gordon's visit to Ivy Court than he had known before.

He glanced at his pocket watch. It was just after two. Havers would be a while with the Cambridge police. He had sufficient time to make the run to Crusoe's Island. If nothing else, that would give him at least a modicum of information. He went to change his clothes.

9

Anthony Weaver stared at the discreet nameplate on the desk—
P. L. Beck, Funeral Director—and felt overcome by a surge
of simple-minded gratitude. This main business office of the
mortuary was as unfuneral as good taste would allow it to be, and while
its warm autumn colours and comfortable furniture did not alter the reality
which had brought him here, at least it did not underscore the finality of
his daughter's death with sombre decorations, canned organ music, and
lugubrious employees dressed in black.

Next to him, Glyn sat with her hands balled into her lap, both feet
flat on the floor, her head and shoulders rigid. She did not look at him.

Upon her continued insistence throughout the morning, he'd taken
her to the police station where, in spite of what he had tried to tell her,
she had fully expected to find Elena's body and be able to see it. When
told that the body had been taken to autopsy, she had demanded to be
allowed to observe the procedure. And when with a horrified look of
supplication in Anthony's direction, the female police constable working
reception had gently said with apologies that it simply wasn't possible,
that it couldn't be allowed, that at any rate the autopsy was performed in
another location, not here at the station, and even if that weren't the case,
family members—

"I'm her mother!" Glyn cried. "She's mine! I want to see her!"

The Cambridge police were not an unsympathetic lot. They took her
quickly to a conference room where a concerned young secretary tried to
ply her with mineral water which Glyn refused. A second secretary brought

in a cup of tea. A traffic warden offered aspirin. And while anxious calls were put out for the police psychologist and the public relations officer, Glyn continued to insist that she see Elena. Her voice was tight and shrill. Her features were taut. When she didn't get what she wanted, she began to shout.

Witness to all of this, Anthony felt only his own growing shame. It was directed at her for causing a humiliating public scene. It was directed at himself for being ashamed of her. So when she finally turned on him and flew in his direction and accused him of being too self-centred to be capable of identifying his own daughter's body so how did they even know it was Elena Weaver whose body they had if they didn't let her mother make the identification, her mother who gave her birth, her mother who loved her, her mother who raised her alone, do you hear me *alone* you bastards he had nothing to do with anything after she was five years old because he had what he wanted he had his precious freedom all right so let me see her LET ME SEE HER . . .

I am wood, he had thought. Nothing she says can touch me. Although this stoic determination to remain inviolate sufficed to keep him from striking out in turn, it was not enough to prevent his unrestrained mind from shooting back through time, sifting through memories in an attempt to recall—let alone understand—what forces had ever brought him together with this woman in the first place.

It should have been something more than sex: a mutual interest, perhaps, a shared experience, a similarity of background, a goal, an ideal. Had any of those been present between them, they might have stood a fighting chance of survival. But instead it had been a drinks party in an elegant house off the Trumpington Road where some thirty postgraduates who had worked for his election had been invited to the victory celebration of the new local MP. At loose ends for the evening, Anthony had gone with a friend. Glyn Westhompson had done the same. Their shared indifference towards the esoteric machinations of Cambridge politics supplied the initial illusion of mutuality. Far too much champagne provided the physical allure. When he'd suggested that they take their own bottle out onto the terrace to watch the moonlight silver the trees in the garden, his intention had been a bit of casual kissing, a chance to fondle the ample breasts which he could see through the sheer material of her blouse, and an opportunity in privacy to slip his hand between her thighs.

But the terrace was dark, the night was quite warm, and Glyn's reaction was not what he'd thought it might be. Her response to his kiss took him by surprise. Her eager mouth hungrily sucked his tongue. One hand unbuttoned her blouse and unhooked her bra while the other insinuated itself into his trousers. She moaned her arousal. She straddled his leg and rotated her hips.

He had no conscious thoughts. He had only the need to be inside her, to feel the warmth and the soft wet suction of her body, to feel his own release.

They didn't speak. They used the terrace's stone balustrade as a fulcrum. He lifted her to it, she spread her legs. He plunged and plunged, panting with the effort to bring himself to climax before anyone should walk out onto the terrace and catch them in the act, while she bit his neck and gasped and tore at his hair. It was the only time in his life that he actually thought of the word *fucking* when he took a woman. And when it was over, he couldn't remember her name.

Five—perhaps seven—graduate students came out of the house before he and Glyn had separated. Someone said "Whoops!" and someone else "I'll have a bit of that myself," and all of them chuckled and went on into the garden. More than anything else, it was the thought of their derision that made him put his arms round Glyn, kiss her, and murmur huskily, "Let's get out of here, all right?" Because somehow leaving with her elevated the act, making them more than two sweating bodies intent upon mating, without intellect or soul.

She'd gone with him to the cramped house on Hope Street which he shared with three friends. She spent the night, and then another, rolling around with him on the thin mattress that served as his bed, eating a quick meal when the mood was upon her, smoking French cigarettes, drinking English gin, and padding again and again to his bedroom, leading him to lie on that mattress on the floor. She'd moved in slowly over two weeks' time—first leaving behind an article of clothing, then a book, then stopping by with a lamp. They never spoke of love. They never fell in love. They merely fell into marriage, which, after all, was the highest form of public validation he could possibly give to a mindless act of sex with a woman he didn't know.

The office door opened. A man—presumably P. L. Beck—entered. Like the office itself, his clothing reflected a careful avoidance of that which might underscore death. He wore a natty blue blazer over soft grey trousers. A Pembroke tie formed a perfect knot at his throat.

"Dr. Weaver?" he said. And then with a crisp turn on his heel to Glyn, "And Mrs. Weaver?" Somehow, he'd done his homework. It was an artful way to avoid linking their names. Rather than offer factitious condolences over the death of a girl he did not know, he said, "The police said you'd be coming. I'd like to get you through this as quickly as possible. May I offer you something? Coffee or tea?''

"Nothing for me," Anthony said. Glyn was silent.

Mr. Beck did not wait for her to reply. He sat down and said, "It's my understanding that the police still have the body. So it may be some days before they release her to us. They've told you that, haven't they?''

"No. Just that they're doing the autopsy.''

"I see." Thoughtfully, he steepled his hands and leaned his elbows on the top of the desk. "It generally takes a few days to run all the tests. They do organ studies, tissue studies, toxicology reports. In a sudden death, the procedure moves fairly rapidly, especially if the''—with a quick, concerned glance in Glyn's direction—"if the deceased has been under a doctor's care. But in a case like this . . .''

"We understand," Anthony said.

"A murder," Glyn said. She moved her eyes off the wall and fixed them on Mr. Beck although her body didn't alter a degree in the chair. "You mean a murder. Say it. Don't slither round the truth. She isn't the deceased. She's the victim. It's a murder. I'm not used to that yet, but if I hear it enough no doubt it'll pop up quite naturally in my speech. My daughter, the victim. My daughter's death, the murder.''

Mr. Beck looked at Anthony, perhaps with the hope that he would say something in answer to the implied invective, perhaps with the expectation of Anthony's offering some word of comfort or support to his former wife. When Anthony said nothing, Mr. Beck continued quickly.

"You'll need to let me know where and when the services are to be held and where she's to be interred. We've a lovely chapel here if you'd like to use that for the service. And—of course, I know this is difficult for you both—but you need to decide if you want a public viewing.''

"A public . . . ?'' At the thought of his daughter being put on display for the curious, Anthony felt the hair bristle on the backs of his hands. "That's not possible. She isn't—''

"I want it." Glyn's nails, Anthony saw, were going completely white with the pressure she was exerting against her palms.

"You don't want that. You haven't seen what she looks like.''

"Please don't tell me what I want. I said I'll see her. I'll do so. I want everyone to see her.''

Mr. Beck intervened with, "We can do some repairs. With facial putty and makeup, no one will be able to see the full extent of—''

Glyn snapped forward. Like a self-preserving reflex, Mr. Beck flinched. "You aren't listening to me. I want the damage seen. I want the world to know."

Anthony wanted to ask, "And what will you gain?" But he knew the answer. She'd given Elena over to his care, and she wanted the world to see how he'd botched the job. For fifteen years she'd kept their daughter in one of the roughest areas of London and Elena had emerged from the experience with one chipped tooth to mark the only difficulty she'd ever faced, a brawl over the affections of an acne-scarred fifth former who'd spent a lunch hour with her instead of his steady girlfriend. And neither Glyn nor Elena had ever considered that uncapped tooth even a minute lapse in Glyn's ability to protect her daughter. Instead, it was for both of them Elena's badge of honour, her declaration of equality. For the three girls whom she had fought could hear, but they were no match for the splintered crate of new potatoes and the two metal milk baskets which Elena had commandeered for defensive weapons from a nearby greengrocer's when she'd come under attack.

Fifteen years in London, one chipped tooth to show for it. Fifteen months in Cambridge, one barbarous death.

Anthony wouldn't fight her. He said, "Have you a brochure we might look at? Something we can use in order to decide . . . ?"

Mr. Beck seemed only too willing to cooperate. He said, "Of course," and hastily slid open a drawer of his desk. From this he took a three-ring binder covered in maroon plastic with the words *Beck and Sons, Funeral Directors* printed in gold letters across the front. He passed this across to them.

Anthony opened it. Plastic covers encased eight-by-ten colour photographs. He began to flip through them, looking without seeing, reading without assimilating. He recognised woods: mahogany and oak. He recognised terms: naturally resistant to corrosion, rubber gasket, crepe lining, asphalt coating, vacuum plate. Faintly, he heard Mr. Beck murmuring about the relative merits of copper or sixteen-gauge steel over oak, about lift and tilt mattresses, about the placement of a hinge. He heard him say:

"These Uniscal caskets are quite the best. The locking mechanism in addition to the gasket seals the top while the continuous weld on the bottom seals that as well. So you've maximum protection to resist the entry of—" He hesitated delicately. The indecision was written plainly on his face. Worms, beetles, moisture, mildew. How best to say it?— "the elements."

The words in the binder slid out of focus. Anthony heard Glyn say, "Have you coffins here?"

"Only a few. People generally make a choice from the brochures. And under the circumstances, please don't feel you must—"

"I'd like to see them."

Mr. Beck's eyes flitted to Anthony. He seemed to be waiting for a protest of some sort. When none was forthcoming, he said, "Certainly. This way," and led them out of the office.

Anthony followed his former wife and the funeral director. He wanted to insist that they make the decision within the safety of Mr. Beck's office where photographs would allow both of them to hold the final reality at bay for just a while longer. But he knew that to call for distance between them and the fact of Elena's burial would be interpreted as further evidence of inadequacy. And hadn't Elena's death already served to illustrate his uselessness as a father, once again underscoring the contention which Glyn had asserted for years: that his sole contribution to their daughter's upbringing had been a single, blind gamete that knew how to swim?

"Here they are." Mr. Beck pushed open a set of heavy oak doors. "I'll leave you alone."

Glyn said, "That won't be necessary."

"But surely you'll want to discuss—"

"No." She moved past him into the showroom. There were no decorations or extraneous furnishings, just a few coffins lined up along the pearl-coloured walls, their lids gaping open upon velvet, satin, and crepe, their bodies standing on waist-high, translucent pedestals.

Anthony forced himself to follow Glyn from one to the next. Each had a discreet price tag, each bore the same declaration about the extent of protection guaranteed by the manufacturer, each had a ruched lining, a matching pillow, and a coverlet folded over the coffin lid. Each had its own name: Neapolitan Blue, Windsor Poplar, Autumn Oak, Venetian Bronze. Each had an individually highlighted feature, a shell design, a set of barley sugar end posts, or delicate embroidery on the interior of the lid. Forcing himself to move along the display, Anthony tried not to visualise what Elena would look like when she finally lay in one of these coffins with her light hair spread out like silk threads on the pillow.

Glyn halted in front of a simple grey coffin with a plain satin lining. She tapped her fingers against it. As if this gesture bade him to do so, Mr. Beck hurried to join them. His lips were pursed tightly. He was pulling at his chin.

"What is this?" Glyn asked. A small sign on the lid said *Nonprotective exterior*. Its price tag read £200.

"Pressed wood." Mr. Beck made a nervous adjustment to his Pembroke tie and rapidly continued. "This is pressed wood beneath a flannel covering, a satin interior, which is quite nice, of course, but the exterior has no protection at all save for the flannel itself and to be frank if I may, considering our weather, I wouldn't be at all comfortable recommending this particular coffin to you. We keep it for cases where there are difficulties . . . Well, difficulties with finances. I can't think you'd want your daughter . . ." He let the drifting quality of his voice complete the thought.

Anthony began to say, "Of course," but Glyn interrupted with, "This coffin will do."

For a moment, Anthony did nothing more than stare at his former wife. Then he found the will to say, "You can't think I'll allow her to be buried in this."

She said quite distinctly, "I don't care what you intend to allow. I've not enough money for—"

"I'll pay."

She looked at him for the first time since they'd arrived. "With your wife's money? I think not."

"This has nothing to do with Justine."

Mr. Beck took a step away from them. He straightened out the small price sign on a coffin lid. He said, "I'll leave you to talk."

"There's no need." Glyn opened her large black handbag and began shoving articles this way and that. A set of keys clanked. A compact snapped open. A ballpoint pen slipped out onto the floor. "You'll take a cheque, won't you? It'll have to be drawn on my bank in London. If that's a problem, you can phone for some sort of guarantee. I've been doing business with them for years, so "

"Glyn. I won't have it."

She swung to face him. Her hip hit the coffin, jarring it on its pedestal. The lid fell shut with a hollow thud. "You won't have what?" she asked. "You have no rights here."

"We're talking about my daughter."

Mr. Beck began to edge towards the door.

"Stay where you are." Angry colour patched Glyn's cheeks. "You walked out on your daughter, Anthony. Let's not forget that. You wanted your career. Let's not forget that. You wanted to chase skirts. Let's not forget that. You got what you wanted. All of it. Every bit. You have no more rights here." Chequebook in hand, she stooped to the floor for the pen. She began to write, using the pressed wood coffin lid as support.

Her hand was shaking. Anthony reached for the chequebook, saying, "Glyn. Please. For God's sake."

"No," she said. "I'll pay for this. I don't want your money. You can't buy me off."

"I'm not trying to buy you off. I just want Elena—"

"Don't say her name! Don't you say it!"

Mr. Beck said, "Let me leave you," and without acknowledging Glyn's immediate "No!" he hurried from the room.

Glyn continued to write. She clutched the pen like a weapon in her hand. "He said two hundred pounds, didn't he?"

"Don't do this," Anthony said. "Don't make this another battle between us."

"She'll wear that blue dress Mum got her last birthday."

"We can't bury her like a pauper. I won't let you do it. I can't."

Glyn ripped the cheque from the book. She said, "Where'd that man get off to? Here's his money. Let's go." She headed for the door.

Anthony reached for her arm.

She jerked away. "You bastard," she hissed. "Bastard! Who brought her up? Who spent years trying to give her some language? Who helped her with her schoolwork and dried her tears and washed her clothes and sat up with her at night when she was puling and sick? Not you, you bastard. And not your ice queen wife. This is my daughter, Anthony. My daughter. Mine. And I'll bury her exactly as I see fit. Because unlike you, I'm not hot after some big poncey job, so I don't have to give a damn what anyone thinks."

He examined her with sudden, curious dispassion, realising that he saw no evidence of grief. He saw no mother's devotion to her child and nothing that illustrated the magnitude of loss. "This has nothing to do with burying Elena," he said in slow but complete understanding. "You're still dealing with me. I'm not sure you even care much that she's dead."

"How dare you," she whispered.

"Have you even cried, Glyn? Do you feel any grief? Do you feel anything at all beyond the need to use her murder for a bit more revenge? And how can anyone be surprised by that? After all, that's how you used most of her life."

He didn't see the blow coming. She slammed her right hand across his face, knocking his spectacles to the floor.

"You filthy piece of—" She raised her arm to strike again.

He caught her wrist. "You've waited years to do that. I'm only sorry you didn't have the audience you'd have liked.'' He pushed her away. She fell against the grey coffin. But she was not spent.

She spit out the words: "Don't talk to me of grief. Don't you ever— *ever*—talk to me of grief.''

She turned away from him, flinging her arms over the coffin lid as if she would embrace it. She began to weep.

"I have nothing. She's gone. I can't have her back. I can't find her anywhere. And I can't . . . I can never . . .'' The fingers of one hand curled, pulling at the flannel that covered the coffin. "But you can. You still can, Anthony. And I want you to die.''

Even through his outrage, he felt the sudden stirring of a horrified compassion. After the years of their enmity, after these moments in the funeral home, he wouldn't have believed it possible that he should feel anything for her save outright loathing. But in those words *you can,* he saw the extent and the nature of his former wife's grief. She was forty-six years old. She could never have another child.

No matter that the thought of bringing another child into the world to take Elena's place was beyond unthinkable, that he'd lost his reason for living the moment he'd looked on his daughter's corpse. He'd spend the rest of his life in a ceaseless involvement in academic affairs so that he would never again have a free moment in which he might have to remember the ruin of her face and the mark of the ligature round her neck, but that was no more than a point of indifference. He could still have another child, whatever the wilderness of his current grief. He still had that choice. But Glyn did not. Her sorrow was doubled by the incontrovertible fact of her age.

He took a step towards her, placing his hand on her shuddering back. "Glyn, I'm—''

"Don't you touch me!'' She rolled away from him, lost her footing, and fell to one knee.

The flimsy flannel covering on the coffin tore. The wood was thin and vulnerable beneath it.

Heart pounding in both his chest and his ears, Lynley staggered to a halt within sight of Fen Causeway. He dug in his pocket for his watch. He flipped it open, panting, and checked the time. Seven minutes.

He shook his head, bent nearly double with his hands on his knees, wheezing like an undiagnosed case of emphysema. Less than a mile's run and he felt completely done for. Sixteen years of cigarette smoking had taken its toll. Ten months of abstinence was not enough to redeem him.

He stumbled onto the worn wooden planks that bridged the stream between Robinson Crusoe's Island and Sheep's Green. He leaned against the metal rail, threw his head back, and gulped in air like a man saved from drowning. Sweat beaded his face and dampened his jersey. What a wonderful experience it was to run.

With a grunt, he turned to rest his elbows against the rail, letting his head hang while he caught his breath. Seven minutes, he thought, and not quite a mile. She would have run the same course in not much more than five.

There could be no doubt about it. She ran daily with her stepmother. She was a long-distance runner. She ran with the Cambridge cross country team. If her calendar was any indication of reality, she'd been running with the University Hare and Hounds as far back as last January and probably before. Depending on the distance she had planned to go that morning, her pacing might have been different. But he couldn't imagine her taking any longer than ten minutes to run to the island, no matter the course she had intended to follow. That being the case, unless she stopped off somewhere along the route, she would have reached the site of her murder no later than six-twenty-five.

Respiration finally slowing, he raised his head. Even without the fog which had shrouded most of the region on the previous day, he had to admit that this was an exceptional spot for a murder. Crack willows, alders, and beeches—none of them yet leafless—created an impenetrable screen which shielded the island not only from the causeway bridge which arched above its south end on the way into the town but also from the public footpath that ran along the stream—Sheehan's bit of a ditch—not ten feet away. Anyone wishing to carry off a crime reaped the benefit of virtual privacy here. And although the occasional pedestrian crossed over the larger bridge from Coe Fen to the island and from there to the footpath, although bicycle riders pedalled across Sheep's Green or along the river, in the nighttime darkness of half past six on a cold November morning the killer could have been fairly certain that no witness would come upon the beating and strangulation of Elena Weaver. At half past six in the morning no one would even be in the area, except her stepmother. And her presence had been eliminated with a simple call placed on the Cee-phone, a call made by someone who presumed on a personal knowledge of Justine to assume that, given the opportunity, she wouldn't run by herself the next morning.

Of course, she had run anyway. But it was the killer's luck that she had chosen a different route. If, indeed, it had been luck at all.

Lynley pushed himself off the railing and walked across the footbridge onto the island. A tall wooden gate leading to the north end stood open, and Lynley entered to see a workshed with punts piled to one side of it and three old bicycles leaning against its green doors. Inside, bundled in heavy pullovers against the cold, three men were examining a hole in a punt. Fluorescent lights along the ceiling yellowed their skin. The scent of marine varnish made a weight of the air. It wafted from a crowded workbench where two gallon cans stood open with paintbrushes resting across their tops. It spread from two other punts, freshly refurbished, that rested on sawhorses, waiting to dry.

"Bloomin idiots, they are," one of the men was saying. "Lookit this bash, will you? It's carelessness, that is. They none of them have a stitch of respect."

One of the other men looked up. Lynley saw that he was young— no more than twenty. His face was spotty, his hair was long, and his earlobe sported a glittering zircon stud. He said, "Help you, mate?"

The other two ceased working. They were middle-aged and tired-looking. One gave Lynley a once-over look that took in his makeshift running clothes of brown tweed, blue wool, and white leather. The other went to the far end of the shed where he fired up an electric sander and began to savage the side of a canoe.

Having seen the official crime-scene notice still marking off the south end of the island, Lynley wondered why Sheehan had done nothing about this section. He discovered soon enough when the younger man said·

"No one shuts us out just 'cause some slag's in the shit."

"Leave off, Derek," the older man said. "It's a killing they're dealing with, not some lady in distress."

Derek tossed his head derisively. He pulled a cigarette from his blue jeans and lit one with a kitchen match which he threw to the floor, casually oblivious of the proximity of several cans of paint.

Identifying himself, Lynley asked if any of them had known the dead girl. Just that she was from the University, they told him. They had no more information than what the police had given them upon their arrival at the workshop yesterday morning. They knew only that a college girl's body had been found on the south end of the island, with her face mashed up and some string round her neck.

Had the police conducted a search of this northern area? Lynley wanted to know.

"Poked their faces everywhere, they did," Derek replied. "Cut right through the gate before we even got here. Ned was right cheesed off about that all day." He shouted through the noise that screeched from the sander at the end of the building, "Weren't you, mate?"

If he heard him, Ned gave no sign. He was fully intent upon the canoe.

"You noticed nothing out of the ordinary?" Lynley said.

Derek blew cigarette smoke from his mouth and sucked it up with his nostrils. He grinned, apparently pleased with the effect. "You mean aside from about two dozen coppers crawling round through the bushes trying to pin what they can on blokes like us?"

"How's that?" Lynley asked.

"It's the regular story. Some college tart got bagged. The coppers are looking to nab a local because if the University nits don't like the nature of the collar, all hell's go'n to break loose. Just ask Bill here how it works."

Bill didn't appear to be willing to hold forth on this particular topic. He busied himself at the workbench where he picked up a hacksaw and went after a narrow piece of wood being held steady by an old red vice.

Derek said, "His boy works on the local rag, he does. Was following a story 'bout some bloke who supposably offed himself last spring. Uni didn't like the way the story was developing and bang on the button they tried to quash it straight away. That's the way it runs round here, mister." Derek stabbed a dirty thumb in the direction of the centre of town. "Uni like the locals to toe the Uni line."

"Isn't that sort of thing dead and gone?" Lynley asked. "I mean the town-and-gown strife."

Bill finally spoke. "Depends on who you ask."

Derek added, "Yeah. It's dead and gone, all right, when you're talking with the toffs down river. They don't see trouble till it smacks them in the face. But it's a bit different, isn't it, when you're rubbing your elbows with the likes of us."

Lynley gave thought to Derek's words as he walked back to the south end of the island and ducked under the established police line. How often had he heard variations on that theme espoused religiously over the last few years? We've no class system any longer, it's dead and gone. It was always stated with well-meaning sincerity by someone whose career, whose background, or whose money effectively blinded him to the reality of life. While all the time those without brilliant careers, those without family trees whose roots plunged deeply into British soil, those without access to ready money or even the hope of saving a few pounds from their weekly pay, those were the people who recognised the insidious social strata of a society that claimed no strata existed at the very same moment as it labelled a man from the sound of his voice.

The University would probably be the first to deny the existence of barriers between gown and town. And why would they not? For those who are the primary architects of ramparts rarely, if ever, feel constricted by their presence.

Still, he had difficulty attributing Elena Weaver's death to the resurrection of a social dispute. Had a local been involved in the killing, his instincts told him that the very same local would have been involved with Elena. But no local had known her from what he had been able to ascertain. And following any pathway that led towards town-and-gown promised, he felt certain, to be a search for nothing.

He walked along the trail of boards which the Cambridge police had laid down from the island's wrought iron gate to the site of the murder. Everything that constituted potential evidence had been swept up and carted away by the crime-scene team. Only a roughly shaped fire ring remained, half-buried in front of a fallen branch. He went to this and sat.

Whatever difficulties existed within the political arena of Cambridge Constabulary's forensic department, the crime-scene team had done their job well. The ashes from the fire ring had been sifted through. It looked as if some of them had even been removed.

Next to the branch, he saw the impression of a bottle in the damp earth and he remembered the list of items which Sarah Gordon had said she had seen. He wondered about this, picturing a killer clever enough to use an unopened wine bottle, to dump the wine in the river afterwards, to wash the bottle inside and out, to tamp it into the earth so that it looked like part of the general rubbish in the area. Smeared with mud, it would appear to have been there for weeks. Moisture inside would be attributed to the damp. Filled with wine, it suited the still-limited description of the weapon which had been used to beat the girl. But if that was the case, how on earth were they to trace a bottle of wine in a city where students kept supplies of drink in their very own rooms?

He shoved himself off the branch and walked to the clearing where the body had been hidden. Nothing was left to indicate that yesterday morning a pile of leaves had camouflaged a killing. Bladder campion, English ivy, nettles, and wild strawberries remained untrampled, despite the fact that every leaf on every plant had been scrutinised and evaluated by people trained to ferret out the truth. He moved to the river and gazed across the wide expanse of marshy land that constituted Coe Fen along whose far edge the beige rise of the buildings of Peterhouse lay. He studied them, admitting the fact that he could see them clearly, admitting that at this distance their lights—especially the light from one building's lantern cupola—would probably glow visibly through all but the most impenetrable fog. He admitted also that he was checking out Sarah Gordon's story. He admitted also that he could not have said why.

He began to turn from the river and caught on the air the unmistakable, sour smell of human vomit, just a solitary whiff of it like the breath of an illness that was passing by. He tracked this to its source on the bank, a coagulating pool of greenish brown slop. It was lumpy and foul, with the tracks and the peck-marks of birds sinking into it. As he bent to examine it, he could hear Sergeant Havers' laconic comment: Her neighbours cleared her, Inspector, her story checks out, but you can always ask her what she had for brekkie and cart this in to forensic for a check-out as well.

Perhaps, he thought, that was the problem he was having with Sarah Gordon. Everything about her story checked out completely. There wasn't a hole anywhere.

Why do you want a hole? Havers would have asked. Your job isn't to want holes. Your job is to find them. And when you can't find them, you just move on.

He decided to do so, following the trail of boards back the way he had come, leaving the island. He walked up the rise in the path that led up to the causeway bridge where a gate gave way to the pavement and the street. Directly across from it was a similar gate, and he went to see what lay beyond it.

A morning jogger, he realised, coming along the river from the direction of St. Stephen's would have three options upon reaching Fen Causeway. A turn to the left and she would run past the Department of Engineering in the direction of Parker's Piece and the Cambridge Police Station. A turn to the right and she would head towards Newnham Road and, if she persisted far enough, to Barton beyond it. Or, he now saw, she could proceed straight ahead, crossing the street, ducking through this second gate, and continuing south along the river. Whoever killed her, he realised, must have not only known her route but also known her options. Whoever killed her, he realised, had known in advance that the only certain chance of catching her was at Crusoe's Island.

He was feeling the cold beginning to seep through his clothes and he headed back the way he had come, maintaining a slower pace this time, one designed merely to keep himself warm. As he made the final turn from Senate House Passage where Senate House itself and the outer walls of Gonville and Caius College were acting like a refrigerated wind tunnel, he saw Sergeant Havers emerging from the gatehouse of St. Stephen's, looking dwarfed by its turrets and its heraldic carving of yales supporting the founder's coat of arms.

She gave his appearance a poker-faced scrutiny. "Going undercover, Inspector?"

He joined her. "Don't I blend in with the environment?"

"You're a regular bit of camouflage."

"Your sincerity overwhelms me." He explained what he had been doing, ignoring the cocked and leery eyebrow which she raised at his references to Sarah Gordon's corroborative vomit, and finishing with, "I'd say Elena ran the course in about five minutes, Havers. But if she was intent on having a fairly long workout, then she may have paced herself. So ten at the extreme."

Havers nodded. She squinted down the lane in the direction of King's College, saying, "If the porter really saw her leave round six-fifteen—"

"And I think we can depend upon that."

"—then she got to the island far in advance of Sarah Gordon. Wouldn't you say?"

"Unless she stopped off somewhere en route."

"Where?"

"Adam Jenn said his digs are by Little St. Mary's. That's less than a block from part of Elena's run."

"Are you saying she stopped off for a morning cuppa?"

"Perhaps. Perhaps not. But if Adam was looking for her yesterday morning, he wouldn't have had much trouble finding her, would he?"

They crossed over to Ivy Court, wound their way through the ubiquitous rows of bicycles, and headed towards O staircase. "I need a shower," Lynley said.

"As long as I don't have to scrub your back."

When he returned from the shower, he found her at his desk, perusing the notes he had written on the previous night. She'd made herself at home, scattering her belongings across the room, one scarf on the bed, another draped across the armchair, her coat on the floor. Her shoulder bag gaped upon the desk top, spilling out pencils, chequebook, a plastic comb with missing teeth, and an orange lapel button printed with the message *Chicken Little Was Right*. Somewhere in this wing of the building, she'd managed to find a stocked gyp room, for she'd made a pot of tea, some of which she was pouring into a gold-rimmed cup.

"I see you've brought out the best china," he said, towelling off his hair.

She tapped her finger against it. The sound snapped sharply rather than sang. "Plastic," she said. "Can your lips endure the insult?"

"They'll soldier through."

"Good." She poured a cup for him. "There was milk as well, but there were white globs floating in it so I left its future to science." She dropped in two sugar cubes, stirred the brew with one of her pencils, and handed him the cup. "And would you please put on a shirt, Inspector? You've got lovely pectorals, but I tend to go light-headed at the sight of a man's chest."

He obliged her by completing the dressing which he'd begun in the icy bathroom down the corridor. He took his tea to the armchair where he saw to his shoes.

"What do you have?" he asked her.

She pushed his notebook to one side and swivelled the desk chair so that she was facing him. She rested her right ankle on her left knee, which gave him his first glimpse of her socks. They were red.

"We've got fibres," she said, "on both armpits of her track jacket. Cotton, polyester, and rayon."

"They could have come from something in her cupboard."

"Right. Yes. They're checking for a match."

"So we're wide open there."

"No. Not exactly." He saw she was holding back a satisfied smile. "The fibres were black."

"Ah."

"Yes. My guess is that he dragged her by the armpits onto the island and left the fibres that way."

He swam by that hook of potential culpability. "What about the weapon? Have they made any headway with what was used to beat her?"

"They keep coming up with the same description. It's smooth, it's heavy, and it left no trace deposit on the body. The only change in what we knew before is that they've moved off calling it your standard blunt object. They've deleted the adjectives, but they're looking like the dickens for some others. Sheehan was talking about bringing in help to have a go with the body because apparently his two pathologists have a history of

being incapable of coming to a clear conclusion—not to mention an agreement—on anything.''

"He indicated there might be trouble with forensic," Lynley said.
He thought about the weapon, pondered the location, and said, "Wood
seems possible, doesn't it, Havers?"

As usual, she was with him. "An oar, you mean? A paddle?"

"That would be my guess."

"Then we'd have trace evidence. A splinter, a speck of varnish.
Something left behind."

"But they've absolutely nothing?"

"Not a sprat."

"That's hell."

"Right. We're nowhere with trace evidence if we're hoping to build
a case out of that. But there's good news otherwise. Lovely news, in
fact." She brought forth several folded sheets of paper from her shoulder
bag. "Sheehan fielded the autopsy results while I was there. We may not
have trace, but we've got ourselves a motive."

"You've been saying that ever since we met Lennart Thorsson."

"But this is better than being turned in for sexual harassment, sir.
This is the real thing. Turn him in for this and he's had it for good."

"Turn him in for what?"

She handed him the report. "Elena Weaver was pregnant."

10

"Which naturally brings up the question of those unused birth control pills, doesn't it?" Havers continued.

Lynley fetched his spectacles from his jacket pocket, returned to the chair, and read the report. She'd been eight weeks pregnant. It was now the fourteenth of November. Eight weeks took them back to sometime during the third week of September, before Cambridge was in session. But, he wondered, was it also before Elena herself had come to the city?

Havers was saying, "And once I told him about them, Sheehan waxed anachronistically eloquent on the subject for a good ten minutes."

Lynley roused himself. "What?"

"The pregnancy, sir."

"What about it?"

She dropped her shoulders in disgust. "Haven't you been listening?"

"I was wondering about the time line. Was she in London when she became pregnant? Was she in Cambridge?" He dismissed the questions momentarily. "What was Sheehan's point?"

"It sounded like a bit of Victoriana, but as Sheehan put it, in this environment we ought to be concentrating on archaic with a capital A. And his conjecture has a nice feel to it, sir." She used a pencil to tap out each point against her knee. "Sheehan suggested that Elena had something going with a senior member of the college. She came up pregnant. She wanted marriage. He wanted his career. He knew he'd be ruined for advancement if the word got out that he'd made a student pregnant. And she threatened to let the word out, thinking that would bend him to her will. But it didn't go as she planned. He killed her instead.''

"You're still hanging on to Lennart Thorsson, then.''

"It fits, Inspector. And that address on Seymour Street that she'd written on her calendar? I checked it out.''

"And?''

"A health clinic. According to the staff doctor who was only too happy to 'help the police with their enquiries,' Elena was there on Wednesday afternoon for a pregnancy test. And we know Thorsson went to see her Thursday night. He was done for, Inspector. But it was worse than that.''

"Why?''

"The birth control pills in her room. The date on them was last February, but they hadn't been taken. Sir, I think Elena was trying to get herself pregnant.'' Havers took a sip of tea. "Your basic entrapment.''

Lynley frowned at the report, removed his spectacles, and polished them on the tail of Havers' scarf. "I don't see how that follows. She merely might have stopped taking them because there was no reason to do so—no man in her life. When one came along, she was unprepared.''

"Rubbish,'' Havers said. "Most women know in advance if they're going to sleep with a man. They generally know the moment they meet him.''

"But they don't know, do they, if they're going to be raped.''

"All right. Given. But you've got to see Thorsson's in line for that as well.''

"Certainly. But he's not alone, Havers. And perhaps not even at the head of the queue.''

A sharp double knock sounded on the door. When Lynley called out in acknowledgement, the St. Stephen's day porter popped his head inside the room.

"Message,'' he said, holding out a folded slip of paper. "Thought it best to bring it over.''

"Thank you.'' Lynley got to his feet.

The porter curled back his arm. "Not for you, Inspector,'' he said. "It's for the sergeant.''

Havers took it from him with a nod of thanks. The porter withdrew. Lynley watched his sergeant read. Her face fell. She crumpled the paper, crossing back to the desk.

He said easily, "I think we've done all we can for today, Havers.''

He took out his watch. "It's after ... Good Lord, look at the time. It's after half past three already. Perhaps you ought to think about—"

She dropped her head. He watched her fumble with her shoulder bag. He didn't have the heart to continue the pretence. They weren't bankers, after all. They didn't work businessmen's hours.

"It's not working," she said. She flung the bit of paper into the rubbish basket. "I wish someone would tell me why the hell nothing ever seems to work out."

"Go home," he said. "See to her. I'll handle things here."

"There's too much for you to do. It's not fair."

"It may not be fair. But it's also an order. Go home, Barbara. You can be there by five. Come back in the morning."

"I'll check out Thorsson first."

"There's no need for that. He's not going anywhere."

"I'll check him out anyway." She took up her shoulder bag and picked her coat off the floor. When she turned to him, he saw that her nose and cheeks had become quite red.

He said, "Barbara, the right thing is sometimes the most obvious thing. You know that, don't you?"

"That's the hell of it," she replied.

"My husband isn't home, Inspector. He and Glyn have gone to make the funeral arrangements."

"I think you can give me the information I need."

Justine Weaver looked beyond him to the drive where the fading afternoon light was winking along the right wing of his car. Brows drawn together, she appeared to be trying to decide what to do about him. She crossed her arms and pressed her fingers into the sleeves of her gabardine blazer. It might have been a gesture to keep herself warm, save for the fact that she didn't move away from the door to get out of the wind.

"I don't see how. I've told you everything I know about Sunday night and Monday morning."

"But not, I dare say, everything you know about Elena."

Her eyes moved off the car to him. Hers, he saw, were morning glory blue, and their colour needed no heightening through an appropriate choice of clothes. Although her presence at home at this hour suggested that she hadn't gone to work that day, she was dressed with nearly as much formality as she had been on the previous night, in a taupe blazer, a blouse buttoned to the throat and printed with the soft impression of small leaves, and slim wool trousers. She'd swept her long hair off her face with a single comb.

She said, "I think you ought to speak with Anthony, Inspector."

Lynley smiled. "Indeed."

In the street, the double tin ringing of a bicycle bell was met by the answering honk of a horn. Closer by, three hawfinches swept in an arc from the roof to the ground, their distinctive call—*tzik*—like a repetitive, single-word conversation. They hopped on the drive and pecked at the gravel and, as one unit, shot into the air again. Justine followed their flight to a cypress on the edge of the lawn. Then she said:

"Come in," and stepped back from the door.

She took his overcoat from him, smoothed it round the newel post at the bottom of the stairs, and led him into the sitting room where they had met on the previous night. Unlike the previous night, however, she made no offer of refreshment. Instead, she went to the glass tea table along the wall and made a small adjustment to its arrangement of silk tulips. That done, she turned to face him, hands clasped loosely in front of her. In that setting, dressed and posed as she was, she looked like a mannequin. Lynley wondered what it took to fracture her control.

He said, "When did Elena arrive in Cambridge for Michaelmas term this year?"

"The term began the first week of October."

"I'm aware of that. I was wondering if she came here in advance, perhaps to stay with you and her father. It would take a few days to settle into the college, I should think. Her father would want to help her."

Her right hand slowly climbed her left arm, stopping just above the elbow where her thumbnail dug in and began to trace a circular pattern. "She must have arrived sometime towards the middle of September because we had a gathering for some of the history faculty on the thirteenth and she was here for the party. I remember that. Shall I check the calendar? Do you need the exact date when she came to us?"

"She stayed here with you and your husband when she first came to town?"

"As much as Elena could be said to stay anywhere. She was on the go, in and out most of the time. She liked to be active."

"All night?"

Her hand climbed to her shoulder, then rested beneath the collar of her blouse like a cradle for her neck. "That's a curious question. What is it you're asking?"

"Elena was eight weeks pregnant when she died."

A quick tremor passed across her face, like a frisson that was emotional rather than physical. Before he could assess it, she had dropped her eyes. Her hand, however, remained at her throat.

"You knew," Lynley said.

She looked up. "No. But I'm not surprised."

"Because of someone she was seeing? Someone you knew about?"

Her gaze went from him to the sitting room doorway as if she expected to see Elena's lover standing there.

"Mrs. Weaver," Lynley said, "right now we're looking directly at a possible motive for your stepdaughter's murder. If you know something, I'd appreciate your telling me about it."

"This should come from Anthony, not from me."

"Why?"

"Because I *was* her stepmother." She returned her gaze to him. It was remarkably cool. "Do you understand? I don't have the sort of rights you seem to think I have."

"Rights to speak ill of this particular dead?"

"If you will."

"You didn't like Elena. That's obvious enough. But all things considered, you're hardly in a unique situation. No doubt you're one of millions of women who don't much care for the children they've been saddled with through a second marriage."

"Children who generally aren't murdered, Inspector."

"The stepmother's secret hope transformed into reality?" He saw the answer in her instinctive shrinking away from him as he asked the question. Quietly, he said, "It's no crime, Mrs. Weaver. And you're not the first person to have your blackest wish granted beyond your wildest dreams."

She left the tea table abruptly and walked to the sofa, where she sat. Not leaning back against it, not sinking into it, but perched on the edge with her hands in her lap and her back like a rod. She said, "Please sit down, Inspector Lynley." When he did so, taking a place in the leather armchair that faced the sofa, she continued. "All right. I knew that Elena was"—she seemed to be searching for an appropriate euphemism—"sexual."

"Sexually active?" And when she nodded, pressing her lips together as if with the intention of smoothing out the salmon lipstick she wore, Lynley said, "Did she tell you?"

"It was obvious. I could smell it on her. When she had sex she didn't always bother with washing herself afterwards, and it's a rather distinctive odour, isn't it?''

"You didn't counsel her? Your husband didn't speak to her?''

"About her hygiene?'' Justine's expression was mildly, if only distantly, amused. "I think Anthony preferred to remain oblivious of what his nose was telling him.''

"And you?''

"I tried to talk to her several times. At first I thought that she might not be aware of how she ought to be taking care of herself. I also thought it might be wise to find out if she was taking precautions against pregnancy. Frankly, I'd never got the impression that she and Glyn engaged in many mother-daughter conversations.''

"She didn't want to talk to you, I take it?''

"On the contrary, she did talk. In fact, she was rather entertained by what I had to say. She informed me that she'd been on the pill since she was fourteen years old when she began fucking—her word, Inspector, not mine—the father of one of her school friends. Whether that's true or not, I have no idea. As to her personal hygiene, Elena knew all about how to take care of herself. She went unwashed deliberately. She wanted people to know she was having sex. Particularly, I think, she wanted her father to know.''

"What gave you that impression?''

"There were times when she'd come by quite late and we were still up and she'd hang on her father and hug him and press her cheek against his and rub up against him and all the time she was reeking like . . .'' Justine's fingers felt for her wedding band.

"Was she trying to arouse him?''

"I thought so at first. Who wouldn't have thought so with her carrying on like that? But then I began to think that she merely was trying to rub his face in normal.''

It was a curious expression. "An act of defiance?''

"No. Not at all. An act of compliance.'' She must have seen the next query on his face, for she went on with, "I'm being normal, Daddy. See how normal I am? I'm partying and drinking and having regular sex. Isn't this what you wanted? Didn't you want a normal child?''

Lynley saw how her words reaffirmed the picture which Terence Cuff had painted obliquely on the previous night about Anthony Weaver's relationship with his daughter. "I know he didn't want her to sign,'' Lynley said. "But as for the rest—''

"Inspector, he didn't want her to be deaf. Nor did Glyn, for that matter."

"Elena knew this?"

"How could she help knowing? They'd spent her entire life trying to shape her into a normal woman, the very thing she could never hope to be."

"Because she was deaf."

"Yes." For the first time, Justine's posture altered. She leaned forward fractionally to make her point. "Deaf—isn't—normal—Inspector." She waited for a moment before going on, looking as if she were gauging his reaction. And he did feel the reaction course swiftly through him. It was an aversion of the sort he always felt when someone made a comment that was xenophobic, homophobic, or racist.

"You see," she said, "you want to make her normal as well. You even want to call her normal and condemn me for daring to suggest that being deaf is different. I can see it on your face: Deaf is as normal as anything else. Which is exactly what Anthony wanted to think. So you can't really judge him, can you, for wanting to describe his daughter in the very same way as you've just done?"

There was sheer, cool insight behind the words. Lynley wondered how much time and reflection had gone into Justine Weaver's being able to make such a detached evaluation. "But Elena could judge him."

"And she did just that."

"Adam Jenn told me he saw her occasionally, at your husband's request."

Justine returned to her original, upright position. "Anthony had hopes that Elena might attach herself to Adam."

"Could he be the one who made her pregnant, then?"

"I don't think so. Adam only met her this past September, at the faculty party I mentioned earlier."

"But if she became pregnant shortly thereafter . . . ?"

Justine dismissed this by quickly raising her hand from her lap to stop his words. "She'd been having sex frequently since the previous December. Long before she knew Adam." Once again, she seemed to anticipate his next question. "You're wondering how I could know that so definitely."

"It was nearly a year ago after all."

"She'd come in to show us the gown she'd bought for the Christmas Ball. She undressed to try it on."

"And she hadn't washed."

"She hadn't washed."

"Who took her to the ball?"

"Gareth Randolph."

The deaf boy. Lynley reflected upon the fact that Gareth Randolph's name was becoming like a constant undercurrent, omnipresent beneath the flow of information. He evaluated the manner in which Elena Weaver might have used him as an instrument of revenge. If she was acting out of a need to rub her father's face in his own desire that she be a normal, functioning woman, what better way to throw that desire back at him than to become pregnant. She'd be giving him what he ostensibly wanted—a normal daughter with normal needs and normal emotions whose body functioned in a perfectly normal way. At the same time, she'd be getting what she wanted—retaliation by choosing as the father of her child a deaf man. It was, at heart, a perfect circle of vengeance. He only wondered if Elena had been that devious, or if her stepmother was using the fact of the pregnancy to paint a portrait of the girl that would serve her own ends.

He said, "Since January, Elena had marked her calendar periodically with the small drawing of a fish. Does that mean anything to you?"

"A fish?"

"A pencil drawing similar to the symbol used for Christianity. It appears several times each week. It's on the calendar the night before she died."

"A fish?"

"Yes. As I've said. A fish."

"I can't think of what it might mean."

"A society she belonged to? A person she was meeting?"

"You make her life sound like a spy novel, Inspector."

"It appears to be something clandestine, wouldn't you agree?"

"Why?"

"Why not just write out whatever the fish stood for?"

"Perhaps it was too long. Perhaps it was easier to draw the fish. It can't mean much. Why would she worry about someone else seeing something she was putting on her personal calendar? It was probably shorthand, a device she used to remind herself of something. A supervision, perhaps."

"Or an assignation."

"Considering how Elena was telegraphing her sexual activity, Inspector, I hardly think she'd be disguising an assignation when it came to her own calendar."

"Perhaps she had to. Perhaps she only wanted her father to know what she was doing but not with whom. And he'd have seen her calendar. He'd have been in her room, so she might not have wanted him to see the name." Lynley waited for her to respond. When she did not do so, he said, "Elena had birth control pills in her desk. But she hadn't taken them since February. Can you explain that?"

"Only in the most obvious way, I'm afraid. She wanted to get pregnant. But that doesn't surprise me. It was, after all, the normal thing to do. Love a man. Have his baby."

"You and your husband have no children, Mrs. Weaver?"

The quick change in subject, tagged logically onto her own statement, seemed to take her momentarily aback. Her lips parted briefly. Her gaze went to the wedding photograph on the tea table. She appeared to straighten her spine even further, but it may have been the result of the breath she took before she replied quite evenly, "We have no children."

He waited to see if she would say more, relying upon the fact that his own silence had so often in the past proved more effective than the most pointed question in pressuring someone into disclosure. Moments ticked by. Outside the sitting room window, a sudden gust of wind tossed a spray of field maple leaves against the glass. They looked like a billowing, saffron cloud.

Justine said, "Will there be anything else?" and smoothed her hand along the perfect, knife-edged crease in her trousers. It was a gesture which eloquently declared her the victor, if only for an instant, in the brief battle of their wills.

He admitted defeat, standing and saying, "Not at the moment."

She walked with him to the front door and handed him his overcoat. Her expression, he saw, was no different from what it had been when she first admitted him into the house. He wanted to marvel at the degree to which she had herself under control, but instead he found himself wondering whether it was a matter of mastering any revealing emotions or a matter of having—or experiencing—those emotions in the first place. He told himself it was to assess this latter possibility rather than to meet the challenge of cracking the composure of someone who seemed so invulnerable that he asked his final question.

"An artist from Grantchester found Elena's body yesterday morning," he said. "Sarah Gordon. Do you know her?"

Quickly, she bent to pick up the stem of a leaf which lay, barely discernible, on the parquet floor. She rubbed her finger along the spot where she had found it. Back and forth, three or four times as if the minuscule stem had somehow damaged the wood. When she had seen to it to her satisfaction, she stood again.

"No," she said. She met his eyes directly. "I don't know Sarah Gordon." It was a bravura performance.

He nodded, opened the door, and walked out onto the drive. Round the corner of the house, an Irish setter bounded gracefully towards them, a dirty tennis ball in his mouth. He vaulted past the Bentley and hurtled onto the lawn, making a joyful racecourse of its perimeter before he leaped over a white wrought iron table and dashed across the drive to land in a happy heap at Lynley's feet. He loosened his jaws and deposited the ball on the drive, tail wagging hopefully and silky coat rippling like soft reeds in the wind. Lynley picked up the ball and flung it beyond the cypress tree. With a yelp of delight, the dog hurtled after it. Once again, he raced round the edge of the lawn, once more he leaped over the wrought iron table, once more he landed in a heap at Lynley's feet. *Again,* his eyes said, *again, again.*

"She always came to play with him in the late afternoon," Justine said. "He's waiting for her. He doesn't know that she's gone."

"Adam said the dog ran with you and Elena in the morning," Lynley said. "Did you take him yesterday when you went alone?"

"I didn't want the trouble. He'd have wanted to head in the direction of the river. I wasn't going that way, and I didn't want him to fight me."

Lynley rubbed his knuckles on the top of the setter's head. When he stopped, the dog used his nose to flip the hand back into appropriate petting position once again. Lynley smiled.

"What's his name?"

"She called him Townee."

Justine didn't allow herself to react until she reached the kitchen. And even then she wasn't aware she was reacting until she saw that her hand—grasping the water glass—was clenched solidly round it as if she'd been suddenly afflicted by a stroke. She turned on the tap, let the water flow, held the glass beneath it.

She felt as if every argument and discussion, every moment of pleading, every second of emptiness over the last few years had somehow been both concentrated and compressed into a single statement: You and your husband have no children.

And she herself had given the detective the opening to make that observation: Love a man, have his baby.

But not here, not now, not in this house, not with this man.

With the water still running, she brought the glass to her lips and forced herself to drink. She filled the glass a second time, forced the water down again. She filled it a third time and drank again. Only then did she turn off the tap, raise her eyes from the sink, and look out the kitchen window into the rear garden where two grey wagtails bobbed up and down on the edge of the birdbath while a plump woodpigeon watched them from the sloping tile roof of the garden shed.

For a while she had harboured the secret hope that she might arouse him to such an extent that he simply lost himself—lost his control—in the desire to have her. She'd even taken to reading books in which she was alternately advised to be playful, to keep him off-guard, to become his fantasy whore, to sensitise her own body to stimulation so that she might more readily understand his, to become aware of erogenous zones, to demand expect require an orgasm, to vary positions locations times and circumstances, to be aloof, to be warm, to be honest, to be submissive. All of the reading and all of the advice left her nothing more than bewildered. It did not change her. Nor did it alter the fact that nothing—no amount of sighing, moaning, coaxing, or stimulating—kept Anthony from rising from her at the crucial moment, fumbling in the drawer, tearing open the package, and sheathing himself with a millimetre's despicable latex protection, her punishment for having threatened, in the heat of a wretchedly futile argument, to stop taking the pills without his knowledge.

He had one child. He would not have another. He could not betray Elena again. He had walked out on her, and he would not make the implied rejection worse by having another child that Elena might see as a replacement for herself or a competitor for her father's love. Nor would he run the risk of her thinking that he was seeking to satisfy his own needs of ego by producing a child who could hear.

They had talked about it all before they married. He had been forthright from the first, letting her know that children between them were out of the question, considering his age and his responsibilities to Elena. At the time, twenty-five years old and just three years into a career at which she was determined to be a success, the idea of having a child had been remote. Her attention had been fixed upon the world of publishing and upon her rise to significance within it. But if the passage of ten years had brought her a fine degree of professional success—thirty-five years old and publishing director of a highly respected press—it also brought her one step closer to the immutable fact of her own mortality and to the need to leave behind something that was her own creation and not the product of someone else.

Each month ticked its way through another cycle. Each egg washed away in a rush of blood. Each gasp of completion her husband experienced marked another wasting of the possibility of life.

But Elena had been pregnant.

Justine wanted to howl. She wanted to weep. She wanted to pull her lovely wedding china from the cupboard and hurl every piece of it against the wall. She wanted to overturn furniture and smash picture frames and drive her fist through the windows. But instead she lowered her eyes to the glass which she held, and she placed it with careful, decided precision into the unblemished porcelain sink.

She thought of the times she had observed Anthony watching his daughter. How that blaze of blind love had burned its way across his face. And all the while confronted with this, she had still managed a disciplined restraint, holding her tongue rather than speaking the truth and running the risk of his concluding that she did not share his love for Elena. Elena. The wild and contradictory currents of life that ran through her—the restless, fierce energy, the probing mind, the exuberant humour, the deep black anger. And always beneath everything, that impassioned need for unequivocal acceptance at continual war with her desire for revenge.

She had managed to achieve it. Justine wondered with what sort of anticipation Elena had looked forward to the moment when she would tell her father about her pregnancy, exacting a payment beyond his every expectation for the well-intentioned but nonetheless revealing crime of wanting her to be like everyone else. How Elena must have triumphed in the potential embarrassment to her father. And how she herself ought to be feeling some small degree of triumph at the idea of being in possession of a fact that would forever dispel Anthony's illusions about his daughter. She was, after all, so decidedly glad that Elena was dead.

Justine turned from the sink and walked into the dining room and from there to the sitting room. The house was still, with only the sound of the wind outside, rushing through the creaking branches of an old liquidambar. She felt suddenly chilled and pressed her palm to her forehead and then to her cheeks, wondering if she was coming down with something. And then she sat on the sofa, hands folded in her lap, and regarded the neat, symmetrical pile of artificial coals in the fireplace.

We'll be giving her a home, he had said when he'd learned that Elena would be coming up to Cambridge. We'll be filling her with love. Nothing, Justine, is more important than that.

For the first time since receiving Anthony's distraught telephone call at work the previous day, Justine thought about how Elena's death might actually affect her marriage. For how many times had Anthony spoken of the importance of providing a stable home for Elena outside the college, and how often had he alluded to the longevity of their ten-year marriage as a shining example of the kind of devotion, loyalty, and regenerative love which every couple sought and few couples found, describing it as an island of tranquillity to which his daughter could retreat and gain sustenance to face the challenges and battles of her life.

We're both Gemini, he had said. We're the twins, Justine. You and I, the two of us against the world. She'll see that. She'll know it. It'll give her support.

Elena would bask and grow in the radiance of their marital love. She would come to her womanhood better for the experience of having been exposed to a marriage that was solid and happy and loving and complete.

That had been the plan, Anthony's dream. And clinging to it in the face of all odds had allowed them both to continue to live in the middle of a lie.

Justine looked from the fireplace to her wedding photograph. They were sitting—had it been some sort of bench?—with Anthony behind her, his hair longer then but his moustache still conservatively trimmed and his spectacles the same wire-rimmed frames. They were both of them gazing intently at the camera, half-smiling as if a show of too much happiness might belie the seriousness of their undertaking. It is, after all, a sober business to embark upon establishing the perfect marriage. But their bodies weren't touching in the picture. His arm wasn't embracing her. His hands didn't reach forward to cover her own. It was as if the photographer who had posed them had somehow seen a truth that they themselves had been unaware of, it was as if the photograph itself would not lie.

For the first time Justine saw what the possibilities were if she did not take action, no matter how little to her liking that action was.

Townee was still playing in the front garden when she left the house. Rather than take the time to shut him up at the rear of the house or in the garage, she called to him, opened the car door, and let him leap inside, unbothered by the fact that he left a muddy paw print on the passenger seat. There wasn't time to consider a minor inconvenience like soiled upholstery.

The car started with the purr of a well-tuned engine. She reversed down the drive and turned east into Adams Road, heading towards the city. Like all men, he was most likely a creature of habit. So he'd be finishing his day near Midsummer Common.

The last of the sunlight fanned out behind the clouds, casting apricot beacons into the sky and throwing the fret-edged shadows of trees like lace silhouettes across the road. In the passenger seat, Townee barked his approval at the sight of hedgerows and cars dashing by. He shifted his weight from right to left front paw, he whined with excitement. Clearly, he thought they were engaged in a game.

And it was a game of sorts, she supposed. But although all the players had taken their positions, the rules were nonexistent. And only the most skilful opportunist among them would be able to shape the horrors of the last thirty hours into a victory that would outlast grief.

The college boathouses lined the north side of the River Cam. They faced south, looking across the river and onto the expanse of Midsummer Common where in the quick-falling darkness, a young girl was grooming one of two horses, her yellow hair streaming out from beneath a cowboy hat and great streaks of mud on the sides of her boots. The horse tossed his head, flicked his tail, and fought against her efforts. But the girl controlled him.

The open land made the wind seem both stronger and colder. As Justine got out of the car, snapping the lead onto Townee's collar, three pieces of orange paper soared like rising birds into her face. She brushed them away. One fell against the bonnet of her Peugeot. She saw Elena's picture.

It was a hand-out from DeaStu calling for information. She grabbed it before it could blow away and stuffed it into the pocket of her coat. She headed towards the river.

At this time of day, none of the rowing teams were out on the water. They generally used the morning for their practices. But the individual boathouses were themselves still open, a row of elegant facades fronting nothing more than capacious sheds. Inside these, some oarsmen and women were ending their day in the way they had begun it, with talk about the season that would come with the end of Lent term. Everything now was focussed upon preparation for that time of competition. Self-confidence and hopes had not yet been dashed by the sight of an unexpected eight flying by as if air and not water were the element against which they matched their strength.

Justine and Townee followed the slow curve of the river, the dog straining at the lead and eager to make the acquaintance of four mallards who swam away from the bank at his approach. He bounded and barked, and Justine wrapped his lead round her hand and gave it a quick tug.

"Behave," she told him. "This isn't a run."

But of course, he would think they were meant to run here. It was water after all. It was what he was used to.

Ahead of them, a lone rower was bringing in a scull, moving against the wind and the current at a furious clip. Justine could imagine that she heard him breathing, for even at this distance and in the failing light she could see the sheen of sweat on his face and she could well envision the heaving of chest that must accompany it. She walked to the edge of the river.

He didn't look up at once as he brought the craft in. Rather, he remained bent over the oars, his head resting on his hands. His hair—thinning at the top and curly elsewhere—was damp and clung to his skull like a newborn's ringlets. Justine wondered how long he had been rowing and whether the activity had done anything at all to assuage whatever emotion he might have felt when first he heard about Elena's death. And he had heard about it. Justine knew that from watching him. Although he rowed daily, he wouldn't have still been here in the dusk, the wind, and the stinging cold, had he not needed to find a physical manner in which he could purge himself of his feelings.

At Townee's whimper to be off and running, the man looked up. For a moment, he said nothing. Nor did Justine. The only sound between them was the scuffling of the dog's nails on the path, the warning honk of ducks who felt the other animal's proximity, and the blare of rock and roll music coming from one of the boathouses. U2, Justine thought, a song she recognised but could not have named.

He got out of the scull and stood on the bank next to her, and she realised, irrelevantly, that she'd forgotten how short he was, perhaps two inches shorter than her own five feet nine.

He said with a futile gesture at the scull, "I didn't know what else to do."

"You might have gone home."

He gave a virtually soundless laugh. It was a reply not of humour, but affirmation. He touched his fingers to Townee's head. "He looks good. Healthy. She took good care of him."

Justine reached into her pocket and pulled out the hand-out which had flown against her. She gave it to him. "Have you seen this?"

He read it. He ran his fingers over the black print and then across the picture of Elena.

"I've seen it," he said. "That's how I found out. No one phoned. I didn't know. I saw it in the senior combination room when I went in for coffee about ten o'clock this morning. And then—" He looked across the river to Midsummer Common where the girl was leading her horse in the direction of Fort St. George. "I didn't know what to do."

"Were you home Sunday night, Victor?"

He didn't look at her as he shook his head.

"Was she with you?"

"For a time."

"And then?"

"She went back to St. Stephen's. I stayed in my rooms." He finally looked her way. "How did you know about us? Did she tell you?"

"Last September. The drinks party. You made love to Elena during the party, Victor."

"Oh God."

"In the bathroom upstairs."

"She followed me up. She came in. She . . ." He rubbed his hand along his jawline. He looked as if he hadn't shaved that day, for the stubble was thick, like a bruise on his skin.

"Did you take off all your clothes?"

"Christ, Justine."

"Did you?"

"No. We stood against the wall. I lifted her up. She wanted it that way."

"I see."

"All right. I wanted it as well. Against the wall. Just like that."

"Did she tell you she was pregnant?"

"Yes. She told me."

"And?"

"And what?"

"What did you plan to do about it?"

He'd been looking at the river, but now he turned back to her. "I planned to marry her," he said.

It wasn't the answer she had come prepared to hear, although the more she thought about it, the less it surprised her. It did leave, however, a slight problem unresolved.

"Victor," she said, "where was your wife Sunday night? What was Rowena doing while you were having Elena?"

11

Lynley was relieved to find Gareth Randolph in the offices of DeaStu, Cambridge University's odd acronym for the Deaf Students' Union. He had tried his room at Queens' College first, only to be directed to Fenners, the central gymnasium for University sports where the boxing team worked out for two hours each day. There, however, in the smaller of the two gyms where he was assailed by the eye prickling smells of sweat, damp leather, athletic tape, chalk, and unwashed workout clothes, Lynley had questioned a lorry-sized heavyweight who had pointed his side-of-beef fist in the direction of the exit and said that the Bant—apparently a reference to Gareth's bantamweight— was sitting by the phones at DeaStu, hoping for a call about the bird who got killed.

"She was his woman," the heavyweight said. "He's taking it hard." And he drove his fists like battering rams into the punching bag which hung from the ceiling, putting his shoulders into each blow with such force that it seemed as if the floor shook beneath him.

Lynley wondered if Gareth Randolph was as powerful a fighter in his own weight class. He considered this question on the way to DeaStu. Anthony Weaver had made allegations about the boy that he could not avoid coupling with Havers' report from the Cambridge police: Whatever Elena had been beaten with, it had left no trace.

DeaStu was housed in the basement of the Peterhouse Library not far from the University Graduate Centre, just at the bottom of Little St. Mary's Lane, little more than two blocks from Queens' College where

Gareth Randolph lived. Its offices were tucked at the end of a low-ceilinged corridor illuminated by bright round globes of light. They had two means of access, one through the Lubbock Room on the ground floor of the library, and the other directly from the street at the rear of the building, not fifty yards away from the Mill Lane footbridge across which Elena Weaver had to have run on the morning of her death. The main office door of opaque glass bore the words *Deaf Students of Cambridge University* and beneath that the less formal *DeaStu* was superimposed over two hands crossed, fingers extended, palms outward.

Lynley had given lengthy thought to how he was going to communicate with Gareth Randolph. He had played round with the idea of calling Superintendent Sheehan to see if he had an interpreter associated with the Cambridge police. He'd never spoken with anyone deaf before, and from what he had gathered over the last twenty-four hours, Gareth Randolph did not have Elena Weaver's facility for reading lips. Nor did he have her spoken language.

Once inside the office, however, he saw that things would take care of themselves. For talking to a woman who sat behind a desk piled with pamphlets, papers, and books was a knobby-ankled, bespectacled girl with her hair in plaits and a pencil stuck behind her ear. As she chatted and laughed, she was signing simultaneously. She also turned in his direction at the sound of the door opening. Here, Lynley thought, would be his interpreter.

"Gareth Randolph?" the woman behind the desk said in answer to Lynley's question and after an inspection of his warrant card. "He's just in the conference room. Bernadette, will you . . . ?" And then to Lynley, "I assume you don't sign, Inspector."

"I don't."

Bernadette adjusted the pencil more firmly behind her ear, grinned sheepishly at this momentary display of self-importance, and said, "Right. Come along with me, Inspector. We'll see what's what."

She led him back the way he had come and then down a short corridor whose ceiling was lined with pipes painted white. She said, "Gareth's been here most of the day. He's not doing very well."

"Because of the murder?"

"He had a thing for Elena. Everyone knew it."

"Did you know Elena yourself?"

"Just to see her. The others"—with a jutting out of her elbows to encompass the area and presumably the membership of DeaStu—"they sometimes like to have an interpreter go with them to their lectures just to make sure they don't miss anything important. That's my function, by the way. Interpreting. I make extra money to see me through the term that way. I get to hear some pretty decent lectures as well. I did a special Stephen Hawking lecture last week. What a job *that* was trying to sign. Astrophysical whatevers. It was like a foreign language.''

"I can well imagine."

"The lecture hall was so quiet you'd have thought God was putting in an appearance. And after it was over, everyone stood and applauded and—'' She rubbed the side of her nose with her index finger. "He's rather special. I quite felt like crying."

Lynley smiled, liking her. "But you never interpreted for Elena Weaver?''

"She didn't use an interpreter. I don't think she liked to."

"She wanted people to think she could hear?''

"Not so much that," Bernadette said. "I think she was proud that she could read lips. It's difficult to do, especially if someone's born deaf. My mum and dad—they're both deaf, you see—they never learned to read much beyond 'three quid please' and 'ta.' But Elena was amazing.''

"How involved was she with the Deaf Students Union?''

Bernadette wrinkled her nose thoughtfully. "I couldn't really say. Gareth'll be able to tell you, though. He's in here."

She led him into a conference room that was roughly the size of an academic classroom. It contained little more than a large, rectangular table covered by green linen. At this, a young man was sitting, bent over a notebook. Lank hair the colour of old wet straw fell across his wide brow and into his eyes. As he wrote, he paused to chew at the fingernails of his left hand.

Bernadette said, "Wait a sec," and from the door she flushed the lights off and on.

Gareth Randolph looked up. He got slowly to his feet, and as he did so, he gathered up from the table a large pile of used tissues, crushing them into a wad in his fist. He was a tall boy, Lynley saw, with a pallid complexion against which the scattered pits of old acne scars stood out in crimson. He wore typical student garb: blue jeans and a sweatshirt onto which had been stencilled the words *What's your sign?* superimposed over two hands making a gesture which Lynley couldn't interpret.

The boy said nothing at all until Bernadette spoke. And even then, since his eyes were on Lynley, he made a rough gesture so that Bernadette had to repeat her first remark.

"This is Inspector Lynley from New Scotland Yard," she said a second time. Her hands fluttered like quick, pale birds just below her face. "He's come to talk to you about Elena Weaver."

The boy's eyes went back to Lynley. He looked him over from head to toe. He replied, hands chopping the air, and Bernadette interpreted simultaneously. "Not in here."

"Fine," Lynley said. "Wherever he likes."

Bernadette's hands flew over Lynley's words, but as they did she continued with, "Speak to Gareth directly, Inspector. Call him *you,* not him. Else it's quite dehumanising."

Gareth read and smiled. His gestures in response to Bernadette's were fluid. She laughed.

"What did he say?"

"He said, Ta, Bernie. We'll make you a deaf woman yet."

Gareth led them out of the conference room and back down the hall to an unventilated office made overly warm by a wheezing radiator. Inside, there was not much space for more than a desk, metal bookshelves on the walls, three plastic chairs, and a separate birch veneer table on which stood a Ceephone identical to those that Lynley had seen elsewhere.

Lynley realised with his first question that he would be at a disadvantage in this sort of interview. Since Gareth watched Bernadette's hands in order to read Lynley's words, there would not be an opportunity to catch a revealing if fleeting expression quickly veiled in his eyes should a question take him unaware. Additionally, there would be nothing to read in his voice, in his tone, in what he stressed or what he deliberately left unaccentuated. Gareth had the advantage of the silence that defined his world. Lynley wondered how, and if, he would use it.

"I've been hearing a great deal about your relationship with Elena Weaver," Lynley said. "Dr. Cuff from St. Stephen's apparently brought you together."

"For her own good," Gareth replied, the hands again sharp and staccato in the air. "To help her. Maybe save her."

"Through DeaStu?"

"Elena wasn't deaf. That was the problem. She could have been, but she wasn't. They wouldn't allow it."

Lynley frowned. "What do you mean? Everyone's said—"

Gareth scowled and grabbed a piece of paper. With a green felt-tip pen he scrawled out two words: *Deaf* and *deaf.* He drew three heavy lines under the upper case *D* and shoved the paper across the desk.

Bernadette spoke as Lynley looked at the two words. Her hands included Gareth in the conversation. "What he means, Inspector, is that Elena was deaf with a lower case *d*. She was disabled. Everyone else round here—Gareth especially—is Deaf with an upper case *D*."

"*D* for different?" Lynley asked, thinking how this assessment went legions to support Justine Weaver's words to him that day.

Gareth's hands took over. "Different, yes. How could we not be different? We live without sound. But it's more than that. Being Deaf is a culture. Being deaf is a handicap. Elena was deaf."

Lynley pointed to the first of the two words. "But you wanted her to be Deaf, like you?"

"Wouldn't you want a friend to run instead of crawl?"

"I'm not sure I follow the analogy."

Gareth shoved his chair backwards. It screeched against the linoleum floor. He went to the bookshelf and pulled down two large leather-bound albums. He dropped them onto the desk. Lynley saw that across each was imprinted the acronym *DeaStu* with the year beneath it.

"This is Deaf." Gareth resumed his seat.

Lynley opened one of the albums at random. It appeared to be a record of the activities in which the deaf students had engaged during the previous year. Each term had its own identifying page on which *Michaelmas, Lent,* or *Easter* had been written in fine calligraphy.

The record consisted of both written documents and photographs. It encompassed everything from DeaStu's American football team whose plays were called by students on the sidelines who beat an enormous drum to signal the team via vibration-code, to dances held with the aid of powerful speakers which conveyed the rhythm of the music in much the same way, to picnics and meetings in which dozens of hands moved at once and dozens of faces lit with animation.

Bernadette said over Lynley's shoulder, "That's called wind-milling, Inspector."

"What?"

"When everyone signs at once like that. All their hands are going. Like windmills."

Lynley continued through the book. He saw three rowing teams whose strokes were orchestrated by coxswains utilising small red flags; a ten-member percussion group who used the movement of an oversized metronome to keep their pulsating rhythm together; grinning men and women in camouflage setting out with banners that read *DeaStu Search and Pellet;* a group of flamenco dancers; another of gymnasts. And in every photograph, participants in an activity were surrounded and supported by people whose hands spoke the language of commonality. Lynley returned the album.

"It's quite a group," he said.

"It's not a group. It's a life." Gareth replaced the albums. "Deaf is a culture."

"Did Elena want to be Deaf?"

"She didn't know what Deaf was until she came to DeaStu. She was taught to think that deaf meant disabled."

"That's not the impression I've been getting," Lynley said. "From what I understand, her parents did everything possible to allow her to fit into a hearing world. They taught her to read lips. They taught her to speak. It seems to me that the last thing they thought was that deaf meant disabled, especially in her case."

Gareth's nostrils flared. He said, "Fug at sht, *fug* 't," and began to sign with hands that pounded through his words.

"There is no fitting into a hearing world. There's only bringing the hearing world to *us*. Make them see us as people as good as they are. But her father wanted her to play at hearing. Read lips like a pretty girl. Talk like a pretty girl."

"That can't be a crime. It is, after all, a hearing world that we live in."

"A hearing world *you* live in. The rest of us without sound get on fine. We don't want your hearing. But you can't believe that, can you, because you think you're special instead of just different."

Again, it was only a slight variation on the theme Justine Weaver had introduced. The deaf weren't normal. But then, for God's sake, neither were the hearing most of the time.

Gareth was continuing. "We are her people. DeaStu. Here. We can support. We can understand. But he didn't want that. He didn't want her to know us."

"Her father?"

"He wanted to make believe she could hear."

"How did she feel about that?"

"How would you feel if people wanted you to play at being something you weren't?"

Lynley repeated his earlier question. "Did she want to be Deaf?"

"She didn't know—"

"I understand that she didn't know what it meant at first, that she had no way of understanding the culture. But once she did know, did she want to be Deaf?''

"She would have wanted it. Eventually.''

It was a telling response. The uninformed, once informed, had not become an adherent to the cause. "So she involved herself with DeaStu solely because Dr. Cuff insisted. Because it was the only way to avoid being sent down.''

"At first that was why. But then she came to meetings, to dances. She was getting to know people.''

"Was she getting to know you?''

Gareth yanked open the centre drawer of the desk. He took out a pack of gum and unwrapped a stick. Bernadette began to reach forward to get his attention, but Lynley stopped her, saying, "He'll look up in a moment.'' Gareth let the moment drag on, but Lynley felt it was probably harder for the boy to keep his eyes fixed upon and his fingers working over the silver wrapper of the Juicy Fruit than it was for himself to wait him out. When at last he looked up, Lynley said,

"Elena Weaver was eight weeks pregnant.''

Bernadette cleared her throat. She said, "My goodness.'' Then, "Sorry.'' And her hands conveyed the information.

Gareth's eyes went to Lynley and then beyond him to the closed door of the office. He chewed his gum with what looked like deliberate slowness. Its scent was liquid sugar in the air.

When he replied, his hands moved as slowly as his jaws. "I didn't know that.''

"You weren't her lover?''

He shook his head.

"According to her stepmother, she'd been seeing someone regularly since December of last year. Her calendar indicates that with a symbol. A fish. That wasn't you? You would have first been introduced to her round then, wouldn't you?''

"I saw her. I knew her. It was what Dr. Cuff wanted. But I wasn't her lover.''

"A bloke at Fenners called her your woman.''

Gareth took a second stick of gum, unwrapped it, rolled it into a tube, popped it into his mouth.

"Did you love her?''

Again, his eyes dropped. Lynley thought of the wad of tissues in the conference room. He looked once again at the boy's pallid face. He said,

"You don't mourn someone you don't love, Gareth," even though the boy's attention was not on Bernadette's hands.

Bernadette said, "He wanted to marry her, Inspector. I know that because he told me once. And he—"

Perhaps sensing the conversation, Gareth looked up. His hands flashed quickly.

"I was telling him the truth," Bernadette said. "I said you wanted to marry her. He knows you loved her, Gareth. It's completely obvious."

"Past. Loved." Gareth's fists were on his chest more like a punch than a sign. "It was over."

"When did it end?"

"She didn't fancy me."

"That's not really an answer."

"She fancied someone else."

"Who?"

"I don't know. I don't care. I thought we were together. And we weren't. That was it."

"When did she make this clear to you? Recently, Gareth?"

He looked sullen. "Don't remember."

"Sunday night? Is that why you were arguing with her?"

"Oh, dear," Bernadette murmured, although she cooperatively continued to sign.

"I didn't know she was pregnant. She didn't tell me that."

"But as to the other. The man she loved. She told you about that. That was Sunday night, wasn't it?"

Bernadette said, "Oh, Inspector, you can't really think that Gareth had anything to do—"

Gareth lunged across the desk and grabbed Bernadette's hands. Then he jerked out a few signs.

"What's he saying?"

"He doesn't want me to defend him. He says there's nothing for me to defend."

"You're an engineering undergraduate, aren't you?" Lynley asked. Gareth nodded. He said, "And the engineering lab's by Fen Causeway, isn't it? Did you know Elena Weaver ran that way in the morning? Did you ever see her run? Did you ever go with her?"

"You want to think I killed her because she wouldn't have me" was his reply. "You think I was jealous. You've got it figured that I killed her because she was giving some other bloke what she wouldn't give me."

"It's a fairly solid motive, isn't it?"

Bernadette gave a tiny mewl of protest.

Gareth said, "Maybe the bloke who got her pregnant killed her. Maybe he didn't fancy her as much as she fancied him."

"But you don't know who he was?"

Gareth shook his head. Lynley had the distinct impression he was lying. And yet he couldn't at the moment come up with a reason why Gareth Randolph would lie about the identity of the man who made Elena pregnant, especially if he truly believed that man might be her killer. Unless he intended to take care of dealing with the man himself, in his own time, on his own terms. And with a blue in boxing, he'd have the odds on his side if it came to taking another by surprise.

Even as Lynley dwelt on this thought, he realised there was yet another possible reason why Gareth might choose not to cooperate with the police. If he was savouring Elena's death at the same time as he mourned it, what better way to prolong his enjoyment than to lengthen the time it would take to bring the criminal to justice. How often had a jilted lover believed that a crime of violence perpetrated by someone else was exactly what the loved one deserved?

Lynley rose to his feet and nodded to the boy. He said, "Thank you for your time," and turned to the door.

On the back of it he saw what he hadn't had the opportunity to notice when he had entered the room. It was hung with a calendar on which the entire year was visible at one glance. So it was not avoidance that had made Gareth Randolph shift his eyes to the door when Lynley had told him of Elena Weaver's pregnancy.

He'd forgotten about the bells. They'd rung at Oxford as well when he was an undergraduate, but somehow the years had taken that memory from him. Now as he stepped out of the Peterhouse Library and began the walk back to St. Stephen's College, the resonant calling of the faithful to Evensong formed an auditory backdrop—like antiphonal chanting—from college chapels across the city. It was, he thought, one of life's most joyous sounds, this ringing of bells. And he found himself regretting the fact that the span of time in which he had given himself over to learning how to understand the criminal mind had allowed him to forget the sheer pleasure of church bells ringing into an autumn wind.

He let sound itself become his most conscious perception as he strolled past the old, overgrown graveyard of Little St. Mary's Church and made the turn onto Trumpington where the jingle of bicycle bells and the metallic clicking of their unoiled gears joined the rumble of evening traffic.

"Go on, Jack," a young man shouted to a retreating bike rider from the doorway of a grocer's shop as Lynley passed. "We'll catch you up at the Anchor. All right?"

"Right." A vague call in return, caught on the wind.

Three girls walked by, engaged in a heated discussion about "that sod, Robert." They were followed by an older woman, high heels snapping against the pavement, pushing a crying baby in a pram. And then lurched by a black-garbed figure of uncertain sex from the folds of whose voluminous coat and trailing scarves came the plaintive notes of "Swing Low, Sweet Chariot" played on harmonica.

Through it all, Lynley heard Bernadette giving voice to Gareth's angry words: We don't want your hearing. But you can't believe that, can you, because you think you're special instead of just bloody different.

He wondered if this had marked the crucial difference between Gareth Randolph and Elena Weaver. *We don't want your hearing.* For because of her parents' well-intentioned if perhaps arguably misguided efforts on her behalf, Elena had been taught to know every moment of her life that something was missing. She had been given something to want. So how could Gareth ever have hoped to win her over to a lifestyle and a culture that she had been taught from birth to reject and overcome?

He wondered what it had been like for the two of them: Gareth dedicated to his people, seeking to make Elena one of them. And Elena merely following the dictates laid down by the Master of her College. Had she feigned interest in DeaStu? Had she feigned enthusiasm? And if she did neither, if she felt contempt, what kind of effect would this have had on the young man who had been given the unwanted assignment of steering her into a society so foreign to that which she had always known?

Lynley wondered what kind of blame—if any—ought to be assessed upon the Weavers for the efforts they had made with their daughter. For in spite of the manner in which they had apparently tried to create an inaccurate fantasy out of the reality of their daughter's life, hadn't they in fact given Elena what Gareth himself had never known? Hadn't they given her her own form of hearing? And if that was the case, if Elena did move with a relative degree of comfort in a world in which Gareth felt himself an alien, how could he come to terms with the fact that he had fallen in love with someone who shared neither his culture nor his dreams?

Lynley paused in front of the multi-spired gatehouse of King's College where lights shone brightly from the porter's lodge. He stared, unseeing, at the collection of bicycles leaning this way and that. A young man was scrawling some sort of notice on a blackboard beneath the gate, while a chatting group of black-gowned academics hurried across the lawn towards the chapel with that self-important stride that appeared to be inherent to senior members of all the colleges who were blessed with the privilege of setting foot to grass. He listened to the continuing echo of the bells, with Great St. Mary's just across King's Parade calling out in a ceaseless, sonorous petition for prayer. Each note cast itself into the emptiness of Market Hill just beyond the church. Each building there caught the sound and flung it back into the night. He listened, he thought. He knew he was intellectually capable of getting to the root of Elena Weaver's death. But as the evening continued to swell with sound, he wondered if he was unprejudicially capable of getting to the root of Elena's life.

He was bringing to the job at hand the preconceptions of a member of the hearing world. He wasn't sure how to shed them—or even if he needed to do so—in order to get at the truth behind her killing. But he did know that only through coming to an understanding of Elena's own vision of herself could he also understand the relationships she shared with other people. And—all previous thoughts on Crusoe's Island aside— for the moment, at least, it seemed that these relationships had to be the key to what had happened to her.

At the far end of the north range of Front Court, an amber rhombus of light melted out onto the lawn as the south door to King's College Chapel slowly opened. The faint sound of organ music drifted on the wind. Lynley shivered, turned up the collar of his overcoat, and decided to join the college for Evensong.

Perhaps a hundred people had gathered in the chapel where the choir was just filing down the aisle, passing beneath the magnificent Florentine screen atop of which angels held brass trumpets aloft. They were led by cross- and incense-bearers, the latter filling the icy chapel air with the heady sweet scent of smoky perfume. And they, along with the congregation, were dwarfed by the breathtaking interior of the chapel itself, whose fan-vaulted ceiling soared above them in an intricate display of tracery periodically bossed by the Beaufort portcullis and the Tudor rose. It formed a beauty that was at once both austere and exalted, like the arcing flight of a jubilant bird, but one who does his sailing against a winter sky.

Lynley took a place at the rear of the chancel from which he could meditate at a distance upon *Adoration of the Magi*, the Rubens canvas that served as the chapel's reredos, softly lit above the main altar. In it, one of the Magi leaned forward, hand outstretched to touch the child while the mother herself presented the baby, as if with the serene confidence that he wouldn't be harmed. And yet even then she must have known what lay ahead. She must have had a premonition of the loss she would face.

A lone soprano—a small boy so tiny that his surplice hung just inches from the floor—sang out the first seven pure notes of a *Kyrie Eleison*, and Lynley lifted his eyes to the stained glass window above the painting. Through it moonlight shimmered in a muted corona, giving only one colour to the window itself, a deep blue faintly touched on its outer edge by white. And although he knew and could see that the crucifixion was what the window depicted, the only section which the moon brought to life was a single face—soldier, apostle, believer, or apostate—his mouth a black howl of some emotion eternally unnamed.

Life and death, the chapel said. Alpha and omega. With Lynley finding himself caught between the two and trying somehow to make sense of both.

As the choir filed out at the end of the service and the congregation rose to follow, Lynley saw that Terence Cuff had been among the worshippers. He had been sitting on the far side of the choir, and now he stood with his attention given to the Rubens, his hands resting in the pockets of an overcoat that was just a shade or two darker than the grey of his hair. Seeing his partial profile, Lynley was struck once again by the man's self-possession. His features did not display the slightest trace of anxiety. Nor did they reveal any reaction to the pressures of his job.

When Cuff turned from the altar, he exhibited no surprise to find Lynley watching him. He merely nodded a greeting, left his pew, and joined the other man next to the chancel screen. He looked round the chapel before he spoke.

"I always come back to King's," he said. "At least twice a month like a prodigal son. I never really feel like a sinner in the hands of an angry God here. A minor transgressor, perhaps, but not a real miscreant. For what kind of God could honestly stay angry when one asks his forgiveness in such architectural splendour?"

"Have you a need to ask forgiveness?"

Cuff chuckled. "I've found it's always unwise to admit one's misdeeds in the presence of a policeman, Inspector."

They left the chapel together, Cuff stopping at the brass collection tray near the door to drop in a pound coin which clanked heavily against an assortment of ten- and fifty-pence pieces. Then they went out into the evening.

"This meets my occasional need to get away from St. Stephen's," Cuff said as they strolled round the west end of the chapel towards Senate House Passage and Trinity Lane. "My academic roots are here at King's."

"You were a senior fellow here?"

"Hmm. Yes. Now it serves as part refuge and part home, I suppose." Cuff pointed towards the chapel spires that rose like sculptured shadows against the night sky. "This is how churches ought to look, Inspector. No one since the Gothic architects has known quite so well how to set fire to emotion with simple stone. You'd think the very material itself would quash the possibility that one might actually feel something at the sight of the finished building. But it doesn't."

Lynley took his lead from the other man's first thought. "What sort of refuge does the master of a college need?"

Cuff smiled. In the weak light, he looked much younger than he had appeared in his library on the previous day. "From political machinations. The battle of personalities. The jockeying for position."

"Everything attending the selection of the Penford Professor?"

"Everything in attendance on a community filled with scholars who have reputations to maintain."

"You've a distinguished enough group set on doing the maintaining."

"Yes. St. Stephen's is lucky in that."

"Is Lennart Thorsson among them?"

Cuff paused, turning to Lynley. The wind was ruffling his hair, and it blew at the charcoal scarf he wore slung round his neck. He cocked his head appreciatively. "You led into that well."

They continued their walk past the back of the old law school. Their footsteps echoed in the narrow lane. At the entrance to Trinity Hall, a girl and boy were engaged in an intent discussion, the girl leaning against the ashlar wall with her head thrown back and tears glittering on her face while the boy spoke urgently in an angry voice, one hand flat against the wall by her head and the other on her shoulder.

"You don't understand," she was saying. "You never try to understand. I don't even think you want to understand any longer. You only want—"

"Can't you ever leave it, Beth? You act like I'm rolling in your knickers every night."

As Lynley and Cuff passed, the girl turned away, her hand to her face. Cuff said quietly, "It always comes down to that sort of give-and-take, doesn't it? I'm fifty-five years old and I still wonder why."

"I should think it's based on the injunctions women grow up hearing," Lynley said. "Protect yourself from men. They only want one thing, and once they get it from you, they'll be fast on their way. Don't give an inch. Don't trust them. Don't trust anyone in fact."

"Is that the sort of thing you'd tell a daughter of yours?"

"I don't know," Lynley said. "I don't have a daughter. I like to think I'd tell her to know her own heart. But then, I've always been a romantic when it comes to relationships."

"That's an odd predisposition in your line of work."

"It is, isn't it?" A car approached slowly, its indicator signalling for Garret Hostel Lane, and Lynley took the opportunity to glance at Cuff as the light from the headlamps struck his face. He said, "Sex is a dangerous weapon in an environment like this. Dangerous for anyone wielding it. Why didn't you tell me about Elena Weaver's charges against Lennart Thorsson?"

"It seemed unnecessary."

"Unnecessary?"

"The girl's dead. There didn't seem to be a point to bringing up something unproved that would only serve to damage the reputation of one of the senior fellows. It's been difficult enough for Thorsson to climb as far as he has at Cambridge."

"Because he's a Swede?"

"A University isn't immune to xenophobia, Inspector. I dare say a British Shakespearean wouldn't have had to jump the academic hurdles Thorsson's had to jump in the last ten years to prove himself worthy. And that despite the fact that he did his graduate work here in the first place."

"Nonetheless, in a murder investigation, Dr. Cuff—"

"Hear me out, please. I don't much like Thorsson personally. I've always had the feeling he's at heart a womaniser, and I've never had time for men of that sort. But he's a sound—if admittedly quixotic—Shakespearean with a solid future ahead of him. To drag his name through the muck in a situation that can't be proved at this point seemed—still seems—a fruitless endeavour."

Cuff shoved both hands back into his overcoat pockets and stopped walking when they came to the gatehouse of St. Stephen's. Two undergraduates hurried by, calling out a hello to him which he acknowledged with a nod of his head. He continued to speak, his voice low, his face in shadow, his back turned to the gatehouse itself.

"It goes beyond that. There's Dr. Weaver to consider. If I bring this matter out into the open with a full investigation, do you think for a moment that Thorsson isn't going to drag Elena's name through the muck in order to defend himself? With his entire career on the line, what kind of tale will he tell about her alleged attempt to seduce him? About the clothes she wore when she came to her supervisions? About the way she sat? About what she said and how she said it? About everything she did to get him into bed? And with Elena not there to argue her case, how will her father feel, Inspector? He's already lost her. Shall we set about destroying his memory of her as well? What purpose does that serve?"

"It might be wiser to ask what purpose it serves to keep everything quiet. I imagine you'd like the Penford Professor to be a senior fellow here at St. Stephen's."

Cuff locked eyes with his. "Your connotation is ugly."

"So is murder, Dr. Cuff. And you can't really argue that a scandal involving Elena Weaver wouldn't cause the search committee for the Penford Chair to think about turning its eyes in another direction. That, after all, is the easiest course of action."

"They're not looking for the easiest. They're looking for the best."

"Basing their decision upon . . . ?"

"Certainly not basing it upon the behaviour of the applicants' children, no matter how outrageous that behaviour may be."

Lynley drew his conclusion from Cuff's use of the adjective. "So you don't really believe Thorsson harassed her. You believe she cooked up this tale because he wouldn't have her when she wanted him."

"I'm not saying that. I'm merely saying there's nothing to investigate. It's his word against hers and she has no word to give us."

"Had you spoken to Thorsson about the charges prior to her death?"

"Of course I'd spoken to him. He denied every one of her accusations."

"What were they exactly?"

"That he'd tried to talk her into sex, that he'd made physical overtures—touching her breasts and thighs and buttocks—that he'd engaged her in discussions about his sex life and a woman he'd once been engaged to and the difficulties she'd had with the enormous size of his erection."

Lynley lifted an eyebrow. "Fairly imaginative material for a young girl to have cooked up, wouldn't you say?"

"Not in this day and age. But it makes no difference because every bit of it was impossible to prove. Unless more than one girl was willing to come forward with an accusation against Thorsson, there was virtually nothing that I could do save speak to the man and warn him off, which I did."

"And you didn't see the harassment accusation as a motive for murder? If there are other girls who might have come forward once the word went out that Elena had turned him in, Thorsson would have been in deeper water then."

"If there are other girls, Inspector. But Thorsson's been a part of the English faculty—and a senior fellow at St. Stephen's—for ten years now without the slightest breath of scandal associated with him. Why this all at once? And why with this one girl who'd already shown herself to be troubled enough to require special regulations just to see that she wasn't sent down?"

"A girl who ended up murdered, Dr. Cuff."

"Not by Thorsson."

"You seem certain enough of that."

"I am."

"She was pregnant. Eight weeks. And she knew it. She seems to have found out the day before Thorsson made a visit to her room. How do you account for that?"

Cuff's shoulders dropped fractionally. He rubbed his temples. "God," he said. "I didn't know about the pregnancy, Inspector."

"Would you have told me about the harassment charges had you known? Or would you have continued to protect him?"

"I'm protecting all three of them. Elena, her father, Thorsson."

"But would you agree that we've just strengthened his motive to kill her?"

"If he's the father of the child."

"But you don't believe he is."

Cuff dropped his hand. "Perhaps I simply don't want to believe it. Perhaps I want to see ethics and morals where they no longer exist. I don't know."

They walked beneath the gatehouse where the porter's lodge stood watch over the comings and goings of the members of the college. They stopped there briefly. The night porter was on duty, and from a room behind the counter that marked his work space, a television was showing scenes from an American cop programme, with lots of fierce gunfire and bodies falling in slow motion, accompanied by fast licks played on an electric guitar. Then a long, slow shot of the hero's face, emerging from the haze, surveying the carnage, mourning its necessity in the life he led as a noble seeker of justice. And a fade-out until next week when more corpses would pile up in the name of justice and entertainment again.

"You've a message," Cuff said from the pigeonholes where he had gone to collect his own. He handed it over, a small piece of paper which Lynley unfolded and read.

"It's from my sergeant." He looked up. "Lennart Thorsson's nearest neighbour saw him outside his house just before seven o'clock yesterday morning."

"That's hardly a crime. He was probably setting off to work a bit early."

"No, Dr. Cuff. He pulled up to the house in his car as the neighbour was opening her bedroom curtains. He was coming home. From somewhere."

12

Rosalyn Simpson climbed the final flight of stairs to her room at Queens' College and not for the first time cursed the choice she had made when her name had been drawn second in the rooms pool last term. Her cursing had nothing to do with the climb itself although she knew that anyone with good sense would have chosen something on the ground floor or something nearer the loo. Instead, she had chosen the L-shaped chamber up under the eaves, with its sloping walls suitable for the dramatic display of her Indian tapestries, its creaking oak floor periodically marred by gaps in the wood, and its extra little room—hardly more than a large cupboard—in which a wash basin stood and into which she and her father had wrestled her bed. It had the added features of half a dozen nooks and crannies where she had placed everything from plants to books, a large storage garret tucked under the eaves into which she sometimes crawled when she wished to disappear from the world—which was generally once a day—and a trap door in the ceiling leading to a passage that gave her access to Melinda Powell's room. This last feature had seemed the most blessed originally, a rather Victorian way in which she and Melinda could be close to each other without everyone knowing the exact nature of their relationship, which at the time was something that Rosalyn had wished to keep to herself. So the passage had been the main reason why she'd chosen the room. It placated Melinda while it preserved her own peace of mind. But now she wasn't so sure about the decision, or about Melinda, or even about their love.

She felt burdened by weights. First was the haversack on her back and the "little package of goodies for you, dear" that her mother had pressed upon her before she left, with tears in her eyes and lips quivering. She had said, "We had such *dreams* for you, Ros," in a fashion that indicated the full extent to which Rosalyn's news—growing out of a mindless birthday promise to Melinda—had hurt her.

"It's just a phase," her father had said more than once during the gruelling thirty-two hours that they'd spent together. And he said it again as Rosalyn left, but this time to her mother. "The dreams are still there, dammit. This is just a phase."

Rosalyn didn't try to disabuse them of the notion. She more than wished it was a phase herself, so she didn't try to tell them that if it was a peculiar, bohemian stage she was going through, she'd been living it actively since she was fifteen years old. She didn't even consider telling them that. It had taken all her energy and courage to bring the subject up in the first place. Arguing against the likelihood of its fading from significance was more than she was willing to take on.

Rosalyn shifted the haversack, felt her mother's package dig into her left shoulder blade, and tried to slough off the heavier, more loathsome weight of her guilt. It seemed to slip and slide round her neck and shoulders like an enormous octopus with tentacles that grew from every part of her life. Her church said it was wrong. Her upbringing said it was wrong. As children, she and her friends had whispered and giggled and shuddered just to think of it. Her own expectations had always called for a man, a marriage, and a family. And still she continued to live in defiance.

Most of the time, she dealt with her life by simply moving forward, one day at a time, filling her time with distractions, keeping her attention focussed upon lectures, supervisions, and practicals, while never giving thought to what the future held for someone like herself. Or if she thought of the future at all, she tried to think of it in the global terms of her childhood when her only dream had been to go to India, to teach and do good and live solely for others.

It was a dream, however, that had lost its definitive clarity on the afternoon five years ago when her fifth form biology mistress had invited her to tea and, along with the cake and scones and clotted cream and strawberry jam, had offered seduction, rich, dark, and mysterious. For a while on the bed in that cottage near the Thames, Rosalyn had felt the contradictory powers of terror and ecstasy driving the blood through her veins. But as the other woman murmured and kissed and explored and caressed, soon enough fear gave way to arousal, which prepared her body for its most acute delight. She hovered on the cutting edge of pain and pleasure. And when pleasure finally took her, she was unprepared for the power of its accompanying joy.

No man had ever been an intimate part of her life since that moment. And no man had ever been as devoted, as loving and concerned as was Melinda. So it had seemed like such a reasonable request, really, that she should tell her parents, coming forward with pride instead of dissembling through paralysis and fear.

"Lesbian," Melinda had said, enunciating each syllable with especial care. "Lesbian, lesbian. It doesn't mean leper."

Entwined in bed one night with Melinda's arms round her and Melinda's slender, splendid, knowing fingers making her body ache with increasing desire, she had made the promise. And she'd just spent the last thirty-two hours at home in Oxford, living through the consequences. She was exhausted.

At the top floor, she paused in front of her door, groping in the pocket of her jeans for the key. It was time for formal dinner—she'd missed the earlier meal—and although she gave a moment's thought to donning her academic gown and joining the others for what was left of the meal, she dismissed the idea. She didn't feel like seeing or talking to anyone.

For that reason primarily, when she opened the door, her spirits drooped further. Melinda was coming across the room. She looked rested and lovely, and her thick sienna hair had been recently washed, for it lay round her face in a wavy mass of natural curls. Rosalyn noted immediately that Melinda wasn't dressed in her usual garb of mid-calf skirt, boots, pullover, and scarf. Instead, she wore white: wool trousers, cowl-necked sweater, and a long gauzy coat that reached just above her ankles. She looked as if she had dressed for celebration. Indeed, she looked disturbingly bridal.

"You're back," she said, coming to Rosalyn's side and grasping her hand as she brushed a kiss across her cheek. "How did it go? Did Mum have apoplexy? Was Dad rushed to hospital clutching weakly at his chest? Did they shriek out *dyke* or just settle for *pervert*? Come on. Tell me. How did it go?"

Rosalyn slipped the haversack from her shoulders and dropped it to the floor. She found that her head was throbbing, and she couldn't remember exactly when it had begun to do so. "It went," she said.

"That's it? No tantrums? No 'How could you do this to your family'? No bitter accusations? No asking what you think granny and the aunts are going to say?"

Rosalyn tried to block from her mind the memory of her mother's face and the look of confusion that had pinched her features. She wanted to forget the sadness in her father's eyes, but more than that she longed to dismiss the guilt that accompanied her realisation of how her parents both were struggling to dismiss their own feelings in the matter, in the process making her feel only so much worse.

"I should think it was quite a scene between you," Melinda was saying with a knowing smile. "Lots of weeping, lots of hair pulling, lots of gnashing of teeth, the requisite blame, not to mention the predictions of hellfire and damnation. The typical middle-class thing. Poor darling, did they abuse you?"

Melinda, Rosalyn knew, had told her own family when she was seventeen in a matter-of-fact, take-it-or-leave-it announcement so typical of her, made during Christmas dinner, sometime between the crackers and the pudding. Rosalyn had heard the story often enough: "Oh, by the way, I'm gay if anyone's particularly interested." They hadn't been. But that was the sort of family Melinda had. So she couldn't imagine what it was like to be the only child of parents who dreamed among other things of a son-in-law and grandchildren and the fragile line of a family continuing into the future for just a bit longer.

"Did your mum push every guilt button there is? She probably did, and I hope you expected it. I did tell you how to answer when she trotted out the 'what about us' line, didn't I? And if you used it properly, then she must have—"

"I really don't want to talk about it, Mel," Rosalyn said. She knelt on the floor, unzipped the haversack, and began unpacking it. Her mother's "goodies from home" she set to one side.

"They really must have gone after you, then. I told you to let me go with you. Why didn't you let me? I could have held my own with both of your parents." She squatted next to Rosalyn. She smelled fresh and clean. "They didn't . . . Ros, they didn't get physical with you, did they? God, your dad didn't *hit* you?"

"Of course not. Look, I just don't want to talk about it. That's it, all right? It's nothing more than that."

Melinda rested back on her heels. She shoved a thick mass of hair behind one ear. She said, "You're sorry you did it, aren't you? I can tell."

"I'm not."

"You are. It had to be done, but you were hoping you could avoid it forever. You were hoping they'd just eventually think you'd become an old maid, weren't you? You didn't want to take a stand. You didn't want to come out."

"That isn't true."

"Or maybe you've been hoping to take the cure. Wake up some morning and whoopee, you're straight. Shove Melinda out of bed and make room for some bloke. Mum and Dad wouldn't ever know anything then."

Rosalyn looked up. She could see the bright shining in Melinda's eyes and the high gloss of colour in her cheeks. It always amazed her that someone so clever and beautiful could also be someone so unsure and afraid.

She said, "I'm not planning on leaving you, Mel."

"You'd like a man, wouldn't you?" Melinda said. "If you could have one. If you could go straight. You'd like it. You'd prefer it. Wouldn't you?"

"Wouldn't you?" Rosalyn asked. She felt terribly weary.

Melinda laughed. The sound was high and giddy. "Men have only one use and we don't even need them for that any longer. Just find a donor and inseminate yourself at home in the loo. They're doing it, you know. I read about it somewhere. In a few more centuries, we'll be generating sperm in laboratories and men as we know them will be completely extinct."

Rosalyn knew it was wiser to say nothing when Melinda felt the spectre of abandonment hovering round her too closely. But she was tired. She was disheartened. She had just endured a marathon session of guilt with her parents largely to please her lover, and she was feeling as most people feel when they have been manipulated into acting in a fashion they might otherwise eschew: resentful. So she replied, against her better judgement:

"I don't hate men, Melinda. I never have. If you do, that's your problem. But it's not one of mine."

"Oh, they're peachy, men are. They're real bricks, the lot of them." Melinda got to her feet and went to Rosalyn's desk. From it she took a bright orange piece of paper, waved it, and said, "These are all over the University today. I saved one for you. This is what men are all about, Ros. Take a look if you like them so much."

"What is it?"

"Just look."

Rosalyn pushed herself to her feet, and, rubbing her shoulders where the haversack had dug into them, she took the piece of paper from Melinda. It was a hand-out, she saw. And then she saw the name in large black letters underneath a grainy photograph: *Elena Weaver*. And then another word: *Murdered*.

A cold chill zig-zagged the length of her spine. She said, "Melinda, what is this?"

"What's been going on round here while you and Mum and Dad were nattering in Oxford."

Numbly, Rosalyn carried the paper to her old rocking chair. She stared at the picture, at the face so familiar to her, at the grin, the chipped tooth, the long flow of hair. Elena Weaver. Her chief competitor. She ran like a god.

"She's in Hare and Hounds," Rosalyn said. "Melinda, I *know* her. I've been to her room. I've—"

"Knew her, you mean." Melinda snatched the paper back, crumpled it, and tossed it into the rubbish basket.

"Don't throw it away! Let me see it! What happened?"

"She was out running by the river early yesterday morning. Someone got her near the island."

"Near the . . . Crusoe's Island?" Rosalyn felt her heart's beating grow heavy and fast. "Mel, that's—" A sudden memory, unbidden, tugged at the fabric of her consciousness, like a shadow becoming substance, like the fragment of a tune. She said slowly, waiting to feel more certain, "Melinda, I need to phone the police."

No matter the fashion she had hoped to use the information about Elena Weaver, colour drained from Melinda's face. Comprehension took its place. "The island. That's where you've been running this term, isn't it? Right along the river. Just like this girl. Rosalyn, promise me you won't run there again. Swear to it, Ros. Please."

Rosalyn was scooping her shoulder bag from the floor. She said, "Come on."

Melinda seemed suddenly to assimilate the intention behind Rosalyn's decision to speak to the police. She said, "No! Ros, if you saw something . . . if you know something . . . Listen to me, you can't do this. Ros, if someone finds out . . . if someone knows you saw something . . . Please. We need to think what might happen. We need to think this through. Because if you saw someone, that means someone probably saw you as well."

Rosalyn was at the door. She was zipping her jacket. Melinda cried out again, "Rosalyn, please! Let's think this through!"

"There's nothing to think about," Rosalyn said. She opened the door. "You can stay here if you want to. I won't be long."

"But where are you going? What are you doing? Rosalyn!" Melinda ran after her frantically.

Having been to Lennart Thorsson's rooms at St. Stephen's and finding them unoccupied, Lynley drove out to the man's house off the Fulbourn Road. It wasn't in an area that seemed at all suited to Thorsson's bad boy, Marxist image, for the trim brick building with its neat tile roof was in a relatively new housing estate, sitting on a street called Ashwood Court. There were perhaps two dozen houses of similar design dotting an area that had once been farmland. Each had its own patch of front lawn, its walled-off rear garden, and its spindly tree, recently planted in the probable hope of creating a neighbourhood that lived up to the street names its developer had chosen: Maple Close, Oak Lane, Paulownia Court.

Somehow, Lynley had expected to find Thorsson's residence in a setting more in line with the political philosophy which he espoused— perhaps one of the terrace houses not far from the railway station or a dimly lit flat above a shop in the city. But he hadn't expected to find his address in the midst of a middle-class neighbourhood whose streets and driveways held Metros and Fiestas and whose pavements were taken up by tricycles and toys.

Thorsson's house at the west end of the cul-de-sac was identical to his neighbour's, and it sat at an angle to the other house so that anyone looking out a front window—from either upstairs or downstairs—would have an unobstructed view of Thorsson's movements. For someone watching for more than a few moments, it would have been difficult to mistake a departure for an arrival. Thus, it would have been impossible to conclude that Thorsson's hurried homecoming at seven in the morning had been anything else.

The lights weren't on in any part of Thorsson's house that could be seen from the street. But Lynley tried the front door anyway, ringing the bell several times. It reverberated hollowly behind the closed door, as if the house held neither furniture nor carpeting to absorb the sound. He stepped back, looked at the upper windows for signs of life. There were none.

He returned to his car and sat for a moment, thinking about Lennart Thorsson, observing the neighbourhood, and reflecting upon the nature of the man himself. He thought of all the young minds, listening to Thorsson expound about his version of Shakespeare, utilising literature more than four hundred years old to promote a political bent that was appearing more and more to be only a convenient guise to hide the basic mundanity of the man beneath. And how dazzling it all was. To take a piece of literature as familiar as one's childhood prayers, to pick and choose lines, to pick and choose scenes, and upon them to hang an interpretation that—under close scrutiny—was potentially more myopic than all the other interpretations it sought to refute. Yet Thorsson's presentation of his material was undeniably beguiling. Lynley had seen that much in the brief time he had stood at the back of the lecture hall in the English Faculty. The man's commitment to his theory was palpable, his intelligence irrefutable, and his manner just dissident enough to encourage a camaraderie that might otherwise not exist with the undergraduates. For what young person could really resist the temptation of rubbing elbows with a rebel?

If this were the case, how unlikely was the possibility that Elena Weaver might have sought out Thorsson, found herself rejected, and cooked up a charge of harassment against him as a bit of revenge? Or how unlikely was the alternative possibility that Thorsson had intentionally involved himself with Elena Weaver, only to discover that she was no easy tumble but rather a woman with entrapment on her mind?

Lynley stared at the house, waiting for answers and knowing that ultimately everything in the case narrowed down to one fact: Elena Weaver was deaf. Narrowed down to one object: the Ceephone.

Thorsson had been to her room. He knew about the Ceephone. All that remained was for him to place the call that had kept Justine Weaver from meeting Elena in the morning. If, in fact, Thorsson knew that Elena ran with her stepmother. If, in fact, he knew how to use the phone in the first place. If, in fact, someone else already with access to a Ceephone hadn't placed the call. If, in fact, there had been a call at all.

Lynley started the Bentley, wound slowly through the streets of the housing estate, and began to evaluate the almost instant antipathy that had developed between Sergeant Havers and Lennart Thorsson. Havers' instincts were generally sound when it came to hypocrisy in her fellow men, and she was anything but xenophobic. She hadn't needed to see Thorsson's home in suburbia to recognise the extent of his affectation. Her play upon Shakespeare earlier in the day indicated that. And Lynley knew her well enough to realise that, having ascertained that Thorsson had been missing from his home in the early hours of the previous day, she would be hot to give him the caution and pin him to the wall of one of Sheehan's interrogation rooms upon her return to Cambridge in the morning. And that's what would happen—that's what solid policework dictated at this point—unless he came up with something else.

In spite of the manner in which their store of facts pointed ineluctably towards Thorsson, Lynley felt discomfited by the very neatness with which everything was falling into place. He knew from experience that murder was often an obviously cut-and-dried affair in which the likeliest suspect was indeed the perpetrator of the crime. But he also knew that some deaths grew from darker places in the soul and from motives far more convoluted than were suggested by the initial evidence. And as the facts and the faces from this particular case drifted in and out of his field of consciousness, he began to weigh the other possibilities, all of them darker than that which was defined by the mere need to dispose of a girl because she was pregnant.

Gareth Randolph, knowing that Elena had a lover, yet loving her all the time himself. Gareth Randolph, with a Ceephone in his office at DeaStu. Justine Weaver, recounting Elena's sexual behaviour. Justine Weaver, with a Ceephone but without her own children. Adam Jenn, seeing Elena regularly at her father's request, his own future tied in to Weaver's promotion. Adam Jenn, with a Ceephone in Anthony Weaver's study in Ivy Court. And everything peculiar about that study, most particularly Sarah Gordon's brief visit to it Monday night.

He made the turn west and began the drive back into Cambridge, recognising the fact that, no matter the day's revelations to the contrary, his mind kept returning to Sarah Gordon. She didn't sit well with him.

You know why, Havers would have argued. You know why she keeps forcing her way into your thoughts. You know who she reminds you of.

He couldn't deny it. Nor could he avoid admitting that at the end of the day when he was most exhausted, he was also most likely to lose the discipline that kept his mind focussed while he was at work. At the end of the day, he was most susceptible to anything and anyone that reminded him of Helen. This had been the case for nearly a year now. And Sarah Gordon was slender, she was dark, she was sensitive, she was intelligent, she was passionate. Still, he told himself, those qualities which she shared with Helen were not the only reasons why he returned to her at a moment when both motive and opportunity were affixing themselves squarely to Lennart Thorsson.

There were other reasons not to eliminate Sarah Gordon. Perhaps they were not as pressing as those which cast blame in Thorsson's direction, but they still existed, nagging at the mind.

You're talking yourself into it, Havers would have said. You're building a case out of dust motes and lint.

But he wasn't so sure.

He didn't like coincidences in the midst of a murder investigation, and—Havers' protests to the contrary—he couldn't avoid seeing Sarah Gordon's presence at the murder scene followed by her presence at Ivy Court that night as coincidental. More than that, he couldn't get away from the fact that she knew Weaver. He had been her student—her private student. She had called him Tony.

Okay, so they were boffing each other, Havers would have continued. So they were doing it five nights a week. So they were doing it in every position known to mankind and in some they invented. So what, Inspector.

He wants the Penford Chair, Havers.

Ah, she would have crowed. Let me get this straight. Anthony Weaver stopped boffing Sarah Gordon—whom, of course, we don't know whether he was boffing in the first place—because he was afraid that if anyone found out, he wouldn't get the Chair. So Sarah Gordon killed his daughter. Not Weaver himself, who probably deserves to be put out of his misery if he's such a gormless twit, but his daughter. Great. When did she do it? How did she carry it off? She wasn't even on the island until seven in the morning and the girl was dead by then. Dead, Inspector, cold, out, kaput, dead. So why are you thinking about Sarah Gordon? Tell me, please, because this is making me nervous. We've walked the path before, you and I.

He couldn't come up with an answer that Havers would find acceptable. She would argue that any exploration of Sarah Gordon at this point was, in fact or fantasy, a pursuit of Helen. She would not accept his essential curiosity about the woman. Nor would she allow for his uneasiness with coincidence.

But Havers wasn't with him at the moment to argue against a course of action. He wanted to know more about Sarah Gordon, and he knew where to find someone with access to the facts. In Bulstrode Gardens.

How convenient, Inspector, Havers would have hooted.

But he made the right turn into Hills Road and dismissed his sergeant's spectral presence.

He arrived at the house at half past eight. Lights were on in the sitting room, filtering through the curtains in lacy strands which fell upon the semi-circle of the drive and glanced off the silver metal of a child's

pantechnicon which lay on its side with one wheel missing. Lynley picked
it up and rang the front bell.

Unlike the previous evening, there was no shouting of children's
voices. Only a few moments of quiet in which he listened to the traffic
passing on the Madingley Road and smelled the acrid odour of leaves
being burnt somewhere in the neighbourhood close by. Then the deadbolt
was drawn and the door was opened.

"Tommy."

It was curious, he thought. For how many years had she greeted him
in this identical fashion, just saying his name and nothing more? Why
had he never before stopped to realise how much it had come to mean to
him—such simplistic idiocy this all was, really—just to hear the cadence
of her voice as she said it?

He handed her the toy. Along with a missing wheel, he noticed that
the lorry's bonnet bore a considerable dent, as if it had been smashed with
a rock or a hammer. "This was in the drive."

She took it from him. "Christian. He's not making a great deal of
progress in the taking-care-of-possessions department, I'm afraid." She
stepped back from the door. "Come in."

He took off his overcoat without invitation this time, hanging it on
a rattan rack just to the left of the front door. He turned to her. She wore
a teal pullover with an ash-coloured blouse beneath it, and the sweater
was smeared in three separate places with what appeared to be spaghetti
sauce. She saw his glance take in the stains.

"Christian again. He's also not making progress in the table manners
area." She smiled wearily. "At least he doesn't offer false compliments
to the cook. And God knows that I've never been much in the kitchen."

He said, "You're exhausted, Helen." He felt his hand go up as if
of its own volition and for a moment the backs of his fingers brushed
against her cheek. Her skin was cool and smooth, like the untroubled
surface of fresh, sweet water. Her dark eyes were on his. A pulse beat
rapidly in the vein on her neck. He said, "Helen," and felt the quick
current of perennial longing that always accompanied the simple, mindless
act of saying her name.

She moved away from him, walked into the sitting room, saying,
"They're in bed now, so the worst is over. Have you eaten, Tommy?"

He found that he still had his hand lifted as if to touch her, and he
dropped it to his side, feeling ever the lovesick fool. He said, "No. Dinner
got past me somehow."

"Shall I make you something?" She glanced down at her pullover.

"Other than spaghetti, of course. Although I don't recall your ever throwing food at the cook."

"Not lately, at least."

"We've some chicken salad. There's a bit of ham left. Some tinned salmon if you like."

"Nothing. I'm not hungry."

She stood near the fireplace where a pile of children's toys leaned against the wall. A wooden puzzle of the United States was balanced on the top. Someone, it appeared, had bitten off the southern end of Florida. He looked from the puzzle to her, saw the lines of weariness beneath her eyes.

He wanted to say, Come with me, Helen, be with me, stay with me. Instead he said merely, "I need to talk to Pen."

Lady Helen's eyes widened. "Pen?"

"It's important. Is she awake?"

"I think so, yes. But"—she glanced warily towards the doorway and the stairs beyond it—"I don't know, Tommy. It's been a bad day. The children. A row with Harry."

"He's not home?"

"No. Again." She picked up the small Florida and examined the damage, then chucked the puzzle piece back with the others. "It's a mess. They're a mess. I don't know how to help her. I can't think what to tell her. She's had a baby she doesn't want. She has a life she can't bear. She has children who need her and a husband who's set on punishing her for punishing him. And my life is so easy, so smooth compared to hers. What can I say that isn't base and blind and entirely useless?"

"Just that you love her."

"Love isn't enough. It isn't. You know that."

"It's the only thing there is, when you cut to the bone. It's the only real thing."

"You're being simplistic."

"I don't think so. If love were simple in and of itself, we wouldn't be in this mess, would we? We wouldn't bother to want to entrust our lives and our dreams into the safekeeping of another human being. We wouldn't bother with vulnerability. We wouldn't expose weakness. We wouldn't risk emotion. And God knows we'd never make a leap of blind faith. We'd never surrender. We'd cling to control. Because if we lose control, Helen, if we lose it for an instant, God knows what the void beyond it is like."

"When Pen and Harry married—"

Frustration seared through him. "This isn't about them. You know that damn well."

They stared at each other. The width of the room separated them. It might have been a chasm. Still, he spoke to her across it, even though he felt the uselessness of saying words that he knew had no power to effect any action, yet saying them anyway, always needing to say them, casting aside caution, dignity, and pride.

"I love you," he said. "And it feels like dying."

Although her eyes looked bright with tears, her body was tense. He knew she wouldn't cry.

"Stop being afraid," he said. "Please. Just that."

She made no reply. But she didn't look away from him, nor did she try to leave the room. He took hope from that.

"Why?" he said. "Won't you tell me that much?"

"We're fine where we are, as we are." Her voice was low. "Why can't that be enough for you?"

"Because it can't, Helen. This isn't about friendship. We aren't chums. We aren't mates."

"We were once."

"We were. But we can't go back to that. At least I can't do it. And God knows I've tried. I love you. I want you."

She swallowed. A single tear slid from her eye, but she brushed it away quickly. He felt torn at the sight of her.

"I always believed it should be jubilation. But whatever it is, it shouldn't be this."

"I'm sorry," she said.

"No more than I," He looked away from her. On the overmantel behind her stood a photograph of her sister and her family. Husband, wife, two children, life's purpose defined. He said, "I still need to see Pen."

She nodded. "Let me get her."

As she left the room, he walked to the window. The curtains were drawn. There was nothing to see. He stared at the rapidly blurring floral pattern on the chintz.

Walk away from it, he told himself fiercely. Make the cut, make it surgical, make it permanent, walk away.

But he couldn't do it. It was, he knew, the great irony of love. That it came out of nowhere, that it had no logic, that it could always be denied and ignored, but that one ultimately paid the price for fleeing it in coin that came from the spirit, from the soul. He'd been witness to the cycle of love and denial in other lives before, generally in womanisers and in men hot after the pursuit of their careers. Hearts were never touched in their cases, so pain was never felt. And why should it be otherwise? The womaniser sought only the conquest of the moment. The career man sought only the glories from his job. Neither was affected by love or sorrow. Either walked off without a backward glance.

His misfortune—if it could be called that—lay in not being of that ilk. Instead of sexual conquest or professional success, he knew only the desire for connection. For Helen.

He heard them on the stairway—quiet voices, slow footsteps—and turned back to the sitting room door. He had known from Helen's words that her sister was not well, but still he was jarred by the sight of her. His face, he knew, was well enough controlled when she walked into the room. But his eyes apparently betrayed him, for Penelope smiled wanly as if in recognition of an unspoken fact and ran ringless fingers through her limp, dull hair.

"You aren't exactly catching me at my best," she said.

"Thank you for seeing me."

Again, the wan smile. She shuffled across the room, Lady Helen at her side. She eased herself into a wicker rocker and drew her dusky pink dressing gown closed at the throat.

"May we offer you something?" she said. "A whisky? Brandy?"

He shook his head. Lady Helen went to the end of the sofa, the nearest spot to the rocking chair, and sat on the edge of it, leaning forward, her eyes on her sister, her hands extended as if to give her support. Lynley took the wingback chair opposite Pen. He tried to gather his thoughts without considering the changes that had come over her and what they meant and how they had to be striking every chord of her younger sister's fear. Deep circles beneath her eyes, complexion mottled and spotty, an angry sore at the corner of her mouth. Unwashed hair, unwashed body.

"Helen tells me you're in Cambridge on a case," she said.

He told her the essentials of the murder itself. As he spoke, she rocked. The chair creaked companionably. He ended with:

"But it's Sarah Gordon who intrigues me. I thought you might be able to tell me something about her. Have you heard of her, Pen?"

She nodded. Her fingers played with the cord of her dressing gown. "Oh yes. For any number of years. There was quite a splash in the local newspaper when she first moved to Grantchester."

"When was this?"

"Some six years ago."

"You're sure about that?"

"Yes. It was"—again the lifeless smile and a shrug—"before the children, and I was working at the Fitzwilliam then. Picture restoring. The museum had a large reception for her. And a showing of her work. Harry and I went. We met her. If you can call it *met*. It was more like being presented to the Queen although that feeling came mostly from the museum directors. Sarah Gordon herself, as I recall, was rather unassuming. Friendly, quite approachable. Not the sort of woman I'd gone expecting to meet, considering all I'd heard and read about her."

"She's that important an artist?"

"Generally speaking, yes. Each piece she creates is a bit of social commentary which usually results in a fair amount of press. At the time I met her, she'd just been named M.B.E., O.B.E., one of the two. I can't recall. She'd done a portrait of the Queen that had been well-received by the critics—some of them were actually calling it 'the conscience of the nation' or some such critical nonsense. She'd had several successful showings at the Royal Academy. She was being touted as the new darling of art."

"Interesting," Lynley said, "because she's not what one might call a modern artist, is she? One would think that the darling of the art world would have to be forging into some kind of new territory. But I've seen her work, and she doesn't seem to be doing that."

"Painting soup tins, you mean?" Pen smiled. "Or shooting herself in the foot, making a film of the event, and calling it performance art?"

"At the extreme, I suppose."

"What's more important than coming up with the fad of the moment is having a style that catches the emotional fancy of collectors and critics, Tommy. Like Jurgen Gorg's Venice carnival pieces. Or Peter Max's early fantasy canvases. Or Salvador Dalí's surrealistic art. If an artist has a personal style, then he *is* forging ahead. If that style gains international approbation, then his career is made."

"Hers is?"

"I should say so, yes. Her style is distinct. It's crisp. Very clear. According to whatever p.r. machine it was that orchestrated her bow to the art world years ago, she even grinds her own pigments like some sort of modern Botticelli—or at least she did at one time—so her colours in oil are wonderful as well."

"She talked about being a purist in the past."

"That's always been part of her persona. As has the isolation. Grantchester, not London. The world comes to her. She doesn't go to the world."

"You never worked with her canvases while you were at the museum?"

"What need would I have? Her work's recent, Tommy. It doesn't need to be restored."

"But you've seen them. You're familiar with them."

"Yes, of course. Why?"

Lady Helen said, "Is her art at the root of this, Tommy?"

He gave his attention to the spotted brown rug that partially covered the floor. "I don't know. She said she hadn't done anything artistically in months. She said she was afraid that she'd lost the passion to create. The morning of the murder was the day she'd designated to start painting—or sketching, or something—again. It seemed like a superstition of hers. Paint on this day, paint at this spot, or give it up forever. Is that possible, Pen? That someone would give over creating—would actually lose it somehow—and find the struggle to come back so enormous that it would end up tied in to exterior influences such as where one paints and what one paints and exactly at what time one paints?"

Penelope stirred in her chair. "You can't be that naive. Of course it's possible. People have gone mad over the belief that they've lost the power to create. People have killed themselves over it."

Lynley raised his head. He saw that Lady Helen was watching him. Both of them had leaped to the same conclusion with Penelope's final words. "Or kill someone else?" Lady Helen said.

"Someone who got in the way of creativity?" Lynley asked.

"Camille and Rodin?" Penelope said. "They certainly killed each other, didn't they? At least metaphorically."

"But how could this University girl have got in the way of Sarah Gordon's creativity?" Lady Helen asked. "Did they even know each other?"

He thought of Ivy Court, her use of the name Tony. He dwelt on every conjecture he and Havers had developed to explain Sarah Gordon's presence there on the previous night.

"Perhaps it wasn't the girl who got in her way," he said. "Perhaps it was her father." Yet even as he spoke, he could list the arguments against that conclusion. The call to Justine Weaver, the knowledge of Elena's running, the entire question of time, the weapon that had been used to beat her, the disposal of that weapon. The relevant issues were motive, means, and opportunity. He couldn't argue that Sarah Gordon had any of them.

"I mentioned Whistler and Ruskin while I was talking to her," he said pensively. "She reacted to that. So perhaps her failure to create over the last year grew out of some critic's hatchet-job of her work."

"That's a possibility, if she'd had negative criticism," Penelope said. "But she hasn't?"

"Nothing major that I know of."

"So what stops the flow of creativity, Pen? What impedes passion?"

"Fear," she said.

He looked at Lady Helen. She dropped her eyes from his. "Fear of what?" he asked.

"Failure. Rejection. Offering something of the self to someone—to the world—and having it stomped to bits. That would do it, I should guess."

"But that didn't happen to her?"

"Not to Sarah Gordon. But that doesn't necessarily mean that she isn't afraid it might happen in the future. Lots of people are felled by their own success."

Penelope looked towards the door as, in the other room, the refrigerator's motor coughed and whirred. She got to her feet. The rocker creaked a final time with her movement.

"I'd not thought about art for at least this last year." She brushed her hair back off her face and smiled at Lynley. "How odd. It was quite nice to talk about it."

"You've got a lot to say."

"Once. Yes. I did have once." She headed towards the stairway and waved him back when he began to rise. "I'm going to check on the baby. Good night, Tommy."

"Good night."

Lady Helen said nothing until her sister's footsteps sounded along the upper corridor, until a door opened and shut. Then she turned to Lynley.

"That was good for her. You must have known it would be. Thank you, Tommy."

"No. Pure selfishness. I wanted information. I thought Pen could provide it. That's all of it, Helen. Well, not quite. I wanted to see you. There doesn't seem to be an end to that."

She got to her feet. He did likewise. They headed for the front door. He reached for his overcoat, but turned to her impulsively before he took it from the stand.

He said, "Miranda Webberly's playing jazz tomorrow night at Trinity Hall. Will you come?" When she glanced towards the stairs, he went on with, "A few hours, Helen. Pen can deal with them alone. Or we can collar Harry at Emmanuel. Or bring in one of Sheehan's constables. That's probably the best bet for Christian anyway. So will you come? Randie plays a mean trumpet. According to her father, she's become a female Dizzy Gillespie."

Lady Helen smiled. "All right, Tommy. Yes. I'll come."

He felt his heart lift, despite the probability that she was accommodating him only as a means of showing her gratitude for having taken Pen away from her malaise for a few minutes. "Good," he said. "Half past seven, then. I'd suggest we have dinner as well, but I won't push my luck." He took his overcoat from the rack and slung it over his shoulder. The cold wouldn't bother him. A moment of hope seemed enough protection against anything.

She knew what he was feeling, as she always did. "It's just a concert, Tommy."

He didn't avoid her meaning. "I know that. Besides, we couldn't possibly make it to Gretna Green and back in time for Christian's breakfast, could we? But even if we could, doing the dread deed in front of the local blacksmith would never be my idea of a way to get married, so you're relatively safe. For an evening, at least."

Her smile widened. "That's an enormous comfort."

He touched her cheek. "God knows I want you to be comfortable, Helen."

He waited for her to move, tried to make her do so through allowing himself if only for a moment to feel the sheer, telling force of his own desire. Her head tilted slightly, pressing her cheek against his hand.

He said, "You won't fail this time. Not with me. I won't let you."

"I love you," she said. "At the bottom of it all."

13

"Barbara? Lovey? Have you gone to bed? Because the lights are out and I don't want to disturb you if you're asleep. You need your sleep. It's your beauty sleep, I know. But if you're still up, I thought we might talk about Christmas. It's early, of course, but still one wants to be prepared with gift ideas and decisions about which invitations to accept and which to decline."

Barbara Havers closed her eyes briefly, as if by that activity she could shut out the sound of her mother's voice. Standing in the darkness at her bedroom window, she looked down on the back garden where a cat was slinking along the top of the fence that separated their property from that of Mrs. Gustafson. Its attention was speared onto the snarl of weeds that grew in place of what once had been a narrow strip of lawn. He was hunting a rodent. The garden was probably swarming with them. Barbara saluted him silently. Have at them, she thought.

Near her face, the curtains gave off the odours of old cigarette smoke and heavy dust. Once a crisp, starched white cotton sprigged with clusters of forget-me-nots, they hung limp and grey, and against this background of grime the cheerful blue flowers had long since given up the effort of contrast. Now they looked largely like smudges of charcoal set against an ever-darkening, bleak field of ash.

"Lovey?"

Barbara heard her mother tottering along the upstairs passage, her mules alternately shuffling and slapping against the bare floor. She knew she ought to call out to her, but instead she prayed that before she reached the bedroom, her mother's fleeting attention would make the jump to something else. Perhaps to her brother's bedroom which, although it long since had been cleared of his belongings, often still proved enough of a lure that Mrs. Havers would wander into it, talking to her son as if he were still alive.

Five minutes, Barbara thought. Just five minutes of peace.

She'd been home for some hours, arriving to find Mrs. Gustafson sitting erect on a kitchen chair at the foot of the stairs and her mother above in her bedroom, crumpled on the edge of the bed. Mrs. Gustafson was curiously armed with the hose of the vacuum cleaner, her mother was bewildered and frightened, a shrivelled figure in the darkness who had lost the simple knowledge of how to operate her bedroom lights.

"We had ourselves a bit of a scuffle. She's been wanting your father," Mrs. Gustafson had said when Barbara came in the door. Her grey wig had been pulled slightly askew so that on the left its curls hung down too far below her ear. "She started looking through the house calling out for her Jimmy. Then she wanted the street."

Barbara's eyes fell to the hose of the vacuum.

"Now, I din't hit her, Barbie," Mrs. Gustafson said. "You know I wouldn't hit your mum." Her fingers first curled round the hose then caressed its worn covering. "Snake," she said confidentially. "She does behave when she sees it, luv. I just wave it a bit. That's all I have to do."

For a moment, Barbara felt as if her blood had congealed, rendering her immobile and incapable of speech. She felt wedged solidly between two conflicting needs. Words and actions were called for, some sort of castigation of the elderly woman for her blind stupidity, for resorting to terrorising instead of tending. But, far more important, placation was required. For if Mrs. Gustafson drew the line on what she was willing to endure, they were lost.

So in the end, despising herself, creating a new, more capacious reservoir in her conscience to hold the guilt, she settled upon saying, "It's hard when she gets confused, I know. But if you frighten her, don't you think she gets worse?" and all the time she hated herself for the tone of reason she employed and the underlying plea for understanding and co-operation. This is your mother, Barbara, she told herself. This isn't an animal we're talking about. But it made no difference. She was talking about caretaking. She had long ago abjured the quality of life.

"She does for a bit," Mrs. Gustafson said, "which is why I phoned you, luv, because I thought she'd lost what few beans she has left. But she's fine now, isn't she? Not a peep out of her. You should have stayed in Cambridge."

"But you phoned for me to come home."

"Yes, I did, didn't I? A bit of a panic that was, when she wanted her Jimmy and she wouldn't drink her tea or eat the nice egg sandwich I'd made. But she's fine now. Go on up. Have a look. She may even have dropped off for a bit of a kip. The way babies do, you know. Just cry themselves to sleep."

Which went a great distance to let Barbara know what the last few hours prior to her arrival had been like in the house. Except that this wasn't a baby crying itself to physical exhaustion. This was an adult, whose exhaustion was one of the mind.

She had found her mother hunched over on the bed, with her head on her knees and her face directed towards the chest of drawers next to the window. When Barbara crossed the room to her, she saw that her mother's spectacles had slipped off her nose and lay on the floor, leaving her vague blue eyes looking even more detached than they normally did.

"Mum?" she said. She hesitated about switching on the light on the bedside table, afraid it might frighten her mother in some further fashion. She touched the older woman's head. Her hair felt very dry, but it was soft like wispy bits of cotton wool. It would be nice to get her a perm, Barbara thought. She'd like that, Mum would. If she didn't forget where she was in the middle of the treatment and try to flee the hairdresser's when she saw her head covered by lumpy coloured rods the purpose of which she no longer understood.

Mrs. Havers stirred, just a small movement of her shoulders as if she were trying to rid herself of an unwanted burden. She said, "Doris and I played this afternoon. She wanted a tea party and I wanted jacks. We tiffed over it. But then we had both."

Doris was her mother's older sister. She'd died as a teenager during the Blitz. She'd not had the courtesy of adding to the family history by being eliminated by a German bomb, however. Instead, it was an inglorious but nonetheless appropriate finish to a life that had been characterised by unfailing rapacity: She'd choked to death on a piece of black market pork which she'd whipped off her brother's plate at Sunday dinner when he left the table to make an adjustment to the wireless out of which, like a saviour, Winston Churchill was due to speak.

Barbara had heard the story often enough as a child. Chew everything forty times, her mother would say, else you'll end up stiff like your auntie Doris.

"I've prep to do for school, but I don't like prep," her mother went on. "I played instead. Mummy won't like that. She'll ask. And I don't know what to say."

Barbara bent over her. "Mum," she said. "It's Barbara. I'm home. I'm going to turn on the light. It won't scare you, will it?"

"But the blackout. We must be very careful. Have you drawn the curtains?"

"It's all right, Mum." She switched on the lamp and sat on the bed at her mother's side. She put her hand on her shoulder and squeezed lightly. "Okay, Mum? That better?"

Mrs. Havers' eyes went from the window to Barbara. She squinted. Barbara reached for her spectacles, polished away a grease spot on one of the lenses by rubbing it against her own trouser leg, and slipped them back on her mother's nose.

"She has a snake," Mrs. Havers said. "Barbie, I don't like snakes and she's brought one with her. She brings it out and she holds it and she tells me what it wants me to do. She says snakes crawl up you. She says they crawl *inside*. But it's so big and if it gets inside me, I'll—"

Barbara put her arm round her mother. She crouched to duplicate her mother's position. They were face-to-face, heads resting on knees. "There's no snake, Mum. It's the vacuum cleaner. She's trying to frighten you. But she wouldn't do that if you'd just manage to do what she says. She wouldn't even bother. Can you try to behave?"

Mrs. Havers' face clouded. "Vacuum cleaner? Oh no, Barbie, it was a snake."

"But where could Mrs. Gustafson have got a snake?"

"I don't know, lovey. But she has it. I've seen it. She holds it and waves it."

"She's holding it now, Mum. Downstairs. It's the vacuum cleaner. Would you like to go down and have a look at it with me?"

"No!" Barbara felt her mother's back go rigid. Her voice began to rise. "Because I don't like snakes, Barbie. I don't want them crawling up me. I don't want them inside. I don't—"

"Okay, Mum, okay."

She saw that she couldn't pit her mother's frail coping skills in psychological warfare against Mrs. Gustafson. *It's just the vacuum, Mum, isn't Mrs. Gustafson silly to try to scare you with it* was not going to work to maintain the fragile peace in the house. Their peace was too volatile, especially when it rested on her mother's failing ability to stay firmly grounded in the here and now.

She wanted to say, "Mrs. Gustafson's as afraid as you are, Mum, that's why she resorts to frightening you when you get a bit wild," but she knew her mother would not understand. So she said nothing. She merely drew her mother close to her and thought with longing and loss of that studio in Chalk Farm where she had stood beneath the false acacia and allowed herself a moment to dream of hope and independence.

"Lovey? Are you still up?"

Barbara turned from the window. Moonlight made the room a place of silver and shadow. It fell in a band across her bed and pooled round the odd, ball-and-claw legs on the chest of drawers. The full-length mirror that hung on the door of the built-in clothes cupboard—"Look at these, Jimmy," her mother had said. "What a nice touch! We won't need wardrobes here."—reflected the light in a shaft of white against the opposite wall. She'd hung a cork board there when she'd turned thirteen years old. It was supposed to hold all the souvenirs of her adolescence: programmes from the theatre, invitations to parties, mementoes from school dances, a dried flower or two. It held nothing at all for the first three years. And then she'd come to realise it never would unless she pinned to it something more than unrealistic dreams. So she'd clipped newspaper articles, first human interest stories about babies and animals, then intriguing pieces about small acts of violence, and finally sensational columns on murder.

"Not the thing for young ladies," her mother had sniffed.

No indeed. Not the thing for young ladies.

"Barbie? Lovey?"

Her door was half-closed and Barbara heard her mother's fingernails scratching against it. If she was absolutely quiet, she knew there was a slight chance that her mother would go away. But it seemed an unnecessary cruelty after what she'd been through that day. So she said:

"I'm awake, Mum. I've not gone to bed."

The door swung inward. Light from the passage behind her acted as accent to Mrs. Havers' gaunt frame. Especially her legs, human spindles with bulbous knees and ankles that were emphasised by the fact that her housecoat was rucked up and her nightdress too short. She toddled into the room.

"I did a bad today, Barbie, didn't I?" she said. "Mrs. Gustafson was to spend the night with me here. I remember you said that this morning, didn't you? You were going to Cambridge. So I must have done a bad if you're home.''

Barbara welcomed the moment of rare lucidity. She said, ''You got confused.''

Her mother stopped a few feet away from her. She'd managed a bath on her own—with just two quick supervisory visits—but she hadn't done as well with the post-ablutionary rites, for she'd doused herself with so much cologne that it seemed to surround her like a psychic aura.

''Is it near Christmas, lovey?'' Mrs. Havers asked.

''It's November, Mum, the second week of November. It's not too far from Christmas.''

Her mother smiled, obviously relieved. ''I *thought* it was near. It gets cold round Christmas, doesn't it, and it's been like that these past few days, so I thought it must be Christmastime. With the fairy lights on Oxford Street and those lovely displays in Fortnum and Mason. And seeing Father Christmas talking to the children. I thought it was near.''

''And you were right,'' Barbara said. She was feeling enormously weary. Her eyelids seemed pricked by thousands of pins. But at least the burden of further dealings with her mother seemed lifted for a moment. She said, ''Ready for bed, Mum?''

''Tomorrow,'' her mother said. She nodded as if satisfied with her decision. ''We'll do it tomorrow, lovey.''

''Do what?''

''Speak to Father Christmas somewhere. You must tell him what you want.''

''I'm a bit old for Father Christmas. And at any rate, I've got to go back to Cambridge in the morning. Inspector Lynley's still there. I can't leave him on his own. But you remember that, don't you? I'm on a case in Cambridge. You remember that, Mum.''

''And we've all the invitations to sort through and the gifts to decide upon. We'll be busy tomorrow. And busy, busy, busy as bees until after the new year.''

The respite had been brief indeed. Barbara took her mother by her bony shoulders and began to guide her gently from the room. She chattered on.

''Daddy's the hardest to buy for, isn't he? Mum's no problem. She's got such a sweet tooth that I always know if I can just find chocolates— you know the kind she loves—I'll be all right. But Dad's a trick. Dorrie, what're you going to get Dad?''

''I don't know, Mum,'' Barbara said. ''I just don't know.''

They managed the passage to her mother's bedroom where the duck-shaped light she loved was burning on the bedside table. Her mother continued her Christmas conversation, but Barbara tuned it out, feeling a tumour of depression begin its slow growth in her chest.

She fought it off by telling herself that there was a purpose behind it all. She was being tested. This was her Golgotha. She tried to convince herself that if nothing else the day had taught her that she couldn't leave her mother for the night with Mrs. Gustafson, and having that knowledge now, under circumstances when she had been close enough to get back home quickly, was so much better than . . .

Than what? she wondered. Than if she had been called home from an exotic holiday she would never take, in a place she would never see, with a man she would never know, in whose arms she would never lie?

She shoved the thought aside. She needed to get back to work. She had to have a focal point for her thoughts that was anywhere else but in this house in Acton.

"Perhaps," her mother was saying as Barbara pulled the covers up and tucked them under the mattress, hoping the gesture would seem like concern for her warmth rather than a desire to keep her anchored to the bed, "perhaps we should take a holiday at Christmas and not worry about a thing. What d'you think of that?"

"It's a grand idea. Why don't you work on it tomorrow? Mrs. Gustafson can help you sort through your brochures."

Mrs. Havers' face clouded. Barbara removed her spectacles and laid them on the table by the bed. "Mrs. Gustafson?" her mother said. "Barbie, who's she?"

14

Lynley saw Sergeant Havers' old Mini trundling its way down Trinity Lane at seven-forty the next morning. He had just left his room in Ivy Court and was walking to his car, which he'd parked in a small space on Trinity Passage, when the familiar rust-eaten sardine-tin-on-wheels that served as Havers' transportation made the turn at the far end of Gonville and Caius College, sending out a noxious cloud of exhaust fumes into the cold air as Havers changed gear round the curve. Seeing him, she tooted the horn once. He lifted a hand in acknowledgement and waited for her to pull to a stop. When she did so, he opened the passenger door without word or ceremony and folded his lengthy frame into the confines of the cramped front seat. Its upholstery was shiny with age and wear. A broken spring bulged against the material.

The Mini's heater was roaring with ineffectual enthusiasm against the morning cold, creating a palpable pool of warmth that rose from the floor to the level of his kneecaps. From his waist up, however, the air was ice tinctured with the odour of the cigarette smoke which had long ago altered the vinyl ceiling from beige to grey. Havers, he saw, was doing her best to contribute to the vinyl's continuing metamorphosis. As he banged the car door shut, she stubbed one cigarette out in the ashtray and immediately lit another.

"Breakfast?" he asked mildly.

"Nicotine on toast." She inhaled with pleasure and brushed some fallen ash off the left leg of her worsted trousers. "So. What's up?"

He didn't answer at once. Rather, he cracked the window a few inches to let in a bit of fresh air and turned back to observe her frankly earnest gaze. Her expression was resolutely cheerful, her manner of dress appropriately haphazard. Every necessary sign was there, painting the picture of all's-right-with-the-world. But her hands gripped the steering wheel far too tightly and a tension round her mouth belied her casual tone.

"What happened at home?" he asked her.

She drew in on her cigarette again and gave its glowing tip her attention. "Nothing much. Mum had a spell. Mrs. Gustafson panicked. It was no big deal."

"Havers—"

"Look, Inspector, you could reassign me and ask Nkata to come up and assist. I'd understand. I know it's rotten with me coming and going and heading back to London so early in the evening. Webberly won't like it much if you sack me on this, but if I make an appointment and go at it with him privately, he ought to understand."

"I can cope, Sergeant. I don't need Nkata."

"But you've got to have someone. You can't do it all alone. This flaming job requires assistance and you've every right to ask for it."

"Barbara, this isn't about the job."

She stared out into the street. At the gatehouse of St. Stephen's College, the porter came out to help a middle-aged woman in a heavy coat and scarf who had climbed off a bicycle and was attempting to manoeuvre it into position among dozens of other bikes against the wall. She gave the handlebars over to him and watched, chatting with great animation, as he shoved the bike among the others and locked it up. They went inside the gatehouse together.

Lynley said, "Barbara."

Havers stirred. "I'm dealing with it, sir. At least, I'm trying to. Let's just get going, shall we?"

He sighed, reached for the seat belt, and brought it over his shoulder. "Head for the Fulbourn Road," he said. "I want to drop in on Lennart Thorsson."

She nodded, reversed the car into Trinity Passage, and turned them in the direction from which she'd come only moments before. All round them the city was coming to life. The occasional early-rising student pedalled off to begin a day of study, as bedders arrived to see to the rooms. On Trinity Street two sweepers unloaded brooms and dustpans from a yellow trolley while three workmen climbed a scaffolding nearby. The merchants in Market Hill were setting up their stalls for the day's business, laying out fruit and vegetables, setting up bolts of bright material, folding T-shirts, blue jeans, and Indian dresses, gathering autumn flowers into dazzling bouquets. Buses and taxis vied for position on Sidney Street, and as Lynley and Havers headed out of town, they passed the morning commuters coming in from Ramsey Town and Cherry Hinton, no doubt ready to take their places behind desks, in the libraries, in the gardens, and before the kitchen stoves of the University's twenty-eight colleges.

Havers didn't speak until they were rumbling their way—with an extensive emission of exhaust and accompanying sputters and belches from the engine—past Parker's Piece, across whose extensive green the police station squatted like an impassive guardian. Its double row of windows, reflecting the cloudless sky, turned it to a draughtboard of blue and grey.

"You got my message, then," Havers said. "About Thorsson. You didn't see him last night?"

"He was nowhere to be found."

"Does he know we're on our way?"

"No."

She crushed her cigarette out, did not light another. "What do you think?"

"Essentially that he's too good to be true."

"Because we've got black fibres on the body? Because we've caught him with motive and opportunity?"

"He does seem to have both. And once we have an idea of what was used to bludgeon her, we may find he had the means as well." He reminded her of the wine bottle which Sarah Gordon had said was left at the scene and told her of the impression of that same bottle which he had seen in the damp earth on the island. He offered his theory of how the bottle might have been used and left behind among the rest of the rubbish.

"But still you don't like Thorsson as our killer. I can see it on your face."

"It seems too clean a case, Havers. I've got to admit I'm not comfortable with that."

"Why?"

"Because murder in general—and this one in particular—is a dirty business."

She slowed for a traffic light and watched as a back-gnarled woman wearing a long black coat slowly negotiated her way across the street. Her eyes were on her feet. She pulled a collapsible luggage trolley behind her. Nothing was in it.

When the light changed, Havers spoke again. "I think Thorsson's dirty as a dog, Inspector. It surprises me that you can't see it as well. Or is seducing school girls not dirty to another man as long as the girls don't complain?"

He was unruffled by the indirect challenge to argue. "These aren't school girls, Havers. We can call them that for want of a better word. But that's not what they are."

"All right. Young women in subordinate positions. Does that make it right?"

"No. Of course not. But we've no direct proof of seduction yet."

"She was pregnant, for God's sake. Someone seduced her."

"Or she seduced someone. Or they seduced each other."

"Or—as you said yourself yesterday—she was raped."

"Perhaps. But I'm having second thoughts about that."

"Why?" Havers' tone was belligerent, a suggestion that Lynley's response implied impossibility. "Or are you of the typical male opinion that she would have lain back and enjoyed the experience?"

He glanced in her direction. "I think you know better than that."

"Then what's your point?"

"She reported Thorsson for sexual harassment. If she was willing to do that and face the possibility of a potentially embarrassing investigation into her own behaviour, I can't see that she'd let a rape go unmentioned."

"What if it was date rape, Inspector? Some bloke she was seeing but didn't expect or want to get involved with?"

"Then you've just put Thorsson out of the picture, haven't you?"

"You *do* think he's innocent." Her fist hit the steering wheel. "You're looking for a way to exonerate him, aren't you? You're trying to pin this on someone else. Who?" She flashed a knowing look at him a second after she asked the question. "Oh no! You *can't* be thinking—"

"I'm not thinking anything. I'm looking for the truth."

She swung the car to the left in the direction of Cherry Hinton, passing a common that was rich with yellow-leaved horse chestnuts wearing a new winter's growth of moss on their trunks. Beneath them, two women pushed prams side by side, their heads tilted together, their eager conversation sending out rapid puffs of steam in the air.

It was just after eight when they drove into Thorsson's housing estate. In the narrow drive of his house on Ashwood Court, a fully restored TR–6 was sitting, its bulbous green wings gleaming in the morning light. They pulled up behind it, so close that the front of the Mini nosed into its boot like a careful insult.

"Nice bit, that," Havers said as she looked it over. "Just the sort of thing one expects one's local Marxist to drive."

Lynley got out and went to inspect the car. Aside from the windscreen, it was beaded with moisture. He pressed his hand to the smooth surface of the bonnet. He could feel the remnants of the engine's warmth. "Another morning arrival," he said.

"Does that make him innocent?"

"It certainly makes him something."

They went to the door where Lynley rang the bell as his sergeant dug through her shoulder bag and brought forth her notebook. When there was no immediate answer and no apparent movement in the house, he rang the bell a second time. A distant shout drifted down to them, a man's voice calling out the words, "A moment." More than one moment passed as they stood waiting on the sliver of concrete that served as the front step, watching two sets of neighbours hurry off to work and a third usher two children into an Escort that idled in the drive. Then behind the five opaque shafts of glass in the door, a shadow moved as someone approached.

The deadbolt turned. Thorsson stood in the entry. He wore a black velour dressing gown which he was in the process of belting. His hair was damp. It hung loose round his shoulders. He had nothing on his feet.

"Mr. Thorsson," Lynley said by way of greeting.

Thorsson sighed, looked from Lynley to Havers. "Christ," he said. "Wonderful. We've got *snuten* again." Roughly, he ran a hand back through his hair. It fell onto his forehead in a boyish tangle. "What is it with you two? What do you want?"

He didn't wait for an answer. Instead, he turned from the door and walked down a short corridor towards the rear of the house where a door opened into what appeared to be the kitchen. They followed and found him pouring himself a mug of coffee from an impressive-looking coffee maker that sat on the work top. He began to drink, making a great deal of noise, first blowing then slurping. His moustache quickly became beaded with the liquid.

"I'd offer you some, but I require the whole pot to wake up in the morning." That said, he added more to his cup.

Lynley and Havers took places at a glass and chrome table sitting in front of French doors. These led into a small rear garden where flagstones formed a terrace which held a set of outdoor furniture. One of the pieces was a wide chaise longue. A rumpled blanket lay across it, limp with the damp.

Lynley looked thoughtfully from the chaise to Thorsson. The other man glanced out the kitchen window in the direction of the furniture. Then he looked back to Lynley, his face a perfect blank.

"We seem to have taken you from your morning bath," Lynley said.

Thorsson swallowed some coffee. He was wearing a flat gold chain round his neck. It glittered like snakeskin against his chest.

"Elena Weaver was pregnant," Lynley said.

Thorsson leaned against the work top, holding his coffee mug balanced against his arm. He looked uninterested, overcome with ennui. "And to think I had no opportunity to join her in celebrating the future blessed event."

"Was a celebration in order?"

"I wouldn't know, would I?"

"I thought you might."

"Why?"

"You were with her Thursday night."

"I wasn't with her, Inspector. I went to see her. There's a difference. Perhaps too subtle for you to grasp, but a difference all the same."

"Of course. But she'd got the results of the pregnancy test on Wednesday. Did she ask to see you? Or did you take it upon yourself to see her?"

"I went to see her. She didn't know I was coming."

"Ah."

Thorsson's fingers tightened their grip on the mug. "I see. Of course. I was the anxious father-to-be waiting to hear the results. Did the rabbit live, precious, or should we start stockpiling disposable nappies? Is that how you have it?"

"No. Not exactly."

Havers flipped over a page in her notebook. She said, "You'd want to know about the test results, I imagine, if you were the father. All things considered."

"What things considered?"

"The harassment charges. A pregnancy is rather convincing evidence, wouldn't you say?"

Thorsson barked a laugh. "What am I supposed to have done, dear Sergeant? Rape her? Tear off her knickers? Ply her with drugs and have at her afterwards?"

"Perhaps," Havers said. "But seduction seems so much more in your line."

"No doubt you could fill volumes with your knowledge of that subject."

Lynley said, "Have you ever had a problem with a female student before?"

"What do you mean problem? What kind of problem?"

"An Elena Weaver kind of problem. Have you ever been charged with harassment before?"

"Of course not. Never. Ask at the college if you don't believe me."

"I've spoken to Dr. Cuff. He confirms what you say."

"But his word's not good enough for you, it seems. You'd prefer to believe the stories cooked up by a little deaf tart who would have spread her legs—or opened her mouth—for any idiot willing to give her a try."

"A little deaf tart, Mr. Thorsson," Lynley said. "Curious choice of words. Are you suggesting that Elena had a reputation for promiscuity?"

Thorsson went back to his coffee, poured another mugful, took his time about drinking it. "Things get around," he settled on saying. "The college is small. There's always gossip."

"So if she was a"—Havers made a production of squinting down at her notes—"'a little deaf tart,' why not poke her yourself along with all the other blokes? What more reasonable conclusion for you to reach than to assume she'd—what was it?—" Again, the deliberately concentrated look at her notes. "Ah yes, here it is ... spread her legs or open her mouth for you? After all, she should have been willing. A man like you could no doubt offer her a real cut above her usual bit of spare."

Thorsson's face washed scarlet. It did battle with the elegant red-gold of his hair. But he said only and with perfect ease, "I *am* sorry, Sergeant. I can't oblige you, no matter how much you'd like the encounter. I prefer women who weigh under ten stone."

Havers smiled with neither pleasure nor amusement, but rather with the knowledge of having trapped her quarry. "Like Elena Weaver?"

"*Djävla skit!* Give it up!"

Lynley said, "Where were you Monday morning, Mr. Thorsson?"

"At the English Faculty.

"I mean early Monday morning. Between six and half past."

"In bed."

"Here?"

"Where else would I be?"

"I thought you might tell us. One of your neighbours saw you arriving home just before seven."

"Then one of my neighbours is mistaken. Who was it, anyway? That cow next door?"

"Someone who saw you drive up, get out of the car, and go into your house. All of it done in a bit of a hurry. Can you elucidate on that? I'm sure you agree that your Triumph would be a difficult car to mistake."

"Not in this instance. I was here, Inspector."

"And this morning?"

"This . . . ? I was here."

"The car's engine was still warm when we arrived."

"And that makes me a killer? Is that how you read it?"

"I don't read it in any particular fashion. I just want to know where you were."

"Here. I told you. I can't help what a neighbour saw. But it wasn't me."

"I see." Lynley looked across the table at Havers. He felt wearied by and bored with the necessity for endless sparring with the Swede. He felt the need for truth. And it appeared there would only be one way to get it. He said, "Sergeant, if you will."

Havers was only too delighted to do the honours. With great ceremony, she flipped her notebook open to the inside of the cover where she kept a copy of the official caution. Lynley had heard her give it hundreds of times, so he was well aware that she knew the words by heart. Her use of the notebook added drama to the occasion, and given his own growing antipathy for Lennart Thorsson, he didn't deny her the pleasure of milking the moment for personal satisfaction.

"Now," Lynley said when Havers had finished. "Where were you Sunday night, Mr. Thorsson? Where were you in the early hours of Monday morning?"

"I demand a solicitor."

Lynley gestured towards the phone which hung on the wall. "Please," he said. "We've plenty of time."

"I can't get one at this hour of the morning and you know it."

"Fine. We can wait."

Thorsson shook his head in an eloquent—if clearly apocryphal—display of disgust. "All right," he said. "I was heading to St. Stephen's early Monday morning. One of the undergraduates wanted to meet with me. I'd forgotten her paper and was in a rush to come back and get it and get to the meeting on time. Is that what you're so determined to know?"

"*Her* paper. I see. And this morning?"

"Nothing this morning."

"Then how do you explain the condition of the Triumph? Aside from being warm, it's covered with damp. Where was it parked last night?"

"Here."

"And you want us to believe that you went out this morning, wiped off only the windscreen for purposes unknown, and returned to the house to have a bath?"

"I don't much care what either of you—"

"And that perhaps you idled the engine for a bit to get the car warmed up although you aren't apparently going anywhere at the moment?"

"I've already said—"

"You've already said a great deal, Mr. Thorsson. And none of it meshes with anything else."

"If you think I murdered that fucking little cunt—"

Lynley got to his feet. "I'd like to have a look at your clothes."

Thorsson shoved his coffee mug the length of the work top. It crashed into the sink. "You need a warrant for that. You damn well know it."

"If you're an innocent man, you have nothing to fear, do you, Mr. Thorsson? Just produce the undergraduate you met with on Monday morning, and hand over everything black that you own. We've found black fibres on the body, by the way, but as they're a mixture of polyester, rayon, and cotton, we should be able to eliminate one or two of your garments right off the top. That ought to cover it."

"That covers *skit*. If you want black fibres, give a thought to trying the academic gowns. Oh, but you won't go sniffing in that direction, will you? Because everyone in the fucking University owns one."

"An interesting point. Is the bedroom this way?"

Lynley headed back in the direction of the front door. In a sitting room at the front of the house, he found the stairway and began to climb. Thorsson followed him with Havers quickly at his heels.

"You bastard! You can't—"

"This is your bedroom?" Lynley said at the doorway closest to the top of the stairs. He walked into the room and opened the clothes cupboard built into one of the walls. "Let's see what we have. Sergeant, a sack."

Havers tossed him a plastic rubbish sack as he began his examination of the clothes.

"I'll have your job for this!"

Lynley looked up. "Where were you Monday morning, Mr. Thorsson? Where were you this morning? An innocent man has nothing to fear."

Sergeant Havers added, "If he's innocent in the first place. If he lives an honest life. If he has nothing to hide."

Every vein on Thorsson's neck swelled. His pulse was throbbing like a drumbeat in his temple. His fingers jerked at the belt of his dressing gown. "Take it all," he said. "You have my bloody permission. Take every rotten piece. But don't forget this."

He ripped the dressing gown from his body. He wore nothing underneath it. He put his hands on his hips.

"I have nothing to hide from you lot," he said.

"I didn't know whether to laugh, applaud, or make an arrest on the spot for indecent exposure," Havers said. "That bloke takes everything right over the top."

"He's in a class all his own," Lynley agreed.

"I wonder if that's what the University environment does."

"Encourages the senior fellows to disrobe before police officers? I don't think so, Havers."

They had stopped at a bakery in Cherry Hinton where they picked up two fresh currant buns and two tepid coffees. These they drank from Styrofoam cups on their way back into the town, Lynley cooperatively operating the gear shift to leave his sergeant with at least one free hand.

"Still, it was a telling sort of thing to do, wasn't it, sir? I don't know about you, but I think he actually was *looking* for the opportunity to . . . I mean I think he was all hot to display . . . Well, you know."

Lynley crumpled the flimsy paper in which his currant bun had been wrapped. He deposited it in the ashtray among what appeared to be at least two dozen cigarette butts. "He was eager enough to make a show of his equipment. There's no doubt of that, Havers. You provoked him to it."

Her head whipped in his direction. "*Me?* Sir, I didn't do a thing and you know it."

"You did, I'm afraid. You've indicated from the first that you aren't about to be dazzled by either his position at the University or any of his accomplishments—"

"Dubious though they probably are."

"—so he felt compelled to give you an adequate idea of the size of the pleasure he was going to withhold as your punishment."

"What a berk."

"In a word." Lynley took a sip of his coffee and changed down into second gear as Havers rounded a corner and stepped on the clutch. "But he did something more, Havers. And if you'll pardon the expression, that's the beauty of it all."

"What, besides provide me with the best morning's entertainment I've had in years?"

"He verified the story Elena told Terence Cuff."

"How? What?"

Lynley changed to third and then fourth before replying. "According to what Elena told Dr. Cuff, Thorsson's approach to her had included, among other things, references to the difficulties he'd had when he was engaged to be married."

"What sort of difficulties?"

"Sexual ones, centring round the size of his erection."

"Too much man for the poor woman to handle? That sort of thing?"

"Exactly."

Havers' eyes lit. "And how would Elena have known about his size unless he'd actually told her himself? He was probably hoping to get her interested in having a look. Perhaps he even gave her one to get her juices flowing."

"Indeed. And taken as a whole it's not the sort of veiled invitation to intercourse that a twenty-year-old girl would cook up on her own, is it? Especially when it so exactly matches the truth. If the story were invention, she'd have been more likely to come up with something far more blatant on Thorsson's part. And he's capable of blatancy, as we've just seen."

"So he was lying about the harassment situation. And"—Havers smiled with undisguised pleasure—"if he was lying about that, why not about everything else as well?"

"He's definitely back in the running, Sergeant."

"I'd say he's about to win the race by a length."

"We'll see."

"But, sir—"

"Drive on, Sergeant."

They headed back into town where, after a minor snarl of traffic created by a collision between two taxis at the top of Station Road, they drove to police headquarters and unloaded the sack of clothing which they'd taken from Thorsson's house. The uniformed receptionist buzzed them through the interior lobby doors with a nod at Lynley's identification. They took the lift up to the superintendent's office.

They found Sheehan standing next to his secretary's vacant desk, the telephone receiver pressed to his ear. His conversation consisted mostly of grunts and *damn*'s and *blast it all*'s. He finally said impatiently, "You've had him jumping through hoops with that girl's body for two days now and we're getting nowhere, Drake . . . If you don't agree with his conclusions, call in a specialist from the Met and have done with it . . . I don't care what the CC thinks at this point. I'll handle him. Just do it . . . Listen to me. This isn't an enquiry into your competence as department head, but if you can't in conscience sign off on Pleasance's report and if he won't change it, there's nothing else to be done . . . I don't have the power to give him the sack . . . That's the way it is, man. Just phone the Met." When he rang off, he didn't appear pleased to see the representatives from New Scotland Yard standing in the doorway as further testimony to the outside help which the circumstances of Elena Weaver's murder had forced him and his police force to endure.

"Trouble?" Lynley asked.

Sheehan picked up a batch of folders from his secretary's desk and riffled through a stack of papers in her IN tray. "What a woman," he said with a nod at her empty chair. "She called in ill this morning. She has a real sixth sense about when things are going to heat up, does Edwina."

"And things are heating up?"

Sheehan grabbed three papers from the tray, stuck them with the folders under his arm, and lumbered into his office. Lynley and Havers followed. "I've got my CC at Huntingdon breathing down my neck about devising a strategy for what he calls 'renewed community relations'—a fancy title for coming up with a way to keep the nobs at the University happy so that you lot don't start making regular appearances here in the future. I've got the funeral home and the parents asking after the Weaver girl's body every quarter hour. And now"—with a look at the plastic sack dangling from Havers' fingers—"I expect you've brought me something else to play with."

"Clothes for forensic," Havers said. "We'd like to make a match with the fibres on the body. If you can give us something positive, we might have what we need."

"To make an arrest?"

"It's looking possible."

Sheehan nodded grimly. "I hate to give those two bickering old biddies something else to fight over, but we'll have a go. They've been sniping over the weapon since yesterday. Maybe this'll take their minds off that for a bit.''

"They've still reached no conclusion?" Lynley asked.

"Pleasance has done. Drake doesn't agree. He won't sign the report, and he's been dragging his heels about calling in the Met for another opinion since yesterday afternoon. Professional pride, if you catch my drift, not to mention competence. He's afraid at this point that Pleasance is in the right. And since he's made such an issue about getting rid of the bloke, he stands to lose a lot more than just face if anyone confirms Pleasance's conclusions.'' Sheehan threw the folders and the papers down on his desk where they mingled with a stack of pages from a computer print-out. He rooted through his top drawer and brought out a roll of mints. He offered them round, sank into his chair, and loosened his tie. Outside, in Edwina's office, the phone began to ring. He ignored it. "Love and death," he said. "Mix up pride with either of them and you're done for, aren't you?''

"Is it the Met's involvement that's bothering Drake or the involvement of any outsider?''

The double ringing of the telephone continued in the outer office. Sheehan continued to let it go unanswered. "It's the Met," he said. "Drake's got himself in a dither over the implication that he's got to be rescued by his London betters. The fact that you're here has our CID boys in a rumble. Drake doesn't want the same to happen in forensic where he already has trouble enough keeping Pleasance in line.''

"But Drake wouldn't object if someone else—someone uninvolved with the Yard—had a look at the body? Especially if that someone worked directly with the two of them—Drake and Pleasance—gave them the information verbally, and allowed them to create the report.''

Sheehan's features sharpened with interest. "What do you have in mind, Inspector?''

"An expert witness.''

"That's not on. We don't have the funding to pay an outsider.''

"You won't have to pay.''

Footsteps rang against the floor in the outer office. A breathless voice answered the phone.

Lynley said, "We'll have the information we need without the Met's presence telegraphing to everyone that Drake's competence is being questioned.''

"And what happens when the time comes for someone to testify in court, Inspector? Neither Drake nor Pleasance can get in the box and give evidence that isn't his.''

''Either one can if he assists, and if his conclusions are the same as the expert's.''

Thoughtfully, Sheehan played the roll of mints back and forth on the top of his desk. ''Can it be arranged discreetly?''

''So that no one aside from Drake and Pleasance knows the expert witness was here in the first place?'' When Sheehan nodded, Lynley said, ''Just hand me the phone.''

A woman's voice called out to Sheehan from the outer office, a diffident ''Superintendent?'' and nothing more. Sheehan got to his feet, joined the uniformed constable who had answered his phone. As they spoke together, Havers turned to Lynley.

''You're thinking of St. James,'' she said. ''Will he be able to come up?''

''Faster than someone from the Met, I dare say,'' Lynley replied. ''Without the attendant paperwork and without the politics. Just pray he's not scheduled to give testimony anywhere within the next few days.''

He looked up as Sheehan plunged back into the office, making for the metal stand upon which his overcoat was hanging. He grabbed this, snatched up the plastic sack which sat next to Havers' chair, and flung it to the constable who had followed him to the door.

''See the forensic boys get this,'' he said. And then to Lynley and Havers, ''Let's go.''

Lynley knew without asking what the set expression on Sheehan's face meant. He'd seen it too many times to wonder what had provoked it. He'd even felt his own features take on the manifestation of that grim anger that always attended the revelation of a crime.

So he was prepared for the inevitable announcement that Sheehan made as they got to their feet. ''We've got another body.''

15

Two panda cars, lights flashing and sirens howling, led the caravan of vehicles on a flight out of Cambridge, tearing down Lensfield Road, soaring over the Fen Causeway and up along the Backs to make the turn west towards Madingley. They left in their wake groups of staring students, bicycle riders veering out of the way, black-gowned fellows setting off to lectures, and two tourist buses disgorging Japanese visitors at the autumn-decked avenue which led to New Court at Trinity College.

Havers' Mini was sandwiched between the second panda car and Sheehan's own vehicle, onto which he had slapped a temporary warning light. Behind him charged the scenes-of-crime van and behind that, an ambulance in the futile hope that the word *body* didn't necessarily mean *death*.

They powered across the flyover that bridged the M11 and swung through the collection of cottages that comprised the tiny village of Madingley. Beyond it, they shot along a narrow lane. It was a farming area, an abrupt change from town to country just minutes away from Cambridge. Hedgerows characterised it—hawthorn, briar, and holly— marking the boundaries of fields newly planted with winter wheat.

They rounded a curve beyond which a tractor stood half on and half off the verge, its enormous wheels crusted with mud. Atop it sat a man in a bulky jacket with its collar turned up round his ears and his shoulders hunched against the wind and the cold. He waved them to a halt and hopped to the ground. A border collie that had been lying motionless at the rear wheel of the tractor got to its feet upon the man's sharp command and came to his side.

"Over here," the man said after introducing himself as Bob Jenkins and pointing out his home about a quarter mile away, set back from the road and surrounded by barn, outbuildings, and fields. "Shasta found her."

Hearing his name, the dog pricked up his ears, gave one extremely disciplined wag of the tail, and followed his master about twenty feet beyond the tractor where a body lay in a tangle of weeds and bracken along the base of the hedge.

"Never seen anything like it," Jenkins said. "I di' know what the ruddy world's comin' to." He pulled at his nose, which was scarlet from the cold, and squinted against the northeast wind. It held the fog at bay—as it had done on the previous day—but it brought along with it the frigid temperatures of the grey North Sea. A hedgerow offered little protection against it.

"Damn" was Sheehan's only remark as he squatted by the body. Lynley and Havers joined him.

It was a girl, tall and slender, with a fall of hair the colour of beechwood. She was wearing a green sweatshirt, white shorts, athletic shoes, and rather grimy socks, the left one of which had become rucked round her ankle. She lay on her back, with her chin tilted up, her mouth open, her eyes glazed. And her torso was a mass of crimson broken by the dark tattooing of unburnt particles of gunpowder. A single glance was enough to tell all of them that the only possible use the ambulance might serve would be to convey the corpse to autopsy.

"You haven't touched her?" Lynley asked Bob Jenkins.

The man looked horrified by the very thought. "Didn't touch nothing," he said. "Shasta here snuffed her, but he backed up quick enough, didn't he, when he caught the smell of the powder. Not one for guns, is Shasta."

"You heard no shots this morning?"

Jenkins shook his head. "I was working over the engine of the tractor early on. I had it going off and on, playing with the carburettor and making a bit of a row. If someone took her down then—" He jerked his head at the body but didn't look at it. "I wouldn't have heard."

"What about the dog?"

Jenkins' hand automatically went for the dog's head which was inches away from his own left thigh. Shasta blinked, panted briefly, and accepted the caress with another single wag of his tail. "He *did* set to with a bit of barking," Jenkins said. "I had the radio going over the engine noise and had to shout him down."

"Do you remember what time this was?"

At first he shook his head. But then he lifted a gloved hand quickly—one finger skyward—as if an idea had suddenly struck him. "It was somewhere near half six."

"You're sure?"

"They were reading the news and I wanted to hear if the P.M.'s going to do something about this poll tax business." His eyes shifted to the body and quickly away. "Girl could of been hit then, all right. But I have to tell that Shasta might of just been barking to bark. He does that some."

Around them, the uniformed police were rolling out the crime scene tape and blocking off the lane as the scenes-of-crime team began unloading the van. The police photographer approached with his camera held before him like a shield. He looked a bit green under the eyes and round the mouth. He waited some feet away for the signal from Sheehan who was peering at the blood-soaked front of the dead girl's sweatshirt.

"A shotgun," he said. And then looking up, he shouted to the scenes-of-crime team, "Keep an eye out for the wad, you lot." He rested on his thick haunches and shook his head. "This's going to be worse than looking for dust in the desert."

"Why?" Havers asked.

Sheehan cocked his head at her in surprise. Lynley said, "She's a city dweller, Superintendent." And then to Havers, "It's pheasant season."

Sheehan went on with, "Anyone wanting to have a bash at the pheasants is going to own a shotgun, Sergeant. The killings begin next week. It's the time of year when every idiot with an itchy finger and a need to feel like some real blood sport's just the way to get him back to his roots will be out blasting away at anything that moves. We'll be seeing wounds every which way by the end of the month."

"But not like this."

"No. This was no accident." He fumbled in his trouser pocket and brought out a wallet from which he extracted a credit card. "Two runners," he said pensively. "Both of them women. Both of them tall, both fair, both long-haired."

"You're not thinking we're looking at a serial killing?" Havers sounded a mixture of doubt and disappointment that the Cambridge superintendent might have reached such a conclusion.

Sheehan used the edge of his credit card to clean off a patch of dirt and leaves that clung to the front of the girl's blood-soaked sweatshirt. Over the left breast the words *Queens' College, Cambridge* were stencilled round the college coat of arms.

"You mean someone with a nasty little bent for bringing down fair-haired college runners?" Sheehan asked. "No. I don't think so. Serial killers don't vary their routines this much. The killing's their signature. You know what I mean: I beat in another head with a brick, you coppers, are you any closer to finding me yet?" He cleaned off the credit card, wiped his fingers on a rust-coloured handkerchief, and pushed himself to his feet. "Shoot her, Graham," he said over his shoulder, and the photographer came forward to do so. At that, the scenes-of-crime team began to move, as did the uniformed constables, beginning the slow process of examining every inch of the surrounding ground.

Bob Jenkins said, "Got to get in that field, if you've a mind to let me," and tilted his chin to direct their attention to where he had been heading in the first place when his dog had come upon the body.

Perhaps three yards away from the dead girl, a break in the hedge revealed a gate giving access to the nearest field. Lynley eyed it for a moment as the crime scene people began their work.

"In a few minutes," he said to the farmer, and added to Sheehan, "They'll need to look for prints all along the verge, Superintendent. Footprints. Tyre prints from a car or a bike."

"Right," Sheehan said, and went to speak with his team.

Lynley and Havers walked to the gate. It was only wide enough to accommodate the tractor, and hemmed in on both sides by a heavy growth of hawthorn. They climbed carefully over. The ground beyond was soft, trodden, and rutted as it gave way to the field itself. But its consistency was crumbly and fragile, so although the imprints of feet were everywhere, nowhere did they leave an impression that was anything more than merely another indentation in the already choppy ground.

"Nothing decent," Havers said as she scouted round the area. "But if it was a lying-in-wait—"

"Then the waiting had to be done right here," Lynley concluded. He worked his eyes slowly over the ground, from one side of the gate to the other. When he saw what he was looking for—an indentation in the ground that didn't fit with the rest—he said, "Havers."

She joined him. He pointed out the smooth, circular impression in the earth, the barely discernible narrow, extended impression behind it, the sharp, deeper fissure that comprised its conclusion. As a unit, the impressions angled acutely perhaps two and a half feet beyond the gate itself, and less than a foot from the hawthorn hedge.

"Knee, leg, toe," Lynley said. "The killer knelt here, hidden by the hedge, on one knee, resting the gun on the second bar of the gate. Waiting."

"But how could anyone have *known*—"

"That she'd be running this way? The same way someone knew where to find Elena Weaver."

Justine Weaver scraped a knife along the burnt edge of the toast, watching the resulting black ash speckle the clean surface of the kitchen sink like a fine deposit of powder. She tried to find a place inside her where compassion and understanding still resided, a place like a well from which she could drink deeply and somehow replenish what the events of the past eight months—and the last two days—had desiccated. But if a well-spring of empathy had ever existed at her core, it had long since dried up, leaving in its place the barren ground of resentment and despair. And nothing flowed from this.

They've lost their daughter, she told herself. They share a mutual grief. But those facts did not eliminate the wretchedness she had felt since Monday night, a replay of an earlier pain, like the same melody in a different key.

They'd come home together in silence yesterday, Anthony and his former wife. They'd been to see the police. They'd gone on to the funeral home. They'd chosen a coffin and made the arrangements, none of which they shared with her. It was only when she brought out the plates of thin sandwiches and cake, only when she had poured the tea, only when she had passed them each the lemon and the milk and the sugar that either of them spoke in anything other than weary monosyllables. And then it was Glyn who finally addressed her, choosing the moment and wielding the weapon, a superficially simple declaration that was skilfully honed by time and circumstance.

As she spoke, she kept her eyes on the sandwich plate which Justine was offering her and which she made no move to accept. "I'd prefer you to stay away from my daughter's funeral, Justine."

They were in the sitting room, gathered round the low coffee table.

The artificial fire was lit, its flames lapping the false coals with a quiet hiss. The curtains were drawn. An electric clock whirred softly. It was such a sensible, civilised place to be.

At first Justine said nothing. She looked at her husband, waiting for him to voice a protest of some sort. But he was giving his attention to his teacup and saucer. A muscle pulled at the corner of his mouth.

He knew this was coming, she thought, and she said, "Anthony?"

"You had no real tie to Elena," Glyn went on. Her voice was even, so extremely reasonable. "So I'd prefer you not to be there. I hope you understand."

"Ten years as her stepmother," Justine said.

"Please," Glyn said. "As her father's second wife."

Justine set the plate down. She studied the neat array of sandwiches, noting how she'd assembled them to form a pattern. Egg salad, crab, fresh ham, cream cheese. Crusts neatly removed, every edge of the bread cut as if it were a perfect plane. Glyn went on.

"We'll take her to London for the service, so you won't have to do without Anthony for longer than a few hours. And then afterwards, you can get directly back to the business of your lives."

Justine merely stared, trying and failing to summon a response.

Glyn continued, as if following a course she'd determined in advance. "We never knew for certain why Elena was born deaf. Has Anthony told you that? I suppose we could have had studies done—some sort of genetic thing, you know what I mean—but we didn't bother."

Anthony leaned forward, put his teacup on the coffee table. He kept his fingers on its saucer as if in the expectation that it would slide to the floor.

Justine said, "I don't see that—"

"The reality is that you might produce a deaf baby as well, Justine, if there's something wrong with Anthony's genes. I thought I ought to mention the possibility. Are you equipped—emotionally, I mean—to deal with a handicapped child? Have you considered how a deaf child might put a spanner in the works of your career?"

Justine looked at her husband. He didn't meet her eyes. One of his hands formed a loose fist on his thigh. She said, "Is this really necessary, Glyn?"

"I should think you'd find it helpful." Glyn reached for her teacup. For a moment, she seemed to examine the rose on the china, and she turned the cup to the right, to the left, as if with the intention of admiring its design. "That's that, then, isn't it? Everything's been said." She replaced the cup and stood. "I won't be wanting any dinner." She left them alone.

Justine turned to her husband, waited for him to speak, and watched him sit motionless. He seemed to be disappearing into himself, bones, blood, and flesh disintegrating into the ashes and dust from which all men were formed. He has such small hands, she thought. And for the first time she considered the wide gold wedding band round his finger and the reason she had wanted him to have it—the largest, the widest, the brightest in the shop, the most capable of heralding the fact of their marriage.

"Is this what you want?" she finally asked him.

His eyelids looked caked, their skin stretched and sore. "What?"

"That I stay away from the funeral. Is this what you want, Anthony?"

"It has to be that way. Try to understand."

"Understand? What?"

"That she's not responsible for who she is right now. She has no control over what she says and does. It goes too deep with her, Justine. You've got to understand."

"And stay away from the funeral."

She saw the movement of resignation—a simple lifting and lowering of his fingers—and knew the response he would make before he made it. "I hurt her. I left her. I owe her this much. I owe both of them this much."

"My God."

"I've already talked to Terence Cuff about a memorial service Friday at St. Stephen's Church. You'll be part of that. All of Elena's friends will be there."

"And that's it? That's all? That's your judgement of everything? Of our marriage? Of our life? Of my relationship with Elena?"

"This isn't about you. You can't take it to heart."

"You didn't even argue with her. You could have protested."

He finally looked at her. "It's the way it has to be."

She said nothing more. She merely felt the hard core of her resentment take on added weight. Still, she held her tongue. Be sweet, Justine, she could hear her mother say over her need to rail like a shrew against her husband. Be a nice girl.

She put the sixth piece of toast into the rack and the rack itself along with boiled eggs and sausage onto a white wicker tray. Nice girls muster up compassion, she thought. Sweet girls forgive and forgive and forgive. Don't think of the self. Go beyond the self. Find a need greater than your own and fill it. That's the Christian way to live.

But she couldn't do it. Into the scales upon which she weighed her behaviour, she put the useless hours that she'd given over to trying to forge a bond with Elena, the mornings on which she'd run at her side, the evenings she'd spent helping her write her essays, the endless Sunday afternoons she'd waited for father and daughter to return from a jaunt which Anthony had declared essential to his recapturing of Elena's love and trust.

She carried the tray into the glassed-in morning room where her husband and his former wife were sitting at the wicker table. They had been picking at grapefruit wedges and corn flakes for nearly half an hour, and now, she supposed, they would do the same with the eggs, the sausage, and the toast.

She knew she ought to say, "You need to eat. Both of you," and another Justine might have managed the seven words and made them sound sincere. Instead, she said nothing. She sat in her accustomed place, with her back to the drive, across the table from her husband. She poured him coffee. He raised his head. He looked ten years older than he had two days ago.

Glyn said, "All this food. I can't eat. It's such a waste really," and she didn't lift her eyes from watching Justine tap off the top of her boiled egg. "Did you run this morning?" she asked, and when Justine didn't reply, "I imagine you'll want to start that up again soon. It's important for a woman to keep working at her figure. Not a stretch-mark anywhere on you, is there?"

Justine stared down at the spoonful of tender white that she'd scooped from her egg. Every admonition from her past rose up to confront her, but they formed an insubstantial barrier that the previous night made easy to surmount. She said, "Elena was pregnant." And then she looked up. "Eight weeks pregnant."

Anthony's face, she saw, went from drained to stricken. Glyn's face offered a curiously satisfied smile.

"That Scotland Yard man was here yesterday afternoon," Justine said. "He told me."

"Pregnant?" Anthony repeated the word in a deadened voice.

"That's what the autopsy showed."

"But who . . . how . . . ?" Anthony fumbled with a teaspoon. It slipped from his fingers and clattered on the floor.

"How?" Glyn gave a tittering laugh. "Oh, I'd think it was how babies usually get made." She nodded at Justine. "What a moment of triumph for you, my dear."

Anthony turned his head. The movement seemed sluggish, as if he were pulling against a great weight. "What's that supposed to mean?"

"You think she doesn't savour this moment? Just ask her if she already knew. Ask her if the information surprised her at all. In fact, you might ask her how she encouraged your daughter to have a man whenever she felt itchy." Glyn leaned forward. "Because Elena told me all about it, Justine. About those heart-to-heart chats, about how she was supposed to take *care* of herself."

Anthony said, "Justine, you encouraged her? You knew?"

"Of course she knew."

"That isn't true," Justine said.

"Don't think for a moment that she didn't want Elena to get pregnant, Anthony. She was willing to settle for anything to drive you away from her. Because if she did that, she'd get what she wanted. You. Alone. With no more distractions."

"No," Justine said.

"She hated Elena. She wanted her dead. I wouldn't be surprised if she killed her herself."

And for a moment—just the fraction of an instant—Justine saw the doubt on his face. She recognised the working of knowledge: she'd been alone in the house when the Ceephone call came, she'd gone out running alone in the morning, she hadn't taken the dog, she could have beaten and strangled his daughter.

She said, "My God, Anthony."

"You knew," he replied.

"That she had a lover. Yes. But that's all. And I spoke to her. Yes. About cleaning   about hygiene. About taking care that she didn't—"

"Who was it?"

"Anthony."

"God damn you, who was it?"

"She knows," Glyn said. "You can see that she knows."

"How long?" Anthony asked. "How long had this been going on?"

"Did they do it here, Justine? In the house? While you were home? Did you let them? Did you watch? Did you listen at the door?"

Justine pushed herself away from the table. She got to her feet. Her head felt empty.

"I want answers, Justine." Anthony's voice rose. "Who did this to my daughter?"

Justine fought to find the words. "She did it to herself."

"Oh yes," Glyn said, her eyes bright and knowing. "Let's have at the truth."

"You're a viper."

Anthony stood. "I want the facts, Justine."

"Then take yourself off to Trinity Lane to find them."

"Trinity . . ." He turned from her to the wall of windows beyond which his Citroën stood on the drive. "No." He was out of the room without another word, leaving the house without a coat, the sleeves of his striped shirt snapping in the wind. He got into the car.

Glyn reached for an egg. "It didn't quite play out as you planned it," she said.

Adam Jenn stared at the neat lines of his handwriting and tried to make sense out of his notes. The Peasants' Revolt. The council of regency. A new query: Was the composition of the council of regency, rather than the imposition of new poll taxes, largely instrumental in the circumstances that led to the revolt of 1381?

He read a few phrases about John Ball and Wat Tyler, about the Statute of Labourers, and about the King. Richard II, well-intentioned but ineffectual, had lacked the skills and the backbone necessary for a man to be a leader. He had tried to please everyone but had succeeded only in destroying himself. He was historical proof of the contention that success requires more than merely a coincidental birthright. Political acumen is the key to arriving unscathed at a personal and professional goal.

Adam himself had been living his academic life according to that precept. He'd made his choice of advisor carefully, spending hours of his time scoping out the candidates for the Penford Chair. He finally made his move in Anthony Weaver's direction only when he felt relatively assured that the St. Stephen's medievalist would be the selection of the University search committee. To have the holder of the Penford Chair as his advisor would virtually guarantee him the benefits he found essential to labelling himself an eventual success—the initial position of academic supervisor to undergraduates, the consequent attainment of a research fellowship, the future movement to lecturer, and finally a professorship before his forty-fifth birthday. All of it seemed within the bounds of reasonable expectation when Anthony Weaver had taken him on as a graduate advisee. So cooperating with Weaver's request that he take the professor's daughter under his wing in order to make her second year at the University a smoother and more pleasant experience than her first had appeared to be yet another fortuitous opportunity for him to demonstrate— if only to himself—that he possessed the requisite amount of political perspicacity to flourish in this environment. What he had not counted on when first told about the professor's handicapped daughter and first envisaging Dr. Weaver's gratitude for the time he expended on smoothing the troubled waters of his daughter's life was Elena herself.

He had been expecting to be introduced to a stoop-shouldered, concave-chested, pasty-skinned fading wildflower of a girl, someone who sat miserably on the edge of a threadbare ottoman with her legs tucked back and clinging to its sides. She'd be wearing an old dress printed with rosebuds. She'd be wearing ankle socks and scruffy-looking brogues. And for Dr. Weaver's sake, he'd do his duty with an appealing blend of gravity and graciousness. He'd even carry a small notebook in the pocket of his jacket to make sure that they could communicate in writing at all times.

He'd held on to this fictional Elena all the way into the sitting room of Anthony Weaver's house, even going so far as to scan the guests who were there for the history faculty's Michaelmas drinks party. He'd had to give up the idea of the threadbare ottoman quickly enough when he saw the nature of the house's furnishings—he doubted that anything threadbare or frayed would be allowed to remain for longer than five minutes in this elegant environment of leather and glass—but he did maintain his mental image of the cringing, retiring, handicapped girl alone in a corner and afraid of everyone.

And then she came swinging towards him, wearing a clingy black dress and dangling onyx earrings, her hair catching her movement and subtly duplicating the sway of her hips. She smiled and said what he took for "Hi. You're Adam, aren't you?" because her pronunciation wasn't clear. He noted the fact that she smelled like ripe fruit, that she didn't wear a bra, that her legs were bare. And that every man in the room followed her movement with his eyes, no matter the conversation in which he was engaged.

She had a way of making a man feel special. He'd learned that soon enough. Astutely, he realised that this feeling of being the sole interest in Elena's life came from the fact that she had to look directly at people in order to read their lips whenever they spoke to her. And for a time he convinced himself that that was the entirety of his attraction to her. But even on the first evening of their acquaintance, he found his eyes continually dropping to the nubs of her nipples—they were erect, they pressed against the material of her dress, they asked to be sucked and moulded and licked—and he found his hands sore with the need to slide round her waist, cup her buttocks, and pull her against him.

He'd done none of that. Ever. Not once in the dozen or more times they'd been together. He'd not even kissed her. And the single time she'd reached out impulsively and ran her fingers the length of his inner thigh, he had automatically knocked her hand away. She laughed at him, amused and unoffended. And he wanted to strike her every bit as much as he wanted to fuck her. He felt the desire like a blaze of fire burning right behind his eyes, needing both at once: the violence of abuse and the sexual act itself; the sound of her pain and the satisfying knowledge of her unwilling submission.

It was always that way whenever he saw too much of a woman. He felt caught within a raging argument of desire and disgust. And perennially playing in the back of his mind was the memory of his father beating his mother and the sound of their frantic coupling afterwards.

Knowing Elena, seeing Elena, dutifully squiring her here and there had all been part of the political process of academic advancement and scholastic success. But like any act of egocentric machination, what posed as selfless cooperation was not without its attendant price.

He had seen as much in Dr. Weaver's face whenever the professor asked him about time spent with Elena, just as he had seen it on the very first night when Weaver's eyes followed his daughter round the room, shining with satisfaction when she paused to talk to Adam and not to someone else. It wasn't long before Adam had realised that the price for success in a milieu in which Anthony Weaver played a major role was likely to be bound up intimately in how things developed in Elena's life.

"She's a wonderful girl," Weaver would say. "She has a lot to offer a man."

Adam wondered what twists and turns and rough roads lay in his future now that Weaver's daughter was dead. For while he'd chosen Dr. Weaver as his advisor strictly for the potential benefits that might accrue from such a choice, he had come to know that Dr. Weaver had accepted him with his own set of benefits in mind. He harboured them in secret, no doubt calling them his dream. But Adam knew exactly what they were.

The study door opened as he was staring at his references to the fourteenth-century riots in Kent and Essex. He looked up, then pushed back his chair in some confusion as Anthony Weaver came into the room. He hadn't expected to see him for at least another several days, so he hadn't done much about straightening up the litter of teacups and plates and essays across the table and on the floor. Even had he done so, the appearance of his advisor directly upon the heels of his having been thinking about him caused the heat to seep up Adam's neck and spread across his cheeks.

"Dr. Weaver," he said. "I wasn't expecting . . ." His voice drifted off. Weaver was wearing neither jacket nor overcoat, and his dark hair was curled and chaotic from the wind. He carried neither briefcase nor textbooks. Whyever he had come, it was not to work.

"She was pregnant," he said.

Adam's throat went dry. He thought about taking a sip of the tea which he'd poured but forgotten about an hour previously. But although he slowly got to his feet, he couldn't manage any other movement, let alone getting his arm to reach out towards the cup.

Weaver shut the door and remained standing next to it. "I don't blame you for it, Adam. Obviously, you were in love with each other."

"Dr. Weaver—"

"I simply wished you'd used some precautions. It's not the best way to start a life together, is it?"

Adam couldn't formulate an answer. It seemed that his entire future depended upon the next few minutes and how he handled them. He danced between the truth and a lie, wondering which would better serve his interests.

"When Justine told me, I left the house in a rage. I felt like some eighteenth-century father storming out to demand satisfaction. But I know how these things happen between people. I just want you to tell me if you'd talked about marriage. Before, I mean. Before you made love to her."

Adam wanted to say that they'd talked about it often, in the late of night typing back and forth furiously on the Ceephone, making plans, sharing dreams, and committing themselves to a life together. But from the roots of such a lie had to grow a convincing performance of grief over the next few months. And while he regretted Elena's death, he did not actually mourn her passing, so he knew that a show of abject sorrow would prove itself more than he could manage.

"She was special," Anthony Weaver was saying. "Her baby—*your* baby, Adam—would have been special as well. She was fragile and working hard to find herself, it's true, but you were helping her grow. Remember that. Hold onto that. You were tremendously good for her. I would have been proud to see you together as man and wife."

He found he couldn't do it. "Dr. Weaver, I wasn't the one." He dropped his eyes to the table. He concentrated on the open texts, his notes, the essays. ''What I mean is I never made love with Elena, sir.'' He felt more colour burn its way into his flesh. ''I never even kissed her. I hardly ever touched her.''

''I'm not angry, Adam. Don't misunderstand. You don't have to deny you were lovers.''

''I'm not denying. I'm just telling you the truth. The facts. We weren't lovers. It wasn't me.''

''But she saw only you.''

Adam hesitated to bring forth the single piece of information which he knew Anthony Weaver was avoiding, perhaps deliberately, perhaps unconsciously. He knew that giving it voice would also mean giving voice to the professor's worst fears. Yet there seemed to be no other way to convince the man of the truth about his own relationship with Elena. And he was an historian, after all. Historians are supposed to be seekers of truth.

He could demand no less of himself. He said, ''No, sir. You've forgotten. I wasn't the only one Elena saw. There was Gareth Randolph.''

Weaver's eyes seemed to unfocus behind his spectacles. Adam hurried on.

''She saw him several times a week, didn't she, sir? As part of the deal she'd struck with Dr. Cuff.'' He didn't want to put anything more into words. He could see the grey curtain of knowledge and misery pass across Weaver's features.

''That deaf—'' Weaver's words stopped. His eyes sharpened once again. ''Did you reject her, Adam? Is that why she looked elsewhere? Wasn't she good enough for you? Did you put you off because she was deaf?''

''No. Not at all. I just didn't—''

''Then why?''

He wanted to say, ''Because I was afraid. I thought she would suck the marrow from my bones. I wanted to have her and have her and have her but not marry her, God not marry her and live on the black edge of my own destruction for the rest of my life.'' Instead, he said, ''It just didn't happen between us.''

''What?''

''The sort of connection one looks for.''

''Because she was deaf.''

''That wasn't an issue, sir.''

''How can you say that? How can you even expect me to believe it?

Of course it was an issue. It was an issue for everyone. It was an issue for her. How could it not be?''

Adam knew this was dangerous ground. He wanted to retreat from the confrontation. But Weaver was waiting for his answer, and his stony expression told Adam how important it was that he answer correctly.

"She was just deaf, sir. Nothing else. Just deaf."

"What's that supposed to mean?"

"That there was nothing else wrong with her. Even being deaf wasn't something wrong. It's just a word people use to indicate something's missing."

"Like blind, like mute, like paralysed?"

"I suppose."

"And if she'd been those things—blind, mute, paralysed—would you still be saying that it wasn't an issue?"

"But she wasn't those things."

"Would you still be saying it wasn't an issue?"

"I don't know. I can't say. I can only say that Elena's being deaf wasn't an issue. Not for me."

"You're lying."

"Sir."

"You saw her as a freak."

"I didn't."

"You were embarrassed by her voice and pronunciation, by the fact that she couldn't ever tell how loud she was speaking so that when you were out in public together, people would hear that odd voice. They'd turn, they'd be curious. And you'd feel embarrassed with all those eyes on you. And ashamed, of her, of yourself, of being embarrassed in the first place. Not the great liberal that you once thought you were. Always wishing that she were normal because if she were—if she just could hear—then you really wouldn't feel as if you owed her something more than you were able to give."

Adam felt his body going cold, but he didn't respond. He wanted to pretend that he hadn't heard, or at the very least, to keep his face from revealing the extent to which he comprehended the underlying meaning of what the professor had said. He saw that he failed to do so on both scores, for Weaver's own face seemed to crumble in on itself and he said, "Oh God."

He walked to the mantel where Adam had continued to place the gathering collection of envelopes and messages. With what appeared to be a tremendous effort, he swept them up and carried them to his desk and sat down. He began to open them, slowly, ponderously, his movements weighted by twenty years of denial and guilt.

Adam cautiously lowered himself into his chair. He went back to his notes, but he saw this time even less than he had managed to see before. He knew that he owed Dr. Weaver some sort of reassurance, a reaching out in fellowship and love. But nothing in his twenty-six years of limited experience provided him with the words to tell the other man that there was no sin in feeling what he felt. The only sin was in running away from it.

He heard the professor quake with a convulsive sound. He turned in his chair.

Weaver, he saw, had been opening the envelopes. And although the contents of at least three of them lay on his lap and another was crumpled into his fist, he was looking at nothing. He had removed his spectacles and covered his eyes with his hand. He was weeping.

16

Melinda Powell was about to wheel her bicycle from Queens' Lane into Old Court when a panda car pulled up less than half a block away. A uniformed policeman got out of it, as did the President of Queens' College along with the senior tutor. The three of them stood talking in the cold, arms folded across their chests, breath clouding the air, faces grave and grim. The policeman nodded at something the President was saying to the senior tutor, and as they moved apart from one another, preparatory to the policeman's taking his leave, a noisy Mini rumbled into the lane from Silver Street and parked behind them.

Two people emerged, a tall, blond man wearing a cashmere overcoat and a squat, square woman swathed in scarves and wool. They joined the others, the blond man producing some sort of identification and the President of the College following up by offering his hand. There was a great deal of earnest conversation, a gesture from the President towards the side entrance to the college, and what appeared to be some sort of direction given by the blond to the uniformed policeman. He nodded and came trotting back to where Melinda stood with her mittened hands curved round the handlebars of her bike, feeling the cold from the metal seeping through the knit wool like strips of damp. He said, "Sorry, miss," as he scooted past her and stepped through the gateway into the college.

Melinda followed him. She'd been gone most of the morning, struggling with an essay she was rewriting for the fourth time in an effort to make her points clear prior to showing it to her supervisor, who would, with his usual bent for academic sadism, no doubt tear it to shreds. It was nearly noon. And although it was typical to see the occasional member of college strolling through Old Court at this time of day, when Melinda emerged from the turreted passage that led to Queens' Lane, she found numerous small clumps of students having hushed conversations on the path between the two rectangles of lawn while a larger group gathered at the staircase door to the left of the north turret.

It was through this door that the policeman disappeared after he stopped for a moment to answer a question. Melinda faltered when she saw this. Her bicycle felt heavy, as if a rusting chain made it difficult to push, and she lifted her eyes to the top floor of the building where she tried to see through the windows of that misshapen room tucked under the eaves.

"What's going on?" she asked a boy who was passing. He wore a sky blue anorak and matching knit cap with the words *Ski Bulgaria* blazed onto it in red.

"Some runner," he said. "Got bagged this morning."

"Who?"

"Another bird from Hare and Hounds, they said."

Melinda felt dizzy. She heard him ask, "You all right?" but she didn't respond. Instead, with every sense numbed, she pushed her bicycle towards the door of Rosalyn Simpson's staircase.

"She *promised*," Melinda whispered to herself. And just for a moment the overwhelming nature of Rosalyn's betrayal was even more devastating than was her death.

She hadn't extracted the promise from her in bed when resolutions weaken in the face of desire. Nor had she engaged in a tear-filled confrontation in which she used Rosalyn's past vulnerabilities as tools of successful manipulation. Instead, she had opted for discussion—trying to remain calm and to avoid falling into the panic and hysteria which she knew would drive Rosalyn away eventually if she didn't learn to get it under control—and she urged her lover to consider the dangers of continuing to run while a killer was at large. She expected a fight, especially since she knew how much Rosalyn regretted the earlier impulsive promise that had led her to Oxford on Monday morning. But instead of an argument or even a refusal to discuss the issue, Rosalyn agreed. She wouldn't run again until the killer was found. Or if she ran, she would not run alone.

They had parted at midnight. Still a couple, Melinda thought, still in love . . . Although they hadn't made love as she had hoped they might in what she'd imagined all Tuesday would be a celebration of Rosalyn's coming forward and admitting her sexual preference to the world. It hadn't worked out that way. Rosalyn had pleaded exhaustion, speaking of an essay she had to work on and expressing a need to be alone in order to come to terms with Elena Weaver's death. All an excuse, Melinda realised now, all part of the beginning of the end between them.

And didn't it always happen that way? The initial rapture of love. The encounters, the hopes. The growing intimacy. A prayer for shared dreams. Joyful communication. And, ultimately, disappointment. She had thought that Rosalyn was going to be different. But it was obvious now. She was a liar and a cheat like all the rest.

Bitch, she thought. Bitch. You promised and you lied what else did you lie about who else did you sleep with did you sleep with Elena?

She leaned her bicycle against the wall—indifferent to the fact that the college rules explicitly required that she take it elsewhere—and elbowed her way into the crowd. She saw that one of the porters stood just inside the entry, barring the doorway to the curious and looking one part grim and one part angry and several other parts disgusted. Over the murmur of voices, she heard him say, "Shot-gun. Blasted her direct in the face."

And her anger dissolved as fast as it had come upon her, melted by the power of those seven simple words.

Shotgun. Blasted her direct in the face.

Melinda found that she was biting down on her wool-covered fingers. Instead of the porter standing in the doorway in Old Court, what she saw was Rosalyn, her face and body shattered, disintegrating before her, blowing away in a roar of gunpowder, shot, and blood. And then directly afterwards, in Rosalyn's place grew the dreadful knowledge of who had to have done this and why and how her own life hung in the balance.

She searched the faces of the students round her, looking for the face that would be looking for hers. It wasn't there. But that didn't mean it wasn't nearby, looking from a window, waiting to see her reaction to the death. He'd be resting a bit from the labours of the morning, but his every intention would be to see the job through to the end.

She felt her muscles coiling as her body reacted to her mind's demand for flight. At the same time, she was acutely aware of the need for an ostensible show of calm. For if she turned and ran in full view of everyone—especially in full view of the watcher who was simply waiting for her to make her move—she was lost for a certainty.

Where to go, she wondered. God, God, where to go.

The crowd of students in which she stood began to part as a man's voice said, "Step to one side, please." And then, "Havers, make that call to London, will you?" And the blond man she had seen in Queens'

Lane shouldered his way through the whispering group in front of the door as his companion headed in the general direction of the junior combination room.

"Porter says it was a shotgun," someone called out as the blond mounted the single step that gave entry to the building. In reaction, the man favoured the porter with a critical glance but he said nothing as he passed him and began climbing the stairs.

"Blew her guts out, I heard," a spotty-faced young man said.

"No, it was her face," someone replied.

"Raped first . . ."

"Tied up . . ."

"Both her tits cut off and—"

Melinda's body sprang into action. She spun from the sound of the speculative voices and shoved her way blindly out of the crowd. If she was fast enough, if she didn't pause to consider where she was going and how she was going to get there, if she scrambled to her room and grabbed a rucksack and some clothes and the money her mother had sent her for her birthday . . .

She dashed across the front of the building to the stairway on the right side of the southern turret. She pushed open the door and flew up the stairs. Scarcely breathing, scarcely thinking, she sought only escape.

Someone called her name when she hit the second landing, but she ignored the voice and continued to dash upward. There was her grandmother's house in West Sussex, she thought. A great-uncle lived in Colchester, her brother in Kent. But none of them seemed safe enough, far enough away. None of them seemed capable of offering her the sort of protection she would need from a killer who seemed to know movements in advance of their being made, who seemed to know thoughts and plans in advance of their being given voice. He was, in fact, a killer who even now might be waiting . . .

At the top floor she paused outside her door, recognising the potential danger that lay within. Her bowels were loosening, and tears were eating at the back of her eyes. She listened at the smudged white panels of the door, but the recessed shape of them did nothing more than act as amplifiers for her own torn breathing.

She wanted to run, she needed to hide. But she had to have that cache of money to do either.

"Jesus," she whispered. "Oh God, oh God."

She would reach for the doorknob. She would fling the door open. If the killer was there she would scream like a banshee.

She filled her lungs with enough air to do the job right and thrust her shoulder against the door. It flew open. It crashed back against the wall. It left her with an unimpeded view of the room. Rosalyn's body was lying on her bed.

Melinda began to scream.

Glyn Weaver positioned herself just to the left of the window in her daughter's bedroom and flicked the sheer material away from the glass so that she could have an unimpaired glimpse of the front lawn. The Irish setter was gambolling there, yelping joyfully in expectation of a run. He was circling frantically round Justine who had changed into a tracksuit and running shoes and who was bending and stretching through a series of warm-ups. She'd taken the dog's lead outside with her, and Townee scooped it up from the lawn on one of his passes by her. He carried it like a banner. He cavorted and pranced.

Elena had sent her a dozen pictures of the dog: as a furry baby curled into her lap asleep, a long-legged pup rooting for his gifts beneath the Christmas tree in her father's house, a sleek adolescent leaping over a dry-stone wall. On the back of each she had written Townee's age—*six weeks, two days; four months, eight days; ten months today!*—like an indulgent mother. Glyn wondered if she would have done the same for the baby she'd carried or if Elena would have opted for abortion. A baby, after all, was different from a dog. And no matter her reasons for getting herself pregnant—and Glyn knew her daughter well enough to realise that Elena's pregnancy had probably been a calculated act—Elena was not so much the fool as to believe her life would be unchanged as a result of bringing a child into it. Children always altered one's existence in unaccountable ways, and their unwavering devotion could hardly be relied upon as could a dog's. They took and took and rarely gave. And only the most selfless sort of adult could continually enjoy the sensation of being drained of every resource and bled of every dream.

And for what reward? Just the nebulous hope that this lovely creature—this complete individual over whom one had absolutely no control—would somehow not make the same mistakes, repeat the same patterns, or know the same pain that the parents had lived through and inflicted on each other.

Outside, Justine was tying back her hair at the nape of her neck. Glyn took note of the fact that to do so she used a scarf that matched both the colour of her tracksuit and the colour of her shoes. Idly, she wondered if Justine ever left the house in anything less than a complete ensemble, and she chuckled at the sight of her. Even if one wished to criticise the fact that Justine chose to go exercising just two days after her stepdaughter's murder, one certainly couldn't condemn her for her choice of colour. It was thoughtfully appropriate.

Such a hypocrite, Glyn thought, her lower lip curling. She turned from the sight of her.

Justine had left the house without a word, sleek and cool and utterly patrician, but no longer as controlled as she liked to be. Their confrontation this morning in the breakfast room had taken care of that, with the real woman smoked out from beneath the guise of dutiful hostess and professor's perfect wife. So now she would run, to tone up that lovely, seductive body, to work up a fragrant rose-scented sweat.

But it was more than that. She had to run now. And she had to hide. Because the fact beneath the fiction that was Justine Weaver had finally been revealed in the breakfast room in that fleeting moment when her normally guileless, butter-wouldn't-melt features became rigid with the culpability that lay beneath them. The truth was out.

She had hated Elena. And now that she was off for her run, Glyn was ready to search out the evidence which would prove that Justine's facade of well-bridled feelings skilfully hid the desperation of a killer.

Outside the house, she heard the dog barking, a happy sound of excitement that rapidly faded towards Adams Road. They were off, the two of them. Whatever time she had until Justine's return, Glyn was determined to use every moment.

She bustled to the master bedroom with its sleek Danish furniture and shapely brass lamps. She went to the long, low chest and began opening drawers.

"Georgina Higgins-Hart." The weasel-faced constable squinted at his notebook, the cover of which bore a stain that looked suspiciously like pizza sauce. "A member of Hare and Hounds. Working on an M.Phil. in Renaissance Literature. Newcastle girl." He snapped the notebook closed. "President of the College and the senior tutor had no trouble identifying the body, Inspector. They've both known her since she came up to Cambridge three years back."

The constable stood posted outside the closed door of the girl's bedsitting room. He was positioned like a guard, legs spread and arms folded across his chest, and his expression—flickering indecisively between smug judgement and outright derision—indicated the degree to which he considered the inadequacies of New Scotland Yard CID responsible for this latest Cambridge killing.

Lynley said only, "Do you have the key, Constable?" and took it from the man's palm when he handed it over.

Georgina, he saw, had been a devotee of Woody Allen, and most of the bed-sit's limited wall space was given over to posters celebrating his films. Bookshelves took up the rest of the space, and on them sat an eclectic display of the girl's possessions, everything from a collection of ancient Raggedy Ann dolls to a seriously extensive selection of wine. She had lined up what few books she owned onto the mantel of the bricked-in fireplace. They were held in place on either end by a dispirited-looking miniature palm.

With the constable outside and the door closed upon him, Lynley sat on the edge of the single bed. A pink duvet covered it, with a large bouquet of yellow paeonies embroidered into its centre. His fingers traced the pattern of flowers and leaves as his mind traced the pattern of the two killings.

The outline comprised the most obvious details: a second runner from Hare and Hounds; a second girl; a second victim who was tall and lithe and long-haired and engaged—in the darkness—in an early morning's work-out. Those were the superficial similarities. But if the killings were connected, there had to be others.

And there were, of course. The most immediately apparent was the fact that Georgina Higgins-Hart, like Elena Weaver, had a relationship with the English Faculty. Although she was a postgraduate, Lynley could not overlook the fact that, in her fourth year at the University, she would have known many of the professors, most of the lecturers, and everyone associated with her own field of Renaissance Literature, those writings—both European and British—of the fourteenth, fifteenth, and sixteenth centuries. He knew what Havers was going to make of this information when she learned of it, and he couldn't deny the connection it suggested.

But he also couldn't ignore the fact that Georgina Higgins-Hart was a member of Queens' College. Nor could he deny the additional connection that Queens' College implied.

He got to his feet and went to the desk which was tucked into an alcove whose walls were hung with a collection of framed stills from *Sleeper, Bananas,* and *Take the Money and Run.* He was reading the opening paragraph of an essay on *The Winter's Tale* when the door opened and Sergeant Havers came into the room.

She joined him at the desk. "Well?"

"Georgina Higgins-Hart," he said. "Renaissance Literature." He could sense her smile as she matched the period of time with its most significant author.

"I knew it. I *knew* it. We need to get back to his house and have a go at finding that shotgun, Inspector. I say we get some of Sheehan's blokes to tear the place apart."

"You can hardly think that a man of Thorsson's intelligence would blast a young girl into oblivion and then simply replace the gun among his belongings. He knows he's under suspicion, Sergeant. He isn't a fool."

"He doesn't need to be a fool," she said. "He just needs to be desperate."

"Beyond that, as Sheehan pointed out, we're standing on the threshold of the pheasant season. Shotguns abound. I wouldn't be surprised to learn that the University itself has an outdoor society devoted to hunting. If there's a student handbook on the mantel, you can check on that yourself."

She didn't move. "You can't mean to suggest that these killings aren't related."

"I don't mean to suggest that. I think they are. But not necessarily in the most obvious fashion."

"Then how? What other connection is there but the most obvious ones which, by the way, we've been handed on a platter? Okay, I know you're going to argue that she was a runner so there's another connection for us to play with. And I know she had the same general appearance as the Weaver girl. But frankly, Inspector, trying to build a case on those two facts seems a lot shakier than building a case on Thorsson." She seemed to sense his inclination to dispute the position she was taking. She went on more insistently. "We *know* there was some truth in what Elena Weaver claimed about Thorsson. He as much as demonstrated that this morning. So if he was harassing her, why not this girl as well?"

"There's another connection, Havers. Beyond Thorsson. Beyond running."

"What?"

"Gareth Randolph. He's a member of Queens'."

She didn't look either pleased with or intrigued by this piece of information. She said, "Right. Quite. And his motive, Inspector?"

Lynley fingered through the items on Georgina's desk. He catalogued them mentally and considered his sergeant's question, trying to develop a hypothetical response that would fit both murders.

"Perhaps we're looking at a primary rejection that's begun seeping into the rest of his life."

"Elena Weaver brushed him off so he killed her and then finding that single killing not enough to wipe the rejection out of his memory, he's bent on killing her again and again? Wherever he finds her?" Havers made no effort to hide her incredulity. She ran a restless hand back through her hair and grabbed onto a fistful which she tugged at impatiently. "I can't even begin to swallow that, sir. The means are too different. The Weaver girl may have been killed in a well-planned attack, but *attack* is the watchword. There was real rage behind what happened to her, a need to hurt as well as to kill. This other—" She waved her hand over the top of the desk as if an indication of its scattering of books and papers would stand as symbol for the death of the second girl—"I think this other was the need to eliminate. Do it fast. Do it simple. But just do it."

"Why?"

"Georgina was in Hare and Hounds. She probably knew Elena. And if that's the case, it stands to reason that she probably also knew what Elena intended to do."

"About Thorsson."

"And perhaps Georgina Higgins-Hart was just the corroboration Elena needed to make that sexual harassment charge stick. Perhaps Thorsson knew it. If he went to argue with Elena about it on Thursday night, she might well have told him that she wasn't the only one going to the authorities. And if that was the case, it wasn't going to be her word against his any longer. It was going to be his against theirs. Those aren't very sweet odds, are they, Inspector? And that wouldn't have looked good to anyone."

Lynley had to admit that Havers' hypothesis was grounded more solidly in reality than was his. And yet unless they could come up with a viable piece of hard evidence, they were stymied. She seemed to realise this.

"We've got the black fibres," she persisted. "If his clothes make a match, we're on our way."

"Do you really think Thorsson would have handed his things over this morning—no matter his frame of mind—had he had even the slightest concern that forensic could match them to the fibres from Elena Weaver's body?" Lynley closed an open text on the desk. "He knows he's clear on that, Havers. We need something else."

"The primary weapon used on Elena."

"Did you get St. James on the phone?"

"He'll be up sometime round noon tomorrow. He was in the middle of messing about with some sort of a polymorphic what-have-you, mumbling about isoenzymes and getting generally bleary-eyed from having looked through his microscopes for more than a week. He'll be glad of the diversion."

"That's what he said?"

"No. Actually, he said, 'Tell Tommy he owes me,' but that's pretty much par for the course with you two, isn't it?"

"Quite." Lynley was looking at Georgina's engagement diary. She was less active than Elena Weaver had been, but like Elena she had kept a record of her appointments. Seminars and supervisions were listed, by subject and by name of supervisor. Hare and Hounds had its places as well. But it took only a moment for him to ascertain that Lennart Thorsson's name appeared nowhere. Nor was there anything that resembled the small fish that Elena had regularly sketched upon her calendar. Lynley riffled through all the pages of the book to find something that suggested the sort of intrigue implied by that fish, but it was completely straightforward. If Georgina Higgins-Hart had secrets, she hadn't hidden them here.

They had little enough to go on, he realised. Mostly a series of unprovable conjectures. Until Simon Allcourt-St. James arrived in Cambridge and unless he gave them something else to work with, they would have to rely on the evidence at hand.

17

With a heaviness of heart and a growing sense that the inevitable was fast approaching between them, Rosalyn Simpson watched as Melinda continued stuffing a mishmash of belongings into two rucksacks. She grabbed knee socks, underwear, stockings, three nightgowns from one drawer; a silk scarf, two belts, four T-shirts from another; her passport, a worn Michelin guide to France from a third. Then she went on to the wardrobe where she removed two pairs of blue jeans, a pair of sandals, and a quilted skirt. Her face was blotched from crying, and all the time she packed, she snuffled. Occasionally she withheld a fractured sob.

"Melinda." Rosalyn tried to sound soothing. "You're not being rational."

"I thought it was you." This had been her most frequent response for the last hour, an hour which had begun with her terrorised screaming, moved quickly on to wildly distraught weeping, and concluded with blind determination to leave Cambridge at once with Rosalyn in tow.

There had been no way to talk to her reasonably, and even if there had been, Rosalyn felt as if she lacked the energy to do it. She had spent a miserable night thrashing round in her bed while guilt spread like a prickly rash on the flesh of her conscience, and the last thing she wanted now was a scene of reproach, recrimination, and reassurance with Melinda. But she was wise enough not to mention any of that at the moment. Rather, she told Melinda only part of the truth: she hadn't slept well the previous night; upon returning from a morning's practical, she'd come to

Melinda's room with nowhere else to go to get a bit of rest when the porter had barred her from climbing her own staircase; she'd fallen asleep and hadn't awakened until the door crashed against the wall and Melinda herself had begun screaming unaccountably. She hadn't known that a runner had been shot that morning. The porter had said nothing, telling her only that the staircase would be closed for a while. And no word had yet gone out among the members of college about the murder, so no one was in front of the building at the time to pass on gossip or information. But if it *was* someone from her staircase who had been shot, she knew it had to be Georgina Higgins-Hart, the only other member of Hare and Hounds who lived in that part of the building.

"I thought it was you," Melinda sobbed. "You promised you wouldn't run alone but I thought you ran anyway to spite me because you were angry that I'd insisted you tell your parents about us so I thought it was you."

Rosalyn realised that she *did* feel some anger. It was a bubbling bit of real resentment that promised to boil over into outright dislike. She tried to ignore it, saying, "Why would I want to spite you like that? I didn't run alone. I didn't run at all."

"He's after you, Ros. He's after us both. He wanted you but he got her instead but he's not done with us and we've got to get away."

She'd taken a tin of money from its hiding place in a shoe carton. She'd rustled up her rucksacks from the back of one of the wardrobe shelves. She'd swept her copious supply of cosmetics into a plastic case. And now she was rolling the blue jeans into cylindrical shapes preparatory to ramming them into the canvas sack with everything else. When she was in this state, there was no real talking to her, but Rosalyn still felt the need to try.

"Melinda, this just doesn't make sense."

"I told you last night not to talk to anyone about it, didn't I? But you wouldn't listen. You've always got to do your precious little duty. And now look where it's got us."

"Where?"

"Here. Needing to clear off, and having nowhere to go. But if you'd thought a bit first . . . If you'd just thought for once . . . And now he's waiting, Ros. He's just biding his time. He knows where to find us. You as good as invited him to blow us both to bits. Well, it's not going to happen. I'm not going to wait round to have him come for me. And neither are you." She took another two pullovers from a drawer. "We're nearly the same size. You won't need to go to your room for clothes."

Rosalyn walked to the window. One lone senior member of the college strolled across the lawn below. The crowd of the curious had long since dispersed, as had all obvious signs of the police, making it difficult to believe that another runner had been murdered that morning, making it impossible to believe that this second killing was tied in any way to the conversation she'd had with Gareth Randolph last night.

She and Melinda—glowering, protesting, and arguing against it every step of the way—had walked the few blocks to DeaStu and found him in his cubicle of an office. With no one there to interpret for them, they'd used the screen of a word processor to communicate. He'd looked awful, Rosalyn recalled. His eyes were rheumy; his skin was unshaven and pinched on his skull. He looked devastated by illness. He looked exhausted and torn. But he didn't look like a killer.

Somehow, she thought, she would have sensed it if Gareth had presented any danger to her. Certainly, there would have been an air of tension surrounding him. He would have shown signs of panic as she told him what she knew about the previous morning's murder. But instead, he evidenced only anger and grief. And faced with that, she had known for a certainty that he had been in love with Elena Weaver.

Quite without warning, she had felt an irrational twist of jealousy. To have someone—all right, a man, she admitted it—love her so much that he would dream about her, think about her, and hope for a life together . . .

Looking at Gareth Randolph, watching his hands move over the keyboard as he typed his questions and responded to hers, she felt overcome by the sudden knowledge that she wanted a conventional future like everyone else. This unexpected desire brought an attendant rush of guilt. It swarmed busily round the issue of betrayal. Yet feeling the tricks and twinges of her conscience, she was roused to anger. For how could there be the slightest degree of treachery in yearning for the simplest prospect that life offered everyone?

They'd returned to her room. Melinda's mood had been black. She'd not wanted Rosalyn to talk to anyone about Robinson Crusoe's Island in the first place and even the compromise of talking to Gareth Randolph and not to the police had been insufficient to quell her displeasure. Rosalyn knew that only seduction would suffice to woo Melinda back to good humour once again. And she understood how the scene would evolve between them, with herself in the role of sexual supplicant and Melinda grudgingly giving reply. Her solicitous advances would eventually melt Melinda's indifference while Melinda's languid and largely uninterested responses would keep her in her place. It would be the delicate dance of expiation and punishment in which they'd engaged so many times. She knew how each movement would play out against the next, all of them acting as a means of proving her love in some way. But while the success of the seduction generally provided a few moments' gratification, the entire procedure had seemed monumentally tiresome last night.

So she'd pleaded exhaustion, an essay, the need to rest and to think. And when Melinda had left her—casting a reproachful glance over her shoulder just before she closed the door—Rosalyn had experienced the most exquisite relief.

That hadn't done much to allow her to sleep, however. The satisfaction of being alone did nothing to stop her from writhing in her bed and trying to wipe from her mind all the elements of her life that seemed to be caving in on her.

You made the choice, she told herself. You are what you are. No one and nothing can change that for you.

But how she wanted to.

"Why don't you think about us?" Melinda was saying. "You never do, Ros. I do. All the time. But you never do. Why?"

"This goes beyond us."

Melinda stopped packing, holding a rolled pair of socks in her hand. "How can you say that? I asked you not to talk to anyone. You said you had to talk anyway. Now someone else is dead. Another runner. A runner from your staircase. He followed her, Ros. He thought it was you."

"That's absurd. He has no reason to hurt me."

"You must have told him something without even being aware of its importance. But he knew what it meant. He wanted to kill you. And since I was there as well, he wants to kill me. Well, he's not getting the chance. If you aren't willing to think of us, I am. We're clearing out until they've nabbed him." She zipped the rucksack and plopped it on the bed. She went to the wardrobe for her coat, scarf, and gloves. "We'll take the train into London first. We can stay near Earl's Court until I get the money to—"

"No."

"Rosalyn—"

"Gareth Randolph's not a killer. He loved Elena. You could see that on his face. He wouldn't have hurt her."

"That's a pile of rubbish. People kill each other all the time over love. Then they kill once again to cover up their tracks. Which is exactly what he's doing, no matter what you think you saw on the island." Melinda glanced round the room as if to make sure she'd forgotten nothing. She said, "Let's get going. Come on."

Rosalyn didn't move. "I did it for you last night, Melinda. I went to DeaStu, not the police. And now Georgina's dead."

"*Because* you went to DeaStu. Because you talked in the first place. If you'd kept your mouth shut, nothing would have happened to anyone. Don't you see that?"

"I'm responsible for this. Both of us are."

Melinda's mouth drew into a hair's width line. "*I'm* responsible? I tried to take care of you. I wanted to protect you. I tried to stop you from putting both of us at risk. And now I'm responsible for Georgina's death? Well, that's rich, isn't it?"

"Don't you see how it is? I *let* you stop me. I should have done what I knew was right in the first place. I should always do that. But I keep getting side-tracked."

"What's that supposed to mean?"

"That it always comes down to a question of love with you. If I really love you, I'll take the room under the eaves. If I really love you, we'll have sex when you want. If I really love you, I'll tell my parents the truth about us."

"And that's what all this is really about, isn't it? That you told your parents and they didn't approve. They didn't fall all over themselves wishing you well. They played it for guilt instead of compassion."

"If I really love you, I'll always do what you want. If I really love you, I'll have no mind of my own. If I really love you, I'll live like a . . ."

"What? Finish it. Say it. Live like a what?"

"Nothing. Forget it."

"Go on. Say it." Melinda sounded giddy. "Live like a dyke. A dyke. A dyke. Because that's what you are and you just can't face it. So you turn it around and shove it on me. You think a man's going to be the answer to your problems? You think a man can make you into something you aren't? You'd better get wise, Ros. You'd better face the truth. The problem's yourself." She shouldered her rucksack and threw the other to the floor at Rosalyn's feet. "Choose," she said.

"I don't want to choose."

"Oh, come on. Don't give me that." Melinda waited for a moment. Somewhere on the staircase, a door opened. Quirky music swelled and a wavering, whimsical voice claimed to be u-n-c-o-u-p-l-e-d. Melinda laughed sardonically. "How appropriate," she said.

Rosalyn reached towards her. But she didn't pick up the rucksack. "Melinda."

"We're born the way we're born. It's a toss of the dice and no one can change it."

"But don't you see? I don't know that. I've never even had a chance to find out."

Melinda nodded, her face quickly becoming both shuttered and cool. "Great. So find out. Just don't come snivelling back when you discover what's what." She grabbed her shoulder bag and pulled on her gloves. "I'm out of here then. Lock up when you leave. Give your key to the porter."

"All this just because I want to see the police?" Rosalyn asked.

"All this just because you don't want to see yourself."

"My money's on the pullover," Sergeant Havers said. She picked up the squat stainless steel teapot and poured, grimacing at the pale colour of the brew with a "what is this stuff, anyway?" to the waitress who was passing their table.

"Herbal blend," the girl said.

Blackly, Havers stirred in a teaspoon of sugar. "Grass cuttings, more likely." She took a tentative sip and scowled. "Grass cuttings undoubtedly. Don't they have the regular bit? P.G. Tips? Something to wear the enamel off your teeth good and proper?"

Lynley poured his own cup. "This is better for you, Sergeant. It has no caffeine."

"It also has no flavour, or don't we care about that?"

"Just one of the drawbacks to the healthy life."

Havers muttered and pulled out her cigarettes.

"No smoking, miss," the waitress said as she brought their sweets to the table, an arrangement of carob-chip biscuits and sugar-free fruit tarts.

"Oh, hell and damnation," Havers said.

They were in the Bliss Tea Room in Market Hill, a small establishment squeezed in between a stationery shop and what appeared to be a gathering place for the local skin heads. *Heavy Mettle* had been scrawled by an obviously untutored hand in red greasepaint across the latter shop's window, and the ear-assaulting screech of electric guitars periodically blasted out the front door. In apparent answer to the window decoration, the stationers had countered with *Waitless Cowardice* across their own glass, a joke that no doubt went unappreciated by the owners and patrons of the neighbouring business.

The Bliss Tea Room—with its plain pine tables and woven grass mats—had been unoccupied by customers when Lynley and Havers entered. And the combination of the music from next door and the health food on the menu was evidence enough that the little restaurant wasn't long for this world.

They'd made their phone call to Cambridge's forensic department from a call box on Silver Street rather than from the junior combination room where Havers had started to direct him upon leaving Georgina Higgins-Hart's bed-sit. He had stopped her, saying:

"I saw a call box on the street. If we've got a match on the fibres, I'd rather the news wasn't overheard and put into the University's gossip mill before we've had a chance to decide what to do with it."

So they had left the college and headed towards Trumpington where an old chipped call box stood near the corner, with three of its front glass panels missing and a fourth taken up by a sticker featuring a drawing of a foetus in a rubbish bin and *Abortion is Murder* printed in crimson letters that dissolved into a garish pool of blood beneath them.

Lynley had made the call because he knew it was the next logical step in the case. But he wasn't surprised by the information which the Cambridge forensic team relayed.

"No match," he said to Havers as they returned to Queens' College where they'd left the car. "They haven't finished with everything yet. But so far, nothing."

What remained to be tested were a coat, a pullover, a T-shirt, and two pairs of trousers. Sergeant Havers was giving her attention to these.

She dipped her carob-chip biscuit into her tea and took a bite before she spoke again, resuming her theme. "It makes perfect sense. The morning was cold. He'd have been wearing a pullover. I think we've got him."

Lynley had chosen the apple tart. He took a bite. It wasn't half-bad. He said, "I can't agree. Not for the fibres we're looking for, Sergeant. Rayon, polyester, and cotton make too light a blend for a pullover, especially one worn in November to cut the morning's chill."

"Okay. I'll buy that. So he wore something over it. An overcoat. A jacket. He took that off before he killed her. Then he put it back on to hide the blood which he got all over himself when he beat in her face."

"And then had it cleaned and ready in anticipation of our coming for it this morning, Sergeant? Because there were no stains on it. And if he anticipated our coming to pick it up, why would he just leave it with the rest of his clothes? Why wouldn't he get rid of it?''

"Because he doesn't quite know how an investigation works."

"I don't like it, Havers. It doesn't feel right. It leaves too much unaccounted for.''

"Like what?"

"Like what was Sarah Gordon doing at the crime scene that morning and prowling round Ivy Court that night? Like why did Justine Weaver run without the dog Monday morning? Like what's the connection between Elena Weaver's presence and performance in Cambridge and her father's attaining the Penford Chair?''

Havers took a second biscuit, broke it in half. "And I thought you had your heart newly set on Gareth Randolph. What happened to him, then? Have you scratched him off the roster? And if you do—if you put Sarah Gordon or Justine Weaver or anyone besides Thorsson, by the way, in his place—what's the story behind the second killing?''

Lynley set his fork down, pushed the apple tart to one side. "I wish I knew.''

The tea room's door opened. They both looked up. A girl stood hesitantly just inside. She was clear-skinned, with a mass of auburn hair swirling round her face like cirrus clouds at the last part of sunset.

"You're . . ." She peered about as if to make sure that she was addressing the proper people. "You're the police, aren't you?" Assured of this, she came to their table. "My name's Catherine Meadows. May I speak with you?''

She removed her navy beret, her matching scarf, and her gloves. She kept on her coat. She sat on the edge of a straight-backed chair, not at their table but at the one next to them. When the waitress approached, the girl looked confused for a moment before glancing at the menu and ordering a single cup of mint tea and a toasted, whole wheat cake.

"I've been trying to find you since half past nine," she said. "The porter at St. Stephen's couldn't tell me where you were. It's only luck that I saw you come in here at all. I was over at Barclay's.''

"Ah," Lynley said.

Catherine smiled fleetingly and worried the ends of her hair. She kept her shoulder bag on her lap and her knees pressed together. She said nothing else until the tea and the teacake were placed before her.

"It's Lenny," she said, her eyes on the floor.

Lynley saw Havers slide her notebook onto the table top and sound-lessly open it. He said, "Lenny?"

"Thorsson."

"Ah. Yes."

"I saw you waiting for him after the Shakespeare lecture on Tuesday. I didn't know who you were then, but he told me later that you'd talked to him about Elena Weaver. He said there was nothing for us to worry about at the time because . . ." She reached for the cup as if about to drink, but then apparently changed her mind. "That doesn't matter, does it? You just need to know that he didn't have anything at all to do with Elena. And he certainly didn't kill her. He couldn't have. He was with me."

"When exactly was he with you?"

She looked at them earnestly, her grey eyes growing dark. She couldn't have been more than eighteen years old. "It's so personal. He could get in such trouble if you were to tell anyone. You see, I'm the only undergraduate Lenny's *ever* . . ." She rolled the corner of her paper napkin into a little tube and said with calm determination, "I'm the only one he's ever allowed himself to get close to. And it's been a struggle for him. His morals. His conscience. What would be right for us. What would be ethical. Because he's my supervisor."

"You're lovers, I take it?"

"You need to know that we went absolute weeks without doing a thing. We fought it every time we were together. Right from the first we both felt the attraction. It was like electricity. Lenny was so open and honest about it. That's the way he's always fought it off in the past. Because he's attracted to women. He does admit that. And in the past he's simply talked it out. He's let women know and they've worked past it—they've worked through it—together. And we tried that, the two of us. We really did try. But in this case, it was bigger than both of us."

"Is that what Lenny said?" Havers asked. Her face was a study of bland, dispassionate interest.

Catherine seemed to hear something in her tone, however. She said a bit archly, "It was my decision to make love with him. Lenny didn't push me. I was ready. And we talked about it for days. He wanted me to know him completely, inside and out, before I made the decision. He wanted me to understand."

"To understand?" Lynley asked.

"Him. His life. What it had been like for him when he'd once been engaged. He wanted me to see him as he truly is so that I could accept him. All of him. Every bit. So that I wouldn't ever be like his fiancée.'' She turned in her chair and faced them squarely. ''She rejected him sexually. She did that to him for all of four years because he was . . . Oh, it doesn't matter. But you need to understand that he couldn't bear it to happen again. He was nearly destroyed by the rejection and sorrow the first time. It's taken him forever to get over the pain and to learn to trust a woman again.''

''Did he ask you to speak to us?'' Lynley asked.

She cocked her pretty head to one side. ''You don't believe me, do you? You think I'm making this up.''

''Not at all. I'm just wondering if and when he asked you to speak to us.''

''He didn't ask me to speak to you. He wouldn't do that. It's just that he told me this morning that you'd been to see him and taken some of his clothes and actually thought . . .'' Her voice wavered momentarily and she reached for the tea, drinking this time. She kept the cup balanced on her small, white palm. ''Lenny had nothing to do with Elena. He's in love with me.''

Sergeant Havers gave a delicate cough. Catherine looked at her sharply.

''I can see what you're thinking, that I'm just some simple-minded tart to him. But that's not how it is. We're going to be married.''

''Quite.''

''We are! When I've graduated.''

Lynley said, ''What time did Mr. Thorsson leave you?''

''Six forty-five.''

''Was this from your room at St. Stephen's?''

''I don't live in college. I share a house with three other girls off Mill Road. Towards Ramsey Town.''

And not, Lynley thought, towards Crusoe's Island. ''Are you certain of the time?''

''I don't have a doubt.''

Havers tapped her pencil against a page of her notebook. ''Why?''

There was a fair degree of pride in Catherine's answer. ''Because I'd looked at the clock when he first woke me up and I looked once again when we finished. I wanted to see how long he lasted this time. Seventy minutes. He finished at 6:40.''

''A real marathon performer.'' Havers nodded. ''You must have felt like chopped meat.''

"Havers," Lynley said quietly.

The girl got to her feet. "Lenny said you wouldn't believe me. He said you especially"—this with a finger pointed at Havers—"wanted to make him pay. Pay for what, I asked him. You'll see, he said, you'll see when you talk to her." She put on her beret and her scarf. She squeezed her gloves into balls. "Well, I see. I do. He's a wonderful man. He's tender. He's loving and brilliant and he's been hurt so badly in his life because he cares too much. He cared for Elena Weaver and she took it the wrong way. And then when he wouldn't sleep with her, she went to Dr. Cuff with this *despicable* story . . . If you can't see the truth—"

"Was he with you last night?" Havers asked.

The girl drew up, hesitated. "What?"

"Did he spend the night with you again?"

"I . . . No. He had a lecture he was working on. And a paper he's been writing." Her voice steadied, grew stronger. "He's working on a study of Shakespeare's tragedies. It's a thesis about the tragic heroes. Victims of their time, he's arguing, conquered not by their own tragic flaws but by the prevailing social conditions. It's radical, brilliant. He was working on it last night and—"

"Where?" Havers asked.

For a moment, the girl faltered again. She gave no response.

"Where?" Havers asked.

"He was at home."

"He told you he was home all night?"

Her hand closed more tightly round her crumpled gloves. "Yes."

"He wouldn't have left sometime? Perhaps to see someone?"

"To see someone? Who? Who would he want to see? I was at a meeting. I got home quite late. He hadn't been by, he hadn't phoned. When I phoned, he didn't answer, but I merely assumed . . . I was the *only* one he'd be seeing. The only one. So . . ." Her eyes dropped. She fumbled with putting on her gloves. "I was the only one . . ." She swung to the door, turned back once as if to say something to them, turned away. The door remained opened behind her when she left. The wind whipped in quickly. It was cold and damp.

Havers took up her teacup and lifted it in a salute to the girl's departure. "Quite a chap, our Lenny."

"He's not the killer," Lynley said.

"No. He's not. At least not Elena's."

18

Penelope answered the door when Lynley rang the bell in Bulstrode Gardens at half past seven that evening. She was carrying the baby against her shoulder, and although she was still garbed only in a dressing gown and slippers, her hair had been washed and it fell round her shoulders in fine, soft waves. There was a scent of fresh powder in the air surrounding her.

She said, "Tommy. Hello," and led him into the sitting room where several large volumes were open on the sofa, competing for space with a child-sized Colt .45, a cowboy hat, and a mound of clean laundry that seemed to consist mostly of pyjamas and nappies.

"You got me interested in Whistler and Ruskin last evening," Penelope said in reference to the volumes which, he saw, were all art books. "The dispute between them is part of art history now, but I hadn't thought about it in years. What a fighter Whistler was. No matter what one thinks of his work—and it *was* controversial enough at the time . . . just consider the Peacock Room in the Leyland house—one simply can't help admiring him."

She went to the sofa and made a nest of the laundry into which she placed the baby who gurgled happily and kicked her feet in the air. She unearthed one book from beneath the stack and said, "This actually has part of the trial transcript in it. Imagine taking on the most influential art critic of your time and suing him for libel. I can't think of anyone who'd have the gumption to do that to a critic today. Listen to his assessment of Ruskin." She picked up the book and ran her finger down the page. "Here it is. 'It is not only when criticism is inimical that I object to it, but when it is incompetent. I hold that none but an artist can be a competent critic.'" She laughed lightly and brushed her hair back from her cheeks. It was a gesture peculiarly like one of Helen's. "Imagine saying that about John Ruskin. What an upstart Whistler was."

"Was he speaking the truth?"

"I think what he said is true of all criticism, Tommy. In the case of painting, an artist bases his evaluation of a piece upon knowledge that's grown from both his education and his experience. An art critic, or any critic for that matter, works from an historical frame of reference—what's been done before—and from theory—how it ought to be done now. That's all well and good: theory, technique, and being grounded in the basics. But, really, it takes an artist to truly understand another artist and his work."

Lynley joined her at the sofa where one of the books was open to *Nocturne in Black and Gold: The Falling Rocket.* "I'm not that familiar with his work," he said. "Other than the painting of his mother."

She grimaced. "To be remembered for such a dreary piece instead of for these. But then, that's not really fair of me, is it? His mother was a fine study in composition and colour—or actually the lack of primary colour and light—but the river pictures are splendid. Look at them. They have a certain glory, don't they? What a challenge to paint the darkness, to see substance in shadows."

"Or in fog?" Lynley asked.

Penelope looked up from the book. "Fog?"

"Sarah Gordon," Lynley explained. "She was getting ready to paint in the fog when she found Elena Weaver's body Monday morning. That's been part of a stumbling block for me when it comes to evaluating her role in what happened. Would you say that painting the fog is the same as painting the darkness?"

"I'd say it's not much different."

"But—like Whistler—it would mean a new style?"

"Yes. But a change in style isn't uncommon among artists, is it? One merely has to consider Picasso. The blue period. Cubism. He was always stretching."

"As a challenge?"

She pulled out another volume. It was open to *Nocturne in Blue and Silver,* Whistler's nighttime depiction of the River Thames and Battersea Bridge. "Challenge, growth, boredom, a need for change, a momentary idea that bursts into a long-term commitment. Artists alter their style for all sorts of reasons.''

''And Whistler?''

''I think he saw art where other people saw nothing. But that's the nature of the artist in the first place, isn't it?''

To see art where other people see nothing. It was, he realised with some surprise, such a logical conclusion to draw from the facts, one he himself should have been capable of drawing.

Penelope was leafing through a few more pages. A car drew up on the drive outside. A door opened and closed. She raised her head.

''What happened to Whistler?'' Lynley asked. ''I can't recall if he won his case against Ruskin.''

Her eyes were on the curtains which were closed. They shifted in the direction of the front door as footsteps approached it, crunching abrasively against the rough shards of gravel on the drive.

She said, ''He won and he lost. The jury awarded him a farthing for contemptuous damages but he had to pay the court costs and ended up going bankrupt.''

''And then?''

''He went off to Venice for a bit, painted nothing, and tried to destroy himself with a vicious sort of wild life. Then he went back to London and continued to try to destroy himself there.''

''He didn't succeed?''

''He didn't.'' She smiled. ''Instead he fell in love. With a woman who also fell in love with him. And that tends to obviate past injustices, doesn't it? One can hardly concentrate on destroying the self when the other becomes so much more important.''

The front door opened. There was a rustle of sound, as of a coat being removed and hung upon the rack. This was followed by a few more footsteps. Then Harry Rodger stopped short at the sitting room door.

He said, ''Tommy. Hullo. I'd no idea you were in town,'' but he remained where he was, looking ill-at-ease in a rumpled suit and a stained red tie. He clutched a worn athletic bag which was unzipped, with the cuff of a white shirt protruding from it. ''You're looking lively,'' he said to his wife. He ventured a few steps into the room, dropped his eyes to the sofa, regarded the books. ''Ah. I see.''

''Tommy was asking about Whistler and Ruskin last night.''

''Was he?'' Rodger cast a cool look in Lynley's direction.

''Yes.'' She went eagerly on. ''You know, Harry, I'd forgotten how interesting the situation between them—''

"Quite."

Slowly, Penelope raised one hand as if to see to the state of her hair. Tiny lines etched their way from the corners of her mouth. She said to Lynley, "Let me get Helen for you. She was reading to the twins. She can't have heard you come in."

When she left them, Rodger went to stand before the sofa. He played the tips of his fingers against the baby's forehead like a restless benediction. "I think we should name you Canvas," he said, running his index finger along the infant's smooth cheek. "Mummy would like that, wouldn't she?" He looked at Lynley, his mouth curving with a sardonic smile.

Lynley said, "People generally have interests outside the sphere of their families, Harry."

"Secondary interests. With their families coming first."

"Life's not that convenient. People don't always fit into the most accommodating mould."

"Pen's a wife." Rodger's voice was smooth, but it had a rock's smoothness, hard and determined. "She's a mother as well. She made that decision more than four years ago. She chose to be the care-giver, the backbone of the family, not someone who leaves her baby in a pile of laundry while she leafs through her art books and dwells on the past."

It was a condemnation that Lynley found particularly unfair, considering the circumstances of Penelope's renewed interest in art. He said, "Actually, I set her off on this yesterday."

"Fine. I understand. But it's over for her, Tommy. That part of her life."

"On whose determination?"

"I know what you're thinking. You're wrong. We both decided what was more important. But she won't accept it now. She doesn't want to adjust."

"Why does she have to? The decision's not written in concrete, is it? Why can't she have both? Her career. Her family."

"There aren't any winners in a situation like that. Everyone suffers."

"Instead of just Pen?"

Rodger's face became chiselled in reaction to the affront. His voice, however, remained perfectly reasonable. "I've seen this sort of thing among my colleagues, Tommy, even if you haven't. Wives go their own way and the family dissolves. And even if that weren't the case—even if Pen could juggle the roles of wife, mother, homemaker, and art conservationist without driving us all mad, which she can't, by the way, which is why she quit her job at the Fitzwilliam when the twins were two—she has everything she needs right here. A husband, a fair income, a decent home, three healthy children.''

"That's not always enough."

Rodger laughed sharply. "You sound just like her. She's lost her *self,* she says. She's just an extension of everyone else. What absolute rubbish. What she's lost is *things.* What her parents provided her. What we used to have when both of us worked. Things.'' He dropped his athletic bag next to the sofa, wearily rubbed the back of his neck. "I've spoken to her doctor. Give her time, he says. It's that post-partum business. She'll be back to herself in a few more weeks. Well, as far as I'm concerned, it had better happen soon. I'm just about at the end of my patience with her.'' He nodded at the baby. "Watch her for me, will you? I've got to get something to eat.''

That said, he left the room, disappearing through the door that led into the kitchen. The baby gurgled once again and clutched at the air. She made a sound like "uh puh" and grinned with happy, toothless pleasure at the ceiling.

Lynley sat down next to her laundry nest and took hold of one of her hands. It wasn't much larger than the pad of his thumb. Her nails teased his skin—odd to think that he'd never once considered the fact that babies *have* nails—and he felt a rush of tenderness towards her. Unprepared to feel anything more than bemusement when left alone with her, he pulled over one of Penelope's art books. Although the words were out of focus because he didn't want to bother—couldn't really bother—with his spectacles, he plunged himself wholeheartedly into distraction with an account of James McNeill Whistler's earliest days in Paris and the typically stuffy, academic revelation of his relationship with his first mistress, who was both introduced and dismissed from Whistler's life within the confines of a single gerund phrase: "He began by assuming a life style he deemed appropriate to a bohemian and by going so far as to attract a young milliner—nicknamed *La Tigresse* with the joyful hyperbolic propensity of the period—to live with and pose for him for a period of time.'' Lynley read on, but there was nothing more of the milliner. To the academic who had written the volume, she merited one sentence in an account of Whistler's life, no matter what she may have been to him, no matter the way in which she may have influenced or inspired his work.

Lynley reflected on the veiled implication behind that simple group of words. *Nonentity,* they declared, someone he painted and took to his bed. She was consigned to history as Whistler's mistress. If she'd ever had a self, it was long forgotten.

He got up restlessly, walked across the room to the fireplace with its display of photographs lined up on the mantel. They depicted Penelope with Harry, Penelope with the children, Penelope with her parents, Penelope with her sisters. But there was not a single picture of Penelope alone.

"Tommy?"

He turned to see that Helen had come into the room. She stood near the door, dressed in brown wool and ivory silk with a trim camel jacket slung over her arm. Penelope was just behind her.

He wanted to say to them both, "I think I understand. Now. In this moment. I think I finally understand." But instead, feeling the depth and breadth of his own inadequacy defined and conditioned by the fact that he was male, he said, "Harry's getting himself something to eat. Thanks for your help, Pen."

Her acknowledgement of this was tentative and brief: a movement of her lips that might have passed for a smile, a quick bob of the head. Then she walked to the sofa and began closing her books. She stacked them on the floor and picked up the baby.

"She's due to be fed," Penelope said. "I can't think why she hasn't begun to fuss." She wandered from the room. They heard her climbing the stairs.

They didn't say anything until they were in the car, driving the short distance to Trinity Hall where the jazz concert was scheduled to be performed in the junior combination room. And then it was Lady Helen who broke the silence between them.

"She actually came to life, Tommy. I can't tell you what a relief it's been."

"Yes. I know. I could see the difference."

"All day she was involved in something beyond the scope of that house. It's what she needs. She knows it. They both do. They must."

"Have you talked to her about it?"

" 'How can I leave them?' she asks me. 'They're my children, Helen. What kind of mother am I if I want to leave them?' "

Lynley glanced at her. Her face was averted. "You can't solve this problem for her, you know."

"I don't see how I can leave her if I don't."

The determination behind her words plunged his spirits. He said, "You're planning to stay on here, aren't you?"

"I'll phone Daphne tomorrow. She can put off her visit for another week. God knows she'd be happy enough to do so. She has a family of her own.''

Without a thought, he said, ''Helen, damn it all, I wish you would—'' and then he stopped himself.

He felt her turn in her seat, knew she was watching him. He said nothing more.

''You've been good for Pen,'' she said. ''I think you've made her face something she didn't want to see.''

He took no pleasure from the information. ''I'm glad I'm good for someone.''

He parked the Bentley in a narrow space on Garret Hostel Lane, a few yards away from the gentle rise of the footbridge that crossed the River Cam. They walked back towards the porter's lodge of the college, just down the street from the entrance to St. Stephen's.

The air was cold, it seemed hung with moisture. A heavy cover of clouds obscured the night sky. Their footsteps echoed against the pave ment, a brisk sound like the sharp tattoo of drums.

Lynley glanced at Lady Helen. She was walking near enough at his side that her shoulder brushed his, and the warmth of her arm, the fresh, crisp scent of her body, acted in concert as a call to action which he tried to ignore. He told himself that there was more to life than the immediate gratification of his own desires. And he tried to believe this even as he felt himself grow lost in the simple contemplation of contrast offered by the dark fall of her hair as it swung forward to touch the pearl of her skin.

He said, as if there had been no break in their conversation, ''But am I good for you, Helen? That's the real question, isn't it?'' And although he managed to keep his voice light, his heart still beat rapidly at the back of his throat. ''I wonder that. I put the sum of what I am into a balance and weigh it against what I ought to be, and I ask myself if I'm really enough.''

When she turned her head, the amber light shafting down from a window above them surrounded her like an aureole. ''Why would you ever think you're not enough?''

He pondered the question, tracing his thoughts and his feelings right back to their source. He found that both of them grew from her decision to remain with her sister's family in Cambridge. He wanted her back in London, available to him. If he was good enough for her, she'd return at his request. If she valued his love, she'd bow to his wishes. He wanted her to do so. He wanted an overt manifestation of the love she claimed to feel for him. And he wanted to be the one to decide exactly what that manifestation would be.

But he couldn't tell her this. So he settled on saying, "I think I'm struggling with a definition of love."

She smiled and slipped her hand through his arm. "You and everyone else, Tommy darling."

They rounded the corner into Trinity Lane and entered the college grounds where a blackboard sign had been decorated with the words *Jazz Up Your Life Tooo-nite* in coloured chalk, and construction paper arrows affixed to the pavement led the way through the main college court to the junior combination room in the northeast corner of the grounds.

Similar to St. Stephen's College, the building that housed Trinity Hall's JCR was modern, little more than alternating panels of wood and glass. In addition to the combination room, it contained the college bar, where a considerable crowd was gathered at small round tables, engaged in boisterous conversation that seemed to be revolving round the good-humoured harassment of two men who were playing darts with rather more intensity than usually accompanied the game. The apparent reason for their avid concentration seemed to be age. One player was a youth of no more than twenty, the other an older man with a close-cropped grey beard.

"Go for it, Petersen," someone shouted when the younger man took position for his turn. "Junior fellows kick arse. Show him."

The young man made an elaborate display of loosening up his muscles and assuming the correct stance before he flung the dart and missed the shot entirely. Jeers roared through the room. In response, he turned around, pointed to his backside meaningfully, and hefted a pint of beer to his mouth. The crowd hooted and laughed.

Lynley guided Lady Helen through the jostling group to the bar and from there they made their way towards the JCR, beers in hand. The JCR was built on several different levels accommodating a line of immovable sofas and a number of uninteresting chairs with lazy, slung backs. At one end of the room, the floor rose to what was being used as a small staging area where the jazz group was getting ready to perform.

There were only six of them, so they didn't need room for anything more than the space required to set up a keyboard and drums, three straight-back chairs for the saxophone, the trumpet, and the clarinet players, and a roughly defined triangular area for the double bass. Electrical extension cords from the keyboard seemed to snake everywhere, and when she turned and saw Lynley and Lady Helen, Miranda Webberly tripped over one in her haste to say hello.

Regaining her footing with a grin, she dashed over to greet them. "You came!" she said. "This is absolutely grand. Inspector, will you promise to tell Dad I'm a musical genius? I'm after another trip to New Orleans, but he's only likely to cooperate if he thinks I've a future playing the changes on Bourbon Street."

"I'll tell him you play like an angel."

"No! Like Chet Baker, please!" She greeted Lady Helen and went on confidentially. "Jimmy—he's our drummer—wanted to cancel tonight's gig. He's at Queens', you know, and he thought with that second girl getting shot this morning . . ." She looked over her shoulder to where the drummer was moodily tapping his sticks in a light spitting rhythm against the cymbals. " 'We shouldn't be out entertaining,' he says. 'It's not right, is it? It doesn't feel right.' But he can't come up with an alternative for us. Paul—he plays double bass—wanted to bash local heads in some Arbury pub. But all in all, it seemed best that we just go ahead and play. I don't know what it'll sound like, though. No one seems very much in the mood." She glanced anxiously round the room as if in the need for some sort of contradiction to reassure her.

A respectable crowd had begun to gather, apparently drawn by the rapid scales and chords which the keyboard player was using to warm up. Lynley took the opportunity before the concert began to say:

"Randie, did you know Elena Weaver was pregnant?"

Miranda shifted on her feet, rubbing the right sole of her high-topped black gym shoe against her left ankle. "Rather," she said.

"How's that?"

"I mean, I suspected. She never told me."

They'd trodden this ground together before. "You mean you didn't know it for a fact."

"I didn't know it for a fact."

"But you suspected? Why?"

Miranda sucked at the inside of her lower lip. "It was the Cocoa Puffs in the gyp room, Inspector. They were hers, the same carton. It'd been there for weeks."

"I'm not sure I understand."

"Her breakfast," Lady Helen said.

Miranda nodded. "She'd left off eating in the morning. And three times—perhaps four—I'd gone to the loo and she'd been in there being sick. Once I found her at it and the other times—" Miranda twisted a button on her navy cardigan. She wore a navy T-shirt beneath it. "It's just that I could smell it."

She belonged on the force, Lynley thought. She was a natural observer. She didn't miss a trick.

She said in a rush, "I would have said something to you Monday night only I didn't know for sure. And other than being sick those mornings, she didn't act any different."

"What do you mean?"

"I mean she wasn't acting like she had anything in particular to worry about, so I thought perhaps I might have been wrong."

"Perhaps she wasn't worried. An out-of-wedlock pregnancy isn't the sort of disaster it might have been thirty years ago."

"Maybe not in your family." Miranda smiled. "But I can't exactly see my dad greeting that kind of news like it was an announcement of the Second Coming. And I never got the impression her dad was any different."

"Randie, come on. Let's do it," the saxophone player called from across the room.

"Right," she said. She gave Lynley and Lady Helen a light-hearted salute. "I'm taking a ride during the second number. Listen for it."

"Taking a ride?" Lady Helen said as Randie scampered back to join the rest of the jazz combo. "What on earth does she mean, Tommy?"

"It must be jazzspeak," Lynley said. "I'm afraid we'd need Louis Armstrong here to translate."

The concert began with a roll of drums and the keyboard player calling out, "Pound the valves down, Randie. One and two and three and—"

Randie, the saxophonist, and the clarinet player lifted their instruments. Lynley glanced down at the sheet of paper that served as programme for the concert and read the name of the number. "Circadian Dysrhythmia." It featured the keyboard player who, huddled over his instrument with effort and concentration, carried the lively melody for the first few minutes before tossing it over to the clarinet player who surged to his feet and took it from there. The drummer provided a steady tip-tapping on the cymbals in the background. As he did so, his narrowed eyes flitted round the room to take in the crowd.

By the middle of the number, more listeners had joined the group in the JCR, wandering in from the bar with drinks in hand, and coming in directly from the college grounds where the music no doubt drifted into the surrounding buildings. Heads bobbed in the sort of second-nature response that is generally the listener's reaction to good jazz while hands rapped against the arms of chairs, the tops of thighs, and the sides of beer glasses. By the end of the number, the audience was won, and when the song ended—with no prior warning or winding down of the musicians' enthusiasm but just upon a single note that was cut off into silence—the moment of stunned surprise that followed was broken by long and enthusiastic applause.

The band didn't acknowledge this approbation with anything more than a nod from the keyboard player. Before the applause died down, the saxophone was twirling through the familiar, sultry melody of "Take Five." After one complete turn through the number, he began to improvise. The double bass player kept up with him through the repetition of three notes and the drummer maintained the beat, but otherwise the saxophone was on his own. And he gave it his heart—eyes closed, his body swayed back, his instrument lifted. It was the sort of music one felt in the solar plexus, hollow and haunting.

As he completed his improvisation, the saxophone player nodded at Randie, who stood and began hers on the last note of his. Again, the double bass played the same three notes, again the drums maintained the same steady beat. But the sound of the trumpet changed the mood of the piece. It became pure and uplifting, a joyous celebration of brassy sound.

Like the saxophone player, Miranda performed with her eyes closed, and she tapped her right foot in time with the drummer. But unlike the saxophonist, when her solo was completed and the improvisation thrown to the clarinet, she grinned with unrestrained pleasure at the applause that greeted the ride she had taken.

Their third number, "Just a Child," changed the mood once again. It featured the clarinet player—an overweight redhead whose face shone with perspiration—and it provided a dusky sound that spoke of rainy evenings and fusty nightclubs, a fog of cigarette smoke and glasses of gin. It invited slow dancing, lazy kissing, and sleep.

The crowd loved it, as they did the fourth, a piece called "Black Nightgown" which featured the clarinet and saxophone. It also ended the first set.

There was a general cry of protest when the keyboard player announced "We're breaking for fifteen," but since it was an opportunity to replenish drinks, most of the audience began to shuffle towards the bar. Lynley joined them.

The two darts players were still at it, he saw, their concentration and dedication having gone unimpaired by the performance in the next room.

The younger man had apparently hit his stride, for the score on the blackboard showed that he had drawn nearly even with his bearded competitor.

"Last toss, this," the younger player announced, displaying the dart with the flare of a magician about to make an elephant disappear. "Over the shoulder and I'll have a bull's-eye and a win. Who wants money on it?"

"Oh, too right!" Somebody laughed.

"Just throw the dart, Petersen," someone else called. "Put an end to your misery."

Petersen clucked in mock dismay. "Oh, you of intolerably little faith," he said. He turned his back to the dart board, threw over his shoulder, and looked as surprised as everyone else when the dart flew like a magnet drawn to metal and lodged in the bull's-eye.

The crowd sent up a satisfied roar. Petersen jumped on top of one of the tables.

"I'm taking all comers!" he shouted. "Step up. Try your luck. Senior members only. Collins here just got bashed and I'm looking for fresh blood." He squinted through the cigarette smoke and the bodies. "You! Dr. Troughton! I see you hulking in the corner. Step up and defend the SCR."

Lynley followed the direction of the boy's gaze to a table at the far end of the room where another senior member of the college sat in conversation with two younger men.

"Drop the history drivel," Petersen went on. "Save it for supervisions. Come on. Have a go. Troughton!"

The man looked up. He waved off the call. The crowd urged him on. He ignored them.

"Blast it, Troughtsie, come on. Be a man." Petersen laughed.

Someone else called, "Let's do it, Trout."

And suddenly Lynley heard nothing more, just the name itself and all its variations, Troughton, Troughtsie, Trout. It was the eternal predeliction of students for giving their instructors some sort of affectionate appellation. He'd done it himself, first at Eton then at Oxford.

And now for the first time, he wondered if Elena Weaver had done the same.

19

"What is it, Tommy?" Lady Helen asked when she came at his beckoning from the doorway to the JCR.

"A premature ending to the concert. For us, at least. Come with me."

She followed him back to the bar where the crush of people was beginning to thin as the jazz audience wandered once again in the direction of the music. The man called Troughton was still sitting at the corner table, but one of his companions had left and the other was getting ready to do the same, donning a green anorak and a black and white scarf. Troughton himself stood and cupped his hand round his ear to hear something that the younger man was saying, and after a moment of further conversation, he too put on a jacket and started across the room to the door.

As he approached, Lynley eyed the older man, taking his measure as the potential lover of a twenty-year-old girl. Although Troughton had a youthful, pixie-like face, he was otherwise perfectly nondescript, an ordinary man no more than five feet eight inches tall whose toast-coloured hair looked soft and was curly but was also decidedly thinning on the top. He appeared to be somewhere in his late forties, and aside from the width of his shoulders and the depth of his chest—both of which suggested that he was a rower—Lynley had to admit that he didn't look at all the type of man to have attracted and seduced someone like Elena Weaver.

As the other man began to pass by them on his way to the door, Lynley said, "Dr. Troughton?"

Troughton paused, looked surprised to have a stranger addressing him by name. "Yes?"

"Thomas Lynley," he said and introduced Lady Helen. He reached into his pocket and produced his police identification. "May we go somewhere to talk?"

Troughton didn't appear the least bewildered by the request. Instead, he looked both resigned and relieved. "Yes. This way," he said and led them out into the night.

He took them to his rooms in the building that comprised the north range of the college garden, two courtyards away from the JCR. On the second floor, situated in the southwest corner, they overlooked the River Cam on one side and the garden on the other. They consisted of a small bedroom and a study, the former furnished only with an unmade single bed and the latter crowded with ancient, overstuffed furniture and a vast and undisciplined number of books. These lent to the room the sort of mouldy mustiness associated with paper too long exposed to air that is heavy with damp.

Troughton picked up a sheaf of essays from one of the chairs and put it on his desk. He said, "May I offer you a brandy?" and when Lynley and Lady Helen accepted, he went to a glass-fronted cabinet to one side of the fireplace where he took out three plain balloon glasses and carefully held each one up to the light before pouring. He didn't say anything until he had taken a seat in one of the heavy, overstuffed chairs.

"You've come about Elena Weaver, haven't you?" He spoke quietly, calmly. "I suppose I've been expecting you since yesterday afternoon. Did Justine give you my name?"

"No. Elena herself did, after a fashion. She'd been making a curious mark on her calendar ever since last January," Lynley said. "A small line drawing of a fish."

"Yes. I see." Troughton gave his attention to his balloon glass. His eyes filled, and he pressed his fingers to them before he raised his head. "Of course, she didn't call me that," he said unnecessarily. "She called me Victor."

"But it was her shorthand method of noting when you'd meet, I should guess. And, no doubt, a way to keep the knowledge from her father should he ever happen to glance at her calendar on a visit to her room. Because, I imagine, you know her father quite well."

Troughton nodded. He took a swallow of his brandy, setting the balloon glass on the low table that separated his chair from Lady Helen's. He patted the breast pocket of his grey tweed jacket and brought out a cigarette case. It was made of pewter, dented in one corner. It bore some sort of crest upon its cover. He offered it round and then lit up, the match flickering in his fingers like an uneasy beacon. He had large hands, Lynley noted, strong-looking with smooth, oval nails. They were his best feature.

Troughton kept his eyes on his cigarette as he said, "The hardest part these last three days has been the pretence of it all. Coming to the college, seeing to my supervisions, taking my meals with the others. Having a glass of sherry before dinner last night with the Master and making small talk while all the time I wanted to throw my head back and howl." When his voice wavered slightly on the last word, Lady Helen leaned forward in her chair as if she would offer him sympathy, but she stopped herself when Lynley lifted his hand in quick admonition. Troughton steadied himself by drawing in on his cigarette and placing it into a pottery ashtray on the table next to him where its smoke rose in a snaking plume. Then he went on.

"But what right have I to any one of the externals of grief? I have duties, after all. I have responsibilities. A wife. Three children. I'm supposed to think of them. I ought to be engaged in picking up the pieces and going on and being thankful that my marriage and my career didn't come crashing down round me because I've spent the last eleven months screwing a deaf girl twenty-seven years my junior. In fact, inside my ugly little soul where no one would ever know the feeling is even there, I ought to be secretly thankful Elena's out of the way. Because there'll be no mess now, no scandal, no titters and whispers behind my back. It's completely over and I'm to go on. That's what men my age do, isn't it, when they've puffed themselves up with a successful seduction that, over time, grows just a little bit tedious. And it was supposed to grow tedious, wasn't it, Inspector? I was supposed to start finding her a sexual millstone, living evidence of an ego-boosting peccadillo that promised to come back to haunt me if I didn't take care of her in one way or another."

"It wasn't like that for you?"

"I love her. I can't even say *loved* because if I put it in the past tense, I'm going to have to face the fact that she's gone and I can't stand the thought of it."

"She was pregnant. Did you know that?"

Troughton closed his eyes. The weak overhead light, which shone down from a cone-shaped shade, cast shadows from his eyelashes onto his skin. It glittered beneath the lashes on the crescent of tears which he appeared to be willing himself not to shed. He pulled a handkerchief out of his pocket. When he could, he said, "I knew."

"I should think that offered the possibility of serious difficulties for you, Dr. Troughton. No matter how you felt about the girl."

"The scandal, you mean? The loss of life-long friendships? The damage to my career? None of that mattered. Oh, I knew I was likely to be ostracised by virtually everyone if I walked out on my family for a twenty-year-old girl. But the more I thought about it, the more I came to realise that I simply didn't care. The sorts of things that matter to my colleagues, Inspector—prestigious appointments, the building of a political base, a stellar academic reputation, invitations to speak at conferences and to chair committees, requests to serve the college, the University, even the nation—those things ceased mattering to me a long time ago when I reached the conclusion that connection to another person is the only item of real value in life. And I felt I'd found that connection with Elena. I wasn't about to give her up. I would have done anything to keep her. Elena."

The saying of her name seemed a necessity to Troughton, a subtle form of release that he had not allowed himself—that the circumstances of their relationship had not allowed him—since her death. But still he didn't cry, as if he believed that to give in to sorrow was to lose control over the few aspects of his life that remained unshattered by the girl's murder.

As if she knew this, Lady Helen went to the cabinet by the fireplace and found the bottle of brandy. She poured a bit more into Troughton's glass. Her own face, Lynley saw, was grave and composed.

"When did you see Elena last?" Lynley asked the other man.

"Sunday night. Here."

"But she didn't spend the night, did she? The porter saw her leaving St. Stephen's to go running in the morning."

"She left me . . . it must have been just before one. Before the gates close here."

"And you? Did you go home as well?"

"I stayed. I do that most weeknights, and have done for some two years now."

"I see. Your home isn't in the city, then?"

"It's in Trumpington." Troughton appeared to read the expression on Lynley's face, adding, "Yes, I know, Inspector. Trumpington's hardly such a distance from the college to warrant having to spend the night here. Especially having to spend most weeknights over a two-year period. Obviously, my reasons for dossing here had to do with a distance of a very different sort. Initially, that is. Before Elena."

Troughton's cigarette had burnt itself to nothing in the ashtray by his chair. He lit another and took more of the brandy. He appeared to have himself once more under control.

"When did she tell you she was pregnant?"

"Wednesday night, not long after she'd got the results of the test."

"But prior to that, she'd told you there was a possibility? She'd told you she suspected?"

"She hadn't said anything to me about pregnancy before Wednesday. I had no suspicion."

"Did you know she wasn't taking precautions?"

"It wasn't something I felt we had to discuss."

Out of the corner of his eye, Lynley saw Lady Helen stir, turning to face Troughton, saying, "But surely, Dr. Troughton, a man of your education wouldn't have left the sole responsibility of contraception to the woman with whom you intended to sleep. You would have discussed it with her before you took her to bed."

"I didn't see the need."

"The need." Lady Helen said the two words slowly.

Lynley thought of the unused birth control pills which Sergeant Havers had found in Elena Weaver's desk drawer. He recalled February's date upon them and the conjectures he and Havers had developed regarding that date. He asked, "Dr. Troughton, did you assume she was using a contraceptive of some sort? Did she tell you she was?"

"As entrapment, you mean? No. She never said a word about contraception one way or another. And she didn't need to, Inspector. It wouldn't have made any difference to me if she had." He picked up his brandy glass and turned it on his palm. It seemed a largely meditative gesture.

Lynley watched the play of uncertainty on his face. He felt irritated at the delicacy with which the circumstances suggested he probe for the truth. He said, "I have the distinct impression that we're caught between talking at cross purposes and engaging in outright prevarication. Perhaps you'd care to tell me what you're holding back."

In the silence, the distant sound of the jazz concert beat rhythmically against the windows in the room, the high wild notes of the trumpet improvising as Randie took another ride with the band. And then the drummer soloed. And then the melody resumed. When it did so, Victor Troughton raised his head, as if the music beckoned him to do so.

He said, "I was going to marry Elena. Frankly, I welcomed the opportunity to do so. But her baby wasn't mine."

"Wasn't—"

"She didn't know that. She thought I was the father. And I let her believe it. But I wasn't, I'm afraid."

"You sound certain of that."

"I am, Inspector." Troughton offered a smile of infinite sadness. "I had a vasectomy nearly three years ago. Elena didn't know. And I didn't tell her. I've never told anyone."

Just outside the building in which Victor Troughton had his study and bedroom, a terrace overlooked the River Cam. It rose from the garden, partially hidden by a brick wall, and it held several planters of verduous shrubs and a few benches on which—during fine weather—members of the college could take the sun and listen to the laughter of those who tried their luck punting down the river towards the Bridge of Sighs. It was to this terrace that Lynley directed Lady Helen. Although he recognised his need to lay before her each singular realisation that the circumstances of the evening had forced upon him, he said nothing at the moment. Instead, he tried to give definition to what those realisations were causing him to feel.

The wind of the previous two days had subsided considerably. All that remained of it was an occasional brief, weak gust of cold that puffed across the Backs, as if the night were sighing. But even those brief gusts would eventually dissipate, and the heaviness of the chill air suggested that fog would replace them tomorrow.

It was just after ten. The jazz concert had ended moments before they left Victor Troughton, and the voices of students calling to one another still rose and fell in the college grounds as the crowd dispersed. No one came in their direction, however. And considering both the hour and the temperature, Lynley knew it was unlikely that anyone would join or disturb them on the secluded river terrace.

They chose a bench at the south end of the terrace where a wall that separated the fellows' garden from the rest of the grounds also afforded them protection from what remained of the wind. Lynley sat, pulling Lady Helen down next to him, drawing her into the curve of his arm. He pressed his lips to the side of her head in what was more a need of physical contact than an expression of affection, and in response her body seemed to yield to his, creating a gentle, constant pressure against him. She didn't speak, but he had little doubt as to where her thoughts lay.

Victor Troughton had seemed to recognise an opportunity to speak for the first time about what had been his most closely guarded secret. And like most people who've lived a lie, when the opportunity presented itself to reveal reality, he was more than willing to do so. But as he began to tell his story, Lynley had seen Lady Helen's initial sympathy towards Troughton—so characteristic of her, really—transform slowly. Her posture changed, drawing her fractionally away from the man. Her eyes grew cloudy. And despite the fact that he was in the midst of an interview crucial to a murder investigation, Lynley found himself watching Lady Helen as much as he was listening to Troughton's story. He wanted to excuse himself to her—to excuse all men—for the sins against women which Troughton was listing without an apparent twinge of conscience.

The historian had lit a third cigarette from the smouldering butt of his second. He had taken more brandy, and as he spoke, he kept his eyes fixed on the liquor in the glass and on the small, swimming oval of yellow-gold that was the reflection in the brandy of the light that hung above him. He never spoke in anything other than a low, frank voice.

"I wanted a life. That's really the only excuse I have, and I know it isn't much of one. I was willing to stay in my marriage for my children's sake. I was willing to be a hypocrite and keep up the pretence of happiness. But I wasn't willing to live like a priest. I did that for two years, dead for two years. I wanted a life again."

"When did you meet Elena?" Lynley asked him.

Troughton waved the question off. He seemed determined to tell the story in his own way, in his own time. He said, "The vasectomy had nothing to do with Elena. I'd merely made a decision about my life-style. These are the days of sexual profligacy, after all, so I decided to make myself available to women. But I didn't want to run the risk of an unwanted pregnancy—or the risk of some scheming female's entrapment—so I had myself fixed up. And I went on the prowl."

He lifted his glass and smiled sardonically. "It was, I must admit, a rather rude awakening. I was just short of forty-five years old, in fairly good condition, in a somewhat admirable and ego-massaging career as a relatively well-known and well-respected academic. I had expectations of scores of women being more than willing to accept my attentions just for the sheer, intellectual thrill of knowing they'd been to bed with a Cambridge don."

"I take it you found that wasn't the case."

"Not among the women I was pursuing." Troughton looked long at Lady Helen, as if he were evaluating the opposing forces at battle within him: the wisdom of saying nothing more versus the overwhelming need to say it all at last. He gave in to need, turning back to Lynley. "I wanted a young woman, Inspector. I wanted to feel young, resilient flesh. I wanted to kiss breasts that were full and firm. I wanted unveined legs and feet without callosity and hands like silk."

"And what about your wife?" Lady Helen asked. Her voice was quiet, her legs were crossed, her hands were folded and relaxed in her lap. But Lynley knew her well enough to imagine how her heart had begun to pound angrily—as any woman's would—when Troughton calmly and rationally offered his list of sexual requirements: not a mind, not a soul, just a body that was young.

Troughton was not reluctant to answer her. "Three children," he replied. "Three boys. Each time, Rowena let herself go a little more. First it was her clothes and her hair, then her skin, then her body."

"What you mean to say is that a middle-aged woman who has borne three children no longer excited you."

"I admit to the worst of it," Troughton replied. "I felt an aversion when I looked at what was left of her stomach. I was mildly disgusted over the size of her hips, and I hated the drooping sacks that her breasts had become and the loose flesh hanging beneath her arms. But most of all I hated the fact that she didn't intend to do a thing about herself. And that she was perfectly happy when I began to leave her alone."

He got up and walked across the room to the window that overlooked the college garden. He pulled back the curtain and studied the outdoors, sipping his brandy.

"So I made my plans. I had the vasectomy to protect myself from any unexpected difficulties, and I began to go my own way. The only problem was that I found I really didn't have the right . . . What do they call it? The right moves? The technique?" He chuckled derisively. "I'd actually thought it would be easy. I'd be joining the sexual revolution two decades too late, but I'd be joining it nonetheless. A middle-aged pioneer. What a nasty surprise it all was for me."

"And then Elena Weaver came along?" Lynley asked.

Troughton stayed by the window, backdropped by the black glass of night. "I've known her father for years, so I'd met her before, on one visit or another when she was up from London. But it wasn't until he brought her to my house last autumn to choose a puppy that I really thought of her as anything other than Anthony's little deaf girl. And even then, it was just admiration on my part. She was lively, good-humoured, a mass of energy and enthusiasm. She got on well in life in spite of being deaf, and I found that—along with everything else about her—immensely attractive. But Anthony's a colleague, and even if a score of young women hadn't already given me sufficient evidence of my undesirability, I wouldn't have had the nerve to approach a colleague's daughter."

"She approached you?"

Troughton made a gesture that encompassed the room. "She dropped by here several times during Michaelmas term last year. She'd tell me about how the dog was doing and chat in that odd-voiced way of hers. She'd drink tea, pinch a few cigarettes when she thought I wasn't looking. I enjoyed her visits. I began to look forward to them. But nothing happened between us until Christmas."

"And then?"

Troughton returned to his chair. He crushed out his cigarette but did not light another. He said, "She came to show me the gown she'd bought for one of the Christmas balls. She said, I'll try it on for you, shall I, and she turned her back and began to undress right here in the room. Of course, I'm not entirely a fool. I realised later that she'd done it deliberately, but at the time, I was horrified. Not only at her behaviour but at what I felt—no, what I knew in an instant that I wanted to do—in the face of her behaviour. She was down to her underthings when I said, For God's sake, what do you think you're doing, girl? But I was across the room and her head was turned, so she couldn't read my lips. She just kept undressing. I went to her, made her face me, and repeated the question. She looked me straight in the eye and said, I'm doing what you want me to do, Vittor. And that was that. We made love in the very chair you're sitting in, Inspector. I was so desperate to have her that I didn't even bother to lock the door." He drank the rest of his brandy, set the balloon glass on the table. "Elena knew what I was after. I've no doubt she'd known the moment her father brought her to my house to see those dogs. If she was nothing else, she was brilliant at reading people. Or at least she was brilliant at reading me. She always knew what I wanted and when I wanted it and just exactly how."

"So you'd found that resilient flesh you'd been seeking," Lady Helen said. Cool condemnation comprised the undercurrent of the statement.

Troughton didn't avoid admitting the worst. "I found it. Yes. But not the way I thought. I didn't count on falling in love. I thought it would just be sex between us. Good, vigorous sex anytime we felt the urge. We were, after all, serving each other's needs."

"In what way?"

"She was accommodating my need to savour her youth and perhaps recapture a bit of my own. I was accommodating her need to hurt her father.'' He poured himself more brandy and added to the other glasses as well. He looked from Lynley to Lady Helen as if gauging on their faces a response to his final statement. He went on with, ''As I said, Inspector, I'm not a complete fool.''

''Perhaps you're judging yourself too harshly.''

Troughton placed the bottle on the table next to his chair and drank deeply of the brandy, saying, ''Not at all. Look at the facts. I'm forty-seven years old and on the downhill plunge. She was twenty, surrounded by hundreds of young men with their entire lives ahead of them. Why on earth would she decide to set her sights on me unless she knew it was the perfect way to strike out at her father? And it *was* perfect, after all. To choose one of his colleagues—indeed, to choose one of his friends. To choose a man who was even older than her father. To choose a man who was married. To choose a man with children. I couldn't actually delude myself with the idea that Elena wanted me because she found me more attractive than any other man she knew, and I never did so. I knew from the first what she had in mind.''

''The scandal we were speaking of earlier?''

''Anthony always had too much of himself tied into Elena's performance here in Cambridge. He involved himself in every aspect of her life. How she acted and dressed, how she took notes in her lectures, how she comported herself in her supervisions. These were weighty matters to him. I think he believed that he would be judged—as a man, a parent, an academic even—dependent upon her success or failure here.''

''Was the Penford Chair tied into all this?''

''In his mind, I should think so. In reality, no.''

''But if he thought judgement of himself was going to be connected to Elena's performance and behaviour—''

''Then he would want to see to it that she performed and behaved as the daughter of a respected professor should. Elena knew that. She could sense that attitude in everything her father did, and she resented him for it. So you can imagine the vast and—to Elena—amusing possibilities for his humiliation and her revenge when it became known that his daughter was having it off on a regular basis with one of his close colleagues.''

''Didn't you mind being used in this way?''

''I was living every fantasy I'd ever entertained about making love to a woman and having a woman make love to me. We met at least three times a week from Christmas on and I loved every moment of it. I didn't care about her motives in the least as long as she kept coming round to see me and taking off her clothes.''

''You met here, then?''

''Generally. I managed to get to London several times during the summer break to see her as well. And on a few weekend afternoons and evenings at her father's house during term.''

''When he was home?''

''Only once, during a party. She found that particularly exciting.'' He shrugged although his cheeks had begun to flush. ''I found it rather exciting as well. I suppose it was the sheer terror of thinking we might be caught going at it.''

''But you weren't?''

''Never. Justine knew—she'd found out somehow, she may well have guessed or Elena may have told her—but she never actually caught us in the act.''

''She never told her husband?''

''She wouldn't have wanted to bear that sort of witness against Elena, Inspector. As far as Anthony was concerned, it would have been a case of kill the messenger, and Justine knew that better than anyone. So she held her tongue. I imagine she was waiting for Anthony to find things out on his own.''

''Which he never did.''

''Which he never did.'' Troughton shifted his position in his chair, crossing one leg over the other and pulling out his cigarette case once again. He merely played it from hand to hand, however. He didn't open it. ''Of course, he would have been told eventually.''

''By you?''

''No. I imagine Elena would have wanted that pleasure.''

Lynley found it hard to believe that Troughton had no conscience in the matter of Elena. He had obviously felt no need to guide her. He had seen no necessity for urging her to deal with her resentment towards her father in another way. ''But, Dr. Troughton, what I don't understand is—''

''Why I went along with the game?'' Troughton set the cigarette case next to the balloon glass. He studied the picture they made, side by side. ''Because I loved her. At first it was her body—the incredible sensation of holding and touching that beautiful body. But then it was her. Elena. She was wild and ungovernable, laughing and alive. And I wanted that in my life. I didn't care about the cost.''

''Even if it meant posing as the father of her child?''

"Even that, Inspector. Once she told me she was pregnant, I nearly convinced myself that the vasectomy had gone wrong all those years ago and that the child was really mine."

"Have you any idea who the father was?"

"No. But I've spent hours since last Wednesday wondering about it."

"Where have your thoughts led you?"

"To the same conclusion again and again. If she slept with me to have revenge on her father, whomever else she slept with, it was for the same reason. It didn't have anything to do with love."

"Yet you were willing to take up a life with her in spite of knowing all this?"

"Pathetic, isn't it? I wanted passion again. I wanted to feel alive. I told myself that I would be good for her. I thought that with me she would be able to let go of her grievances against Anthony eventually. I believed I'd be enough for her. I'd be able to heal her. It was an adolescent little fantasy that I clung to till the end."

Lady Helen placed her balloon glass on the table next to Troughton's. She kept her fingers carefully on its rim. She said, "And what about your wife?"

"I hadn't told her about Elena yet."

"That's not what I meant."

"I know," he said. "You meant what about the fact that Rowena bore my children and did my laundry and cooked my meals and cleaned my house. What about those seventeen years of loyalty and devotion. What about my commitment to her, not to mention my responsibilities to the University, to my students, to my colleagues. What about my ethics and my morals and my values and my conscience. That's what you meant, isn't it?"

"I suppose it is."

He looked away from them, eyes focussed on nothing. "Some kinds of marriages wear at a person until the only thing left is a body that's simply going through the motions."

"I wonder if that's your wife's conclusion as well."

"Rowena wants out of this marriage as much as I do. She just doesn't know it yet."

Now, in the darkness on the terrace, Lynley felt burdened not only by Troughton's assessment of his marriage but also by the mixture of revulsion and indifference he had expressed towards his wife. More than anything, he wished Helen had not been with him to hear the story of his attachment to Elena Weaver and his maddeningly level-headed rationale for that attachment. For as the historian had calmly outlined his reasons for turning away from his wife and seeking the company and the love of a woman young enough to be his daughter, Lynley believed he had finally come to understand at least part of what lay at the root of Helen's refusal to marry him.

The understanding had been an uneasiness churning within him— asking to be noticed—since the start of the evening in Bulstrode Gardens. It had demanded some sort of spoken release in the musty confines of Victor Troughton's study.

What we ask of them, he thought. What we expect, what we demand. But never what we will give in return. Never what they want. And never a moment's thorough consideration of the burdens which our desires and requirements place upon them.

He looked up at the vast grey darkness of the cloud heavy sky. A distant light winked in it.

"What are you seeing?" Lady Helen asked him.

"A shooting star, I think. Close your eyes, Helen. Quickly. Make a wish." He did so himself.

She laughed at him quietly. "You're wishing on a plane, Tommy. It's heading for Heathrow."

He opened his eyes, saw that she was right. "I've no viable future in astronomy, I'm afraid."

"I don't believe that. You used to point out all the constellations to me. In Cornwall. Don't you remember?"

"It was all show, Helen darling. I was trying to impress you."

"Were you? Well, I was suitably impressed."

He turned to look at her. He reached for her hand. In spite of the cold, she wasn't wearing gloves, and he pressed her cool fingers against his cheek. He kissed her palm.

"I sat there and listened and realised that he may as well have been me," he said, "because it all boils down to what men want, Helen. And what we want is women. But not as individuals, not as living, breathing, vulnerable human beings with a set of desires and dreams of their own. We want them—you—as extensions of ourselves. And I'm among the worst."

Her hand moved in his, but she didn't withdraw it. Rather, her fingers entwined with his.

"And as I listened to him, Helen, I thought of all the ways I've wanted you. As my lover, as my wife, as the mother of my children. In my bed. In my car. In my home. Entertaining my friends. Listening to me talk about my work. Sitting next to me quietly when I don't feel like speaking. Waiting up for me when I'm out on a case. Opening your heart to me. Making yourself mine. And those are the operative words I kept hearing: I, me, my, mine.'' He looked across the Backs to the smudgy forms of English oaks and common alders that were little more than shadows against a charcoal sky. When he turned back to her, her expression was grave, but her eyes were still on him. They were dark and kind.

"There's no sin in that, Tommy."

"You're right," he replied. "There's only self in it. What I want. When I want it. And you're meant to cooperate because you're a woman. That's how I've been, isn't it? No better than your brother-in-law, no better than Troughton."

"No," she said. "You're not like them. I've not seen you that way."

"I've wanted you, Helen. And the hell of it is that I want you right now as much as I ever have. I sat there and listened to Troughton and had my own eyes opened in a thousand different ways about what goes wrong between men and women and it all comes down to the same damned fact with absolutely no change in it. I love you. I want you."

"If you had me once, could you let it all go? Could you let me go?"

His answering laugh was mordant and painful. He looked away. "I wish it were as simple as taking you to bed. But you know it isn't. You know I—"

"But could you, Tommy? Could you let me go?"

He turned back to her slowly, recognising something in her voice, an urgency, a plea, an inherent call for a degree of understanding he'd never been able to establish with her. It seemed to him as he studied her face—and saw the thin line of worry between her brows—that the attainment of every dream he'd ever harboured depended upon his ability to know what she meant.

He looked at her hand, still held in his own. So fragile, he could feel the bones of her fingers. So smooth that he could easily conceive of its tender passage against his skin.

"How do I answer that?" he said at last. "I feel you've placed my whole future on the line."

"I don't mean to do that."

"But you've done it, haven't you?"

"I suppose I have. In a way."

He released her hand and walked to the low brick wall that edged the river terrace. Below, the Cam glinted in the darkness, green-black ink drifting lazily towards the Ouse. It was an inexorable progress—this movement of water—slow and sure and as unstoppable as time.

"My longings are the same as every other man's," he said. "I want a home, a wife. I want children, a son. I want to know at the end that my life hasn't been for nothing, and the only way I can know that for a certainty is to leave something behind, and to have someone to leave it to. All I can say right now is that I finally understand what kind of burden that places on a woman, Helen. I understand that no matter how the load is shifted between partners, or divided or shared, the woman's burden will always be greater. I do know that. But I can't lie to you about the reality that remains. I still want those things."

"You can have them with anyone."

"I want them with you."

"You don't need them with me."

"Need?" He tried to read the expression on her face, but she was just a pale blur in the darkness beneath the tree that threw a cavernous shadow over the terrace bench. He pondered the oddity of the word she had chosen, reflecting on her decision to remain with her sister in Cambridge. He considered the canvas of the fourteen years he had known Lady Helen. And finally, the realisation struck him.

He sank onto the concrete ledge that comprised the top of the brick river wall. He regarded her evenly. Faintly, he heard the click-clacking of a bicycle passing across Garret Hostel Bridge, the grinding clang of a lorry shifting gears as it made its way down the distant Queens' Road. But neither sound did more than stir against his consciousness as he studied Lady Helen.

He wondered how he could have come to love her so much and all the time know her so very little. She had been before him for more than a decade, never attempting to disguise who and what she was. Yet for all that time, he had failed to see her in the light of reality, imbuing her instead with a set of qualities which he wished her to possess while all along, her every relationship had been acting as a cogent illustration of what she saw as her role, her way of getting on. He couldn't believe he had been such a fool.

He spoke more to the night than to her. "It's all because I can function by myself. You won't marry me because I don't need you, Helen, not the way you want me to. You've decided I don't need you to stand on my own, or to get on in life, or even to be whole. And it's the truth, you know. I don't need you that way."

"So you see," she said.

He heard the finality in her three quiet words and felt his own quick anger in response to them. "I see. I do. I see that I'm not one of your projects. I see that I don't need you to save me. My life is more or less in order now, and I want to share it with you. As your equal, your partner. Not as some emotional mendicant, but as a man who's willing to grow at your side. That's the beginning and end of it. Not what you're used to, not even what you've had in mind for yourself. But it's the best I can do. It's the best I can offer. That and my love. And God knows that I love you."

"Love isn't enough."

"God damn it, Helen, when are you going to see it's the only thing there is!"

In answer to his angry words, a light snapped on in the building behind them. A curtain flicked back and a disembodied face appeared at one window. Lynley pushed himself off the concrete ledge and rejoined Lady Helen beneath the tree.

"What you're thinking," he said to her, quietly now for he could see how she had begun to withdraw from him, "is that if I need you enough, I'll never think of leaving you. You'll always be safe. That's how it is, isn't it?"

She averted her head. Gently, he caught her chin with his fingers and turned her back towards him.

"Helen, isn't it?"

"You're not being fair."

"You're in love with me, Helen."

"Don't. Please."

"Every bit as much as I'm in love with you. You want me as much, you long for me as much. But I'm not like all the rest of the men you've involved yourself with. I don't need you in a way that makes it safe for you to love me. I don't depend upon you. I stand on my own. If you take up life with me, you jump into the void. You risk it all, without a single guarantee."

He felt her tremble slightly. He saw her throat work. He felt his heart open.

"Helen." He drew her into his arms. He took strength from knowing each gentle curve of her, from feeling the rise and fall of her chest, from the feathering touch of her hair against his face, from the slender hand that caught at his jacket. "Darling Helen," he whispered and ran his hand along the length of her hair. When she looked up, he kissed her. Her arms slipped round him. Her lips softened and opened beneath his. She smelled of perfume and Troughton's cigarette smoke. She tasted of brandy.

"Do you understand?" she whispered.

In reply, he drew her mouth back to his, giving himself over to nothing more than the separate sensations attendant to kissing her: the soft warmth of her lips and her tongue, the faint sound of her breathing, the heady pleasure of her breasts. Desire built in him, slowly obliterating everything but the knowledge that he had to have her. Now. Tonight. He wasn't prepared to wait another hour. He would take her to bed and to hell with the consequences. He wanted to taste her, to touch her, to know her completely. He wanted to take every lovely part of her body and to make her body his. He wanted to lower himself between her upraised thighs and hear her gasp and cry out when he sank inside her and . . .

I wanted to feel young resilient flesh I wanted to kiss breasts that were full and firm I wanted unveined legs and feet without callosity and IwantedIwantedIwanted . . .

He released her. "Good Christ," he whispered.

He felt her hand touch his cheek. Her skin was so cool. His own, he knew, was probably burning.

He stood. He felt shaken. He said, "I ought to get you back to Pen's."

"What is it?" she asked.

He shook his head blindly. It was, after all, so easy to construct lofty, intellectual, self-denigrating comparisons between himself and Victor Troughton, especially when he felt relatively sure that her response would be a loving and generous reassurance that he was not like other men. It was far more difficult to look at the matter when his own behaviour—his desires and his intentions—delineated the truth. He felt as if he'd spent the last few hours earnestly gathering the seeds of understanding, all of which he'd just flung mindlessly into the wind.

They started walking back across the lawn, towards the porter's lodge and Trinity Lane beyond it. She was silent beside him, although her question still hung in the air, waiting for an answer. He knew she deserved one. Still, he didn't reply until they'd reached his car and he'd unlocked the door and opened it for her. And then, he stopped her just before she got inside. He touched her shoulder. He fumbled for words.

"I was standing in judgement of Troughton," he said. "I was naming the sin and deciding the punishment."

"Isn't that what police are meant to do?"

"Not when they're guilty of the same crime, Helen."

She frowned. "The same—"

"Wanting. Not giving, not even thinking. Just wanting. And blindly taking what they want. And not caring a damn about anything else."

She touched her hand to his. For a moment, she looked to the rise of the footbridge and the Backs beyond it where the first ghost puffs of fog were beginning to curl like misty fingers round the trunks of the trees. Then her eyes moved back to his. "You weren't alone in the wanting," she said. "You never have been, Tommy. Not before this. And certainly not tonight."

It was an absolution that filled his heart with a sense of completion that he'd never had with her before. "Stay in Cambridge," he said. "Come home when you're ready."

"Thank you," she whispered—to him, to the night.

20

The fog lay heavily on the city the next morning, a grey blanket of mist that rose like a gas from the surrounding fens and billowed into the air in amorphous clouds that shrouded trees, buildings, roadways, and open land, changing everything from common and recognisable substance into mere shape. Cars, lorries, buses, and taxis inched their way along the damp pavements of the city streets. Bicyclists slowly swayed through the gloom. Pedestrians huddled into heavy coats and dodged the constant spattering of the drops of condensation that fell from rooflines, window ledges, and trees. The two days of wind and sunshine might never have existed. Fog had returned like a pestilence in the night. This was Cambridge weather with a vengeance.

"Makes me feel like a case for the tubercular ward," Havers said. Encased in her pea-soup coat with its hood pulled up and a pink knit cap on her head for additional protection, she beat her hands against her upper arms and stamped her feet as they walked to Lynley's car. The heavy mist was creating a beadwork of damp on her clothing. Across her brow, her sandy fringe was beginning to curl as if exposed to steam. "No wonder Philby and Burgess went over to the Soviets while they were here," she continued darkly. "They were probably looking for a better climate."

"Indeed," Lynley said. "Moscow in the winter. That's certainly my idea of heaven on earth."

He glanced at his sergeant as he spoke. She'd arrived nearly half an hour late and he'd been in the process of gathering his things to start without her when she'd clumped down the corridor to his room in Ivy Court and rapped on his door.

"Sorry," she'd said. "Bleeding fog this morning. The M11 was a glorified car park." But despite the deliberately casual tone of her voice, he noted the fact that her face was drawn with weariness and she sauntered about the room restlessly as she waited for him to don his coat and his scarf.

"Rough night?" he asked her.

She settled the strap of her bag high on her shoulder in what seemed to be a metaphorical gathering of personal resources before she replied. "Just a bit of the old insomnia. I'll survive it."

"And your mother?"

"Her as well."

"I see." He draped his scarf round his neck and shrugged into his overcoat. At the mirror, he ran a brush through his hair, but it was just an excuse to observe Havers in reflection rather than doing so directly. She was staring down at his open briefcase on the desk. She didn't appear to be taking note of anything in it. He stood at the mirror, giving her time, saying nothing, wondering if she would speak.

He felt a mixture of guilt and shame, faced with the diversity of their positions. Not for the first time, he was forced to acknowledge that the differences between them were not confined to birth, class, and money. For her struggles took their definition from a range of circumstances that far exceeded the family into which she had been born and the manner in which she pronounced her words. These circumstances rose from simple ill-fortune, dominoes of bad luck that had tumbled one upon the other so quickly in the last ten months that she had not been able to stop their progress. That she could stop them now with a simple phone call was the single fact he wished her to acknowledge. Yet he had to admit that that very phone call, so easy for him to recommend, represented to her a sloughing off of responsibility, coveted salvation rather than obvious solution. And he could not deny that, in similar circumstances, he would not have found himself as equally tied to the idea of filial obligation.

When he reached the point that only narcissism could possibly explain why he was still admiring his own reflection, he set down his brush and turned to her. She heard his movement and looked up from her study of the briefcase.

"Look, sorry I was late," she said in a rush. "I know you're covering for me in all this, sir. I know you can't do it indefinitely."

"That's not the point, Barbara. We cover for each other when things get rough personally. That's understood."

She reached out for the back of an armchair, not so much for support, it seemed, but for something to do with her hands, because she watched her fingers pick at a frayed cord of its upholstery. She said, "The funny thing is she was right as rain this morning. Last night was a real horror, but this morning she was fine. I keep thinking that must mean something. I keep telling myself it's a sign."

"If you're looking for signs, you can find them in anything. They don't tend to change reality, however."

"But if there's a chance she's taken a turn for the better . . ."

"What about last night? And what about you? What sort of turns are you taking here, Barbara?"

She was working an entire section of the cording loose, twisting it round and round her fingers. "How can I move her from her home when she doesn't understand what's even going on? How can I do that to her? She's my mother, Inspector."

"It's not a punishment."

"Then why does it feel like one? Worse, why do I feel like a criminal who's getting away scot free while she takes the rap?"

"Because you want to do it in your heart, I expect. And what greater source of guilt could there be than the guilt that arises from finally trying to decide if what you want to do—which seems momentarily and superficially selfish—is also the right thing to do? How can you tell if you're really being honest or just trying to talk yourself into dealing with the situation in a way that meets with your own desires?"

She looked utterly defeated. "That's the question, Inspector. And I'll never have the answer. The whole situation goes too far beyond me."

"No, it doesn't. It starts and stops with you. You hold the power. You can make the decision."

"I can't stand to hurt her. She won't understand."

Lynley snapped the briefcase closed. "And what does she understand as things are now, Sergeant?"

That put an end to it. As they walked to his car, which was shoe-horned into the same narrow space he'd used last night on Garret Hostel Lane, he told her about his conversation with Victor Troughton. When he was finished, she said before getting into the Bentley:

"D'you suppose Elena Weaver felt real love for anyone?"

He switched on the ignition. The heater sent out a stream of cold air

on their feet. Lynley thought of Troughton's final words about the girl—
"Try to understand. She wasn't evil, Inspector. She was merely angry.
And I, for one, can't condemn her for that."

"Even though, in reality, you were little more than her choice of
weapons?" Lynley had asked him.

"Even though," he'd replied.

Now, Lynley said, "We can never really come to know any victim's
heart completely, can we, Sergeant? In this sort of job, we look at a life
backwards, starting with death and working forward from there. We patch
pieces together and try to make truth from them. And with that truth we
can only hope for an understanding of who the victim was and what
provoked her murder. But as to her heart—as to the real, lasting truth of
her—we can never really get to that. In the end, we have only facts and
whatever conclusions we draw from them." The little street was too
narrow to turn the Bentley around, so he slowly reversed towards Trinity
Lane, braking for a shadowy, well-bundled group of students who came
out the side gate of Trinity Hall. Beyond them, fog lapped eagerly at the
college garden.

"But why would he want to marry her, Inspector? He knew she
wasn't faithful. She didn't love him. How could he believe that a marriage
between them would have ever worked out?"

"He thought his love would be enough to change her."

Havers scoffed at this. "People never change."

"Of course they do. When they're ready to grow." He headed the
car past St. Stephen's Church and on towards Trinity College. The headlamps fought with the heavy bank of fog, and their illumination bounced
uselessly back into the car. They moved at the pace of a somnolent insect.
"It would be a fine and certainly less complicated world if people only
had sex with those they loved, Sergeant. But the reality is that people use
sex for a variety of reasons, most of which have nothing to do with love,
marriage, commitment, intimacy, procreation, or any other lofty motive.
Elena was one of them. And Troughton, evidently, was willing to accept
that."

"But what kind of marriage could he have expected to have with
her?" Havers asked in protest. "They were starting life with a lie."

"Troughton wasn't bothered by that. He wanted her."

"And she?"

"No doubt she wanted that triumphant moment of seeing her father's
face when she broke the news to him. But there would have been no news

to break if she hadn't been able to manoeuvre Troughton into marrying her in the first place.''

"Inspector." Havers' voice sounded thoughtful. "D'you think there's a chance that Elena told her father? She got the news on Wednesday. She didn't die till Monday morning. His wife was out running. He was home alone. D'you think . . . ?''

"We certainly can't discount it, can we?''

That appeared to be as close as the sergeant was willing to come to voicing her suspicions, for she went on in a more decided tone with, "They couldn't have expected to be happy together, Elena and Troughton.''

"I think you're right. Troughton was deluding himself about his ability to heal her anger and resentment. She was deluding herself into believing she'd get lasting pleasure from dealing her father such an excruciating blow. One can't build a marriage on that sort of foundation.''

"Are you saying, in effect, that one can't get on with living unless one puts ghosts from the past to rest?''

He glanced at her warily. "That's a quantum leap, Sergeant. I think one can always muddle on through life. Most people do. I just couldn't tell you how well they do it.''

Because of the fog, the traffic, and the capricious nature of Cambridge's one-way streets, it took them just over ten minutes to drive to Queens' College, the same time it would have taken them to walk it. Lynley parked in the same spot he had used the day before, and they entered the college through the turreted passage.

"So you think this is the answer to everything?'' Havers asked, looking round Old Court as they walked across its central path.

"I think it may be one of them.''

They found Gareth Randolph in the college dining hall, a hideously unappealing combination of linoleum, long cafeteria tables, and walls panelled in what appeared to be mock golden oak. It was a modern architect's salute to the utterly banal.

Although there were other students present, Gareth was at a table by himself, hunching disconsolately over the remains of a late breakfast which consisted of a half-eaten fried egg with its yolk punched out and a bowl of cornflakes and bananas grown, respectively, soggy and grey. A book was open on the table in front of him, but that seemed mostly for show since he wasn't reading. Nor was he writing in the notebook next to it although he held a pencil poised as if to do so.

His head raised with a jerk when Lynley and Havers took seats across from him. He glanced round the hall as if for quick escape or assistance from the other members of the college who were present. Lynley took his pencil and dashed nine words across the top of the notebook: *You were the father of her baby, weren't you?*

Gareth raised a hand to his forehead. He squeezed his temples, then brushed the lank hair from his brow. His chest heaved once before he seemed to draw himself together by standing and canting his head in the direction of the door. They were meant to follow.

Like Georgina Higgins-Hart's, Gareth's bed-sitting room was tucked into Old Court. On the ground floor, it was a perfectly square room of white walls upon which were hung four framed posters advertising the London Philharmonic and three photographic enlargements of theatrical performances: *Les Miserables, Starlight Express, Aspects of Love.* The former featured the name Sonia Raleigh Randolph prominently above the words *at the piano.* The latter featured an attractive young woman in appropriate costume, singing.

Gareth pointed first to the posters, then to the photographs. "Mutha," he said in his strange guttural voice. "Sisser." He watched Lynley shrewdly. He seemed to be waiting for a reaction to the irony of his mother's and sister's modes of employment. Lynley merely nodded.

On a wide desk beneath the room's only window, a computer sat. It was also, Lynley saw, a Ceephone, identical to the others he had already seen in Cambridge. Gareth switched the unit on and drew a second chair to the desk. He gestured Lynley into it and quickly accessed a word processing programme.

"Sergeant," Lynley said, when he saw how Gareth intended them to communicate, "you're going to have to make notes from the screen." He took off his coat and scarf and sat at the desk. Havers came to stand behind him, the hood of her coat thrown back, her pink cap removed, a notebook in her hand.

Were you the father? Lynley typed.

The boy looked long at the words before he replied with: *Didn't know she was pg. She never said. Told you already.*

"Not knowing she was pregnant doesn't mean sod-all," Havers remarked. "He can't take us for fools."

"He doesn't," Lynley said. "I dare say he just takes himself for one, Sergeant.'' He typed: *You had sex with Elena*, deliberately making it a statement, not a question.

Gareth answered by hitting one of the number keys: *1*.

Once?

Yes.

When?

The boy pushed away from the desk for a moment. He remained in his chair. He looked not at the computer screen but at the floor, his arms on his knees. Lynley typed the word *September* and touched the boy's shoulder. Gareth glanced up, read it, dropped his head again. A hollow sound, akin to a stricken bellow, rose from his throat.

Lynley typed: *Tell me what happened, Gareth* and touched the boy's shoulder again.

Gareth looked up. He had begun to cry, and as if this display of emotion angered him, he drew his arm savagely across his eyes. Lynley waited. The boy moved back to the desk.

London, he typed. *Just before term. I saw her for my birthday. She fucked me on the floor of the kitchen while her mum was out buying milk for tea. HAPPY BIRTHDAY, YOU BLOODY STUPID BERK.*

''Great.'' Havers sighed.

Loved her, Gareth went on. *I wanted us special. To be*—he dropped his hands to his lap, stared at the screen.

You thought the lovemaking meant more than Elena intended it to mean, Lynley typed. *Is that what happened?*

Fucking, Gareth answered. *Not lovemaking. Fucking.*

Is that what she called it?

Thought we build something. Last year. I took real care. To make it last. Didn't want to rush anything. Never even tried with her. Wanted it to be real.

But it wasn't?

Thought it was. Because if you do that with a woman it means like a pledge. Like you say something you wouldn't say to anyone else.

Saying that you love each other?

Want to be together. Want to have a future. I thought that's why she did it with me.

Did you know she was sleeping with someone else?

Not then.

When did you learn it?

She came up this term. I thought we'd be together.

As lovers?

She didn't want that. Laughed when I tried to talk to her about it. Said what's matter with you Gareth it was only a fuck we did it it felt good that's the end of it right why you getting so moon-eyed over it it's not a big deal.

But it was to you.

Thought she loved me that's why she wanted to do it with me didn't know— He stopped. He looked sapped of energy.

Lynley gave him a moment, glancing round the room. Over a hook on the back of the door hung his scarf, the distinctive blue of the University letterman. His boxing gloves—smooth, clean leather with a look of having been lovingly cared for—hung on a second hook beneath them. Lynley wondered how much of Gareth Randolph's pain had been worked out against one of the punching bags in the small gymnasium on the upper floor of Fenners.

He turned back to the computer. *The argument you had with Elena on Sunday. Is that when she told you she was involved with someone else?*

I talked about us, he responded. *But there was no us.*

That's what she told you?

How could there not be us. I said what about London.

That's when she told you it hadn't meant anything?

Just a poke for fun Gareth we were randy we did it don't be such a twit and make it more than that.

She was laughing at you. I can't imagine you liked it.

Kept trying to talk. How she acted London. What she felt London. But she wouldn't listen. And then she told.

That there was someone else?

Didn't believe her at first. I said she was scared. Said she was trying to be what her father wanted her to be. Said all sorts of things. Wasn't even thinking. Wanted to hurt her.

"That's a telling remark," Havers noted.

"Perhaps," Lynley said. "But it's a fairly typical reaction to being hurt by someone you love: Measure still for measure."

"And when the first measure is murder?" Havers asked.

"I haven't discounted that, Sergeant." He typed, *What did you do when she'd convinced you there was another man?*

Gareth lifted his hands but did not type. In a nearby room, a vacuum began to thunder as the building's bedder made her daily rounds, and Lynley felt the answering urgency of concluding this interview before they were disturbed by anyone. He typed again: *What did you do?*

Hesitantly, Gareth touched the keys. *Hung about at St. Stephen's till she left. I wanted to know who.*

You followed her to Trinity Hall? You knew it was Dr. Troughton? When the boy nodded, Lynley typed: *How long did you hang about there?*

Till she came out.

At one?

He nodded. He'd waited in the street for her to emerge, he told them. And when she'd come out, he'd confronted her again, furiously angry at her rejection of him, bitterly disappointed in the loss of his dreams. But most of all he was disgusted with her behaviour. For he thought he'd understood her intentions in involving herself with Victor Troughton. And he saw those intentions as an attempt to attach herself to a hearing world that would never fully accept or understand her. She was acting deaf. She wasn't acting Deaf. They'd argued violently. He'd left her in the street.

Never saw her again, he finished.

"Doesn't look good to me, sir," Havers said.

Where were you Monday morning? Lynley typed.

When she was killed? Here. In bed.

But no one, of course, could verify that. He had been alone. And it would not have been an impossibility for Gareth simply to have failed to return to Queens' College that night, going instead to Crusoe's Island to lie in wait for Elena Weaver and to put a permanent end to the dispute between them.

"We need those boxing gloves, Inspector," Havers said as she snapped her notebook closed. "He's got motive. He's got means. He's got opportunity. He's got a temper as well and the talent to channel it right through his fists."

Lynley had to admit that a blue in boxing could not be overlooked when the murder victim had been beaten before she was strangled.

He typed, *Did you know Georgina Higgins-Hart?* And after Gareth nodded, *Where were you yesterday morning? Between six and half past.*

Here. Asleep.

Can someone verify that?

He shook his head.

We need your boxing gloves, Gareth. We need to give them to the forensic lab. Will you let us take them?

The boy gave a slow howl. *Didn't kill her didn't kill her didn't didn't didn't didn't did—*

Gently, Lynley moved the boy's hands to one side. *Do you know who did?*

Gareth shook his head once, but he kept his hands in his lap, balled into fists, as if they might betray him of their own volition should he raise them to the keyboard and allow them to type again.

"He's lying." Havers paused in the doorway to drape Gareth's boxing gloves round the strap of her shoulder bag. "Because if anyone ever had a motive to bag her, he's the one, Inspector."

"I can't disagree with that," Lynley said.

She pulled her cap firmly down over her forehead and drew up the hood of her coat. "But you can—and no doubt will—disagree with something else. I've heard that tone of yours before. What?"

"I think he knows who killed her. Or thinks he knows."

"Of course he does. Because he did it himself. Directly after he pounded her face in with these." She flipped the gloves in his direction. "What have we been looking for as a weapon all along? Something smooth? Have a feel of this leather. Something heavy? Imagine being on the receiving end of a boxer's punch. Something capable of inflicting face-shattering damage? Look at a few post-prize-fight photos for the proof if you want it."

He couldn't disagree. The boy had all the necessary requirements. Save one.

"And the gun, Sergeant?"

"What?"

"The shotgun used on Georgina Higgins-Hart. What about that?"

"You said yourself that the University probably has a gun club. To which, I have no doubt, Gareth Randolph belongs."

"So why follow her?"

She frowned, jabbing the toe of her shoe against the icy stone floor.

"Havers, I can understand why he would lie in wait at Crusoe's Island for Elena Weaver. He was in love with her. She'd rejected him. She'd made it plain that their lovemaking was just a bit of sweaty frolic on her mother's kitchen floor. She'd declared her attachment to another man. She'd teased and humiliated and made him feel a perfect fool. I agree with all that."

"So?"

"What about Georgina?"

"George . . ." Havers only stumbled over the thought for a moment before going on stoutly. "Perhaps it's what we thought before. Symbolically killing Elena Weaver again and again by seeking out all the young women who resemble her.''

"If that's the case, why not go to her room, Havers? Why not kill her in the college? Why follow her all the way out past Madingley? And *how* did he follow her?''

"How . . .''

"Havers, he's deaf.''

That stopped her.

Lynley pressed his advantage. "It's the country, Havers. It was pitch dark out there. Even if he got a car and followed her at a distance until they were safely out of town and then drove beyond her to lie in wait in that field, wouldn't he have had to hear something—her footfalls, her breathing, anything, Havers—in order to know exactly when to shoot? Are you going to argue that he went out there before dawn on Wednesday morning and blithely relied upon there being adequate starlight in this weather—which, frankly, would have been a fairly bad bet—to see a running girl well enough and soon enough to aim at her, discharge the weapon, and kill her? That's not premeditated murder. That's pure serendipity.''

She lifted one of the boxing gloves with the palm of her hand. "So what're we doing with these, Inspector?''

"Making St. James work for his money this morning. As well as hedging our bets.''

She pushed open the door with a weary grin. "I just love a man who keeps his options open.''

They were heading towards the turreted passage and Queens' Lane beyond it when a voice called out to them. They turned back into the court. A slender figure was coming along the path, the mist breaking before her like a curtain as she jogged in their direction.

She was tall and fair, with long silky hair that was held back from her face by two tortoise shell combs. These glittered with damp in the light that shone from one of the buildings. Beads of moisture clung to her eyelashes and skin. She was wearing only an unmatched sweatsuit whose shirt, like Georgina's, was emblazoned with the name of the college. She looked terribly cold.

"I was in the dining hall,'' she told them. "I saw you come for Gareth. You're the police.''

"And you're . . . ?''

"Rosalyn Simpson.'' Her eyes fell to the boxing gloves, and her brow furrowed in consternation. "You don't think Gareth's had anything to do with this?"

Lynley said nothing. Havers crossed her arms. The girl continued.

"I would have come to you sooner, but I was in Oxford until Tuesday evening. And then . . . Well, it gets a bit complicated." She cast a glance in the direction of Gareth Randolph's room.

"You have some information?" Lynley asked.

"I went to see Gareth at first. It was the DeaStu handout he'd printed, you see. I saw it when I got back, so it seemed logical to talk to him. I thought he'd pass the information on. Besides, there were other considerations at the time that . . . Oh, what does it matter now? I'm here. I'm telling you."

"What, exactly?"

Like Sergeant Havers, Rosalyn too crossed her arms, although it seemed more in a need to keep warm than a desire to project implacability. She said, "I was running along the river Monday morning. I went by Crusoe's Island round half past six. I think I saw the killer."

Glyn Weaver edged part way down the stairs, just far enough to hear the conversation between her former husband and his current wife. They were still in the morning room—although it had been some hours since breakfast—and their voices were just polite and formal enough to give a clear indication of the state of things between them. Cool, Glyn decided, frosting over into glacial. She smiled.

"Terence Cuff wants to give some sort of eulogy," Anthony was saying. He spoke without any evident feeling, the information given like a recitation. "I've talked to two of her supervisors. They'll also speak, and Adam's said he'd like to read a poem she was fond of." There was a clink of china, a cup being placed carefully into a saucer. "We might not have the body back from the police before tomorrow, but the funeral parlour will have a coffin there all the same. No one will know the difference. And as everyone's been told she's to be buried in London, no one will be expecting an interment tomorrow."

"As to the funeral, Anthony. In London . . ." Justine's voice was calm. Glyn felt her spine tingle when she heard that tone of cool determination.

"There can't be a change in the plans," Anthony said. "Try to understand. I have no choice in the matter. I must respect Glyn's wishes. It's the least I can do."

"I'm your wife."

"As she was once. And Elena was our daughter."

"She was your wife for less than six years. Six miserable years, as I recall your telling me. More than fifteen years ago at that. While you and I—"

"This situation has nothing to do with how long I was married to either of you, Justine."

"It has everything to do with it. It has to do with loyalty, with vows I made and promises I've kept. I've been faithful to you in every way, while she slept around like a whore and you know it. And now you say that respecting her wishes is the least you can do? Respecting hers over mine?"

Anthony had begun to respond with, "If you still can't see that there are times when the past—" when Glyn got to the doorway. She took only a moment to survey them before speaking. Anthony was sitting in one of the wicker chairs, unshaven, desiccated. Justine was at the bank of windows where the fog that shrouded the wide front garden pressed long streaks of moisture against the glass. She was dressed in a black suit and pearl grey blouse. A black leather briefcase leaned against her chair.

Glyn said, "Perhaps you'd like to say the rest, Justine. Like mother, like daughter. Or don't you have the nerve to carry your special brand of honesty to its logical conclusion?"

Justine began to move towards her chair. She brushed a strand of blonde hair off her cheek. Glyn caught her arm, dug her fingers into the fine wool of her suit, and enjoyed a fleeting moment of delight when she saw Justine flinch.

"I said why don't you finish what you were saying?" she insisted. "Glyn put Elena through her paces, Anthony. Glyn turned your daughter into a little deaf whore. Elena gave a poke to anyone who wanted it, just like her mum."

"Glyn," Anthony said.

"Don't try to defend her, all right? I was standing on the stairs. I heard what she said. My only child dead for just three days, myself struggling to make some kind of sense of it, and she can't wait to tear into the both of us. And she chooses sex to do it. I find that most interesting."

"I won't listen to this," Justine said.

Glyn tightened her grip. "Can't you bear to hear the truth? You use sex as a weapon, and not merely against me."

Glyn felt Justine's muscles go rigid. She knew that her dagger had hit the mark. She drove it in farther. "Reward him when he's been a good little boy, punish him when he's bad. Is that how it is? So. How long will he pay for keeping you from the funeral?"

"You're pathetic," Justine said. "You can't see beyond sex any more than—"

"Elena?" Glyn dropped Justine's arm. She looked at Anthony. "Ah. There it is."

Justine brushed at her sleeve as if to cleanse herself of the contact she'd had with her husband's former wife. She picked up her briefcase.

"I'm off," she said calmly.

Anthony stood, his eyes going from the briefcase to her, moving his gaze from her head to her feet as if he had only just become aware of the manner in which she had dressed for the day. "You can't be intending—"

"To go back to work just three days after Elena was murdered? To expose myself to public censure for having done so? Oh yes, Anthony, that's exactly what I intend."

"No. Justine, people—"

"Stop it. Please. I'm not at all like you."

For a moment, Anthony stared after her as she left the house, taking her coat from round the newel post on the stairway and closing the front door behind her. He watched her walk through the fog towards her grey Peugeot. Glyn kept her eyes on him warily, wondering if he would run out and try to stop her. But he seemed, if anything, too exhausted to care about changing anyone's mind. He turned from the window and trudged towards the back of the house.

She went to the table upon which the breakfast things still lay: bacon congealing in slim jackets of grease, egg yolks drying and splitting like yellow mud. A piece of toast still stood in the silver rack, and Glyn reached for it thoughtfully. Dry and abrasive beneath her fingers, it crumbled easily, leaving a shower of dust upon the clean parquet floor.

From the back of the house, she could hear the metallic sound of file drawers sliding open. And over it, the high whine of Elena's Irish setter, longing to be allowed into the house. Glyn walked to the kitchen from whose window she could see the dog sitting on the back step, his black nose pressed into the doorjamb, his feathery tail sweeping back and forth in innocent anticipation. He took a step backwards, looked up, and saw her watching him through the window. His tail picked up rhythm, he gave a joyful bark. She regarded him evenly—taking a small degree of pleasure in allowing his hopes to rise—before she turned and made her way to the rear of the house.

At the doorway to Anthony's study, she paused. He was crouched by an open drawer of the filing cabinet. The contents of two manila folders lay on the floor, comprising perhaps two dozen pencil sketches. Next to them was a canvas rolled like a tube.

For a moment, Glyn watched as Anthony's hand passed slowly over the drawings in a gesture like an incomplete caress. Then he began to go through them. His fingers seemed clumsy. Twice he gasped for breath. When he paused to remove his spectacles and wipe their lenses on his shirt, she realised that he was crying. She entered the room to get a better look at the drawings on the floor and saw that they were all sketches of Elena.

"Dad's got himself into drawing these days," Elena had told her. She'd pronounced it *dawing,* and she'd laughed about the idea. They'd often chuckled over Anthony's attempts to find himself through one activity or another as he approached middle age. First it had been long distance running, after that he had begun to swim, then he'd taken up bicycling like a zealot, and finally he had learned to sail. But of all the activities which he had pursued, drawing amused them the most. "Dad t'inks he's got the soul of Van Gogh," Elena would say. And she'd mimic her father's wide-legged stance with sketch pad in hand, eyes squinting towards the distance, hand shading her brow. She'd draw a moustache like his on her upper lip and pull her face into a contorted frown of concentration. "Doe move an inch, Glynnie," she would command of her mother. "Hol' that pose. Hol'—that—pose." And they would laugh together.

But now Glyn could see that the sketches were quite good, that he had managed to achieve something far more in them than was depicted in the still lifes that hung in the sitting room, or the sailboats, the harbours, and the fishing villages here on the study walls. For in the series of drawings he'd spread out on the floor, she could see that he had managed to capture the essence of their daughter. Here were the exact tilt of her head, the elfin shape of her eyes, the wide chipped-tooth grin, the contour of a cheekbone, of nose, and of mouth. These were studies only, they were quick impressions. But they were lovely and true.

As she took a step closer, Anthony looked up. He gathered the drawings together and replaced them in their respective folders. Along with the canvas which fit into the back, he shoved them into the drawer.

"You don't have any of them framed," she said.

He didn't answer. Instead, he closed the drawer and went to the desk, where he played restlessly with the computer, switching on the Ceephone and watching the screen. A series of menu instructions appeared. He stared at them but did nothing with the keyboard.

"Never mind," Glyn said. "I know why you hide them." She went to stand behind him. She spoke near his ear. "How many years have you lived like this, Anthony? Ten? Twelve? How on earth have you managed?"

His head lowered. She studied the back of his neck, remembering unexpectedly how soft his hair was and how, when overlong, it curled like a child's against his skin. It was greying now, with scattered strands like white threads woven against black.

"What did she hope to gain? Elena was your daughter. She was your only child. What on earth did she hope to gain?"

His reply was a whisper. He spoke as if answering someone not in the room. "She wanted to hurt me. There was nothing else she could do to make me understand."

"Understand? What?"

"How it felt to be devastated. How I'd devastated her. Through cowardice. Selfishness. Egocentricity. But mostly through cowardice. You want the Penford Chair only for your ego, she said. You want a beautiful house and a beautiful wife and a daughter who'll be your marionette. So that people will look at you with admiration and envy. So that people will say the lucky bloke's got it all. But you don't have it all. You have practically nothing. You have less than nothing. Because what you have is a lie. And you don't even have the courage to admit it."

A sudden fist of knowledge squeezed at Glyn's heart as the full meaning of his words slowly dawned upon her, even though he spoke them in a fugue. "You could have prevented it. If only you'd given her what she wanted. Anthony, you could have stopped her."

"I couldn't. I had to think of Elena. She was here in Cambridge, in this home, with me. She was starting to come round, to be free with me at last, to let me be her father. I couldn't run the risk of losing her again. I couldn't take the chance. And I thought I *would* lose her if I—"

"You lost her anyway!" she cried, shaking his arm. "She's not going to walk through that door. She's not going to say Dad, I understand,

I forgive you, I know you did your best. She's gone. She's dead. And you could have prevented it.''

"If she had a child, she might have understood what it felt like to have Elena here. She might have known why I couldn't face the thought of doing anything that might have resulted in losing her again. I'd lost her once. How could I face that agony again? How could she expect me to face it?''

Glyn saw that he wasn't really responding to her. He was ruminating. He was speaking in tongues. Behind a barrier that shielded him from the worst of the truth, he was talking in a canyon where an echo exists, but throws back different words. Suddenly, she felt the same degree of anger towards him that she'd felt during the worst years of their marriage when she'd greeted his blind pursuit of his career with pursuits of her own, waiting for him to notice the late nights she was keeping, wanting him to notice the nature of the bruises on her neck, her breasts, and her thighs, anticipating the moment when he would finally speak, when he'd give an indication that he really did care.

"This is all about you, isn't it?" she asked him. "It always has been. Even having Elena here in Cambridge was for your benefit, not for herself. Not for her education, but to make you feel better, to give you what you want.''

"I wanted to give her a life. I wanted us to have a life together.''

"How would that have been possible? You didn't love her, Anthony. You only loved yourself. You loved your image, your reputation, your wonderful accomplishments. You loved being loved. But you didn't love her. And even now you can stand here and look at your daughter's death and think about how you caused it and how you feel about it now and how devastated you are and what kind of statement it all makes about *you*. But you won't do anything about any of it, will you, you won't make any declaration, you won't take any stand. Because how might that reflect upon you?''

Finally, he looked at her. The rims of his eyes appeared bloody and sore. "You don't know what happened. You don't understand.''

"I understand perfectly. You plan to bury your dead, lick your wounds, and go on. You're as much a coward as you were fifteen years ago. You ran out on her then in the middle of the night. You'll run out on her now. Because it's the easiest thing to do.''

"I didn't run out on her,'' he said carefully. "I stood firm this time, Glyn. That's why she died.''

"For you? Because of you?"

"Yes. Because of me."

"The sun rises and sets on the same horizon in your world. It always has."

He shook his head. "Perhaps once," he said. "But it only sets now."

21

Lynley pulled the Bentley into a vacant space at the southwest corner of the Cambridge police station. He stared at the vaguely discernible shape of the glass-encased notice board in front of the building, feeling drained. Next to him, Havers fidgeted in her seat. She began to flip through her notebook. He knew she was reading what she'd just recorded from Rosalyn Simpson.

"It was a woman," the Queens' undergraduate had said.

She had walked them along the same route she had taken early Monday morning, through the thick, dun, cotton wool of fog in Laundress Lane where the open door to the Asian Studies Faculty shot a meagre light out into the gloom. Once someone slammed it shut, however, the mist seemed impenetrable. The universe became confined to the twenty square feet which comprised the boundary of what they could see.

"Do you run every morning?" Lynley asked the girl as they crossed Mill Lane and skirted the metal posts that kept vehicles off the pedestrian bridge which crossed the river at Granta Place. To their right, Laundress Green was obscured by the fog, an expanse of misty field intermittently disturbed by the hulking forms of crack willows. Beyond it, from across the pond, a single light winked from an upper floor in the Old Granary.

"Nearly," she answered.

"Always the same time?"

"As close to a quarter past six as I can make it. Sometimes a bit later."

"And on Monday?"

"Mondays are slower for me, getting out of bed. It was probably round six-twenty-five when I left Queens' on Monday."

"So you'd reach the island . . ."

"No later than half past."

"You're certain of that. It couldn't have been later?"

"I was back in my room by half past seven, Inspector. I'm quick, it's true, but I'm not that quick. And I did a good ten miles Monday morning, with the island at the start of it. It's part of my training circuit."

"For Hare and Hounds?"

"Yes. I fancy a blue this year."

She hadn't noticed anything unusual on the morning of her run, she told them. It was still quite dark when she left Queens' College, and aside from overtaking a workman who was pushing a cart down Laundress Lane, she hadn't seen another soul. Just the usual assortment of ducks and swans, some already floating on the river, others still placidly dozing on the bank. But the fog was heavy—"At least as heavy as it is today," she said—so she had to admit that anyone might have been lurking in a doorway or waiting, hidden by the fog, on the green.

When they reached the island, they found a small fire burning, sending up weak puffs of acrid, soot-coloured smoke to melt into the fog. A man in a peaked cap, overcoat, and gloves was feeding autumn leaves, trash, and bits of wood into the blue-tipped flames. Lynley recognised him as Ned, the surlier of the two older boat repairmen.

Rosalyn indicated the footbridge that crossed not the Cam itself, but the secondary stream that the river became as it flowed round the west side of the island. "She was crossing this," she said. "I heard her because she stumbled against something—she might have lost her footing, everything was quite damp—and she was coughing as well. I assumed she was out running like me and was feeling worn out, and frankly I was a bit peeved to come upon her like that because she didn't appear to be watching where she was going and I nearly bumped into her. And—" She seemed embarrassed. "Well, I suppose I have the University mind set about townees, don't I? What was she doing, I thought, invading my patch?"

"What gave you the impression she was a local?"

Rosalyn looked thoughtfully at the footbridge through the mist. The damp air was catching on her eyelashes, spiking them darkly. Childlike curls of hair were forming against her brow. "It was something about her clothes, I should guess. And perhaps her age, although I suppose she could have been from Lucy Cavendish."

"What about her clothes?"

Rosalyn gestured at her own mismatched sweat suit. "University runners generally wear their college colours somewhere, their college sweatshirts as well."

"And she wasn't wearing a sweat suit?" Havers asked sharply, glancing up from her notebook.

"She was—a tracksuit actually—but it wasn't from a college. I mean, I don't recall seeing a college name on it. Although, now I think of it, considering the colour, she might have been from Trinity Hall."

"Because she was wearing black," Lynley said.

Rosalyn's quick smile indicated affirmation. "You know the colleges' colours, then?"

"It was just a good guess."

He walked onto the footbridge. The wrought iron gate was partially open upon the south end of the island. The police line was gone now, the island available to anyone who wished to sit by the water, to meet surreptitiously, or—like Sarah Gordon—to attempt to sketch. "Did the woman see you?"

Rosalyn and Havers remained on the path. "Oh yes."

"You're sure?"

"I nearly ran into her. She couldn't have helped seeing me."

"And you were wearing the same clothes you're wearing now?"

Rosalyn nodded, and plunged her hands into the pockets of the anorak she'd taken from her room prior to their setting out into the fog. "Without this, of course," she said with a lift of her shoulders to indicate the anorak. She added ingenuously, "One gets warm enough running. And"—her face brightened—"she didn't have a coat or a jacket on, so that must have been another reason why I assumed she was a runner. Although . . ." A marked hesitation as she looked into the mist. "She might have been carrying one, I suppose. I can't recall. But I think she was carrying something . . . I think."

"What did she look like?"

"Look like?" Rosalyn frowned down at her gym shoes. "Slender. She wore her hair pulled back."

"Colour?"

"Oh dear. It was light, I think. Yes, quite light."

"Anything unusual about her? A feature perhaps? A mark on her skin? The shape of her nose? A large forehead? A pointed chin?"

"I can't recall. I'm terribly sorry. I'm not much help, am I? You see, it was three days ago and I didn't know at the time that I'd have to remember her. I mean, one doesn't really *study* everyone one meets. One doesn't expect to have to recall them.'' Rosalyn blew out a breath of frustration before going on to say earnestly, ''Perhaps if you'd like to hypnotise me the way they do sometimes when a witness can't recall the details of a crime . . .''

''It's fine,'' Lynley said. He rejoined them on the path. ''Do you think she got a clear look at your sweatshirt?''

''Oh, I dare say she did.''

''She would have seen the name?''

''Queens' College, you mean? Yes. She would have seen that.'' Rosalyn looked back in the direction of the college, although even had there been no fog, she wouldn't have been able to see it in the distance. When she turned back to them, her face was sombre, but she didn't say anything until a young man, coming across Crusoe's Bridge from Coe Fen, descended the ten iron steps—shoes ringing loudly against the metal—and plodded past them, head bent into the mist which quickly enveloped him. ''Melinda was right, then,'' Rosalyn said quietly. ''Georgina died in my place.''

A girl her age didn't need to carry round that sort of responsibility for a lifetime, Lynley thought. He said, ''You can't know that for a certainty,'' although he was fast arriving at the same conclusion.

Rosalyn reached for one of the tortoise shell combs in her hair. She pulled it out and grasped a long lock in her fingers. ''There's this,'' she said, and then she unzipped her anorak and pointed to the emblem across her breast. ''And this. We're the same height, the same weight, the same colouring. We're both from Queens'. Whoever followed Georgina yesterday morning thought she was following me. Because I saw. Because I knew. Because I might have told. And I would have, I *should* have . . . And if I had done—as by rights I should have and I know it, you don't have to tell me, I know it—Georgina wouldn't be dead.'' She whipped her head away and blinked furiously at the cloudy mass of Sheep's Green.

And he knew there was little or nothing he could say to lessen her guilt or lighten her burden of responsibility.

Now, more than an hour later, Lynley drew a deep breath and let it out, staring at the sign in front of the police station. Across the street, the wide green that was Parker's Piece might not even have existed, hidden as it was by the mat-work of fog. A distant beacon blinked off and on in its centre, serving as a guide to those trying to find their way.

''So it had nothing to do with the fact that Elena was pregnant,'' Havers said. And then, ''What now?''

"Wait here for St. James. See what he's able to conclude about the weapon. And let him have a go at eliminating the boxing gloves as well."

"And you?"

"I'll go to the Weavers'."

"Right." Still, she didn't move from the car. He could feel her looking at him. "Everyone loses, don't they, Inspector?"

"That's always the case with a murder," he said.

Neither of the Weaver cars was in the drive when Lynley pulled up to the front of the house. But the garage doors were closed and, assuming that the cars would be kept out of the damp, he went to ring the bell. From the back of the house, he could hear the dog's answering bark of welcome. It was followed moments later by a woman's voice calling for quiet behind the door. The bolt was drawn back.

Since she'd met him at the door on his two previous visits, Lynley had been expecting to see Justine Weaver when the broad oak panels slid soundlessly open. So he was taken aback when in her place stood a tall, somewhat beefy middle-aged woman carrying a plate of sandwiches. These gave off the distinct odour of tuna. They were surrounded by a substantial nest of crisps.

Lynley recalled his initial interview with the Weavers, and the information that Anthony Weaver had given him about his former wife. This, he realised, would be Glyn.

He produced his warrant card and introduced himself. She took her time about scrutinising it, giving him time to scrutinise her. Only in height was she like Justine Weaver. In every other way, she was Justine's antithesis. Looking at her heavy tweed skirt that stretched wide across her hips, her line-weary face with its loose flesh on the jaw, her wiry hair liberally streaked with grey and pulled back into an unflattering chignon, Lynley found himself hearing once again Victor Troughton's assessment of his wife's middle age. And he felt a surge of mortification when he realised that he too was in the process of judging and dismissing based upon what time had done to a woman's body.

Glyn Weaver looked up from her perusal of his card. She held the door open. "Come in," she said. "I was just having lunch. Would you like something?" She offered the plate in his direction. "You'd think there might be something other than tinned fish in the larder, but Anthony's Justine likes to watch her weight."

"Is she here?" Lynley asked. "Is Dr. Weaver here?"

Glyn led him into the morning room and fluttered a hand in dismissal. "Both out. One couldn't really expect Justine to hang about the house for more than a day or two over something as inconsequential as a family death—and as for Anthony, I don't know. He went off a while ago."

"By car?"

"Yes."

"To the college?"

"I have no idea. One moment he was here in the house talking to me. The next moment he was gone. I expect he's out there somewhere in the fog, trying to think what he's going to do next. You know how it is. Moral obligation versus cock-throbbing lust. He's always had trouble when it comes to conflict. In his case, I'm afraid, lust usually wins."

Lynley didn't respond. He would have had to be a complete dullard not to recognise what was roiling beneath the thin veneer of Glyn's civility. Anger, hatred, bitterness, envy. And a terror of abjuring any of them in order to allow her heart to begin to feel the full strength of what had to be a multifurcate grief.

Glyn set her plate on the wicker table. Its breakfast dishes had not yet been removed. On the floor surrounding it, a noticeable patina of toast crumbs lay on the wood, and she walked right through this, either oblivious or unconcerned. She stacked the breakfast plates one upon the other, mindless of the cold and congealing food upon each. But rather than take them into the kitchen, she merely pushed them to one side, ignoring a dirty knife and teaspoon that fell from the table onto the crisp floral pillow that covered the seat of one of the chairs.

"Anthony knows," she said. "I expect you know as well. I expect that's why you've come. Will you arrest her today?" She sat down. Her chair's willow strands creaked as they rubbed together. She picked up the sandwich and took a hefty bite, chewing with a pleasure that seemed only marginally related to the food.

He said, "Do you know where she's gone, Mrs. Weaver?"

Glyn picked among the crisps. "At what point exactly do you make an arrest? I've always wondered that. Do you need an eyewitness? What about hard evidence? You've got to have something to give to the prosecutors, don't you? You've got to have a case that solidly sticks."

"Did she have an appointment?"

Glyn wiped her hands against her skirt and began to tick items off on her fingers. "There's the Ceephone call that she claimed she received on Sunday night. There's the fact that she ran without the dog on Monday morning. There's the fact that she knew exactly where and how and what time to find her. And there's the fact that she hated her and wanted her dead. Do you need something more? Fingerprints? Blood? A single hair, a bit of skin?''

"Has she gone to see family?"

"People loved Elena. Justine couldn't stand that. But mostly, she couldn't stand that Anthony loved her. She hated his devotion, how he always tried to make things right between them. She didn't want that. Because if things went right between Anthony and Elena, things would go wrong between Anthony and Justine. That's what she thought. And she was sick with jealousy. You've finally come for her, haven't you?''

Eagerness appeared in wet glimmers at the corners of her mouth. She reminded Lynley of the crowds that once gathered to watch public executions, revelling in the vengeful taking of a life. Had there been a possibility to see Justine Weaver drawn and quartered, he had no doubt that this woman would be more than willing to grasp the opportunity. He wanted to tell her that there was, in the end, no real taking of an eye for an eye and no real satisfaction to be found at any bar of justice. For even if the most barbarous kind of punishment were meted out against the perpetrator of a crime, the rage and grief of the victimised remained.

His eyes dropped to the mess on the table. Near the stacked plates and beneath a knife that was smeared with butter lay an envelope with the crest of the University Press on it and Justine's name—but not her address—written in a firm, masculine hand.

Evidently, Glyn saw the direction of his gaze for she said, "She's an important executive. You couldn't really have thought she'd be hanging round here."

He nodded and began to take his leave.

"Will you arrest her?" she asked again.

He responded with, "I want to ask her a question."

"I see. Just a question. Quite. Well. Would you arrest her if you had the proof in your hand? If I gave you the proof?'' She waited to see the reaction to her questions. She smiled like a perfectly satisfied cat when his steps faltered and he turned to face her. "Yes," she said slowly. "Oh yes, indeed, Mister Policeman."

She pushed away from the table and left the room. In a moment, he heard the Irish setter begin barking again and her answering shout from the back of the house: "Shut up, will you!" The dog persisted.

"Here," she said, returning. She carried two manila folders and, under her arm, what appeared to be an artist's canvas rolled up. "Anthony had these in the study, hidden at the back of a filing drawer. I found him snivelling over them an hour or so ago, just before he left. Have a look for yourself. I've no doubt what conclusion you'll reach.''

She handed over the folders first. He flipped through the sketches that each contained. All of them were studies of the dead girl, all appeared done by the same hand. They were undeniably skilful, and he admired their quality. None, however, could possibly serve as a motive for murder. He was about to say this when Glyn thrust the canvas at him.

''Now look at this,'' she said.

He unrolled it, squatting to place it on the floor because it was quite large and had been doubled over prior to being rolled and stored in the first place. It was, he saw, a spattered piece of canvas with two large rips moving diagonally towards the middle and a central, shorter rip meeting them there. The spattering on it had been created by large gobs of paint —mostly white and red—that looked as if they'd been smeared haphazardly onto the canvas with a palette knife and with no regard for artistic expression. Where they did not meet or overlap, the colours of another oil painting showed through. He stood up and gazed down at it, feeling the first stirring of final comprehension.

''And this,'' Glyn said. ''It was wrapped up in the canvas when I first unrolled it.''

She slapped into his hand a small brass plaque—perhaps two inches long and three quarters of an inch wide. He took it from his palm and held it to the light, knowing what it was that he would likely see. ELENA was engraved in fine script across it.

He looked up at Glyn Weaver and saw the exultant pleasure she was taking from the moment. He knew she was expecting him to comment upon the nature of the motive she'd just presented him. Instead, he asked, ''Has Justine gone running while you've been in Cambridge?''

This didn't seem to be the response she expected from him. But she answered well enough although her eyes narrowed with sharp suspicion as she did so. ''Yes.''

''In a tracksuit?''

''Well, she wasn't exactly dressed by Coco Chanel.''

''What colour, Mrs. Weaver?''

''Colour?'' With a hint of outrage that he wasn't keying into the ruined painting and what it implied.

''Yes. The colour.''

''It was black.''

•   •   •

"So just how much more proof do you want that Justine hated my daughter?" Glyn Weaver had followed him out of the breakfast room, leaving behind the smell of old eggs, tuna, butter, and crisps vying with one another in the air for domination. "What's it going to take to convince you? How much more proof?"

She'd put a hand on his arm and pulled on him till he faced her, standing so close that he could feel her breath on his face and could smell the oily odour of fish each time she exhaled. "He sketched Elena, not his wife. He painted Elena, not his wife. Imagine watching that. Imagine hating each moment as it was going on before your eyes. Right here in this morning room. Because the light's good here, and he would have wanted to paint her in light that was good."

Lynley turned the Bentley into Bulstrode Gardens where the street-lamps did not so much cut through the mist as merely colour the top layer of it gold while the rest remained a mass of wet grey. He pulled directly into the semi-circular drive, through a mat of damp leaves fallen and blown from the stand of slim birches at the edge of the property. Without taking particular note of it, he gazed at the house before getting out of the car, considering the nature of the evidence he had with him, reflecting upon the sketches of Elena and what they suggested about the ruined canvas, thinking of the Ceephone, and, above all, playing with time. For it was time upon which the entire case hung.

She would have obliterated the image first and, taking no real or lasting satisfaction in that, she would have moved on to the girl herself second, Glyn Weaver had asserted. She would have pounded her face just as she'd hacked and stabbed at the painting, brutalising and destroying, living out her rage.

But most of that constituted hopeful conjecture, Lynley thought. Only part of it skirted close to the truth. He tucked the canvas under his arm and went to the door.

Harry Rodger answered, Christian and Perdita at his heels. He said only, "It's Pen you want?" to Lynley's request, and then to his son, "Go fetch Mummy, Chris."

When the little boy scampered up the stairway to do so, shouting "Mummy!" and bashing the worn head of a hobbyhorse against the balusters with additional cries of "Ker-blowey, Ker-*blew*!" Rodger nodded Lynley into the sitting room. He swung his daughter onto his hip and glanced without speaking at the canvas beneath Lynley's arm. Perdita curled herself against her father's chest.

Above them Christian's footsteps thumped along the upstairs corridor. His hobbyhorse banged against the wall. "Mummy!" Small fists pounded on a door.

"You've brought her some work, haven't you?" Rodger's words were polite, his face deliberately impassive.

"I'd like her to look at this, Harry. I need her expertise."

The other man's lips offered a brief smile, one which accepted information without indicating that it was at all welcome. He said, "Excuse me, please," and he walked into the kitchen, shutting the door behind him.

A moment later, Christian preceded both his mother and his aunt into the sitting room. Somewhere in his sojourn through the house, he'd picked up a tot-sized vinyl holster, and he was wrestling it inexpertly round his waist, its companion toy gun dangling to his knees. "I shoot you, mister," he said to Lynley, dragging on the gun's handle and knocking himself into Lady Helen's legs in his effort to get it out. "I shoot, Auntie Leen."

"Those aren't the wisest words to say to a policeman, Chris." Lady Helen knelt in front of him, and saying, "Don't be such a wiggle-worm," she fastened the holster round his waist.

He giggled and shouted, "Ker-blang you, mister!" and ran to the sofa where he beat the pistol against the pillows.

"If nothing else, he has a fine future in crime," Lynley noted.

Penelope raised both hands in futility. "It's nearly his naptime. He gets a bit wild when he's tired."

"I'd hate to think what he's like when he's fully awake."

"Ker-plough!" Christian yelled. He rolled onto the floor and began crawling in the direction of the hall, making shooting noises and taking aim at imaginary foes.

Penelope watched him and shook her head. "I've considered sedating him until his eighteenth birthday, but what would I do for laughs?" As Christian began an assault on the stairway, she said with a nod towards the canvas, "What have you brought?"

Lynley unrolled it along the back of the sofa, gave her a moment to observe it from across the room, and said, "What can you do with it?"

"Do?"

"Not a restoration, Tommy," Lady Helen said doubtfully.

Penelope looked up from the canvas. She said, "Heavens. You must be joking."

"Why?"

"Tommy, it's a ruin."

"I don't need it repaired. I just need to establish what's underneath the top layer of paint."

"But how do you even know there's something underneath it?"

"Look closer. There has to be. You can see it. And besides, it's the only explanation."

Penelope asked for no further details. She merely walked to the sofa for a closer look and touched her fingers to the surface of the canvas. "It would take weeks to clean this off," she said. "You've no idea what it would entail. This sort of thing is done inches at a time across a canvas, a single layer at a time. One doesn't just dump a bottle of solvent on it and wipe it off like a window being cleaned."

"Blast," Lynley muttered.

"Ker-blooey!" Christian yelled from his position of potential ambush on the stairs.

"Still . . ." Penelope tapped her index finger against her lip. "Let me take it into the kitchen and have a look under stronger light."

Her husband was standing at the stove, flipping through the day's post. His daughter leaned against him, one arm encircling his leg, one apple cheek pressed against his thigh. Sleepily, she said, "Mummy," and Rodger raised his head from the letter he was perusing. His eyes took in the canvas that Penelope carried. His face was unreadable.

Penelope said, "If you'll just clear off the work top," and waited with the canvas in her hands while Lynley and Lady Helen moved aside the mixing bowls, lunch dishes, story books, and silverware. Then she flopped the canvas down and looked at it thoughtfully.

"Pen," her husband said.

"In a moment," she replied. She went to a drawer and took out a magnifying glass, fondly running her fingers through her daughter's hair as she passed.

"Where's the baby?" Rodger asked.

Penelope bent over the work top and scrutinised first the individual blotches of paint and then the rips in the canvas itself. "Ultraviolet," she said. "Perhaps infrared." She looked up at Lynley. "Do you need the painting itself? Or would a photograph do?"

"Photograph?"

"Pen, I asked—"

"We have three options. An X-ray would show us the entire skeleton of the painting—everything that's been painted on the canvas no matter how many layers have been used. An ultraviolet light would give us whatever work's been done on top of the varnish—if there's been re-painting, for instance. An infrared photo would give us whatever comprised the initial sketch for the painting. And any doctoring that's been done to the signature. If there is a signature, of course. Would any of that be helpful?"

Lynley looked at the lacerated canvas and considered the options. "I should guess an X-ray," he said reflectively. "But if that doesn't do it, can we try something else?"

"Certainly. I'll just—"

"Penelope." Harry Rodger's face had mottled, although his voice was determinedly pleasant. "Isn't it time that the twins had a lie down? Christian's been acting like a madman for the past twenty minutes, and Perdita's falling asleep on her feet."

Penelope glanced at the wall clock that hung above the stove. She chewed on her lip and looked at her sister. Lady Helen smiled faintly, perhaps in acknowledgement, perhaps in encouragement. "You're right, of course," Penelope said with a sigh. "They do need to nap."

"Good. Then—"

"So if you'll see to them yourself, darling, the rest of us can pop this canvas round to the Fitzwilliam to see what can be done with it. The baby's been fed. She's already asleep. And the twins won't give you much trouble so long as you read them something from *Cautionary Verses*. Christian's quite partial to that poem about Mathilda. Helen must have read it to him half a dozen times before he dropped off yesterday." She began rolling up the canvas. "I'll just need a moment to dress," she told Lynley.

When she'd left the room, Rodger lifted up his daughter. He looked at the doorway as if in the expectation of Penelope's return. When that did not occur, when instead they heard her saying, "Daddy will help you have a lie down, Christian darling," he gave his attention to Lynley for a moment as Christian pounded down the stairs and across the sitting room towards the kitchen.

"She isn't well," Rodger said. "You know as well as I that she shouldn't be leaving this house. I hold you responsible—both of you, Helen—if anything happens."

"We're merely going to the Fitzwilliam Museum," Lady Helen replied, sounding for all the world like a model of reason. "What on earth could possibly happen to her there?"

"Daddy!" Christian flung himself into the room and crashed euphorically against his father's legs. "Read 'Tilda to me! Now!"

"I'm warning you, Helen," Rodger said, and stabbing a finger in Lynley's direction, "I'm warning the both of you."

"Daddy! Read!"

"Duty appears to be calling, Harry," Lady Helen replied serenely. "You'll find their pyjamas beneath the pillows on their beds. And the book—"

"I know where the damn book is," Rodger snapped and took his children from the room.

"Oh dear," Lady Helen murmured. "I'm afraid there's going to be hell to pay for this."

"I don't think so," Lynley said. "Harry's an educated man. At the very least we know he can read."

"*Cautionary Verses?*"

Lynley shook his head. "The handwriting on the wall."

"After an hour, we all managed to come to an agreement. The strongest likelihood is that it was glass. When I left, Pleasance was still holding out for his theory that it was a champagne or wine bottle—preferably full—but he's fresh from graduate school and still attached to any opportunity to expatiate. Frankly, I expect he's more attracted to the sound of his arguments than to their viability. No wonder the head of forensic—is it Drake?—wants his neck in a noose."

Forensic scientist Simon Allcourt-St. James joined Barbara Havers at her solitary table in the officers' mess at Cambridge Police Station. For the past two hours, he'd been holed up at the regional police laboratory with the disputing parties of Superintendent Sheehan's forensic team, examining not only the X-rays of Elena Weaver but the body itself and comparing his conclusions with those developed by the younger scientist in the Cambridge group. It was an activity that Barbara had begged off attending. The brief period during her police training that had been given to watching autopsies had more than sated whatever nugatory interest she may once have had in forensic medicine.

"Please note, officers," the forensic pathologist had intoned as he stood before the draped cart under which was the corpse that would be their object lesson, "that the mark of the ligature used in strangling this woman can still be plainly observed although our killer made what he apparently believed would be an ingenious attempt at obfuscation. Step closer, please."

Like idiots—or automatons—the probationary DC's had done so. And three of them had fainted dead away when, with a tiny smile of malicious anticipation, the pathologist whipped back the sheet to display the grisly remains of a body that had been saturated with paraffin and set afire. Barbara herself had remained on her feet, but only just. And she had never been in a tearing hurry to stand in on an autopsy from that time forward. Just bring me the facts, she always thought when a body was carted away from a murder scene. Don't make me watch you gather them.

"Tea?" she asked St. James as he lowered himself into one of the chairs, adjusting his position to make allowances for the brace he wore on his left leg. "It's fresh." She gave a glance to her watch. "Well, okay. Only moderately fresh. But it's riddled with enough caffeine to paste your eyelids permanently open if you're feeling clapped out."

St. James accepted the offer and ministered to his cup with three overlarge spoonfuls of sugar. After a taste of it, he added a fourth, saying, "Falstaff is my only defence, Barbara."

She lifted her cup to him. "Cheers," she said, and watched him drink.

He was looking well, she decided. Still too thin and angular, still too lined about the face, but there was an appealing sheen to the undisciplined dark hair, and his hands on the table seemed utterly relaxed. A man at peace with himself, she thought, and she wondered how long it had taken St. James to achieve such psychic equilibrium. He was Lynley's oldest and closest friend, an expert witness from London upon whose forensic services they had called more than once.

"If not a wine bottle—and there was one at the crime scene, by the way—and not a champagne bottle, then what was used to beat her?" she asked. "And why have the Cambridge people been scrapping over this issue in the first place?"

"A case of male posturing, to my way of thinking," St. James replied. "The head of forensic is just over fifty. He's been on the job for a good twenty-five years. Along comes Pleasance, twenty-six years old and acting the upstart crow. So what you have is—"

"Men," Barbara said in simple conclusion. "Why don't they just go outside and settle their dispute by seeing who can pee the farthest?"

St. James smiled. "Not a bad idea."

"Ha! Women should run the world." She poured herself more tea. "So why couldn't it have been a wine or champagne bottle?"

"The shape doesn't make a match. We're looking for something with a slightly broader curve making the connection between bottom and sides. Like this." He cupped his right palm to form half an oval.

"And the leather gloves wouldn't work for that curve?"

"For the curve, perhaps. But leather gloves of that weight wouldn't shatter a cheekbone in a single blow. I'm not sure a heavyweight could even do that, and from what you said, the boy who owns the gloves isn't a heavyweight by any stretch of the imagination."

"Then what?" Barbara asked. "A vase perhaps?"

"I don't think so. Whatever was used had some sort of handgrip. And it was quite heavy, enough to do maximum damage with minimum effort. She'd only been struck three times."

"A handgrip. That suggests the neck of a bottle."

"Which is why Pleasance is continuing to propound his full-champagne-bottle theory despite compelling evidence to the contrary. Unless, of course, it's the most oddly shaped champagne bottle on record." St. James removed a paper napkin from the table dispenser and roughed out a sketch, saying, "What you're looking for is flat on the bottom, with a broad curve on the sides, and, I imagine, a sturdy gripping neck." He handed it over. Barbara studied the drawing.

"This looks like one of those ship's decanters," she said, pulling on her upper lip thoughtfully. "Simon, did someone cosh the girl in the face with the family Waterford?"

"It's as heavy as crystal," St. James replied. "But smooth-surfaced, not cut. Solid as well. And if that's the case, it's not a container of any sort."

"What, then?"

He looked at the drawing which she placed between them. "I have no idea."

"You won't go for something metal?"

"Doubtful. Glass—especially if it's smooth and heavy—is the likelier substance when there's no trace evidence left behind."

"Need I ask if you were able to find trace evidence where the Cambridge team found none?"

"You needn't. I didn't."

"What a balls-up." She sighed.

He didn't disagree. Rather, he shifted position in his chair and said,

"Are you and Tommy still intent on connecting the two killings? That's an odd approach when the means are so different. If you're working with the same killer, why weren't both victims gunned down?"

She picked at the gelatinous surface of a cherry tart that was doing service as the edible portion of her afternoon tea. "We're thinking that the motive determined the means in each killing. The first motive was personal, so it required a personal means."

"A hands-on means? Beating then strangling?"

"Yes. If you will. But the second murder wasn't personal at all, just a need to eliminate a potential witness who could place the killer at Crusoe's Island right at the time Elena Weaver was strangled. A shotgun sufficed to carry that out. Of course, what the killer didn't know is that the wrong girl got shot."

"A nasty business."

"Quite." She speared a cherry. It looked disturbingly like a large clot of blood. Shuddering, she tapped it onto her plate and tried another. "But at least we've got a tab on the killer now. And the Inspector's gone to—" She stopped, brow furrowed, as Lynley came through the swinging doors, his overcoat slung over his shoulder and his cashmere scarf fluttering round him like carmine wings. He was carrying a large manila envelope. Lady Helen Clyde and another woman—presumably her sister —were right behind him.

"St. James," he said by way of greeting his friend. "I'm in your debt again. Thank you for coming. You know Pen, of course." He dropped his coat over the back of a chair as St. James greeted Penelope and brushed a kiss across Lady Helen's cheek. He pulled extra chairs over to their table as Lynley introduced Barbara to Lady Helen's sister.

Barbara watched him, perplexed. He'd gone to the Weaver house for information. As soon as he had it, his next step was supposed to be to make an arrest. But clearly, no arrest had been made. Something had taken him in another direction.

"You haven't brought her with you?" she asked.

"I haven't. Look at this."

From the envelope, he took out a thin stack of photographs, telling them about the canvas and the set of sketches that Glyn Weaver had given him. "There was dual damage to the painting," he said. "Someone had defaced it with great smears of colour and then finished the job with a kitchen knife. Weaver's former wife assumed that the subject was Elena and that Justine had destroyed it."

"She was wrong, I take it?" Barbara asked, picking up the photographs and flipping through them. Each of them showed a different section of the canvas. They were curious pieces, some of them looking like nothing so much as double exposures in which one figure was superimposed over another. They depicted various portraits of a female, from childhood up to young adulthood. "What are these?" Havers asked, passing each photograph on to St. James after she perused it.

"Infrared photographs and X-rays," Lynley said. "Pen can explain. We did it at the museum."

Penelope said, "They show what was originally on the canvas. Before it was smeared with paint."

There were at least five head studies in the group, one of which was more than double the size of all the rest. Barbara puzzled her way through them, saying, "Odd sort of painting, wouldn't you say?"

"Not when you assemble them," Penelope said. "Here. I'll show you."

Lynley cleared away the tea debris, piling the stainless steel teapot, the cups, the plates, and the silverware onto a table nearby. "Because of its size, it could only be photographed in sections," he explained to Barbara.

Pen went on. "When the sections are assembled, it looks like this." She laid the photographs out to form an incomplete rectangle from whose right-hand corner a quadrilateral was missing. What Barbara saw on the table was a semi-circle of four head studies of a growing girl—depicted as a baby, a toddler, a child, an adolescent—and offset by the fifth and larger head study of the young adult.

"If this isn't Elena Weaver," Barbara said, "then who—"

"It's Elena all right," Lynley said. "Her mother was dead on the money about that. Where she went wrong was in the rest of the scenario. She saw sketches and a painting hidden in Weaver's study and reached a logical conclusion based upon her knowledge that he dabbled in art. But obviously this isn't dabbling."

Barbara looked up, saw that he was removing another photograph from the envelope. She held her hand out for it, put it into the empty spot at the bottom right-hand corner, and looked at the artist's signature. Like the woman herself, it was not flamboyant. Just the simple word *Gordon* in thin strokes of black.

"Full circle," he said.

"So much for coincidence," she replied.

"If we can just connect her to some sort of weapon, we're starting to fly home free." Lynley looked at St. James as Lady Helen gathered the pictures into a neat stack and replaced them in the folder. "What did you come up with?" he asked.

"Glass," St. James said.

"A wine bottle?"

"No. Not the right shape."

Barbara went to the table where Lynley had stacked their tea things and rooted through them to find the drawing St. James had made. She pulled it from beneath the teapot and tossed it their way. It fell to the floor. Lady Helen picked it up, looked at it, shrugged, and handed it to Lynley.

"What is it?" he asked. "It looks like a decanter."

"My thought as well," Barbara said. "Simon says no."

"Why?"

"It needs to be solid, heavy enough to shatter a bone with one blow."

"Damn and blast," Lynley said and flipped it to the table.

Penelope leaned forward, drew the paper towards her. "Tommy," she said thoughtfully, "you know, I can't be certain, but this looks awfully like a muller."

"A muller?" Lynley asked.

Havers said, "What the dickens is that?"

"A tool," Penelope said. "It's what an artist first uses when he's making his own paint."

22

Sarah Gordon lay on her back and fixed her eyes on the ceiling in her bedroom. She studied the patterns made in the plaster, urging out of the subtle swirls and indentations the silhouette of a cat, the gaunt face of an old woman, the wicked grin of a demon. It was the only room of the house on whose walls she had hung no decoration, establishing in it a monastic simplicity that she had believed would be conducive to the flights of imagination that had always in the past led her to creation.

They led her only to memory now. The thud, the crunch, the crushing of bone. The blood unexpectedly hot when it flew up from the girl's face to speckle her own. And the girl herself. Elena.

Sarah turned on her side and drew the woollen blanket closer round her, curling herself into a foetal position. The cold was intolerable. She'd kept a fire burning downstairs for most of the day, and she'd turned the heat up as far as it would go, but still she couldn't escape the chill. It seemed to seep from the walls and the floor and the bed itself like an insidious contagion, determined to have her. And as the minutes passed, the cold became ever more the victor as her body convulsed with new spasms of shivering.

A small fever, she told herself. The weather's been bad. One can't expect to remain unaffected by the damp, the fog, or the ice-driven wind.

But even as she repeated key words—damp, fog, and wind—like a hypnotic chant designed to focus her thoughts on the narrowest, most bearable and acceptable pathway, the single part of her mind that she had been unable to discipline from the very beginning forced Elena Weaver forward again.

She'd come to Grantchester two afternoons a week for two months, rolling up the drive on her ancient bicycle with her long hair tied back to keep it out of her face and her pockets filled with contraband treats to slip to Flame when she thought Sarah was least likely to notice. Scruff-dog, she called him, and she tugged affectionately on his lopsided ears, bent her face to his, and let him lick her nose. "Wha' d' I have for li'l Scruffs?" she said, and she laughed when the dog snuffed at her pockets, his tail thumping happily, his front paws digging at the front of her jeans. It was a ritual with them, generally carried out on the drive where Flame dashed out to meet her, barking a frantic, delighted greeting that Elena claimed she could feel vibrating through the air.

Then she'd come inside, slinging off her coat, untying her hair, shaking it out, smiling her hello, a little embarrassed if Sarah happened to have caught her in the act of greeting the dog with such an open display of affection. She seemed to feel it wasn't quite adult of her to love an animal, especially one that she didn't even own.

"Ready?" she'd say in that half-swallowed manner that made the word sound much more like *reh-y*. She seemed shy at first, when Tony brought her by those few nights to model for the life-drawing class. But it was only the initial reserve of a young woman conscious of her difference from others, and even more conscious of how that difference might somehow contribute to others' discomfort. Once she sensed another's ease in her presence—at least once she'd sensed Sarah's ease—she herself grew more forthright, and she began to chat and to laugh, melding into the environment and the circumstances as if she'd always been a part of them.

She hopped onto the tall stool in Sarah's studio at precisely half past two on those free afternoons. Her eyes danced round the room, scouting out whatever pieces had been worked on or were new since her last visit. And always she talked. She was, at heart, so like her father in that.

"You never married, Sarah?" Even her choice of topics was the same as her father's, except unlike his, her question came out more like *You ne'r mah-weed, Seh-ah?* and it was a moment before Sarah mentally worked through the careful if distorted syllables to comprehend their meaning.

"No. I never did."

"Why?"

Sarah examined the canvas on which she was working, comparing it to the lively creature perched atop the stool and wondering if she would ever be able to capture completely that quality of energy which the girl seemed to exude. Even in repose—holding her head at an angle with her hair sweeping round and the light glancing off it like sun hitting summer wheat—she was electric and alive. Restless and questioning, she seemed eager for experience, anxious to understand.

"I suppose I thought a man might get in my way," Sarah replied. "I wanted to be an artist. Everything else was secondary."

"My da' wan's to be an ar'ist as well."

"Indeed he does."

"Is he good, d'you think?"

"Yes."

"An' d'you like him?"

This last with her eyes riveted on Sarah's face. It was only so that she could easily read the answer, Sarah told herself. But still she said abruptly, "Of course. I like all my students. I always have done. You're moving, Elena. Please put your head back as it was."

She watched the girl reach her toe forward and rub it along the top of Flame's head where he lay on the floor, anticipating the treat he hoped would fall from her pocket. She waited, breath held, for the moment's question about Tony to pass. It always did. For Elena excelled at recognising boundaries, which went far to explain why she also excelled at obliterating most of them.

She grinned, said, "Sorry, Sarah," and resumed her position while Sarah herself escaped from the girl's scrutiny by going to the stereo and switching it on.

"Dad'll be s'prised when he sees this," Elena said. "When c'n I see it?"

"When it's done. Position again, Elena. Damn, we're losing light."

And afterwards with the easel covered and the music playing, they'd sit in the studio and have their tea. Shortbread which Elena slipped into Flame's eager mouth—his tongue lapping bits of sugar from her fingers—tarts and cakes that Sarah made from recipes she'd not thought about in years. As they munched and talked, the music continued, and Sarah's fingers tapped its rhythm against her knee.

"Wha's it like?" Elena asked her casually one afternoon.

"What?"

She nodded towards one of the speakers. "That," she said. "You know. That."

"The music?"

"Wha's it like?"

Sarah dropped her gaze from the girl's earnest eyes and looked at her hands as the haunting mystery of Vollenweider's electric harp and Moog synthesiser challenged her to answer, the music rising and falling, each note like a crystal. She thought about how to reply for such a length of time that Elena finally said, "Sorry. I jus' thought—"

Sarah raised her head quickly, saw the girl's distress, and realised that Elena thought she herself was embarrassed by being accosted with an unthinking act of mentioning a disability, as if Elena had asked her to look upon a disfigurement she'd prefer to avoid seeing. She said, "Oh no. It's not that, Elena. I was trying to decide . . . Here. Come with me." And she took her first to stand by the speaker, turning the sound up full volume. She placed her hand against it. Elena smiled.

"Percussion," Sarah said. "Those are the drums. And the bass. The low notes. You can feel them, can't you?" When the girl nodded, pulling on her lower lip with her chipped front teeth, Sarah looked round the room for something else. She found it in the soft camel hairs of dry fine brushes, the cool sharp metal of a clean pallet knife, the smooth cold glass of turpentine in a jar.

"All right," she said. "Here. This is what it sounds like."

As the music changed, shifted, and swelled, she played it against the girl's inner arm where the flesh was tender and most sensitive to touch. "Electric harp," she said, and with the pallet knife she tapped the light pattern of notes against her skin. "And now. A flute." This was the brush, in a wavering dance. "And this. The background, Elena. It's synthetic, you see. He's not using an instrument. It's a machine that makes musical sounds. Like this. Just one note now while all the rest are playing," and she rolled the jar smoothly in one long line.

"All at once it happens?" Elena asked.

"Yes. All at once." She gave the girl the pallet knife. She herself used the brush and the jar. And as the record continued to play, they made the music together. While all the time above their heads on a shelf not five feet away sat the muller that Sarah would use to destroy her.

Now on her bed in the dim afternoon light, Sarah clutched the blanket and tried to stop quaking. There had been no other alternative, she thought. There was no other way that he might learn to face the truth.

But she herself had to live with the horror of it all for the rest of her life. She had liked the girl.

She'd moved beyond sorrow eight months ago, into a limbo in which nothing could touch her. So that when she heard the car on the drive,

Flame's answering bark, and the footsteps approaching, she felt nothing at all.

"Okay, I accept the fact that the muller looks like a go for the weapon," Havers said as they watched the panda car pull away from the kerb, taking Lady Helen and her sister home. "But we *know* that Elena was dead round half past six, Inspector. At least, she was dead round half past six if we can trust what Rosalyn Simpson said, and I don't know about you, but I think we can. And even if Rosalyn wasn't definite about the time she reached the island, she knows for certain that she got back to her room by half past seven. So if she did make an error, it's probably in the other direction, putting the killing earlier, not later. And if Sarah Gordon—whose account is supported by two of her neighbours, mind you—didn't leave her house until just before seven . . ." She squirmed in her seat to face Lynley. "Tell me. How was she in two places at once, at home having her Wheetabix in Grantchester at the same time as she was on Crusoe's Island?"

Lynley guided the Bentley out of the car park and slid it into the spotty traffic heading southeast on Parkside. "You're assuming that, when her neighbours saw her leaving at seven, it was the first time she left that morning," he said. "Which is exactly what she wanted us to assume, exactly what she wanted her neighbours to assume. But by her own account, she was up that morning not long after five—and she would have had to tell the truth about that because one of the very same neighbours who saw her leaving at seven might well have seen her lights on earlier and told us about that. So I think it's safe to conclude that she had plenty of time to make another, earlier trip to Cambridge."

"But why go a second time? If she wanted to play discoverer of the body once Rosalyn saw her, why not just head out to the police station right then?"

"She couldn't," Lynley said. "She had no real choice in the matter. She had to change her clothes."

Havers stared at him blankly. "Right. Well. I'm a real looby, then. What have clothes got to do with it?"

"Blood," St. James responded.

Lynley nodded at his friend in the rearview mirror before saying to Havers, "She could hardly go dashing into the police station to report having found a body if she was wearing a tracksuit whose jacket front was spotted with the victim's blood."

"Then why even go to the police station at all?"

"She had to place herself at the crime scene just in case—when the news broke about Elena Weaver's death—Rosalyn Simpson remembered what she had seen and went to the police. As you said yourself, she had to play discoverer of the body. So that even if Rosalyn had been able to give the police an accurate description of the woman she'd seen that morning, even if the description led the local CID to Sarah Gordon—as it might have done once Anthony Weaver got wind of it—why on earth would anyone conclude that she had been to the island twice? Why on earth would anyone conclude that she'd kill a girl, go home, change her clothes, and return?"

"Right, sir. So why the hell did she?"

"To hedge her bets," St. James said. "In case Rosalyn got to the police before she got to Rosalyn."

"If she was wearing different clothes from those Rosalyn had seen the killer wear," Lynley went on, "and if one or more of her neighbours could verify that she hadn't left her house till seven, why would anyone think she was the killer of a girl who'd died round a half hour earlier?"

"But Rosalyn said that the woman she saw had light hair, sir. It was practically the only thing she remembered."

"Quite. A scarf, a cap, a wig."

"Why bother with that?"

"So that Elena would think she was seeing Justine." Lynley circled through the roundabout at Lensfield Road before he continued. "Time has been the issue that we've stumbled over from the first, Sergeant. Because of it, we've spent two days following an assortment of blind leads about sexual harassment, pregnancy, unrequited love, jealousy, and illicit affairs when we should have recognised the single point of similarity which everyone shares, both of the victims and every last suspect. All of them can run."

"But everyone can run." And, with an apologetic glance at St. James who, in his best moments, could only manage a moderate hobble, "I mean, generally speaking."

Lynley nodded grimly. "That's exactly my point. Generally speaking."

Havers gave a sigh of frustration. "I'm getting flummoxed. I see means. I see opportunity. But I don't see motive. It seems to me that if anyone was going to get beat up and strangled by anyone else in this case—and if Sarah Gordon did it—it doesn't make sense that the victim was Elena when our Justine is the far better bet. Look at the facts. Not bothering to consider that it probably took Sarah half an age to paint it in the first place, that portrait was probably worth hundreds of pounds—possibly more, although what I don't know about the value of art could fill a good-sized library—and Justine destroyed it. Having a bit of a tantrum, some real splatter and slash on an original oil sounds like a motive for something, if you ask me. And, mind you, it wasn't a bit of dabbling by her husband that she was venting her feelings on, but the real thing. By a real artist with a real reputation. Even Weaver himself couldn't have been too chuffed by that. As a matter of fact, *he* might have been the one to do the killing once he saw what she'd done to the picture. So why bag Elena?'' Her voice became thoughtful. ''Unless, of course, Justine didn't do the slashing at all. Unless Elena herself . . . Is that what you're thinking, Inspector?''

Lynley didn't reply. Instead, just before they reached the bridge that crossed the river on Fen Causeway, he pulled off the road and onto the pavement. Leaving the motor running, he turned to the others and said, ''I'll just be a moment.'' Ten steps from the Bentley, he was enveloped by the fog.

He didn't cross the street to look at the island for a third time. He knew it had no further secrets to reveal. From the causeway, he knew, he would see the shapes of trees, the mist-washed form of the footbridge that crossed the river, and perhaps the etching of birds on the water. He would see Coe Fen as an opaque screen of grey. And that would be all. If the lights of Peterhouse managed to cut through the vast and tenebrous expanse of fog on this day, they would be mere pinpricks, less substantial than stars. Even Whistler, he thought, would have found it a challenge.

For the second time, he walked to the end of the causeway bridge where the iron gate stood. And for the second time, he made note of the fact that anyone running along the lower river from Queens'—or from St. Stephen's—would have three options upon reaching Fen Causeway. A turn to the left and she would run past the Department of Engineering. A turn to the right and she would head towards Newnham Road. Or, as he had seen for himself on Tuesday afternoon, she could proceed straight ahead, crossing the street to where he now stood, ducking through the gate, and continuing south along the upper river.

What he had failed to consider on Tuesday afternoon was that someone running *into* the city from the opposite direction would have had three options as well. What he had failed to consider on Tuesday afternoon was that someone could have run in the opposite direction in the first place, starting from the upper rather than the lower river, and hence following the upper rather than the lower path on which Elena Weaver had been running on the morning of her death. He observed this upper path now, noting how it disappeared into the fog like a thin line of pencil. As on Monday, visibility was poor—perhaps less than twenty feet—but the river and hence the path next to it flowed due north at this particular section, with scarcely a bend or a wrinkle to cause a walker or a runner—either of them familiar with the lay of the land—any need for marked hesitation.

A bicycle came wheeling towards him out of the mist, a headlamp affixed to the ten-speed's handlebars providing a weak beam of light not much wider than an index finger. When the rider—a young, bearded man wearing a rakish trilby as an odd accent piece to his faded jeans and black oilskin jacket—dismounted to open the gate, Lynley spoke to him.

"Where does this path lead?"

Making an adjustment to his hat, the young man looked back over his shoulder as if a perusal of the path would help him answer the question. Thoughtfully, he pulled on the end of his beard. "Along the river for a bit."

"How far?"

"Couldn't say for certain. I always pick it up round Newnham Driftway. I've never headed in the other direction."

"Does it go to Grantchester?"

"This path? No, mate. It doesn't go there."

"Blast." Lynley frowned at the river, realising that he might have to reassess what he had thought of as a plausible explanation for how Elena Weaver's death had been orchestrated on Monday morning.

"But you can get there from here if you've a mind for the walk," the young man said, perhaps anticipating that Lynley was anxious for a fog-dampened stroll. He slapped a spattering of mud from his jeans and waved his arm vaguely from south to southwest. "Down the river path there's a car park, just past Lammas Land. If you cut through there and nip down Eitsley Ave, there's a public footpath that goes through the fields. It's posted well enough, and it'll take you straight to Grantchester. Although—" He eyed Lynley's fine overcoat and his hand-tooled Lobbs shoes. "I don't know if I'd try it in the fog if you don't know the route. You could end up doing nothing but thrashing round in the mud."

Lynley found his excitement quickening as the young man spoke. The facts were going to support him after all. "How far is it?" he asked.

"The car park's under half a mile, I should guess."

"I mean Grantchester itself. If you go through the fields."

"Mile and a half, mile and three-quarters. No more than that."

Lynley looked back at the path, at the untroubled surface of the sluggish river. Timing, he thought. It all centred round timing. He returned to the car.

"Well?" Havers said.

"She wouldn't have driven her car on the first trip," Lynley said. "She couldn't have taken the risk that one of her neighbours might see her leaving—as two did later in the morning—or that anyone might see it parked near the island."

Havers looked in the direction from which he'd just come. "So she walked in on a footpath. But she must have had to run like the devil all the way back."

He reached for his pocket watch and unhooked it from his waistcoat. "Who was it—Mrs. Stamford?—who said she was in a tearing hurry when she left at seven? At least now we know why. She had to find the body before anyone else did." He flipped the watch open and handed it to Havers. "Time the drive to Grantchester, Sergeant," he said.

He slid the Bentley into the traffic which, although slow-moving, was sparse at this time of afternoon. They descended the gentle slope of the causeway and, after one quick pause when an oncoming car veered into their lane in order to avoid hitting a postal van that was parked half on the pavement with its hazard lights blinking, they made their way into the Newnham Road roundabout. From there traffic diminished noticeably, and although the fog was still thick—swirling round the Granta King pub and a small Thai restaurant as if it were being stage-managed to do so— Lynley was able to increase his speed marginally.

"Time?" he asked.

"Thirty-two seconds so far." She pivoted in her seat so that she faced him again, the watch still in her hand. "But she's not a runner, sir. Not like the rest of them."

"Which is why it took her nearly thirty minutes to get home, change her clothes, load her car, and get back to Cambridge. It's little more than a mile and a half over the field to Grantchester," he said. "A distance runner could have done the same course in less than ten minutes. And had Sarah Gordon been a runner, Georgina Higgins-Hart wouldn't have needed to die."

"Because she would have got home, changed clothes, and returned in good enough time that even if Rosalyn described her accurately, she could have said that she was stumbling off the island after having discovered the body?"

"Right." He drove on.

She examined the watch. "Fifty-two seconds."

They drove along the west side of Lammas Land, a broad green of picnic tables and play areas that sprawled for three-quarters of the length of Newnham Road. They swung through the dogleg where Newnham became Barton and spun past a line of dismal pensioners' flats, past a church, past a steamy-windowed laundrette, past the newer, brick buildings of a city in the midst of economic growth.

"One minute fifteen," Havers said as they made the turn south towards Grantchester.

Lynley looked in the rearview mirror at St. James. The other man had picked up the material which Pen had assembled at the Fitzwilliam Museum—welcomed by her former colleagues with the sort of delight one expects to greet only visiting royalty—and he was flipping through the X-rays and the infrared photographs in his usual deliberate and thoughtful fashion. "St. James," Lynley asked, "what's the best part of loving Deborah?"

St. James raised his head slowly. He looked surprised. Lynley understood. Considering their history, these were straits which they did not generally navigate. "That's an unusual question to ask a man about his wife."

"Have you ever considered it?"

St. James glanced out the window where two elderly women—one supporting herself by means of an aluminum walker—were making their way towards a cramped-looking green grocer's where an outdoor display of fruit and vegetables wore a sequin covering of mist. Orange string sacks dangled limply from their arms.

"I don't think I have," St. James said. "But I suppose it's that feeling of being thoroughly struck by life. *Feeling* alive, not just being alive. I can't merely go through the motions with Deborah. I can't make do. She doesn't allow it. She demands my best. She engages my soul." He looked into the mirror once again. Lynley caught his gaze. Sombre, thoughtful, it seemed at odds with his words.

"That's what I would imagine," Lynley said.

"Why?"

"Because she's an artist."

The last buildings—a row of old terrace houses—on the outskirts of Cambridge melted away, enclosed by the fog. Country hedges replaced them, dusty grey hawthorn preparing for winter. Havers looked at the watch. "Two minutes, thirty seconds," she said.

The road was narrow, undivided, and unmarked. It swept past fields where a nimbus seemed to rise from the land, creating a solid, two-dimensional, mouse-coloured canvas on which nothing was drawn. If farm buildings existed somewhere in the distance round which a farmer worked and animals grazed, the heavy fog hid them.

They drove into Grantchester, passing a man in tweeds and black Wellingtons who was watching his collie explore the verge as he himself leaned heavily on a cane. "Mr. Davies and Mr. Jeffries," Havers said. "Doing their usual number, I expect." As Lynley slowed through the turn into the high street, she examined the face of the watch again. Using her fingers to help her with her calculations, she said, "Five minutes, thirty-seven seconds," and jerked forward in her seat with a "Whoa, what're you doing, sir?" when Lynley abruptly applied the brakes.

A metallic blue Citroën was parked squarely in the drive of Sarah Gordon's house. Seeing it with the mist lapping at its tyres, Lynley said, "Wait here," and got out of the Bentley. He pressed the door closed to shut it without sound and walked the remaining distance to the remodelled school.

The curtains on the front panel of windows were closed. The house itself seemed calm and uninhabited.

One minute he was here in the house talking to me. The next moment he was gone. I expect he's out there somewhere in the fog, trying to think what he's going to do next.

What had she called it? Moral obligation versus cock-throbbing lust. It was, on first and superficial glance, as much an inadvertent reference to the demise of her own marriage as it was an assessment of her former husband's dilemma. But it was more than that. For while Glyn Weaver saw her words as relating to Weaver's duty towards a daughter's death versus his continuing desire for a beautiful wife, Lynley was certain now that they had another application, one of which Glyn could not possibly be aware, one which was presented pellucidly in the simple form of a car in a driveway.

I knew him. For a time we were close.

He's always had trouble when it comes to conflict.

Lynley approached the car and found it locked. It was also empty save for a small, tan and white carton that lay partially open on the passenger seat. Lynley froze momentarily when he saw it. His eyes snapped to the house, then back to the carton and the three red cartridges that were sliding out of it. He jogged back to the Bentley.

"What's—?"

Before Havers could finish the question, he switched off the ignition and turned to St. James.

"There's a pub just a bit beyond the house on the left," he said. "Go there. Phone the Cambridge police. Tell Sheehan to get out here. No sirens. No lights. But tell him to come armed."

"Inspector—"

"Anthony Weaver's in her house," Lynley said to Havers. "He's got a shotgun with him."

They waited until St. James had disappeared into the fog before they turned back to the house some ten yards beyond them in the high street.

"What do you think?" Havers said.

"That we can't afford to wait for Sheehan." He peered back the way they had come into the village. The old man and the dog were just ambling round the bend in the road. "There's a footpath somewhere that she had to have used on Monday morning," he said. "And it seems to me that if she got out of her house without being seen, she can't have left the front way. So . . ." He looked back at the house, and then again down the road. "This way."

They set off on foot in the direction from which they had just driven. But they hadn't gone more than five yards when the old man and the dog accosted them, the man raising his cane and poking it at Lynley's chest.

"Tuesday," he said. "You lot were here Tuesday. I remember that sort of thing, you know. Norman Davies. Good with my eyes, I am."

"Christ," Havers muttered.

The dog sat at attention at Mr. Davies' side, ears pricked forward and an expression of friendly anticipation on his face.

"Mr. Jeffries and I"—this with a nod at the dog who seemed to dip his head politely at the sound of his name—"have been out for an hour now—Mr. Jeffries having a bit of a time answering the calls of nature at his advanced age—and we saw you pass, didn't we, Mister? And I said those folks have been here before. And I'm right, aren't I? I don't forget things."

"Where's the footpath to Cambridge?" Lynley asked without ceremony.

The man scratched his head. The collie scratched his ear. "Footpath, you ask? You can't be meaning to take a walk in this fog. I know what you're thinking: If Mr. Jeffries and I are out in it, why not you two? But we're out taking a ramble in order to see to the necessary. Otherwise, we'd be snug inside.'' He gestured with his cane to a small thatched cottage just across the street. ''When we aren't out seeing to the necessary, we mostly sit in our own front window. Not that we spy on the village, mind you, but we like to have a look at the high street now and again. Don't we, Mr. Jeffries?'' The dog panted agreeably.

Lynley felt his hands itch with the need to grab the old man by the lapels of his coat. ''The footpath to Cambridge,'' he said.

Mr. Davies rocked back and forth in his Wellingtons. ''Just like Sarah, aren't you? She used to walk to Cambridge most days, didn't she? 'I had my constitutional this morning already,' she'd say when Mr. Jeffries and I would stop by of an afternoon and ask her out on a ramble with us. And I'd say to her, 'Sarah, anyone as attached to Cambridge as you are ought to live there just to save yourself the walk.' And she'd say, 'I'm planning on it, Mr. Davies. Just give me a bit of time.''' He chuckled and settled into his story by digging his cane into the ground. ''Two or three times a week she was heading over the fields and she never took that dog of hers with her which, frankly, is something I have never been able to understand. Now, Flame—that's her dog—doesn't get near enough exercise to my way of thinking. So Mr. Jeffries and I would—''

''Where's the bloody path!'' Havers snarled.

The man started. He pointed down the road. ''Just there on Broadway.''

They set off immediately, only to hear him call, ''You might express some appreciation, you know. Folks never do think . . .''

The fog shrouded his body and muffled his voice as they rounded the bend where the high street became Broadway, as misnamed as a country lane could possibly be, narrow and thickly hedged on either side. Just beyond the last cottage, not two-tenths of a mile past the old school, a wooden kissing gate—green with its growth of winter moss—hung from rusty hinges at a lopsided angle, its corner in the mud. A large English oak spread its branches above it, partially hiding a metal sign that was posted on a pole nearby. *Public footpath,* it said. *Cambridge 1½ miles.*

The gate opened onto pasture land, thick and lush with grass that bent under the weight of the day's heavy fall of moisture. Drops showered their trouser legs and their shoes as they hurried down the track that ran along the rear garden fences and walls which marked the property boundaries of the cottages along the high street of the village.

''D'you really think she made a hike into Cambridge in fog like this?'' Havers asked, jogging at Lynley's side. ''And then ran back? Without getting lost?''

''She knew the way,'' he said. ''You can see the path itself well enough. And it probably skirts the fields rather than heads across them. If you were familiar with the lay of the land, you could probably do it blindfolded.''

''Or in the dark,'' she finished for him.

The rear garden of the old school was contained by a barbed wire fence, rather than a wall. It consisted of a vegetable garden gone extensively to seed and an overgrown lawn. Beyond this was the back door of the house, set above three steps. On the top one of these stood Sarah Gordon's mongrel, pawing at the bottom of the door, giving a low, worried whine.

''He's going to set up a row the moment he sees us,'' Havers said.

''That depends on his nose and his memory,'' Lynley replied. He gave a soft whistle. The dog's head darted up. Lynley whistled again. The dog gave two rapid barks—

''Damn!'' Havers said.

—and bounded down the steps. He trotted briskly across the lawn to the fence, one ear perked up and the other drooping over his forehead.

''Hello, Flame.'' Lynley extended his hand. The dog sniffed and examined and began wagging his tail. ''We're in,'' Lynley said and slipped through the barbed wire. Flame leaped up with a single yelp, eager to say hello. He planted muddy paws on the front of Lynley's coat. Lynley grabbed him, lifted him, and turned back to the fence as the dog licked his face and squirmed in delight. He handed the animal over to Havers and pulled off his own muffler.

''Put this through his collar,'' he said. ''Use it as a lead.''

''But I—''

''We've got to get him out of here, Sergeant. He's willing to say hello, but I doubt he's willing to sit on the back step quietly while we slip into the house.''

Havers was struggling with the animal who seemed to be mostly tongue and legs. Lynley looped his muffler through Flame's leather collar and handed the ends to Havers as she set the dog on the ground.

''Take him to St. James,'' he said.

''What about you?'' She looked towards the house and came up with an answer that she clearly didn't like. She said, ''You can't go in there alone, Inspector. You can't go in at all. You said he's armed. And if that's the case—''

"Get out of here, Sergeant. Now."

He turned away from her before she could speak again and, in a crouch, quickly crossed the lawn. On the far side of the house, lights were on in what had to be Sarah Gordon's studio. But the rest of the windows stared blankly into the fog.

The door was unlocked. The knob was cold, wet, and slippery in his hand, but it turned without a sound, admitting him into a service porch beyond which was the kitchen where cupboards and work tops threw long shadows across the white linoleum floor.

Somewhere in the gloom nearby, a cat mewled. The sound was followed a moment later by the appearance of Silk, slithering in from the sitting room like a professional housebreaker. The cat paused abruptly when he saw Lynley in the doorway, scrutinising him with an undaunted stare. Then, he leapt onto one of the work tops where he sat with Egyptian-like tranquillity, his tail curling round his front feet. Lynley walked past him—his eyes on the cat, the cat's eyes on him—and edged to the door which led into the sitting room.

Like the kitchen, the room was empty. And with the curtains drawn, it was filled with by shadows and illuminated only by what little daylight made its way through the curtains and through a small chink that kept those same curtains from being completely closed. A fire was burning low in the fireplace, hissing gently as wood turned to ash. A small log rested next to this on the floor, as if Sarah Gordon had been in the act of adding it to the others that were already burning when Anthony Weaver had arrived to interrupt her.

Lynley shed his overcoat and passed through the sitting room. He entered the corridor that led to the rear of the house. Ahead of him, the door to the studio was partially closed, but light streamed out from the narrow aperture in a transparent triangle on the bleached oak floor.

He heard the murmur of their voices first. Sarah Gordon was talking. Her voice was drained. She sounded exhausted.

"No, Tony, that isn't how it was."

"Then tell me, damn you." In contrast Weaver's voice was hoarse.

"You've forgotten, haven't you? You never asked me to return the key."

"Oh God."

"Yes. After you ended things between us, I thought at first that you'd simply overlooked the fact that I could still get into your rooms. Then I decided you must have changed the locks because that would have been easier for you than asking me to give the key back and risking another scene between us. Then later, I''—a lifeless, brief laugh, sounding mostly self-directed—''I actually started to believe that you were just waiting until you'd secured the Penford Chair before you'd phone and ask me to meet you again. And I'd need the key for that, wouldn't I?''

''How can you think what happened between us—all right, what I *made* happen between us—had anything to do with the Penford Chair?''

''Because you can't lie to me, Tony. Not at the heart of things. No matter how much you lie to yourself and to everyone else. This is about the Chair. It always was. It always will be. You merely used Elena as an excuse that was nobler in your mind and far more attractive than academic greed. Better to end your affair with me because of your daughter than because you might lose a promotion if everyone knew you walked out on your second wife for another woman.''

''It was Elena. *Elena*. You know it.''

''Oh, Tony. Don't. Please. Not now.''

''You never tried to understand anything about us. She'd finally begun to forgive me, Sarah. She'd finally begun to accept Justine. We were building something together. The three of us were a family. She needed that.''

''You needed it. You wanted the appearance it offered to your public.''

''I stood to lose her if I left Justine. They'd started to develop a relationship together, and if I left Justine—just as I'd left Glyn—I stood to lose Elena for good. And Elena came first. She had to.'' His voice grew louder as he moved in the room. ''She came to our home, Sarah. She saw what a loving marriage could be like. I couldn't destroy that— I couldn't betray what she believed about us—by leaving my wife.''

''So you destroyed what was best about me instead. It was, after all, the more convenient thing to do.''

''I had to keep Justine. I had to accept her terms.''

''For the Penford Chair.''

''No! God damn you! I did it for Elena! For my daughter. For Elena. But you could never see that. You didn't want to see it. You didn't want to think I could possibly feel anything beyond—''

''Narcissism? Self-interest?''

In answer, metal slid savagely against metal. It was the unmistakable sound of a round being chambered within a shotgun. Lynley moved to within two inches of the studio door, but both Weaver and Sarah Gordon stood outside his line of vision. He tried to gauge their positions by listening to their voices. He rested one hand lightly against the wood.

"I don't think you really want to shoot me, Tony," Sarah Gordon was saying, "any more than you want to hand me over to the police. In either case, a scandal will come crashing down round you, and I don't think you want that. Not after everything that's happened already between us."

"You killed my daughter. You phoned Justine from my rooms on Sunday night, you arranged that Elena would run alone, and then you killed her. Elena. You killed Elena."

"Your creation, Tony. Yes. I killed Elena."

"She never touched you or hurt you. She never even knew—"

"That you and I were lovers? No, she never knew. I was good about that. I kept my promise. I never told her. She died thinking you were devoted to Justine. And that's what you wanted her to think, isn't it? Isn't that what you wanted everyone to think?"

Although enormously weary, her voice was more clearly defined than his. She would, Lynley thought, be facing the door. He pressed on it gently. It swung inward a few more inches. He could see the edge of Weaver's tweed coat. He could see the gunstock resting at his waist.

"How could you bring yourself to it? You met her, Sarah. You *knew* her. She sat in this room and let you sketch her and pose her and talk to her and . . ." His voice caught on a sob.

"And?" she said. "*And,* Tony? And?" She gave a small, pain-stricken laugh when he didn't respond. "And paint her. That's how the story goes. But it doesn't end there. Justine made certain of that."

"No."

"Yes. *My* creation, Tony. The only copy. Just like Elena."

"I tried to tell you how sorry—"

"Sorry? *Sorry?*" For the first time, her own voice broke.

"I had to accept her terms. Once she knew about us. I had no choice."

"Neither did I."

"So you murdered my daughter—a human being, flesh and blood, not a lifeless piece of canvas—to get your revenge."

"I didn't want revenge. I wanted justice. But I wasn't going to get it in a court of law because the painting was yours, my *gift* to you. What did it matter how much of myself I'd put into it because it no longer belonged to me. I had no case. So I had to balance the scales myself."

"As I'm about to do now."

There was movement in the room. Sarah Gordon passed in line with the door. Her hair matted, her feet bare, she was wrapped in a blanket.

Her face was colourless, even to her lips. "Your car's in the drive. No doubt someone saw you arrive. How do you intend to get away with killing me?"

"I don't particularly care."

"About the scandal? Oh, but there won't be much of one, will there? You're the grieving father driven to violence by his daughter's death." She straightened her shoulders and faced him directly. "You know, I think you ought to thank me for killing her. With public opinion so much on your side, you're guaranteed the Chair now."

"Damn you—"

"But how on earth will you manage to pull the trigger without Justine here to steady the gun?"

"I'll manage it. Believe me. I will. With pleasure." He took a step towards her.

"Weaver!" Lynley shouted and at the same instant threw open the door.

Weaver whirled in his direction. Lynley dived for the floor. The gun discharged. A deafening explosion roared through the room. The stench of gunpowder filled the air. A cloud of blue-black smoke seemed to rise out of nowhere. Through it, he could see Sarah Gordon's crumpled form not five feet away from him, prone on the floor.

Before he could go to her, he saw rather than heard the click and slither of metal once again as Weaver reloaded. He surged to his feet a moment before the history professor turned the gun awkwardly on himself. Lynley leapt at the other man, shoving the gun to one side. It discharged a second time just as the front door to the house was kicked open. Half a dozen men from the police firearms unit stormed down the corridor and into the studio, guns extended, ready to fire.

"Hold off," Lynley shouted over the tremendous ringing in his ears.

And indeed there was no need for further violence. For Weaver sank dully onto one of the stools. He removed his spectacles and dropped them to the floor. He crushed their lenses.

"I had to do it." he said. "For Elena."

It was the same crime-scene team that had done the honours at Georgina Higgins-Hart's death. They arrived only minutes after the ambulance had roared off towards the hospital, cutting a wide path through the curious who had gathered in a cluster at the foot of the drive where Mr. Davies and Mr. Jeffries were holding court, proud to name themselves first at the scene, proud to be able to announce to all listeners that they'd known something was wrong the minute they'd seen that plump little lady leading Flame towards the pub.

"Sarah'd never give Flame to just anyone," he said. "And him not even on his lead. I knew there was something wrong the minute I saw that, didn't I, Mr. Jeffries?"

In other circumstances, Mr. Davies' continued presence might have been irksome to Lynley. But as it was, the man was a godsend, for Sarah Gordon's dog knew him, recognised his voice, and was willing to go with him even when his owner was carried out of the house, swathed in temporary bandages, with a pressure pack applied to stop arterial bleeding.

"I'll take the cat as well," Mr. Davies said as he shuffled down the drive with Flame in tow. "Not much for cats, Mr. Jeffries and I, but we won't want to see the poor thing go begging for somewhere to lodge till Sarah comes home." He gazed uneasily in the direction of her house where several members of the firearms unit stood talking together. "She's coming home, Sarah is, isn't she? She'll be all right?"

"She'll be all right." But she'd taken the shot straight on in her right arm, and from the look the ambulance attendants had given the extent of the damage, Lynley wondered how *all right* would be defined. He walked back to the house.

From the studio, he could hear the sound of Sergeant Havers' sharp questions and Anthony Weaver's deadened responses. He could hear the crime scene team gathering evidence. A cupboard closed and St. James said to Superintendent Sheehan: "This is the muller." But Lynley didn't join them.

Instead, he went into the sitting room and studied a few of the pieces of Sarah Gordon's work that hung on the walls: four young blacks—three crouched, two standing—round a doorway in one of London's most disastrous tower blocks; an old chestnut seller hawking his product outside the underground in Leicester Square as well-furred and well-garbed theatre-goers passed him by; a miner and his wife in the kitchen of their tumbledown Welsh cottage.

Some artists, he knew, make their work a mere showcase for a clever technique in which little is risked and less is communicated. Some artists merely become experts in their medium, working clay or stone or wood or paint as proficiently and effortlessly as an ordinary craftsman. And some artists try to make something out of nothing, order out of chaos, demanding of themselves that they ably communicate structure and composition, colour and balance, and that each piece they create serve to communicate a predetermined issue as well. A piece of art asks people to stop and look in a world of moving images. If people take the time to pause before canvas, bronze, glass, or wood, a worthy effort is one which does something more than act as nonverbal panegyric to the talents of its creator. It doesn't call for notice. It calls for thought.

Sarah Gordon, he saw, was that kind of artist. She had played her passions out on canvas and stone. It was only when she had tried to play them out in life that she had failed.

"Inspector?" Sergeant Havers entered the room.

With his eyes on the painting of Pakistani children, he said, "I don't know if he really intended to shoot her, Barbara. He was threatening her, yes. But the gun may well have gone off accidentally. I'll have to say that in court."

"It won't look pretty for him no matter what you say."

"His culpability is moot. All he needs is a decent lawyer and public sympathy."

"Perhaps. But you did the best that you could." She extended her hand. In it she held a folded piece of white paper. "One of Sheehan's men found a shotgun in the boot of her car. And Weaver, he had this thing with him. He wouldn't talk about it, though."

Lynley took the paper from her and unfolded it to see a sketch, a beautifully rendered tiger pulling down a unicorn, the unicorn's mouth opened in a soundless scream of terror and pain.

Havers went on. "All he said was that he found it in an envelope in his rooms at the college when he went by yesterday to talk to Adam Jenn. What do you make of it, sir? I remember that Elena had posters of unicorns all over her walls. But the tiger? I don't get it."

Lynley returned the paper to her. "It's a tigress," he said and finally understood why Sarah Gordon had reacted to his mention of Whistler on the first day they had spoken to her. It wasn't about John Ruskin's criticism, nor was it about art or painting the night or the fog. It was because of a woman who had been the artist's mistress, the unnamed milliner he had called *La Tigresse*. "She was telling him that she'd murdered his daughter."

Havers' jaw dropped. She snapped it closed. "But why?"

"It was the only way to complete the circle of ruin they'd inflicted on each other. He destroyed her creation and her ability to create. She knew he'd done so. She wanted him to know that she'd destroyed his."

23

Justine met him at the front door. He'd only inserted his key into the lock when she opened it for him. She was, he saw, still dressed for her working day, and although she had worn the black suit and pearl grey blouse for at least thirteen hours now, they remained unwrinkled. She might have just put them on.

She looked beyond him to the receding lights of the panda car in the drive. "Where have you been?" she asked. "Where's the Citroën? Anthony, where are your glasses?"

She followed him to his study and stood in the doorway while he rooted through his desk for an old pair of horn-rimmed spectacles that he hadn't used in years. His Woody Allen specs, Elena had called them. *You look like a clod with those on, Dad.* He hadn't worn them again.

He looked up at the window in whose reflection he could see himself and his wife behind him. She was a lovely woman. For the ten years of their marriage, she had asked for little enough from him, only that he love her, only that he be with her. And in return she had created this home, into it she had welcomed his colleagues. She had given him support, she had believed in his career, she had been perfectly loyal. But she had not been able to give him that ineffable connection that exists between people when their souls are one.

As long as they'd had a mutual goal towards which they were working—scouting round for a house, painting and decorating, purchasing furniture, looking at cars, designing a garden—they'd existed quite securely within the illusion of their ideal marriage. He had even thought:

I've got a happy marriage this time round. It's regenerative, devoted, committed, tender, loving, and strong. We're even the same astrological sign, Gemini, the twins. It's as if we were meant for each other from birth.

But when the superficial commonalities had disappeared—when the house had been purchased and furnished to perfection, when the gardens had been planted and the sleek French cars sat shining in the garage—he had found himself left with an indefinable emptiness and a sense of vague, uneasy incompletion. He wanted something more.

It's the absence of an outlet for creativity, he had thought. I've spent more than twenty years of my life in dusty academia, writing, giving lectures, meeting students, climbing up. It's time to broaden my horizons and stretch my experience.

As in everything else, she had supported him in this. She did not join him—she had no abiding interest in the arts—but she admired his sketches, she mounted and framed his watercolours, and she clipped out of the local newspaper the announcement of the class that Sarah Gordon would teach. This is something you might like to take, darling, she had told him. I've never heard of her myself, but the paper says she's quite an astounding talent. Wouldn't it be wonderful for you to get to know a real artist?

That, he felt, was the greatest of the ironies. That Justine should have been the instrument of their acquaintance. But then, her having made him aware of Sarah Gordon's presence in Grantchester in the first place actually completed the circle of the story in a well-balanced fashion. Justine, after all, was uniquely responsible for the final set of events in this obscene tragedy, so it was only appropriate that she also would have been instrumental in setting in motion the initial events that began with a life-drawing class in Sarah Gordon's studio.

If it's over between you, get rid of the painting, Justine had said. Destroy it. Get it out of my life. Get her out of my life.

But it hadn't been enough when he defaced it with oils. Only its complete destruction would appease Justine's anger and assuage the pain of his infidelity. And at only one time, in only one place, could this act of destruction be carried out in order to convince his wife of the sincerity with which he was putting an end to his affair with Sarah. So three times he had driven the knife through the canvas as Justine looked on. In the end, however, he'd been unable to bring himself to leave the ruined painting behind.

If she'd only been what I needed in the first place, none of this would have happened, he thought. If she'd only been willing to open her heart, if she'd got in touch with her spirit, if creating meant more to her than merely possessing, if she'd done more than just listen and appear sympathetic, if she'd had something to say about herself, about life, if she'd tried to understand me at the deepest level of who and what I am . . .

"Where's the Citroën, Anthony?" Justine repeated. "Where are your glasses? Where on earth have you been? It's after nine o'clock."

"Where's Glyn?" he asked.

"Having a bath. And using most of the hot water in the house to do it."

"She'll be gone tomorrow afternoon. I'd think you could manage to put up with her that much longer. After all—"

"Yes. I know. She's lost her daughter. She's been crushed and devastated and I ought to be able to overlook everything she does—and every rotten thing she says—because of that fact. Well, I won't buy it. And you're a fool if you do."

"Then I suppose I'm a fool." He turned from the window. "But that's something you've used to your advantage more than once, isn't it?"

A spot of deep ruby appeared on each of her cheeks. "We're husband and wife. We made a commitment. We made vows in a church. At least I did. And I've never broken them. I wasn't the one—"

"All right," he said. "I know." The room was too warm. He needed to take off his coat. He couldn't summon the will to do so.

She said, "Where have you been? What have you done with the car?"

"It's at the police station. They wouldn't allow me to drive it home."

"They . . . The police? What's happened? What's going on?"

"Nothing. Not any longer at least."

"What's that supposed to mean?" She seemed to grow taller as some sort of realisation dawned upon her. Under the fine material of her suit, he could imagine her muscles ripple and coil. "You've been with her again. I can see it in your face. You promised me, Anthony. Anthony, you *swore* to me. You said it was over."

"It is. Believe me." He left the study and headed for the sitting room. He heard the sound of her high heels tapping along behind him.

"Then what . . . Have you been in an accident? Have you wrecked the car? Are you hurt in some way?"

Hurt, an accident. There could be no greater truth. He wanted to chuckle at the grim, gallows humour. She would always assume that he was victim, not avenger. She couldn't conceive that he might take matters into his own hands for once. She couldn't conceive that he might finally act at his own behest, without regard for opinion or condemnation any longer, because he believed it was right to do so. And why should she, really? When had he ever acted on his own before? Other than to walk out on Glyn and he'd paid for that decision for the last fifteen years.

"Anthony, answer me. What's happened to you today?"

"I finished things. Finally." He went into the sitting room.

"Anthony . . ."

He'd once thought the still lifes hanging above the sofa represented his very best work. *Paint something that we can hang in the sitting room, darling. Use colours that match.* He had done so. Apricots and poppies. One could tell what they were at a single glance. And isn't that what true art is all about? An accurate duplication of reality?

He'd taken them off the wall and carted them proudly to show her on the first night of class. No matter that it was life drawing she was teaching, he wanted her to know from the very start that he was a cut above all the rest, raw talent just waiting for someone to mould him into the next Manet.

She'd surprised him from the first. Perched on a stool in the corner of her studio, she began by offering no instruction at all. Instead, she talked. She hooked her feet round the rungs of the stool, put her elbows on her thoroughly paint-spattered knees, cupped her face in her hands so that her hair spilled through her fingers, and talked. At her side stood an easel holding an unfinished canvas, depicting a man sheltering a tousle-haired little girl. She never pointed to it as she spoke. It was clear that she expected they would make the connection.

"You're not here to learn how to put paint on canvas," she had said to the group. There were six of them: three elderly women in smocks and brogues, the wife of an American serviceman with time on her hands, a twelve-year-old Greek girl whose father was spending a year as a guest lecturer at the University, and himself. He knew at once that he was the serious student among them. She seemed to be speaking directly to him.

"Any fool can make splatters and call it art," she had said. "That's not what this course is all about. You're here to put part of yourself on canvas, to reveal who you are through your composition, your choice of colour, your sense of balance. The struggle is to know what's been done before and to push beyond it. The job is to select an image but to paint a concept. I can give you techniques and methods, but whatever you produce ultimately has to come from your self if you want to call it art.

And—'' She smiled. It was an odd, bright smile, completely without self-conscious affectation. She couldn't have known that it wrinkled her nose in an unattractive fashion. But if she did know, she probably didn't care. Externals did not seem to have much importance to her. ''—if you have no real self, or if you have no way of discovering it, or if for some reason you're afraid to find out who and what it is, then you'll still manage to create something on canvas with your paints. It'll be pleasant to look at and a pleasure to you. But it'll be technique. It won't necessarily be art. The purpose—our purpose—is to communicate through a medium. But in order to do that, you must have something to say.''

Subtlety is the key, she had told them. A painting is a whisper. It isn't a shout.

At the end of it all, he'd felt ashamed of his arrogance in having brought his watercolours to show her, so confident of their having merit. He resolved to slink unobtrusively out of the studio with them safely tucked, in their protective—and suitable—brown wrapping paper, under his arm. But he wasn't quick enough. As the others filed out, she said, ''I see you've brought some of your work to show me, Dr. Weaver,'' and she came to his worktable and waited while he unwrapped them, feeling as he hadn't felt in years, in a welter of nerves and completely outclassed.

She'd gazed on them thoughtfully. ''Apricots and . . . ?''

He felt his face grow hot. ''Oriental poppies.''

''Ah,'' she said. And then quite briskly, ''Yes. Very nice.''

''Nice. But not art.''

She turned her gaze to him. It was friendly and frank. He found it disconcerting to be engaged so directly by a woman's eyes. ''Don't misunderstand me, Dr. Weaver. These are lovely watercolours. And lovely watercolours have a place.''

''But would you hang them on your wall?''

''I . . . ?'' Her gaze flickered under his, then held quite firmly. ''I tend to like a painting that challenges just a bit more. It's a matter of taste.''

''And these don't challenge?''

She studied the watercolours once more. She perched on the worktable and held the paintings on her knees, first one then the other. She pressed her lips together. She blew out her cheeks.

''I can take it, you know,'' he said with a chuckle that he realised was far more anxious than amused. ''You can give it to me straight.''

She took him at his word. "All right," she said. "You can certainly copy. Here's the evidence of that. But can you create?"

It didn't hurt nearly as much as he thought it might. "Try me," he said.

She smiled. "A pleasure."

He'd thrown himself into it for the next two years, first as a member of one class or another which she offered the community, then later on as a private student, alone with her. In winter they used a live model in the studio. In summer they took easels, sketch pads, and paints out into the country and worked off the land. Often they sketched each other as an exercise in understanding the human anatomy—the sternocleidomastoid muscles, Tony, she would say and put her fingertips to her neck, try to think of them like cords right beneath the skin. And always she filled the environment with music. Listen to me, if you stimulate one sense, you stimulate others, she explained, art can't be created if the artist himself is an insensate void. See the music, hear it, feel it, feel the art. And the music would start—a haunting array of Celtic folktunes, a Beethoven symphony, a *salsa* band, an African mass called the *Missa Luba,* the nerve-shaving whine of electric guitars.

In the presence of her intensity and dedication, he'd begun to feel as if he'd emerged from forty-three years of darkness to find himself walking in sunlight at last. He felt completely renewed. He felt his interest engaged and his intellect challenged. He felt emotions spring to life. And for six straight months before she became his lover, he called it all the pursuit of his art. There was, after all, a certain safety in that. It did not beg an answer for the future.

Sarah, he thought, and he marvelled at the fact that even now—after everything, even after Elena—he could still wish to murmur the name that he hadn't allowed himself to say for the past eight months since Justine had accused and he had confessed.

They'd pulled up to the old school on a Thursday evening, just at the time he'd usually arrived. The lights were on and a fire was burning—he could see its shifting glow through the drawn front curtains—and he knew that Sarah was expecting him and that music would be playing and a dozen or more sketches would be strewn among the pillows on the floor. And that she would come to meet him when the doorbell rang, that she would run to meet him, throw open the door, and draw him inside saying Tonio I've had the most marvellous idea about how to compose that picture of the woman in Soho, you know the one that's been making me wild for a week . . .

I can't do this, he said to Justine. Don't ask me to do this. It's going to destroy her.

I don't much care what it's going to do to her, Justine replied and got out of the car.

She must have been passing the door when they rang the bell, because she answered it just as the dog began to bark. She called over her shoulder, Flame, stop it it's Tony you know Tony you silly thing. And then she turned back to the door, to the sight of them both—he in the foreground and his wife in the background and the portrait wrapped in brown paper and held under his arm.

She didn't say anything. She didn't even move. She merely looked beyond him to where his wife stood, and her face summed up the count of his sin. Betrayal works in two directions, Tonio, she'd said in the past. And he understood that clearly when she dropped into place that insubstantial patina of breeding and civility that she actually believed was going to protect her.

Tony, she said.

Anthony, Justine said.

They walked into the house. Flame trotted out of the sitting room with an old knotted sock between his teeth and he barked through it happily at the sight of a friend. Silk looked up from a doze by the fire and undulated his long serpent tail in lazy greeting.

Now, Anthony, Justine said.

He lacked the will: to do it, to refuse, even to speak.

He saw Sarah look at the painting. She said, What have you brought me, Tonio, as if Justine were not standing at his side.

There was an easel in the sitting room and he unwrapped the painting and set it there. He expected her to fly to it when she saw the great smears of red, white, and black that obscured the smiling faces of his daughter. But instead she simply approached it slowly, and she gave a low cry when she saw what she had to have known she would see on the bottom of the frame. The little brass plaque. The scrolled ELENA.

He heard Justine move. He heard her say his name, and he felt her press the knife into his hand. It was a sturdy vegetable knife. She'd taken it from the drawer in the kitchen of their house. She'd said get it out of my life, get her out of my life, you'll do it tonight and I'll be there to make sure.

He made the first cut in a blaze that mixed both anger and despair. He heard Sarah cry No! Tony! and felt her fingers on his fist and saw the red of her blood when the knife slid across the back of her knuckles to carve a pathway through the canvas again. And then the third cut, but by that time, she had backed away with her bleeding hand held like a child against her, not crying because she wouldn't do that, not in front of him, not in front of his wife.

That's enough, Justine said. She turned and left.

He followed her out. He hadn't said a single word.

She had talked one night in class about the risk and the reward of making art personal, of offering little here-and-there bits of one's essence to a public who might misunderstand, ridicule, or reject. Although he had listened dutifully to her words, he had not understood the meaning behind them until he had seen her face when he destroyed the painting. It wasn't a reaction to the weeks and months of effort it had taken her to complete it for him, nor was it a response to his mutilation of a gift. It was simply that three times he had driven the knife through what had represented to Sarah the most singular manner in which she could show him compassion and love.

This was, perhaps, the greatest of his sins. To have prompted the gift. To have ripped it to pieces.

He took his watercolours—those terribly safe apricots and poppies— from the wall above the sofa. They left two darker spots on the wallpaper, but that couldn't be helped. No doubt Justine would find something suitable to replace them.

She said, ''What are you doing? Anthony, answer me.'' She sounded frightened.

''Finishing things,'' he said.

He carried the paintings out into the hall and balanced one carefully, thoughtfully, on the tips of his fingers. *You can copy,* she said, *but can you create?*

The last four days had given him the answer that two full years with her had failed to provide. Some people create. Others destroy.

He smashed the painting against the newel post at the foot of the stairway. Glass shattered and fell onto the parquet floor like crystal rain.

''Anthony!'' Justine grasped his arm. ''Don't! Those are your paintings. They're your art. Don't!''

He smashed the second with even greater force. He felt the pain of connecting with the wooden post shoot like a cannonball through his arm. Glass flew up at his face.

''I have no art,'' he said.

• • •

Despite the cold, Barbara took her cup of coffee out into the ruined rear garden of her house in Acton and sat down on the cold block of concrete that served as the back step. She pulled her coat more closely round her and balanced the coffee cup on the top of one knee. It was not black dark outside—it never could be when one was surrounded by several million people and a teeming metropolis—but the heavy night shadows still made the garden a less familiar place than was the inside of the house, and thus a place less weighted down by the conflict that sprang from the opposing forces of guilt-ridden memory and simple necessity.

What kind of bond truly exists between a parent and child, she wondered. And at what point does it finally become necessary to break or perhaps redefine that bond? And in either case, is breaking or redefining even possible?

During the last ten years of her life, she had grown to believe that she would never have children. At first, the realisation was a source of pain to her, inextricably connected as it was to the knowledge that she would probably never marry. She knew quite well that marriage was not a prerequisite for parenthood. Single-parent adoptions happened more and more, and with her career finally off the ground, she would be a serious contender in the pool of prospective single parents seeking a child. Should she volunteer for a hard-to-place child, her success would be virtually guaranteed. But, perhaps too conventionally, she had always seen parenthood as a joint venture between two partners. And as the likelihood of a partner in her life grew more remote every year, the distant possibility of becoming a mother grew more hazy-edged, more like a fantasy ungrounded even slightly in the reality of her circumstances.

It wasn't something she thought of very often. Most of the time she was simply too busy to dwell upon a future that felt like ice. But while most people, getting older, experienced the growth of family and the increase in connection brought about by the ties of marriage and children, her own family was steadily diminishing now, and her own connections were being severed one by one. Her brother, her father, both dead and buried. And now she faced the prospect of cutting the final tie with her mother as well.

In the end, life is all about seeking reassurance, she thought, we're all engaged in looking for some kind of sign that will tell us we're not really alone. We want a bond, an anchor that will hold us fast to a landmass of belonging somewhere, of being close to someone, of having something more than the clothes on our backs or the houses we live in or the cars that we drive. And in the end we can only gain that reassurance through people. No matter how we fill our lives with the trappings of a carefree independence, we still want the bond. Because a vital connection with another human being always carries the potential to act as a viable approbation of the self. If I am loved, I am worthy. If I am needed, I am worthy. If I maintain this relationship in the face of all difficulties, I am somehow whole.

What, indeed, was the real difference between Anthony Weaver and herself? Wasn't her behaviour—like his—governed inherently by an anxiety that the world might withdraw its approval of her? Didn't her behaviour—like his—mask a desperation which rose from the same insidious source, guilt?

"Mum had a fine day today, Barbie," Mrs. Gustafson had said. "She started out a bit rough round the edges, though. At first, she wouldn't mind me at all and she kept calling me Doris. Then she wouldn't eat her teacakes. And she wouldn't have her soup. When the postman came, she thought it was your dad and she wouldn't let me hear the end of wanting to be off with him. To Majorca, she said. Jimmy promised me Majorca, she said. And when I wanted to tell her that it wasn't Jimmy, she tried to chuck me out the door. But she finally settled down." Her hand fluttered nervously upwards towards her wig like an indecisive bird and she touched her fingers to the stiff, grey curls. "She hasn't wanted to go to the loo, though. I can't think why. But the telly's on for her. And she's been as good as gold for the last three hours."

Barbara found her in the sitting room, in her husband's tattered easy chair, lolling back into the greasy indentation which his head had made over the years. The television was roaring at a volume that accommodated Mrs. Gustafson's failing hearing. It was Humphrey Bogart and Lauren Bacall. The film that had that line about whistling. Barbara had seen it at least a dozen times, and she shut it off just as Bacall made her final shimmy across the room in Bogart's direction. Barbara had always liked that moment best. She'd always liked its veiled promise of the future.

"Now she's all right, Barbie," Mrs. Gustafson said anxiously from the doorway. "You can see she's all right."

Mrs. Havers was slumped to one side in the chair. Her mouth was slack. Her hands played with the hem of her dress which she'd drawn up to the height of her thighs. The air surrounding her was foetid with the odour of excrement and urine.

"Mum?" Barbara said.

She didn't respond although she hummed four notes as if with the intention of beginning a song.

"See how quiet and nice she can get?" Mrs. Gustafson said. "She can be a real jewel, can your mum, when she wants."

On the floor just inches from her mother's feet, the hose of the vacuum cleaner was curled into a coil.

"What's that doing here?" Barbara asked.

"Now, Barbie, it does help keep her—"

Barbara felt something inside her give way, like a dam that crumbles when it cannot contain the pressure-build of standing water any longer. "Didn't you even notice that she'd messed herself?" she said to Mrs. Gustafson. She found it a miracle that her voice sounded so calm.

Mrs. Gustafson blanched. "Messed? Why, Barbie, you must be mistaken. I asked her twice. She didn't want the loo."

"Can't you smell her? Haven't you checked her? Have you left her alone?"

Mrs. Gustafson's lips quivered with a hesitant smile. "I can see you're feeling a bit put out, Barbie. But if you've spent some time with her—"

"I've spent years with her. I've spent my whole life with her."

"I only meant to say—"

"Thank you, Mrs. Gustafson. You won't be needed again."

"Why, I—" Mrs. Gustafson clutched at the front of her dress, approximately in the location of her heart. "After all I've done."

"That's right," Barbara said.

Now, she stirred restlessly on the back step, feeling the cold seeping through her trousers, trying to force from her mind the image of her mother as flaccid as a rag doll in that chair, reduced to inertia. Barbara had bathed her, feeling struck to sadness at the sight and the feeling of her withered flesh. She led her to bed, tucked in the covers, and turned out the light. Through it all, her mother did not say a word. She was like the living dead.

Sometimes the right thing to do is also the most obvious thing to do, Lynley had said. There was truth in that. She had known from the first what had to be done, what was right, what was best, what would serve her mother. It was in the fear of being judged as a callous and indifferent child—by what she knew was largely a callous and indifferent world— that Barbara had floundered, waiting for direction, instruction, or permission that wasn't going to come. The decision rested with her, as it always had. What she hadn't realised was that judgement rested with her as well.

She pushed herself off the step and went into the kitchen. The smell of mouldy cheese was in the air. There were dishes to be washed and a floor to be scrubbed and a dozen distractions to allow her to avoid the inevitable for at least another hour. But she'd been avoiding it since her father's death in March. She couldn't do so forever. She went to the phone.

Odd to think that she'd memorised the number. She must have known from the first that she'd be using it again.

The phone rang four times on the other end. A pleasant voice said, "Mrs. Flo here. Hawthorn Lodge."

Barbara spoke on a sigh. "This is Barbara Havers. I wonder if you remember meeting my mother Monday night?"

24

Lynley and Havers arrived at St. Stephen's College at half past eleven. They'd spent the early part of the morning assembling their reports, meeting with Superintendent Sheehan, and discussing what sort of charges might be filed against Anthony Weaver. Lynley knew that his hope for attempted murder was a futile one at best. Weaver was, after all, the originally injured party when one considered the case from a purely legal standpoint. No matter what intimacies, oaths, and lovers' betrayals had led up to the killing of Elena Weaver, no real crime had been committed in the eyes of the law until Sarah Gordon had taken the girl's life.

Driven by his grief, the defence would argue. Weaver himself— who would wisely not stand in his own defence and thus run the risk of cross-examination—would emerge as loving father, devoted husband, brilliant scholar, Cambridge man. If the truth about his affair with Sarah Gordon managed to work its way into the courtroom, how easily it could be dismissed as a sensitive, artistic man's giving way to a lethal temptation in a moment of weakness or during a time of marital estrangement. How easily he could be depicted as having done his best—done everything in his power, in fact—to put the affair behind him and get on with his life once he became aware of the extent to which he was hurting his faithful and long-suffering wife.

But *she* could not forget, the defence would argue. She was obsessed with the need to avenge herself for his rejection of her. So she killed his daughter. She stalked her as she and her stepmother ran in the morning, she noted the clothes which her stepmother wore, she created the means to have the girl run alone, she lay in wait, she beat in her face, and she killed her. Having done so, she went to Dr. Weaver's college rooms by night and left him a message that revealed her culpability. Faced with that, what was he to do? What would any man—driven to despair by the sight of his child's corpse—do?

Thus, the focus would subtly turn from Anthony Weaver to the crime that had been committed against him. And what jury would ever be able to consider the crime Weaver had committed against Sarah Gordon in the first place? It was only a painting, after all. How could they hope to understand that while Weaver struck out at a piece of canvas, he carved cleanly through a unique human soul?

. . . when one stops believing that the act itself is superior to anyone's analysis or rejection of it, then one becomes immobilised. That's what happened to me.

But how could a jury hope to understand that if its members had never felt the call to create. Far easier to limn her a woman scorned than to try to understand the extent of her loss.

Sarah Gordon taught bloody instructions, the defence would argue, and they came back in full measure to plague her.

There was truth in this. Lynley thought of his final sight of the woman—so late into the night that milk delivery was already rumbling in the streets—five hours after they had wheeled her out of the operating theatre. She was in a room outside of which a uniformed constable sat as a guard, a ludicrous formality required to guarantee that the official prisoner—the killer of record—not try to escape. She seemed such a small figure in the bed that the form of her barely disturbed the covers. She lay heavily bandaged and heavily sedated, her lips blue-edged and her skin bruised snow. Still alive, still breathing, and still unaware of the additional loss she would have to face.

We managed to save the arm, the surgeon told him, but I can't say she'll ever be able to use it again.

Lynley had stood by the bed, looked down on Sarah Gordon, and thought about the alternative merits of seeking justice and obtaining revenge. In our society the law calls out for justice, he thought, but the individual still craves revenge. Yet to allow a man or woman to pursue a course of retaliation is to invite further violence as a result. For outside a courtroom, there is no real way to balance the scales when an injury has been done to an innocent party. And any attempt to do so only promises grief, additional injury, and further regret.

There is no eye for an eye, he thought. As individuals, we cannot design the means of another's retribution.

But now he wondered about that facile philosophy—so appropriate to a hospital room at dawn—as he and Sergeant Havers left the Bentley on Garret Hostel Lane and walked back towards the college to clear his belongings from the small room in Ivy Court. Directly in front of St. Stephen's Church, a hearse was parked. Lined up before it and behind it were more than a dozen other cars.

"Did she say anything to you?" Havers asked. "Anything at all?"

" 'She thought it was her dog. Elena loved animals.' "

"That's it?"

"Yes."

"No regrets? No remorse?"

"No," Lynley said. "I can't say she acted as if she felt either."

"But what did she think, sir? That if she killed Elena Weaver, she'd be able to paint again? That murder would somehow free up her creativity?"

"I think she believed that if she made Weaver suffer as she was suffering, she'd be able to go on with her life somehow."

"Not very rational, if you ask me."

"No, Sergeant. But human relationships aren't rational in the least."

They skirted the graveyard. Havers squinted up at the church's Norman tower. Its slate roof was only a few shades lighter than the sombre colour of the late morning sky. It was a suitable day for the dead.

"You were right about her from the very start," Havers said. "Nice policework, Lynley."

"No need for compliments. You were right as well."

"Right? How's that?"

"She reminded me of Helen from the moment I saw her."

It was only a few minutes' work to gather his belongings and see to his suitcase. Havers stood by the window, looking down on Ivy Court while he emptied cupboards and packed up shaving gear. She seemed more at peace with herself than she had been in months. She wore with a fair degree of comfort the relief that comes from effecting a closure.

He said casually as he threw a final pair of socks into his case, "Did you take your mother to Greenford?"

"Yes. This morning."

"And?"

Havers picked at a flaking patch of white paint on the window sill. "And I'll have to get used to it. Letting go, I mean. Being alone."

"That's what one has to do sometimes." Lynley saw her look in his direction, saw her start to speak. "Yes. I know, Barbara. You're a better man than I am. I haven't been able to manage it yet."

They left the building and crossed the court, skirting the graveyard through which a narrow path wound between sarcophagi and tombstones. It was old and bent, cracked in places where tree roots lifted it and weeds pushed through.

From the church, they could hear a hymn coming to an end, and rising out of its concluding notes came the high, sweet sound of a trumpet playing "Amazing Grace." Miranda Webberly, Lynley guessed, giving Elena her own public form of farewell. He felt unaccountably touched by the unadorned melody and he marvelled at the human heart's capacity to be moved by something as simple as sound.

The church doors opened, and the even-paced procession began to file out, headed by the bronze-coloured coffin which was carried on the shoulders of six young men. One of them was Adam Jenn. The immediate family followed: Anthony Weaver and his former wife, behind them Justine. And then the mourners, a large crowd of University dignitaries, colleagues and friends of both the Cambridge Weavers, and countless junior and senior fellows of St. Stephen's. Among them, Lynley noted Victor Troughton with a pear-shaped woman leaning on his arm.

Weaver's face registered neither reaction nor recognition as he passed by Lynley, following the coffin which was draped with a sheet of pale pink roses. Their odour was sweet in the heavy air. As the rear door of the hearse closed upon the coffin and one of the undertakers scuttled inside to rearrange the cave of additional flowers in which the coffin rode, the crowd pressed in round Weaver, Glyn, and Justine, black-garbed men and women with melancholy faces, earnestly offering affection and condolence. Among them was Terence Cuff, and it was to Cuff that the college porter—crossing the lane from the gatehouse—excused his way through the crowd to see. He carried a thick, creamy envelope which he handed to the Master of the College with a quiet word which Cuff bent to hear.

Cuff nodded, tore open the envelope. His eyes scanned the message. His face flashed briefly with a smile. He was not standing far from Anthony Weaver, so it took only a moment for him to reach his side and only another moment for the words he murmured to filter back through the crowd.

Lynley heard it coming from several directions at once.

"Penford Chair."

"He's been named . . ."

"So deserved . . ."

". . . an honour."

Next to him, Havers said, "What's going on?"

Lynley watched Weaver lower his head, press a clenched fist to his moustache, then raise his head again, shaking it, perhaps stunned, perhaps touched, perhaps humbled, perhaps disbelieving. He said, "Dr. Weaver has just reached the pinnacle of his career before our very eyes, Sergeant. He's been awarded the University's Penford Chair in History."

To which she replied, "He has? Bloody hell."

My sentiments exactly, Lynley thought. They stayed for a moment longer, watching the condolences change to quiet congratulations, hearing the murmurs of conversation that spoke of triumph coming upon the heels of tragedy.

Havers said, "If he's charged, if he goes to trial, will they take the Chair from him?"

"Chairs are for life, Sergeant."

"But don't they *know*—"

"About what he did yesterday? The committee? How could they? The decision was probably made by then anyway. And even if they did know, even if they decided this morning, he was, after all, only a father driven wild by his grief."

They edged round the crowd and headed in the direction of Trinity Hall. Havers was dragging her feet on the ground, her attention given to the tops of her shoes. She drove her fists into the pockets of her coat.

"Did he do it for the Chair?" she asked abruptly. "Did he want Elena to go to St. Stephen's because of the Chair? Did he want her to behave because of the Chair? Did he want to stay married to Justine because of it? Did he want to end his affair with Sarah Gordon because of it?"

"We'll never know, Havers," Lynley replied. "And I'm not sure Weaver will ever know either."

"Why?"

"Because he still has to look at himself in the mirror every morning. And how can he do that if he ever starts digging through his life for the truth?"

They rounded the corner into Garret Hostel Lane. Havers stopped abruptly, slapping a hand to her forehead with a loud groan. "Nkata's book!" she said.

"What?"

"I promised Nkata I'd pop into a few bookshops—they're supposed to have a decent place called Heffers—and look for . . . now what was it . . . where did I put the flipping . . .'' She zipped open her shoulder bag and began mauling her way through its contents, saying, ''You go on without me, Inspector.''

''But we've left your car—''

''No problem. The station's not far and I want to have a word with Sheehan before I head back to London.''

''But—''

''It's okay. Really. Fine. See you. Bye.'' And with a wave of her hand, she whipped back round the corner.

He stared after her. Detective Constable Nkata hadn't read a book in a decade or more, as far as he knew. His idea of an evening's entertainment was having the senior officer on the bomb squad retell the story of how, as a member of the Met's PSU, he lost his left eye in a brawl in Brixton which, no doubt, Nkata himself had probably instigated during his salad days as chief battle counsel for the Brixton Warriors. They would talk and argue and laugh over scotch eggs, pickled onions, and beer. And if they moved on to other topics, none of them were likely to be centred round literature. So what was Havers up to?

Lynley turned back to the lane and saw the answer, sitting on the top of a large tan suitcase at the side of his car. Havers had seen her as they turned the corner. She had read the moment and left him to face it alone.

Lady Helen stood. ''Tommy,'' she said.

He walked to join her, trying to keep his eyes off the suitcase lest looking at it make the purpose for its presence something other than what he hoped it would be.

''How did you find me?'' he asked.

''Luck and the telephone.'' She smiled at him fondly. ''And knowing that you have a need to finish things, even when you can't finish them the way that you'd like.'' She looked towards Trinity Lane where cars were starting and people were calling out quiet farewells. ''It's over, then.''

''The official part of it.''

''And the rest?''

''The rest?''

''The part where you blame yourself for not being quicker, not being more clever, not being able to stop people from doing the worst to each other?''

''Ah. That part.'' He let his eyes follow the progress of a group of students who passed them, pedalling their bicycles in the direction of the Cam as the bells of St. Stephen's Church started tolling the hollow, stately accompaniment to a funeral's conclusion. "I don't know, Helen. That part never seems to be over for me."

"You look exhausted."

"I was up all night. I need to go home. I need to get some sleep."

"Take me with you," she said.

He turned back to her. Her words were smooth enough and said with conviction, but she looked uncertain about their reception. And he was unwilling to risk misunderstanding or to allow hope even a moment to plant roots in his breast.

"To London?" he asked.

"Home," she replied. "With you."

How odd it was, he thought. It felt as if someone had cut into him quite painlessly and all of his life force were pouring out. It was the strangest sensation in which blood, bones, and sinews transformed into a palpable deluge which flowed from his heart to encompass her. Caught in the midst of it, he saw her clearly, felt his own body's presence, but couldn't speak.

She faltered under his gaze, seemed to think she had made an error in judgement. She said, "Or you could drop me in Onslow Square. You're tired. You won't be in the mood for company. And no doubt my flat could use a good airing out. Caroline won't be back yet. She's with her parents—did I tell you?—and I ought to see what sort of state things are in because—"

He found his voice. "There are no guarantees, Helen. Not in this. Not in anything."

Her face grew soft. "I know that," she said.

"And it doesn't matter?"

"Of course it matters. But you matter more. And you and I matter. The two of us. Together."

He didn't want to feel any happiness yet. It seemed too ephemeral a condition in life. So for a moment he stood there and merely let himself feel: the cold air washing from the Backs and the river, the weight of his overcoat, the ground beneath his feet. And then, when he was sure that he could bear any reply she might make, he said:

"I still want you, Helen. Nothing's changed there."

"I know," she said, and when he would speak again she stopped him with, "Let's go home, Tommy."

He loaded their suitcases into the boot, his heartbeat light and his spirit soaring free. Don't make too much of it, he told himself roughly, and don't ever believe your life depends on it. Don't ever believe your life depends upon anything at all. That's the way to live.

He got into the car, determined to be casual, determined to be the one in control. He said, "You took quite a chance, Helen, waiting like that. I might not have come back and found you for hours. You might have been sitting in the cold all day."

"It doesn't matter." She drew her legs up beneath her and settled companionably into the seat. "I was quite prepared to wait for you, Tommy."

"Oh. How long?" Still, he was casual. Still, he was the one in control.

"Just a bit longer than you've waited for me."

She smiled. She reached for his hand. He was lost.